A SWEET OBSCURITY

Also by Patrick Gale

PATRICK GALE

A SWEET OBSCURITY

Flamingo
An Imprint of HarperCollins*Publishers*

Flamingo
An imprint of HarperCollins*Publishers*
77–85 Fulham Palace Road,
Hammersmith, London W6 8JB

Flamingo is a registered trade mark of
HarperCollins*Publishers* Limited

www.fireandwater.com

Published by Flamingo 2003
1 3 5 7 9 8 6 4 2

ISBN 0 00 715099 7

Typeset in Apollo MT by Palimpsest Book Production Limited,
Polmont, Stirlingshire

Printed and bound in Great Britain by
Creative Print and Design Wales

For Aidan Hicks

As still she would not speak I said, 'Could we be happy?' She said, 'This has nothing to do with happiness, nothing whatever.' That was true. I took in the promise of her words. I said, 'I wonder if I shall survive it.'

(*A Severed Head*: IRIS MURDOCH)

Reason is true to itself,
But pity breaks open the heart.

(*A Child of our Time*: MICHAEL TIPPETT)

1

Eliza woke in the night and heard the dog was dying. He was whimpering and his breath came only in laboured lungfuls that must be costing him what little energy they gave.

'I'm here,' she called out, fumbling into a dressing gown. 'Don't worry. I'm coming.'

He was in the tiny room off her small one. She kept the door between the two ajar so that she could listen out for him and so that he would not wake in the dark and be frightened. He hated to be shut in, always had. She sat on the floor beside his bed. 'Ssh,' she said.

He was struggling to sit up, eyes wide with fear at what was happening to him, this final mutiny of heart and lungs. She placed a hand on his shoulder and gently pushed. He resisted only a second then sank back on his bed, teeth bared in his effort to suck in enough breath. She spread her palm and ran it back across his brow. His eyes shut a moment, breathing checked, then they opened, staring into space as his struggle continued. She slid her hand down to the hair on his chest, feeling the heat there and the wild knocking of his swollen heart.

'Don't fight,' she murmured. 'It's okay. You can stop now, poor, old man. Let go. Let go now.'

But he fought on tenaciously for another hour, filling

the room with fetid breath, held on, as people said, for grim death.

Dawn was revealing the unreachable grime on the window panes when he breathed his last. He did so abruptly, as though someone had pulled his plug. His tongue protruded. She pushed it back behind his teeth but it slid out again as if suddenly doubled in size. Neither would his eyes stay closed. She would have hugged him but death had relieved him of every social restraint and his bowels and bladder now gave out, driving her from the room. Eliza shut the door, sank to her bed, pulled the quilt about her and gave way to exhaustion.

He had been dying for six months or more.

'You must prepare yourself,' she had been told. 'He could go any day.'

At first she believed them, taking care to bid him good night with extra tenderness in case he went in his sleep, jumping up at the least sound of discomfort and fearing the worst if she woke to a silent flat. Then he defied all predictions. With the aid of prescriptions she could ill afford – ACE inhibitors, diuretics and digitalis – he rose from his sickbed and began to take walks again. Far from dying in the night, he developed only a maddeningly weak bladder and started waking her two, even three times a night to go out. Night after night would find her leaning, blank-eyed in her dressing gown in the draughty lobby while he took longer and longer to trawl the sad patch of grass and bushes outside. Repeatedly, mornings found her with the grey complexion and poor concentration of a nursing mother. Often she woke to find him slumped, seemingly lifeless. She would call his name and feel guiltily disappointed when he slowly opened his eyes and raised his head.

'When his appetite goes and he stops wagging his tail,' she told people, 'I'll let him go, I'll stop the pills.'

But his appetite showed no signs of abating, he continued

to wag his tail and he became something of a prodigy so that all the staff at the vet's would come out to greet him when Eliza called in for more pills.

A month's supply cost as much as her food bill for a fortnight. She tried to economise, giving up coffee and wine, but the withdrawal symptoms – punishing headaches and a dull, flu-like throbbing in her joints – frightened her so she gave up lunch instead. This morning the electricity bill had come due and the pills had almost run out so she was faced with the stark choice: do without light and heat or let the dog die. Foolhardy or sentimental – she was, she knew, often both – she had bought more pills with the last of her funds and rang the number on the back of the electricity bill for people in financial difficulties. She told them she had a child. Shamelessly, she cried. She won both a fortnight's precious grace and the right to pay in instalments.

But Carlo heard her, or at least heard the tone in her voice. And now he was dead and she could sell back the unopened pills to the understanding vet and pay the bill. He had even spared her the cost she had been dreading of having him put to sleep. Just before his eyes turned glassy, she fancied she saw reproach in them. He had perhaps been fighting to stay alive all this time for her sake and would have surrendered long ago had he only known how things stood.

Thank God Dido was away and could be left with only happier memories of him.

The thought of her daughter gave her uselessly meandering thoughts a momentary purposeful channel. Eliza rose and pulled on whatever clothes came to hand. She spread Carlo's old bath towel on the floor then, wrinkling her nose against the smell, fetched his body from next door, laid him on it and gathered its corners around him as a makeshift shroud. Then she heaved him into her arms and left. Illness had left his body pounds underweight and she carried him down the stairs with relative ease.

It was only ten minutes' walk from her flat to Giles' house on Starcross Road. Eliza felt mildly self-conscious carrying her tragic bundle along Caledonian Road but it was only as she stood on his well-swept stairs with their spiral-clipped box trees and left finger marks on his old brass bell pull that she began to feel like the bag lady she resembled.

After the distant jangling of the bell there was a long pause. Eliza pulled again a little harder, just in case.

'Hello?' Julia's voice sounded uncertain, even guilty, like a surprised intruder's, which was gratifying.

'It's me. Eliza,' she said.

Two locks and a bolt were unfastened, the door opened a foot and Julia peered around it. Her skin was without a crease and she appeared to have brushed her hair. She was, as ever, Snow White to Eliza's disordered Goldilocks yet with the dangerous hauteur of Snow White's queenly stepmother.

'Eliza, it's Sunday and it's barely seven,' she sighed. 'And Dido's not here. Giles took her to Winchelsea for the weekend.'

'I know that,' Eliza bluffed. She had forgotten it was Sunday. She still had a day's grace before Dido came back. She reached down to where she had laid her bundle. 'It's Carlo,' she explained, catching Julia's small moue of distaste as a shaggy paw swung free of the towel. 'He died finally and I thought we could put him under the apple tree. Giles always said that would be best. And he was his dog.'

'But the apple tree's gone.'

Eliza took this in then asked, 'Why?'

'It wasn't fruiting any more and it was casting too much shade so I had it pulled out.'

'Well under that copper-leafed prunus would do just as

well. I don't mind doing it. You go back to bed. I know where the tools are.'

Coerced, Julia stood back and opened the door wider.

Black and white floor tiles, stripped oak stairs, a huge and faintly sinister pot of fleshy green cymbidiums. Had she really once lived here? Crossing the polished threshold, Eliza felt entirely not at home. There was an alien smell she did not immediately recognise as furniture polish and a terrible sense of everything being arranged in order to impress rather than comfort. Flower arrangements, forbiddingly plumped up cushions, printed invitations on the mantelpiece.

Momentarily forgetting her mission in her curiosity to see what other changes Julia had wrought, Eliza wandered into what she remembered as the telly room and set off the burglar alarm. Wincing against the noise as Julia said a crisp *fuck sorry* and hurried to turn the thing off, Eliza was chilled to find the cosiness of ramshackle sofas and Dido's play things replaced by the austere, dead space of a dining room. Whatever must Dido think, passing between their spartan flat and all this? The child was too diplomatic to say, but she must have made comparisons and formed a preference. Could it be that, with her natural taste for order and control, she preferred here to there?

'Let me.' Julia was back at her side and taking the bundle from Eliza's grasp. She took it with surprising gentleness and, following her towards the garden, Eliza assumed she was going to assist at the burial. But Julia turned abruptly aside into the utility room, where she laid Carlo on the floor. 'If you don't mind,' she said, 'I'll bury him later. I don't want to wake people and . . . and there are bulbs and things I don't want dislodged at this time of year.'

'But we ought to get him buried before Dido gets back.'

'Don't worry, Eliza. I'll do it. I've got all day. Now go home and get some rest.'

Eliza found herself steered efficiently to the hall then shut out on the doorstep before she could protest further. Doubts beset her. Julia was the kind of woman who bought rubber gloves on a weekly basis. It was hard to imagine her stuffing a chicken, still less burying a sizeable dog. The dog pre-dated her, however, so perhaps she would do the deed with a glad heart, burying the first of two rivals for Giles' heart. First of three, if one counted Dido.

Eliza walked home in a daze, fell back into bed and cried herself to sleep.

Initially she wept because she was so tired and because Carlo's long illness was over but the deeper reason was one she could barely have spelled out, even to herself. Carlo was not her dog, not strictly. Strictly speaking he belonged to Giles. But he had bought him on a whim, had never loved him as he ought and had found less and less time in which to give him walks. He had also acquired a mistress with a fur allergy but hid this motive behind the characteristically barbed pronouncement that a dog had no place in a childless house.

There remained the small matter of their legal bond, but Carlo had been the last palpable vestige of a marriage gone awry.

And now she was finally cut adrift.

Eliza spent Sunday in bed, stirring only to brew cups of tea, slap the used teabags into the sink and smear margarine onto bread before retreating with this meagre nourishment to her room. Her room smelt neglected but she could not care. Occasionally a draught through one of the cracked windows brought worse smells under the door from the dog's deathbed. The telephone was silent, disconnected when she failed to keep up payments against the last bill.

She had read once that sleepiness was a symptom of depression, that the depressed sought negation of their pain in slumber. If this was true, she had been suffering from depression all her life. Even as a small child, she had faced the bossy arrival of daylight with a kind of horror and retired each night with relief. Dressed or naked, asleep or watchful, to be curled within or sprawled upon a bed was her natural state, from which every other activity was a resented departure. She was a born nester, whose animal affinities had always lain with sloths, lemurs and dormice rather than with nature's predatory adventurers. Alone, shoeless and horizontal, she felt more truly herself than when she was upright and out in the world.

Unless she could guarantee a deep and dreamless sleep however, taking to her bed was hardly a depressive's escape since, once there, she had nothing to distract her from the steady contemplation of herself.

2

As usual Giles began with purely physical exercises; a sequence of stretches, deep, slow breaths and artificial yawns he had performed in the same order and at roughly the same time of the morning for so long that he could be half-asleep still and his body would shift from one gentle exertion to another without his conscious mind being involved. He had once shared a dressing room with a hatha yoga adherent who had said the same of the unvarying sequence of *asanas* with which he began and closed each day.

Then, blood buzzing nicely, Giles moved to Trudy's piano and began humming arpeggios at the lower end of his register. It was said that the vibrations from a hum helped to relax the vocal cords, though he could never see how this could be, given that it was the vocal cords which produced the hum in the first place. He then ran through the same sequence of lower register arpeggios at half-tempo, beginning each note as an open mouthed hum – actually an *ng* sound at the back of his throat – then opening it out to a fully sung *ah*.

At home, in Islington, Sunday was a practice-free day unless he had a concert in the evening. He had long striven to spend Sunday mornings the way the rest of the population did or at least pretended to; a long leisurely breakfast blurring into a slow, superficial browse through two or more Sunday papers. On Sundays at Trudy's, however, he had to practise because he knew she went to some expense to have the piano tuned in his honour and would have been hurt if he spent the morning ignoring it.

He suspected that she liked to feel that his needing to use her piano was a significant link between his art and her nurturing. The sad truth was that, beyond the odd stabbed chord or melodic line picked out with one finger, he did not need the thing at all. He didn't have perfect pitch but he knew his own range and could pitch any piece he had learnt more or less accurately simply from where its opening notes felt most natural in his voice. With works as familiar as the one he was currently singing, the process was like repositioning furniture by the dents left in the pile of a carpet.

'Despair no more shall wound me,' he sang. Then he repeated the incomplete sequence of notes, adjusting the pitch minutely. 'Despair no more shall wound me.' The intervals were useful this morning, a kind of spiralled arpeggio. 'Shall wound me. Shall wound me. Wound. Shall wound me,' he sang, then allowed himself the brief indulgence of a complete phrase, its incurling flourish like a perfect Grinling Gibbons curlicue. 'Despair no more shall wound me/Since you so kind do prove.' Then he allowed himself the first of the aria's fiendish little runs. 'Wou-ou-ou-ou-ound'. 'Sounds like a constipated owl,' he muttered and tried some more humming.

He swung aside on the piano stool to look out of the window. The others were in the garden. Trudy talked incessantly while flicking through a *Country Life* backwards. She persisted in wearing white and in dying her hair an approximation of the blonde it used to be.

'I know I'm too old for it,' she said, 'but Ron prefers me this way so what can I do?'

Last night she had worn a white off-the-shoulder thing,

far too dressy considering they were en famille, and far too revealing. This morning she had gone to the other extreme and pulled on jaunty white shorts, a tee shirt and white strappy sandals. She changed two or more times a day, ostensibly because it was hard to wear white and not be forever soiling it but secretly, Giles liked to imagine, so she could snatch a few minutes in which to howl into her pillow or bounce naked off the bathroom walls to release her tension.

He wondered if he was alone in finding that, in his mid-thirties, he regarded his mother with the same unsparing revulsion he had as a teenager. He had only to glance at her to relive his shock at discovering how boys at school rated her a kind of pin-up, to hear again husky voices singing *Mrs Robinson* as she collected him on Sundays.

Dido was dutifully playing Swingball with is stepfather. The game had been bought for her just as the piano had been tuned for Giles. She would far rather be flopped in the distant hammock with a book.

Puffing, dangerously red, Ron was trying not to win but his competitive instincts were too deeply instilled. Dido's clumsiness and lack of interest offered too great a challenge to even his sense of fair play. Once more he could not resist thwacking the ball, once more it flew off the spring and once more Trudy, who failed to understand the game, gave a sort of cheer as Dido gamely ran off to fetch the thing. She hooked it back onto the spring, politely assisting in her own torment.

'All joy and bliss surround me, My—' he sang out at her through the glass. He had meant to sing the entire phrase through to *love* but something in the flourish on *surround* snagged like a hangnail and he was compelled to go back and repeat the flourish in isolation, smoothing it out, folding it up again, faster, slower, and again in context. 'All joy and bliss surround.' Again the snag. He frowned, turned from the window absorbed again. He had been practising for so long, it seemed, that sometimes he felt the process engaged his intellect no more than was a bird's on grooming its plumage.

Ignorance occasionally led people to assume that his high voice was artificial, and thus especially strenuous to maintain. It was true that his range, which unusually could tackle roles written for soprano as well as alto castrati, shrank on the occasions when sickness or a bad cold prevented his keeping his voice muscles limber. But then all full-voice, operatic singing, all *produced singing* as his first teacher had called it, was artificial. As with most counter-tenors, his natural, non-falsetto voice was fairly deep, a lightish baritone, but his high voice felt the more comfortable of the two. On his rare visits to church, for funerals or weddings, it amused him to startle friends by singing hymns at an ordinary blokeish pitch and timbre.

The English choral tradition, based on a network of cathedral and college choir schools, produced many counter-tenors. Most of them, though, however agile their technique, had essentially domestic voices which could no more carry in an opera house than exquisite real jewellery could compete with fat and gaudy paste when it came to being seen from the back of the upper circle. Giles was lucky. His counter-tenor was big, making up for what it lacked in nuance with its ability to cut through an orchestra of scrubbing strings like any trumpet or triangle.

Giles had found his gift by accident. When his nice enough treble voice broke he had not minded, looking forward to singing less and playing football more. As in most all-boy schools, however, altos were needed to balance the choir and likely candidates would be press-ganged into squawking a falsetto line whenever possible. There was no option. A choir audition was a compulsory start to each school year until one was fifteen, no more avoidable than vaccinations or

Latin. It was no use fluffing the required scales on purpose; the choirmaster was an old hand, adept at telling faked tone-deafness from the real thing.

Giles remembered the fateful audition vividly. A football game had overrun so he had come straight from the pitch without changing. He remembered the sacrilegious sensation of walking up the chapel aisle in studded boots and his self-consciousness at singing out in an apparently empty space while the choirmaster shouted down instructions from the organ loft. When he asked Giles, after an initial gruff phrase or two, to try a few falsetto notes, he had to explain.

'Pretend you're imitating a woman singing. Just see what happens . . .'

Even then Giles' falsetto sound was big, but it was like a powerful car in the hands of a non-driver and he began a lifetime's practice of being entirely dependent on others to show him what to do with it.

The discovery that he could sing changed his life. It paid his school fees. It landed him a place at a university he could never have entered on academic ability alone. It gave a boy with no particular ambitions a career.

His darkest professional secret remained that he was gifted with a voice but not naturally musical. He had a horror of sight-reading in public. Every inflexion in every role he sang was taught by a precious teacher and memorised. Directors liked him because he was entirely reliable but he knew that, for all the size of his voice, he would never attract the adulation of a Kowalski or a Scholl because his performance of a piece was the same night after night, too perfectly controlled to admit the risks of genius.

'All joy and bliss surround me,/My soul is tun'd to love.'

Dido heard him and smiled, completely missing her chance to hit the ball back in a different direction, so that Ron won again. Trudy came to the rescue, patting the cushions on the bench beside her and continuing to chatter as Dido went to sit there and flick through a magazine too. Freed from his killer instincts, Ron took down the Swingball and prepared to mow the lawn.

Weekends with his mother and stepfather were fragile affairs, painstaking constructions of good manners and enthusiasm forever tearing at their papery edges. By *weekend at home*, most sons would mean two or even three nights. For Giles that would have proved unsustainable. His practice was to arrive at teatime on Saturday then leave precisely twenty-four hours later. His mother always baked a cake, slices of which framed the visit like sticky bookends.

He often had performances or concerts to sing on Saturday nights, so visits like this were not a regular thing. Neither side could have borne them if they were. But he felt they were good for Dido, as she saw so little of her maternal grandmother and had so little family life. He worried she was being dragged down and limited by her mother's straitened style of living and he was not above entertaining wicked fantasies in which, through timely interventions of Justice or Death, he became sole parent.

On the weekends when Dido was with him, he tried to fill her time with things he felt it might lack when she was with her mother: beauty, sophistication, above all a sense of possibilities, a sense of all the places she might go and all the things she might become. In the event, she often simply watched television or spent an evening in one of the opera houses before he took her out to dinner. She did not like music much, not real music, but she enjoyed the opera because of the costumes and drama and in spite of any sounds the singers made. This had taken time. When she first saw *The Magic Flute*, in a fluffy, witty production which he had thought the ideal introduction, she kept covering her ears and complained of the singers afterwards, 'It's as if they're putting their insides outside. They're *showing* too much!'

Showing too much was something Giles keenly understood and feared in himself. His father died when he was eight, which sent his mother spiralling into lost years of alcoholism. Boarding school was a kind of prison for other boys; for him it brought blessed release from a mother's incoherent moods and unwanted confidences, a place of orderly restraint as respite from a damaging lack of boundaries. She saw the light only when, old enough at seventeen to stand up to her, he flatly refused to come home one summer holiday and instead spent two months visiting friends and working on farms. At the end of the summer, realising he had survived and would survive without her dubious protection, he wrote a short, brutal letter telling her so and telling her why. In an effort to make her just another adult, he addressed the letter to *Dear Trudy* rather than *Dear Mum* and had called her nothing else since.

Stung (she later brightly admitted to having attempted suicide), she took herself off to the local chapter of Alcoholics Anonymous where she began carefully to rebuild herself and where she met Ron.

He was an insurance salesman. The kind of man she had raised Giles to ignore. But he worshipped her, in his bluff way, and seemed content never to find out who she really was. They shared a life of unimpeachable normality, in a household shorn of stimulants, took bird-watching holidays, played golf and continued to attend AA together as other couples attended church.

Oddly she was no longer contrite as she had frequently been when drunk. Instead sobriety made her honest.

'Oh no,' she blurted out once. 'I'm not happy. You can't be happy when you're always being careful. But I'm calm and I've stopped being frightened all the time.'

Built over an abyss, her life with Ron was a neatly hedged

Hell but looked happy and ordinary enough in twenty-four-hour doses.

There was a lunch of roast chicken and a trifle unredeemed by sherry, then a short walk with binoculars and bird books before yesterday's cake made a second appearance and set them free. Giles indulged Dido on the train ride home, letting her listen to the radio on his personal stereo and sit with her shoeless feet on the seat opposite. The wind blowing across her from an open window set her uneven pigtails flapping and brought him the tart, nutty scent of hot little girl. It was time she started using a deodorant perhaps. Rather than embarrass her by mentioning this, he had a quiet word with Julia when they arrived.

Bath times overseen by Julia were a Sunday evening ritual on her precious weekends with them. The general idea was an indulgent fix of girlydom, a scented bath, the run of Julia's beauty tools and pampering products. As often as not she would come down to supper spangled, painted and crudely curled, smelling like an overheated flower shop. She glowed in Julia's full attention, however, enjoying the brief sense of sisterly conspiracy and the moment of revelation before the household's man.

Julia enjoyed these sessions too. She said it was like having a baby sister to play with, but hearing their laughter from another room gave him a pang of regret; it made him imagine Julia as a mother, a subject he knew better than to pursue.

Dido had chosen pizza for supper, her side of the bargain being to let him make it from scratch, yeast dough and all, and to eat whatever grown up or healthy toppings he chose to use. While the dough was rising and the girls had fun in the bathroom with crimping tongs, he flopped onto the small kitchen sofa to watch whatever banalities the television could offer. Visits to his mother left him fit for nothing more.

There were footsteps overhead, the tell-tale thump of Dido's trainers into his study. The phone rang and he heard Julia answer it at the other side of the house and laugh at something. After a while the footsteps left his study more slowly then came downstairs. He smelt Julia's crazily expensive bath essence and turned down the noise on the television.

Seeing Dido pink from her bath, in a cast-off tee shirt of Julia's, hair crazily crimped, lips glossed, he felt his habitual Sunday night remorse at having wasted so much of the weekend. He felt he had barely seen her, had barely spoken with her. They had not talked about school or her friendships or her dreams and not even her mother – none of the things a father should discuss – and now she had almost left him again.

'Who can that be?' he asked. 'Who let a princess in?'

Once she would have wriggled at this and smiled but tonight she gave only a half-smile, almost a shrug. She was getting too old for such daddy's-girlisms. She came solemnly over to his chair and leant against his knees, picking at the seams of his chinos with a blue-painted fingernail.

'What is it, kitten?' he asked.

She bumped against his knees. 'Nothing,' she said and climbed onto his lap, reaching for the remote control and flicking channels idly. She had not done this since she was very small. Perhaps she regretted Sunday nights too. Touched, he put an arm around her and held her close. 'I saw the photos you'd hidden,' she mumbled into his shoulder. 'I went to look for something else and they sort of fell out.'

Julia had finished her phone call and he heard her sandals clacking across the landing and entering the study overhead. He suffered a convulsion of guilty panic.

'Where did you leave them?' he asked.

'It's okay,' she said. 'I slipped them back between the books. Why did you hide them?'

'I don't know. I didn't think you'd like them.'

If she could see his face, she would know this for a lie; he had hidden the things out of shame.

Trudy and Ron had given him a digital camera for his birthday and he had surprised himself by spending a whole weekend snapping this and that, enjoying the near silent zoom and intelligent flash, the small, steely neatness of the new toy.

He had few pictures of Dido and she was changing so fast. He stole into her room, hoping to surprise her deep in her bedtime reading and found her asleep. She had borrowed an unsuitably adult magazine of Julia's, all blow-job techniques and saucy pictures of half-naked hunks and, reassuringly bored, had fallen asleep over it.

It was a hot night and she had pushed the bedding down to her waist. Her tee shirt had ridden up so that the golden light from her bedside lamp fell on the scrawny line of her stretched out belly. One nipple was laid bare, puppy fat giving the illusion of an incipient breast.

His initial reaction was that she looked sweet, enchanting precisely because of the lack of innocence in the discarded magazine crumpled beside her. The act of taking her photograph laid another layer of meaning on the scene, however; when he had fed it into his computer and printed it out a few times, he realised it looked like kiddie porn.

He had meant to throw the prints away and wipe away all computerised traces, but it was a beautiful picture. A sweet picture. And throwing it away was like throwing her away. He kept every picture anyone had ever taken of her, failed ones included. He had wiped it off the computer memory but could not bring himself to destroy the prints. He had thought, however, that he had hidden them better. Now she had seen, of course, it was too late.

'What did you think?' he asked her cautiously.

'Dunno,' she mumbled, face still pressed into his shoulder.

He could feel her hand on the back of his head. The curliness of his hair had always fascinated her because hers was flat and needed the electricity of brushing to give it body. When she was little, she never tired of pulling a curl straight then watching it spring back into place. 'I was a bit scared at first but it's nice really. I'm glad you kept them for me to see.'

'Oh, darling.' He held her to him more tightly and pressed his lips into her shampooey hair to kiss her. Her hair smelt intensely clean and disconcertingly like Julia's. He felt crazily moved, as though she had forgiven him and declared love to him simultaneously. He kissed her again, moving his hand down her back and suddenly she was pulling away from him.

'What?' he asked but she climbed down and backed away from him, dropping the remote.

'Creep,' she said. 'Fucking creep.'

'Dido!'

She had never sworn at him before. He made to follow her and realised that, thanks to her sitting on his lap, he had a hard-on. He stumbled to a halt, awkwardly rearranging himself, and of course that made it worse. Her eyes narrowed briefly in disgust then she hurried out.

Giles sank defeated in his chair and listened to her telling Julia that no thanks, she wasn't hungry and thought she'd go to bed now.

'What was that all about?' Julia asked, bringing him a glass of wine. She sat on the sofa arm and reached for the TV remote almost exactly as Dido had. 'Have you had a row?'

'No,' he said in all honesty.

'She was fine earlier. Very giggly.' She sighed. 'Must be reaching that difficult age.'

'She's not yet ten.'

'Well don't bite *my* head off.'

'Sorry. It's been a long weekend. Trudy was a bit full-on for her, I think. She's probably just tired.'

Somehow he got through the evening, ate his share of pizza, drank his wine, made self-exonerating love to his girlfriend. But through it all he was aware of the shut door into the attic bedroom, which was quite possibly locked against him, and the seeming impossibility of saying anything that would not make a terrible situation worse. Most fathers would have knocked on the door, demanded a talk, cleared the air with a joke. They would certainly have brought their partner onside by explaining the situation. But his relationship to Dido was far more delicate and vulnerable than ordinary fatherhood and he was paralysed by guilt that, in misreading a particular situation, she had stumbled onto a general damning truth.

3

Julia had grown up in an atmosphere of physical and legal disorder among undisciplined people so had naturally developed an instinct that control was all-important. If a bill was paid on receipt there would be no shaming final demand. If food was eaten carefully there would be no stains. If one thought a sentence through before beginning to speak it there was less risk of ill effect. If a room was kept tidy, if everything was returned to its proper place after use, if no unpleasant task was ever deferred, life became less nebulous, its unavoidable problems uncluttered by needless ones.

She had never understood girls who complained that their mothers were always on at them to tidy their rooms, since her room had always been the only tidy one in the house, a small, still refuge of neatly labelled shoeboxes and underfilled, orderly drawers. Now that most households had nobody keeping house full time, a new career had arisen which would have suited her perfectly. She could have been a clutter counsellor, paid to show people how to remove every possession from a room, put only one fifth of them back and survive the trauma. Julia knew better than to say so aloud but she intuitively understood the appeal of little clips to keep socks in pairs through the wash, of drawer dividers to keep bras and knickers untangled, of electronic diaries that reminded one when to post a birthday card.

She was swiftly smitten with Giles because he was beautiful, the first truly beautiful man she had known and because he needed her. But she only became emotionally involved when she recognised him as a fellow refugee from disorder, damaged first by his appalling mother, then by Eliza. The moment Dido first appeared, in tights with holes in them and without a sensible coat, the child similarly awakened in her a desire to rescue her from an unregulated life.

This was odd because, if questioned closely, she would have admitted to being godless and selfish, still enough the refugee for her principal instinct to be self-preservation rather than the succouring of others. When she thought about them however, the anomalies pleased her as small but significant proofs that she had a heart.

It had occurred to her recently, when obliged to attend a colleague's wedding and thus made party to the envies and recriminations of single girlfriends on such occasions, that she was happy. It was an astonishing, even risky conclusion to draw but she was happy, she realised, because for the first time in her life she wanted for nothing.

She had an interesting, fairly well paid job with good benefits, a beautiful, talented lover, an attractive house. She was not married to Giles, but what would marriage have added? They had each seen enough of marriage to know the disorder it could bring. She was not yet a mother either but in a way she was. Dido was in their lives just enough to gratify parenting instincts but not enough to overwhelm with a sense of responsibility.

When she first encountered Dido's sharp mind and suspicious nature she saw the temptation to be a wicked stepmother, to begrudge the emotional territory the girl had invaded and to waste no opportunity to highlight Eliza's deficiencies and undermine her standing. Her heart was snared, however, so she took the other way.

Dido reminded her so much of herself at that age. She was so cross and plain and funny, her face in a state of awkward transition. She wanted longer hair but became impatient with the effort of keeping it clean and under control so she tended to wear it twisted at random into uneven pigtails, fastened with whatever came to hand: Julia's scrunchies but also rubber bands or even coloured pipe-cleaners.

It was a real pleasure to make subtle, flattering changes to her appearance, to buy her clothes and to teach her things. Eliza had no computer so Julia set Dido free on hers before finding her one of her own, encouraging her to explore her creativity (without mess) in the computer's paint-box and to broaden her horizons through the Internet. Eliza went outside her immediate district so rarely she might as well have been living in a remote village as in London so Julia made a point, when Dido was with them, of arranging regular excursions into town for doses of high and low culture. In a sense she was arming Dido, preparing her for battle and she thought of her as a comrade rather than a stepdaughter. Dido returned the compliment, coming to treat her with the respect and guarded affection she might show an older sister.

When the three of them went out together Julia was aware, as Giles was not, that they were only playing at being a family. She could see what a good father Giles could make and had no doubt that he watched her with Dido and assessed her in the same way, but it was always a relief to let Dido go again and return to their quietly selfish selves. She secretly loved it when waitresses or sales assistants mistook them for mother and daughter but had no desire to lose her freedom and figure in the chaos of real, blood parenthood.

Weekends like this one, when Giles took Dido to his mother's house, left Julia vulnerable to doubt however.

She had gone home with him once but had not seen eye to eye with Mrs Easton so had hastily agreed when Giles suggested she might prefer not to go next time. For all her insincere parade of welcoming curiosity, Trudy Easton could not forgive her for not being Eliza, so whenever Giles went to Winchelsea without her, discretion felt ever so slightly like ostracism.

Weekends on her own in town would have offered any other woman an ideal opportunity to catch up with old friends. Julia had no close friends, however, had never acquired the knack of charming women without arousing their suspicion. Such times tended to begin with a sort of nervous collapsing in on herself, an instinctive grasping at the easy pleasures of chocolate and alcohol. But her habit of control was so ingrained that bad behaviour swiftly gave rise to good. She would devote the rest of her free time to self-maintenance – hair, nails, feet, to self improvement – mugging up on a new client's repertoire, going to hear old ones perform. Or to snooping.

In the name of tidying up she had been through most drawers and cupboards in the house but she continued to feel a near-erotic excitement on sliding her hands into the pockets of trousers and jackets Giles had recently worn. Occasionally she would come across a mystery, a photograph of him with someone she did not know, a restaurant bill or some entirely unnamed, unitemised till receipt and would pass the time by chafing at it, feeding her mental itch with supposition.

She abhorred hoarding and was so instinctive in her throwing out of scraps of paper and old diaries that she routinely had to check herself, to retain those documents the Inland Revenue liked kept. It amazed her how reckless Giles was, not only in the things he kept but in the casualness with which he left them lying about. He had always been especially careless with photographs people gave him. She would find them tucked into coat pockets or muddled up with people's holiday postcards in the kitchen or they would spring out at her from half-read books in which he had been using them to mark his place.

Were they married, she sometimes thought, she would have met all these smiling mysteries at their wedding reception, all the ones that mattered. Being what she was, less than wife, more than mistress, she made do with meeting them in dribs and drabs. When introduced she would say something like, 'No, we haven't met, but I know you so well from that photograph, the nice one with the sundial,' partly to break the ice, partly to see a person's small glow of gratification at knowing themselves remembered and discussed.

Today was to have been different. She had planned there would be no snooping, no sad hanging around the house in fact. She had plans to take herself into town for lunch at one of the Tates and then, perhaps, unless it seemed a waste of good weather, to an afternoon screening. The trouble with her job was that she saw countless operas and heard five or more recitals a week which rarely left time or energy for plays or films, once a passion of hers. Never mind the good weather, she decided. If she went into town early enough, she could fit in an exhibition in the morning, watch two matinees back to back and still be home in time for supper with Giles and Dido.

But then Eliza arrived with the dog and the day's plans uncurled.

It was so typical of Eliza to think nothing of calling so early. She had that selfishness and one-track mind that came so easily to depressives. It was a squandered ruthlessness, if one thought about it cynically. She was so relentlessly superior, too; whenever they had to meet, usually because of Dido, she managed to make Julia feel not only less clever but, more woundingly, less sensitive and artistic. If a woman found time to brush her hair before answering the door it made her unfeeling. If she took care of herself it meant she could not care for others.

It was hard to believe Giles' mother had ever been fond of her. They could have had little in common. Some mothers regarded loving their son's wives as a necessary but ennobling form of martyrdom. Perhaps now the marriage had collapsed, Trudy continued to support the estranged daughter-in-law out of guilt, believing Giles and his behaviour to be all a mother's fault? Julia suspected Trudy Easton's dislike of herself was inevitable even had she been the first and only woman Giles had brought home; it was the gut reaction of one wary, self-created woman for another. Some kindred spirits could not afford to get on.

Having seen Eliza off, Julia dealt with the dog. She began by throwing on some old clothes and walking into the garden with a spade. But it was July and there was nowhere obvious she could dig a grave without disturbing plants in flower and she had taught herself just enough about gardening to know that this was the one time not to trouble them. Then irritation seized her. Why should she suddenly play host, sexton indeed, to someone else's canine corpse? Eliza's effrontery had been disguised in such tearful ditheriness it had taken a few minutes to sink in.

She smacked on a pair of rubber gloves, slid the dog – which stank – into a black bin liner then slid two more around that before binding the grisly package with parcel tape. Still gloved, she carried it to the wheelie bin, then remembered there was no collection until midweek. The stink would grow still worse in the heat, even through bags. There would be flies. Worse, Dido might find it.

She thanked God the chest freezer in the utility room was not particularly full. They were nearing the stewy end of half an organic bullock from Islington Farmers' Market so she was able to make a few rearrangements and stash the dog at one end where its packaging could not touch even the plastic surrounding something else.

She slammed shut the lid, clicked the thing onto super-freeze, threw away the tainted gloves then hurried into the lavatory to be sick. After that the house seemed to be full of things that smelled bad – a vase of stagnant flower water, a box of liquefied camembert, a load of washing Giles had forgotten to take out of the machine, her hair which smelled of last night's second-hand smoke.

So she stayed home to clean, then to brood, then to eat lunch because vomiting had left her ravenous, then to brood more deeply because, in the name of tidiness, she had finished a bottle of Merlot with her lunch.

She had not killed the wretched animal so why did she feel as though she had? Experience had immunised her against animal-love. She had grown up in a household where there was always a dog or a cat suffering the incontinence of extreme youth or age, always an infestation of fleas in warm weather, always the lingering smells of ancient teeth, dirty dog beds, the tripe her mother boiled in bulk to save money on tinned feed and the clouds of evil gas this drew from whichever creature ate it. Only the canaries did not smell – there were always two or three canaries – but they made up for the shortfall by showering the carpet with their seed, filling the air with nervous fluttering and scratching sounds and by capping any mechanical or human outburst with their ear-scouring song.

When Julia met Giles there was no dog in his life. At first. When Carlo had so rudely re-entered it, never walking when he could bound, shaking himself on newly washed walls, chewing, with sinister accuracy, only those shoes that really mattered, she was nearly driven away by the stress he caused her.

Then something Giles let slip struck home, something light-hearted but flattering, said to the dog in her hearing, about *knowing what side his bread was buttered*. Carlo, she realised, was just another pitiful refugee from disorder. She had found him a trainer and a walker so that he was too exhausted to be bad. She had borrowed a colleague's baby gate to confine him to the kitchen and arranged for fortnightly visits from a mobile dog-washing service. The shoe-chewing, the trainer told her, was a sign of respect, even love towards an alpha bitch. Won over, Julia began to admit that he was quite sweet, for a dog. Had he not started to make her sneeze, she would have been sad to see him go.

She was not superstitious but when she found the pictures they linked with the dog in her mind and made her think of the sudden arrival of the corpse on her doorstep as a bad portent. She truly found the pictures. She was tidying, not snooping, in Giles' office. It was *their* office really. She used the computer more than he did. She kept his books and filled out his tax return. But because she had a desk and computer at work and did not want him to feel emasculated, the room was always referred to as his.

The photographs startled her so badly she had to sit down. She had long made a habit of thinking of her life as unconnected episodes and had lived it so as to minimise the risk of people and events from one section spilling over into another. The pictures before her were as damaging an overspill from her unhappy youth as the dead dog's stink had been from her childhood.

Guiltily she hid them back precisely where she had found them. It would not do for Giles to know she knew, not before she had decided how to deal with the situation.

Then she pictured Eliza, maddeningly, effortlessly pretty, like some Hardy waif in her down-at-heel floral clothes and unwashed hair, and suddenly understood things about her that had mystified her before. Perhaps she should have gone to the cinema after all and watched the wildest piece of escapist nonsense she could find? Its narrative might have provided useful confusion and driven out the storylines now unspooling in her head.

By the time Giles and Dido returned from Kent, the house was spotless and Julia was composed. But her calm was wafer thin. Helping Dido through their Sunday night ritual, washing and drying her hair, indulging with tongs and mascara the child's covert desire to be beautiful, she felt burdened by secrets, torn between the urge to love and the cruel impulse to enlighten.

4

The steers were ready to be moved. Pearce could always tell at a glance. Often they would tire of a particular field even though there was still plenty of grass for them to crop. There was no point forcing them to stay put or their boredom would register itself as restlessness or destructiveness. In this case they had tried to destroy a water trough. The concrete lid of the ballcock chamber had been cracked through on an earlier occasion. Now one of them must have nudged the two parts around until one of them fell inside, pressing the ballcock hard down and causing a small flood.

He waded into the muddy puddle, pulled up his overall sleeves, reached into the water, heaved out the piece of concrete slab and set it back in place alongside its neighbour. For now a rock from the hedge would serve to hold the thing in place.

His mobile rang, startling him. Molly had insisted he buy one after the twin horrors of their father's death and a character in *The Archers* being run over by his own tractor. If he left it on its bracket in the tractor cab it enraged her.

'You can't call an ambulance if you can't reach the thing, you lummock,' she had shouted. 'Pocket. Always in a pocket, okay?'

It took him a few minutes to find the phone as it was in a shirt pocket, not an overall one. His niece, Lucy, had fiddled with it and changed the ringing tone from a snatch of Mozart to some pop tune he could not name.

'Hello?'

'You've forgotten, haven't you?'

'Shit.'

'Pearce!'

'Half an hour. I'll be there in half an hour.'

'You know I don't like leaving her on her own.'

'She'll be okay for half an hour. We were always on our own at that age.'

'On a farm. Not here. Where are you?'

'I'm in the yard,' he fibbed. 'I'm just headed in for a shower.'

'Half an hour. You promise?'

'Promise.'

He hung up and called the cattle, in the same way his father used to, a wordless shout somewhere between 'Come on' and 'Hiya'. Inquisitive and hopeful, several were already making their way towards him. More lumbered, mooing, round a hedge to join them from the field beyond. As always the burly Angus-Limousin cross was in the lead. As always they followed the eccentric line of a cattle path. He waited, standing on a hedge for a better view, until they were in a close, hard breathing mass below him and he had counted all seventy-two, then he opened the gate.

They needed no calling through and several soon broke into a short-lived charge. The last one safely through, he doubled back to fix the gate shut with the tangle of barbed wire that looped every gate post on the farm. Then he walked amongst them, leading them as much as driving them to a temporary holding field nearer the house. Looking back he saw the stragglers, one of them with a limp that would need investigating tomorrow, calmly following the cattle path, nose to tail.

The paths traversed the farm and were a mystery. They did not always offer the most direct route but had been trod down hard by so many generations of animals that they seemed to represent rights of way as fixed in tradition as any church way or bridle path. Whereas rabbits or foxes ran at will across open grassland where there was no route trodden out, cattle seemed incapable of moving from field to field without following a track their forefathers had made. At several points a marked wiggle took the path out of true by several feet and every time they would follow it religiously, each wiggling in turn. During the BSE crisis and, more recently, during the last outbreak of foot and mouth, there had been a few weeks when the farm was unstocked. When new animals were introduced to the fields they found the paths immediately and followed them. When grass fields were ploughed up for a few years of other crops – potatoes or barley – then resown with grass, he could have sworn the cattle re-established their path along the same line.

Odder still, if you walked with your mind on other things you soon looked down to find your boots had found the line of impacted soil a few inches below the level of the more comfortable grass.

As a boy Pearce had once been taken to a hill above Barrowcester. The purpose had been to admire the view of the cathedral and Tathams, the city's ancient school, and to examine Iron Age fortifications. His attention had been entirely absorbed however in an old turf maze cut into a flat expanse on the hill's crest. While the others in the school party had been taking photographs of the distant buildings, he had been occupied with treading out the maze, understanding instinctively how its simple pathways were designed to still and thereby free the busy mind.

He loved walking with cattle about him. It amused him that such heavy, powerful creatures should be so playful, acting out a grandmother's footsteps pantomime close behind him, hitching lewd rides on one another's haunches, occasionally kicking up their heels in sheer joy at a fresh piece of pasture. He liked their warm, beery smell, less pungent than cows, and their reassuring snorts of breath on his hands and back.

He showered quickly then drove his Land Rover up the lane to Kelynack then over Carn Bosavern, then down through St Just towards Cape Cornwall and Molly's cottage. There was a honk and she waved to him from a carful of women heading in the other direction. She flashed fingers at him to indicate eleven, meaning she'd be back by then, then headed on into Penzance while he continued towards the terrace where she lived now.

It never ceased to surprise him that they had passed through the same childhood, rarely apart, yet somehow she had emerged with a cluster of friends she still saw while most of his old mates had moved away or were swallowed up in religion or marriage or a deadly combination of the two. Continuity played a part too; those of Molly's friends who had gone on to study after school had mostly done it within the region – in Falmouth, Truro, Exeter or Plymouth. Those who had married had done so locally, finding men whose surnames would be familiar to their parents.

Pearce had only been away two years but that brief interval had been long enough to sever ties he had in any case been neglecting. When he found himself unexpectedly back here, he fell between generations, then was drawn into the unsociable habits of agriculture.

Molly had not divorced but her marriage to Morris had fallen apart and she now lived alone with Lucy. Far from sliding into self-pity or bitterness, she had simply taken up

again with the friendships marriage had temporarily interrupted. Where their parents' generation had used words like
duty and obligation with reference to the community, Molly
used them cheerfully of self. 'I owe it to myself,' she would
say or, 'You've a duty to yourself, Pearce.'

Now that she was socialising again, she had begun to put
pressure on Pearce to go out more. Whenever he plucked
up courage to ask someone out or accepted an invitation,
she would make encouraging noises the way one did when
training a puppy, patiently affirming good behaviour. This
would irritate him into taking things no further. Occasionally
she had tried to set him up with one of her friends but it was
hopeless. He knew too much about them and vice versa and
they would spend most of a wretched evening or two talking
about Molly for want of more interesting common ground. He
was touched that Molly tried, however irritating he found it,
but relieved when she called on him as a babysitter instead.
It was all very well waxing nostalgic about their parents' day,
when farmers had met girls through chapel picnic or hunt ball
but he suspected he would have fared no better in the Fifties
than now.

Lucy must have heard his car because she opened the front
door as he was walking up the garden path. She was on the
phone but she gave him what in her current manifestation
passed for a smile. He left her to talk in the conservatory in
peace and headed for the kitchen.

Molly worried Lucy was eating nothing but junk. As well
as making sure she spent long enough on Friday night's
unfinished homework, his job was to cook himself something
wholesome and tempt her to join him.

Lucy was ten and had been dressing as a boy most of her
short life. One could blame it on nothing in particular; it had
predated any trouble between her parents or her father losing
his farm. It seemed to Pearce she had been a boy as soon as

she had the ability to choose – her life a brief flourish of pinks and frills before a sturdy continuum of jeans and beanies. It saddened Molly, he suspected, because in unguarded sleep Lucy dropped her habitual scowl and became pretty, really pretty. Morris teased the girl about it, called her Tom or Jim-Me-Lad, which only made her more cussed and scowly. Pearce saw no harm in it. Jeans were more practical than skirts, especially for skateboarding which Lucy loved. He guessed Molly's unspoken fear but could see no risk that the child was butch to the core. Beneath the gruff exterior, she adored boys and had simply found a way of retaining their company and respect beyond the age when football and instinct usually dictated a ruthless gender divide.

And her life was not as protected as it would have been growing up on her father's farm. For all its remoteness St Just was becoming a tough little town. Unemployment was high, as was illiteracy. Bored gangs of boys hung around the car park and pavements playing with skateboards or bikes beyond the age when it was cool to do so. Inevitably there were drugs, regular outbreaks of tedium-fuelled arson and, when the recycling bins weren't being set on fire or the British Legion's windows smashed, there were ugly vendettas against targets picked at random – rehoused problem families, foster children, asylum seekers. There were jokes about neighbouring communities, like Pendeen deemed more inbred, more problematic. Kids in Pendeen probably mocked the ones up the road in the hamlet of Morvah and so on. The bottom of the pecking order was probably someone's pig up in Cripplesease.

If dressing like a boy enabled Lucy to hold her head up among her peers and survive without becoming another teenage pregnancy statistic, so much the better for her. Pearce's only worry, knowing how much pleasure and support Molly had always found in girlfriends, was that his niece would miss out. Male conversation was so limited and innutritious.

'Lo,' she said when her mumbled phone conversation was over at last. She had made a brave show on the phone of manly reluctance – 'Yeah. Gotta go. No. My uncle's here. Yeah.' – but now they were without witnesses, she allowed herself a sweet smile and a little girlishness. This was the side of her Molly rarely saw.

'Hi,' he said.

'What you making?'

'Fried chicken,' he said, knowing this was a favourite of hers. 'And fried bananas.'

'Can we have corn fritters instead of the bananas?'

'If you make them. Yeah. You have that pan and I'll have this one.'

He showed her how to soak the chicken in milk for a while first to keep it moist and ground up a mixture of stale bread, garlic and dried out cheddar to roll it in. Lucy then stirred together a can of creamed corn, an egg and a spoonful of flour as though this were the height of culinary sophistication. He set two pans to heat up, sloshed in olive oil and together they cooked, raising a cloud of greasy smoke.

'What's your homework?'

'Photothingy. Synthetics. I should have done it on Friday as soon as I got in. I always do this. Hate it. It hangs over me and spoils Sunday night. I hate plants.'

'It's easy.'

'No it's not.'

'What don't you understand?'

'I've got the green stuff, yeah? The chloro you know.'

'Phyll.'

'Yeah and I know that uses sunlight but then I get muddled.'

'You need sunlight and what else?'

'Water,' she said.

'Which is H_2O which means what?'

'Hydrogen twice and some oxygen.'

'Good. Then anything else?'

'No.'

'Wrong. Water in its natural state has salts in it. Minerals from the soil, which the plant needs. What then?'

'Then I don't know.'

'Okay. Do those need turning?' He gestured to the darkening fritters with his spatula.

'No. So what else?'

'Carbon dioxide. Plants take in CO_2, keep the carbon and let the oxygen out again. Carbon's the building block they use to make formaldehyde and simple sugars and from those they make starch. Carbohydrates. Sugar. Sugar beet. Potatoes. The sweetness in that sweetcorn. But the gas is important too because we keep each other going. Animals use oxygen and give out carbon dioxide but while plants are photosynthesising they take in carbon dioxide and give out oxygen. No waste.'

'Provided there are enough plants.'

'And not too many animals. That make sense?'

'Not really. What happens at night?'

'That's when plants give out carbon dioxide like animals. It's why nurses always used to take all the plants out of a patient's room at night.'

'Huh?'

'Look. We'll eat. Then I'll do you a drawing you can copy. And there's a groovy experiment you can do with tin foil and a growing leaf. It takes a day or two but you could write down how to do it.'

'Yeah?' She looked distinctly unconvinced. 'Thanks.'

'Any time. How's stuff otherwise? How's school?'

'Okay.'

'How's your dad?'

'I dunno. How's yours?'

'Cheeky. Come on. Wash hands. Lay table.'

'Can I have Coke?'

'Will it help your homework?'

'Yeah.'

'Do it then, and get me a beer.'

After supper he talked her through the experiment to prove starch production in leaves, amazed that he could still remember the details of it. They set it up on one of the houseplants, wrapping a leaf in a piece of silver foil out of which LUCY had been carefully cut with kitchen scissors. Then he watched as she drew a few diagrams and a flow chart before leaving her at the kitchen table to write it up while he slipped upstairs to use her computer.

It was a sad addiction but a harmless one. Like a lot of men, he suspected, married and single, his first weeks of being connected to the Internet had passed in a dazed frenzy of porn. Apart from a few dog-eared pictures passed around at school and college, he had little experience of smutty pictures in printed form, having never overcome his fear of handing a magazine across the counter or being caught leafing through one in Smith's. The Internet was crammed with them, catering to every taste, from glossily professional to touchingly amateur. There were even live women, as it were, jerkily posing and shifting in front of cameras in their own homes.

He wanted contact however. Before long he realised that the parade of unattainable, anonymous breasts and groins, lust-stupid, wet-lipped pouts and proffered parts and, worse, the plastic technology he needed to summon them, only emphasized that he was on his own. He still found that the odd flirty chat with one of the nice, well-informed girls in Cornwall Farmers gave him a more lasting fulfilment. Porn had such a limited repertoire and so few ingredients, which of course was why it could answer a specific need with such accuracy, but conversation excited because it was less predictable and left room for emotional as well as erotic fantasy.

He had been wary of chat rooms at first, being half-ignorant of the technology involved and fearing they might require actual talking. Once he understood what they were, thanks to a remark by the diesel delivery man, there was no stopping him. He went online for two or more hours a night.

There were as many chat rooms as there were topics for discussion, but it was amazing how many of the tapped-in conversations soon came down to sex. He had been to sites connected with farming, with history, with Cornwall, even suicide and in all of them, sooner or later, established that a person he was talking to was a woman and horny. There was a limit to what could be done with words but it was still wilder than mere pictures and he came away sensing he had been given a glimpse of someone's deeper wishes. He had been left feeling not quite so alone.

After a while he had given up pretending and headed straight for a chat room about love, in other words sex. It was called, with breathtaking originality, lonesometonight.co.uk. You gave yourself a name when you logged on and he enjoyed being different people. John the fireman with the big hose, Peter the carpenter with a woody, Jud the butcher who liked the feel of flesh beneath his hands, and so on.

He had become a very fast two-finger typist.

He had soon guessed that he was not the only one being someone he wasn't, subtracting years, adding inches, changing job, name, hair colour with a few blithe key strokes. Few of the women could be the curvaceous, tanned, devil-may-care temptresses they said they were or they'd have too much of a social life to be spending an evening with a computer. Some would be plain. Some would be married. Some might be old enough to be his mother. Some might be scared of meeting people in the flesh. Some might not even be women. It did not matter. They would never meet and their words and fantasies combined to flatter and fulfil each other.

Then one day a woman he had been chatting to, who had described herself as a size 8 and billed herself as Tina, a voracious, twenty-something brunette who liked two-on-ones and having her insteps licked by a man with a day's growth of beard and hands with engine grime around the nails, broke through the glass barrier between them. Breaking all the unwritten rules, she had stopped halfway through telling him how she'd like it if he'd handle her just after stripping a truck engine and left grimy fingerprints all over her full but still pert breasts.

Suddenly she typed, *Oh sod it. My name's Janet. I'm a size 12 and a mother of three under-8s. I'm 38, bored as fuck and living in Hayle.*

He had been so startled he typed back that he was Pearce, not a black mechanic from Detroit but a white farmer from West Penwith and just turned 40. She had asked him where he went to school and they had established that her clever younger brother had gone to Humphrey Davy too, but only after it had stopped being a grammar school. A cousin of his had taught RE at her school. A distant cousin. He had asked about her children. She had asked about his farm. He had found himself telling her about his dead parents, about Molly's marriage and how her husband had been ruined by buying too many pigs and getting into debt during the BSE crisis, about how he loved children, how he was babysitting his niece as they typed.

What about you? he had typed. *What do you like doing?*

TV she had said, *Lots of TV*, which depressed him until he remembered she had small children. *And I go dancing at The Barn when I get the chance, which is about once a year, but . . . it makes me feel ancient until I've had a few.*

38's a very sexy age, he had typed back daringly. *You know a thing or two. You know what you want.*

Yeah, she had responded. *That's easy for a 40-year-old to say. Sorry. Gotta go. C U.*

He had told her too much and scared her off. And she had regretted being so open and grown inhibited. He had logged onto the site punctiliously for the last ten days or so looking for Tina3Way among the usual suspects but she was never there. Either she had changed her moniker or she had given up and switched to a different chat room entirely, regretting her honesty. Try as he might, he suddenly found he could muster no interest in anyone else, in Lulu or Sabina or Greasemonkey or Hotlips and their predictable come-ons soon turned to surly defensiveness when he failed to respond. For all that they were sparing themselves, hiding behind false names and artificial language, the chat room now felt as bleak and humiliating as any singles night in a half-empty bar. Lonesome Tonight indeed.

When he logged on this evening he meant only to check his e-mails. But one of these was from Billy Pender with a query about the next day's cattle auction and how many lots Pearce was interested in. To answer it he had to stay online a little longer to visit the auctioneer's website and online catalogue. He noted down the lot numbers, e-mailed Billy back the response then lingered just a little too long and found himself tapping in www.lonesometonight.co.uk.

She was there.

Janet? he typed. He guessed that by using her real name he could gauge immediately how she felt now about their early honesty.

There was a pause. She had forgotten his name. Of course she had.

Pearce? How RU?

Fine. How RU, Janet?

Never better. Hot. Wet. What RU wearing?

He paused. So that was how it was going to be.

Just got in from the garage, he typed. *Oily overalls. Nothing much underneath.*

Buttons or zip?

Buttons. Rubber buttons. Most of them are missing. U?

Black negligee. Red lace knickers.

Bra?

No. 2 hot. That feels good. Cup me from behind. R your hands dirty?

Filthy. I'm leaving fingerprints all over you and I don't care. Janet?

What? What are you doing now?

Giving you my mobile number, he typed. *And logging off. I hate this.*

He typed in the phone number before he had time for second thoughts, then logged off and switched off the computer before he had a chance to see if she logged off too or simply started chatting to someone else.

He stepped out onto the landing to listen out for Lucy. He heard gunshots and the whinnying of frightened horses so knew her homework was finished. She was the only girl he had ever known who liked Westerns. It was not something she shared with mates – Westerns were not cool like horror films – but a private obsession. At ten she was already a connoisseur. She had acquired the taste off Morris who was

41

a country-and-western fan, but had gone far beyond him. For Morris, cowboy culture was essentially a sentimental construct and a way to meet women. For his daughter, Westerns by John Ford or Howard Hawks were almost sacred texts, tough lessons in morality and honour undiluted by romance.

Her uncle had taken up where her father left off. Pearce kept a little card in his wallet listing the films she had on video or DVD so he could know when to buy a rarity for her collection. He always approached the films with a slight feeling of dread, fearing that their limited, masculine stories would be as dry as their settings, then found himself surprised by the beauty of the cinematography or the archetypal power of the storylines. *Red River* remained a favourite of his because of the cattle-driving scenes but he occasionally had great heroic dreams in which he was riding into the sunset with a woman in a Quakerish Grace Kelly bridal gown.

It took him a second or two to realise his mobile was ringing because its unfamiliar pop jingle tone was competing with the noise of the shootout from the TV. He had to run downstairs to the kitchen to snatch it from his denim jacket.

'Hello?'

'Pearce?' she whispered.

'Janet?'

'Yeah.'

'Why are you whispering?'

'Er . . . kids are asleep.'

'Oh.' He pictured her in an old-fashioned nursery with brass bedsteads and a rocking horse, an eroticised Mrs Darling. 'Do you want me to call you back? This'll be costing.'

'No. It's fine. We're on the same network. Free local call.'

'Oh. Great.'

'So . . . d'you want to meet or what?'

'Sure.' His blood raced. He quietly closed the kitchen door. 'Where are you?'

'Hayle. 34 Portreath Way.'

'That's easy.'

'Yeah. Er. Can you come over now?'

'I'm looking after my sister's kid.'

'Oh. Right.'

'Tomorrow?' he suggested.

'No,' she said. 'How about Tuesday?'

'Tuesday'd be fine. What time shall I pick you up.'

'How'd you mean?'

'To go out.'

'Oh . . .'

'Or we could stay in.'

'Yeah. Er. Eight? Give the kids time to get off.'

'Okay. 34 Pentreath Way.'

'Portreath. Yeah.'

'See you there, Janet.'

'Yeah. Great. Bye.'

He hung up and remained leaning on the cluttered dresser as he took it in. From what he could tell from her whisper, her voice had been rough, as if she had just woken up, but warm, definitely warm. Hot, as she would have put it. 34 Portreath Way. Not Street or Road. A modern house, therefore. As different from his as could be imagined. He could bring her into Penzance, perhaps, to the tapas bar or the fish place. Or a film, maybe? No. Eight was too late for a film. Perhaps she'd have eaten already. A drink, then. Could he take wine? What was the form for a date with a woman you had never met and didn't know? And what should he wear?

He had a fleeting vision of turning up in oily overalls with nothing underneath to find her sleepily welcoming in a black negligee and not much else then realised he was getting crazily

43

horny which felt dreadful in Molly's kitchen with Lucy next door. So he made them a pot of tea and took it through with a packet of fig rolls to watch the rest of the Western with her. Happily it was an Alan Ladd one; scarcely a lily white breast or pouting squaw in sight, just the relative innocence of men, guns and horseflesh.

5

Eliza woke to find Dido standing by the bed with a cup of tea.

'You're not due back until tomorrow.'

'It *is* tomorrow,' Dido said. 'I made you tea. Sit up or you'll go to sleep again.' Her brow furrowed. 'Where's Carlo?'

'Oh. Oh, Dido.' Eliza sat up. She worried she was going to cry again.

'It's okay. I know he's dead. I cleared up the mess. I just wondered where you put his body.'

'Giles' garden. Under the copper cherry. He'll be happy there.' With dim gratitude Eliza registered that Julia had not broken the news herself.

'Oh.' Dido shrugged. 'So you can pay that bill.'

'Yes.' Eliza felt herself blush. She sat up and obediently sipped her tea. 'Mmm,' she said. 'Thank you.' Dido was eyeing her sceptically in the way that always made Eliza think *caught red-handed*. 'I must get up,' she added. 'This is awful. I was going to buy food.'

'I bought food.'

'How?'

Dido spoke over her shoulder as she returned to the kitchen. 'Granny gave me money.'

'She's not your granny.'

'I know, I know. She's just Giles' mother but I don't mind calling her that. She's nice. And she gives me money.'

'Yes but it's your money, to spend on things you want.'

'I wanted food. I bought bacon and bread and bananas and beans.'

'B food.'

'And milk and tea and sugar. Giles gave me money as well. Twenty pounds. I think that was supposed to come to you. And *She* gave me money, too.'

'Why?' Eliza knew Dido was shrugging.

'To shut me up? Buy me off? I dunno. Money's money.'

Eliza heard cupboards open and close, the frying pan clunk onto the stove, the menacing, electric click-click of the gas lighter.

She must have fallen asleep again, for the next moment Dido was holding out a bacon sandwich and a glass of orange juice. Breakfast was one of the things they did together, as a rule, Dido sitting at the opposite end of the bed while they chewed over toast and the day's prospects. This morning, however, Dido must have eaten already.

'Are you ill?' she asked as Eliza sipped her juice. 'Or just sad?'

Eliza shook her head. 'Sad, mainly.'

'He was a good age.'

'I know.'

'And he was costing a lot.'

Eliza smiled at this frank assessment. 'I know,' she said. 'Where are you going?'

'School. I'm late. Sign this. It's to say you can't come to the Parents' Evening tonight. I've got to go because Meera and I are helping with coffees but there's food so . . . oh. Sticky fingers. Don't worry. I'll do it.' Eliza watched Dido execute a perfect copy of her signature after only a moment's thought.

'Bye.' Dido kissed her shortly. 'Don't forget to eat again later. You're getting too thin.'

Eliza lay listening to Dido brushing her teeth, washing up breakfast then letting herself out. It was monstrous to let the child mother her, she knew this, but Dido's capability was hard to withstand. Increasingly the little girl – not so little, she was ten next birthday – was coming not only to display traces of her grandmother's bracing lack of humour but to resemble Hannah too, neither greatly comforting.

Dido was not really Eliza's daughter but her niece, her sister Hannah's unplanned daughter. Her senior by two years, Hannah was everything Eliza was not: sporty, rebellious, popular, courageous, startlingly plain. Until she was seven or eight, she was a nice enough looking, chubby-cheeked child who more than made up for her failure to turn heads with her dynamic ability to make friends. Then she began to grow and her troubles started. The strain of coping with what came next drove her father to walk out on them. Eliza would have walked out too, only she was still a child and knew of nowhere better to walk to.

So she ran away into study. Encouraged by her mother, who taught Latin to ever dwindling classes, she concentrated on work as Hannah had done on sport, and found that she was good at it. She discovered a technique for assimilating, mentally filing, then reproducing information that could be applied equally well to physics or history. But these were cold, unstirring successes quite unlike Hannah's sweaty triumphs on the sports track.

It was only in music that she found any real delight. Musicians were famously unconscious of fashion and accommodating of outcasts. She was quiet and had no dress sense beyond aspiring to invisibility. She fitted right in. She was not a star but she played the piano well enough to accompany those who thought they might be, and she sang soprano in a clear tone with barely a hint of vibrato, so was a natural for close harmony and madrigal groups. She was not particularly popular but she went unnoticed, which was the best she could hope for.

The real escape came at university. The family had no money but she won a music scholarship to Oxford and, for the first time in her life, found herself hundreds of miles from home, among people who knew nothing of Hannah or her problem. Impulsively, when first asked, she said that, no she had no brothers or sisters, and the lie brought a heady buzz that outweighed any dull pang of guilt. So she repeated it until it became a kind of truth. Hannah was far away, studying sociology on a sports scholarship in America, so there was no risk she would visit.

Having avoided involvements with boys throughout her teens, it became ever easier to do so; resistance rather than exposure, it seemed, was the surest inoculation. By her second year of studies, she was comfortably established as the girl to whom men brought their confidences and girls their complaints. Merely by withholding herself and standing back to observe, she found she had acquired a wholly unfounded reputation for wisdom. Whereas virginity in her teens had been a mark of ridiculous shame, in her twenties it was so unimaginable a state that her friends assumed she had lost it long ago and decided men were not worth the emotional expense.

So, while her friends' second and third year rooms acquired the appurtenances of sin – ashtrays, joss stick holders, wine racks, cunningly concealed extra mattresses – and while many of them opted to move out to sordid, mixed-gender house shares, Eliza's room in the weeks of her Finals remained as studious and tidy as in her first week. Fruit bowl, music stand

and a second-hand *Grove Encyclopaedia of Music* were totemic of her withheld state.

She graduated with a first-class degree and calmly accepted the research place her tutor had already hinted would be offered her. The thought of going back into the world after these three years of self-regarding peace left her queasy with fear.

Her doctoral research was to be on the Elizabethan madrigal, focussing on the two surviving works of a young Cornish courtier, Roger Trevescan (*Ave Verum* and *Go, Dissembler, I Care Not*). She believed she could furnish a case for his being the hand behind *The Revels of Cybele*, an unfinished cycle of madrigals in praise of the monarch.

She still played the piano, still sang, but had no illusions about pursuing either as a career. She would finish her doctorate, become a lecturer, carve herself out a quietly comfortable niche which would change nothing in the world and where the world would leave her alone. Not for her Hannah's climbing of mountains and battling with prejudice.

Then she was pressed to sing the soprano solos in a small performance of the Pergolesi *Stabat Mater*. Her fellow soloist was Giles, a choral scholar at one of the grander colleges and quite unreasonably beautiful. Almost bloodlessly Aryan, he looked barely eighteen, although he was actually twenty. His voice was that rare thing, a counter tenor which did not immediately make her want to laugh, perhaps because, for once, its high, bright tone was emerging from a face that matched it.

She was embarrassed to be singing with him, not being in his league, but he softened his tone to complement hers, followed her lead in the way she sang the ornaments (sensing that, unlike him, she had researched them) and congratulated her afterwards without so much warmth as to sound patronising. When he insisted she join him for dinner after-wards, it was a perilous moment. Assailed by his beauty and charm, she accepted but insisted no less vehemently on bringing along two friends from the orchestra, both of them plainly smitten with him, one of them exceedingly pretty. She was thus able to spend the meal feasting on his looks with impunity and at a safe distance while he basked in the adoration of the others. He left with the pretty one, with whom he had an affair for the rest of that term.

Believing herself proof against further meetings with him, she thought no more about it. Two weeks later, in the summer holidays, Hannah was reported dead and Eliza had to rush home.

Not long before, Hannah had amazed everyone by returning from America with a baby girl in tow and joking that she had no idea who the father was because there were so many candidates. Thinking back, Eliza realised her mother and her friends were too startled to remember to be scandalized. Undaunted by everyone's assumption that raising the little girl, Dido, would now be her occupation, Hannah settled in London and threw herself into fundraising work for a charity that provided support for people with facial disfigurement. Dido slept peacefully in her carrycot in a corner of an office plastered with images of burn victims, Paget's disease, leontism and cherubism. Months later Dido was still only a babe in arms, barely weaned, sleeping peacefully on the veranda of a boarding house in Kathmandu when Hannah fell to her death off a mountain. She had left Dido in the care of an *amah* while she led an all-woman team on a sponsored hike up Sharpu 1. Characteristically she died saving the life of a team member, a guilt-wracked cartographer who escorted Hannah's ashes, along with Dido, back to England.

It was Hannah's fourth such expedition but her first as a

mother. Under the terms of the will she had drawn up before setting out, she gave Eliza sole guardianship of the baby, to raise her as her own. Informed by fleeting postcard, Eliza had not for one moment thought of the document as anything but a superstitious formality, like taking out holiday insurance.

Tucked in Dido's carrycot, Eliza found a guidebook which she pored over obsessively in her shock. *From the campsite Sharpul looks awesome but behind the well-named facade lies an easier but still intimidating route to a tiny summit perch over 4000 ft above the valley floor. Around 2 weeks walk from Kathmandu via the airstrip at Taplejung, it is reached after a fitness-testing hike over three mountain passes.* She found the spot on the book's fold-out map and showed it to her mother but what her reeling mind needed was a chart of the mountain seen from the side, with drops and distances; she needed to be able to say *here's where she fell and there's where she landed.*

Her sorrow at losing Hannah was heightened by her guilty sense of relief that her troublesome sister was gone. And the gift of Dido, the entrusting of a baby to her, brought a confusion of joy and dismay. Befuddled by grief, and by antidepressants pressed on them by a kind GP, she and her mother were thrust into a world of potty training and *Ready Brek*. Robbed of a funeral, cheated of goodbyes, they grew briefly close again as they had not been since Hannah blew the family apart. The merciful tedium of child-rearing enfolded them even as they were ostracised in the way the bereaved are when everyone considers the death a blessing. Despite the announcement in the papers, Eliza's father did not use the occasion to resume contact, which was also a cause for relief.

The possibility that Dido would take after her mother was discussed even less than the identity of her mystery father. Just once, when they were bathing her, Eliza asked,

'So do you think she's going to . . . ?'

And her mother replied, 'No, of course she's isn't. Just look at her. She's a little angel!' with a religious certainty that silenced fear.

Her mother was startled and upset when Eliza began preparing to return to her studies and to take Dido with her.

'I thought you weren't going back,' she said. 'Not now. I thought you'd both stay here. How will you manage? University's no place for a baby!'

'We'll be fine,' Eliza assured her. 'She's so good. She'll be no bother.' Though in truth she was giving little thought to how they would manage, such was her growing desperation to escape the desolation of her mother's house.

At first Dido was, indeed, little more trouble than a cat. Other students managed to keep far more problematic pets. It was simply a matter of anticipating when Dido was going to fall asleep and seizing that moment to leave her in her pushchair while Eliza raced to the library and found what she needed. Even wide awake she was an affable baby, easily placated. When people asked, Eliza told them half the truth, that she had adopted Dido, that she had known Dido's mother all her life, that Dido's mother had died in a mountaineering accident. Friends were charmed at the idea. Married ones, with children of their own, welcomed her into their unofficial club with something like relief, recommended babysitters and made offers of outgrown clothing. Eliza had always found that work expanded to fill the time you gave it and now her research actually benefited from the disruption the baby represented, obliged as she was to channel her efforts into increasingly concentrated intervals of peace and clear thinking.

Such a chasm of years seemed to yawn between the gurgler in the pushchair and the dear, severe, forgiving person who had just washed up breakfast. Her manner was so much older than was fair, a consequence of Eliza's failure to protect her.

Eliza had no camera but there was a recent snap of Dido, taken by Giles, tucked into her wallet. Head thick with the past, she made herself sit up and lunge over the side of the bed to retrieve it.

Dido was in a dressing room at the Coliseum, playing at actresses and surprised by the camera. She had on a crazy feathered headdress and had frozen in the act of lifting a powder puff to her nose. Eliza stared at the picture hard, fighting to see truth beneath familiarity. Yes, the features were quite large and her teeth weren't entirely straight, but then whose teeth were at that age? It was more comforting, Eliza decided, to hope that the stranger slowly emerging from the child's soft beginnings was not Hannah at all, but the unnamed, unaware father.

6

Giles got up at the same time as Julia because it was a working morning and his voice would need time to warm up and settle. His first thought was of Dido but she had got up even earlier and already left the house.

'Don't worry,' Julia told him. 'She'll be cooking breakfast for Eliza before school. It's one of their things together. At least I had a chance to clean her uniform. It was filthy. And I slipped in some money for food. God knows what they eat half the time.'

'You are good. You think of everything.'

'I know.'

He lifted her hair and kissed the back of her neck as she pored over the day's paper. (She rarely had time to read more than the arts pages and a headline or two.) For a moment she softened under his touch, remembering him with her last night, then he felt her pull herself together. She sighed.

'I must go.'

'Russians at the airport?'

'Czechs this week,' she said. 'And Alexy.' She stood, folding the paper in the neat way he had never mastered.

She had been up no longer than him but managed to look amazingly groomed. Her dark hair was glossy smooth, her make-up perfect. An American client, a tenor they both knew, called her awesome.

'How do you *do* that?' Giles asked, admiring her as she picked up the leather document case he had bought her back from his trip to the *Maggio Musicale*. He noticed she had managed to find shoes which subtly echoed it.

'Do what?' she said, worried.

'You look wonderful.'

'Thanks,' she said but her smile was warmer than her words.

'Wish me luck.'

'Why? Shit. I forgot. Of course! Your cab's booked for nine but I was going to put your music out.'

'It's okay.' He opened the paper, saw the word *paedophile* in a headline and immediately closed it. 'I can find it myself. Bye.'

As soon as she was gone, he took his orange juice (he never took coffee within two hours of performing) and climbed the stairs to Dido's room.

He could not say what he hoped to find there. An angry note or a letter of guarded apology? There was nothing, of course, not even a vengeful mess. This had always been her room, even since she was old enough to move down to one of the larger ones. A maid's room, with crazily sloping ceilings which would soon be making even Dido duck, it had begun as an ideal nursery, close enough to hear a cry in the night, far enough away for noise not to reach dining table or music room. It was easy, now, to imagine it as a shy teenager's bolt-hole, an eyrie dank with neglected laundry and unwashed thoughts.

When Julia oversaw the complete redecoration of the house recently they consulted Dido about what she wanted. She pored for a few minutes over a range of 'heritage' paint colours and opted for Uppark Dairy Blue. 'And I want to be able to put everything away and I want curtains and a lock on the door.'

The result was a sort of nun's cell; undoubtedly cooler and less childish than anything Julia would have chosen. The clothes she kept here were all tidied away behind doors or in drawers built in under the bed. They had fixed her up with a desk and a computer, although she rarely did homework here, and her books were ranged along a pair of shelves.

There was no clutter. She had even made her bed before leaving and pulled up and smoothed the bedspread. (It was not really a bedspread but a fanciful blue silk robe Giles had worn in a production of *Rodelinda*.) There were no toys. Dido was not really a toy-loving child. Apart from the contents of the bookshelves, the only childish touch in sight was a poster from Berlin Zoo of a hippopotamus calf swimming and displaying tombstone teeth.

Giles stretched out on the bed, his feet dangling over the edge, and wondered how it must be to be her. This room was precious to him as concrete proof that she was still in his life but he knew it for a brave gesture, knew that most of her days were quite unlike this, spent at school or with friends or in Eliza's flat.

He could not begin to imagine what Eliza's flat was like inside but had stood below it often enough gazing up, seeing the sort of desperate, down-at-heel people who came in and out, noting the sheets and towels draped on strings in place of curtains, the broken panes of glass, the junk huddled on cramped balconies. He had guiltily pieced the rest together from what he saw in police dramas on the television and from the poverty that clung to Dido like the smell of damp wool or sour towels when she first arrived after several days with her mother.

Guiltily, not because he felt it was his fault that Eliza was there, the doing and choosing was most definitely all her own, but because he could never stop hoping that staying in this place, with comfort and carpets and culture could not help but change the way Dido viewed her life in that one. He would never stop fantasising that one day she would call a halt to the relentless toing and froing and make a devastating choice in his favour. He had gone so far as to consult a lawyer. He knew there were precedents in his favour, that such things could happen. A mother could be deemed unfit, a step-parent recognised by law as a more suitable guardian. He told no one, least of all Julia, who had such a terrifying ability to take action and make a finality of passing whim. If the wish came true it must be on his own merits, not through lobbying or subterfuge.

The doorbell brought him to his senses. He raced down to the nearest intercom and found it was the cab Julia had ordered for him. Asking them to wait, he hurriedly gathered his music, snatched a bottle of his preferred mineral water (still, unchilled) and left, cursing himself.

Whatever trouble he was having, his voice had to come first. Like any athlete, a singer's livelihood and reputation depended upon health and a handful of trained, specialised muscles. A hint of rhinitis could affect tuning, a drying effect of coffee or red wine affect his upper register, while milk, cheese or chocolate cake left his larynx feeling clogged and phlegmy which was disastrous for trills. An outright cold or sore throat was a crisis but the effects of mere domestic carelessness could be almost as dire.

The interval between Julia's leaving and the cab's arrival should have been spent gently warming his voice. The recording was happening in a church which might be as chilly as its acoustic was moist.

Throat wrapped in a silk scarf he superstitiously always wore to recordings, he sat in the back of the car reading over the books of Dowland much as a film actor must run through the day's shooting script. Today was nothing very grand; a budget recording of Elizabethan lute songs, but then, Giles was not a grand singer and could not afford not to treat every broadcast or recording, however minor, as though he were singing for Rattle and the Berlin Phil. As he read and changed a few breath marks, Giles buzzed softly, tongue against teeth. Occasionally he forced an artificial yawn. He had been doing this for years and was heedless of the driver's reaction.

He took minicabs everywhere. He had not owned a car since he was a student. He never saw the point. The money he saved in petrol, insurance, repairs and parking permits more than covered cab fares. Still, it embarrassed him when the subject arose. People always said how sensible he was, think of the money you save and the bother and so on but he saw them looking at him and thinking *pathetic*. He saw they suspected he did not actually know how to drive or had lost his licence. It was like confessing to having only one ball.

Counter-tenors always had *that* cross to bear. It was assumed they were gay or eunuchs or not quite manly. After their brief flirtation with principal-boy mezzos in unconvincing breastplates or frock coats, Handel and Glück revivalists had long since gone back to casting men in the high voiced, heroic roles but there were still titters. Even in the most formal opera house. Titters one could hear quite plainly over the orchestra. Present a martial figure, in Roman costume, muscular legs, a little leather jerkin, swirling red cloak, the whole *Gladiator* thing, and it was sexy. But the moment he opened his mouth to sing as high or higher than a woman there was always some fool who laughed.

After nearly ten years in the business, live performances, especially in opera, still left him sick with fear. There was so much to think about, so much that could go wrong – costumes, props, moves, words, memory, other people – and one was entirely exposed. This was different. He had worked with Douglas, the lutenist, on many occasions and they had rehearsed all the pieces twice the previous week so he was on secure ground. Wearing comfortable clothes, sitting face to face in a deserted Kilburn church, all they had to do was sing and play. Then listen. Then sing and play again. And their only audience was the recording engineer. Giles could focus all his energies on his voice and a perfect understanding with Douglas and forget all the rest.

Compared to opera, lute songs were an intimate, unshowy medium – bedroom music in fact. Sighs in a lover's ear rather than public declamations. If they were difficult to sing it was precisely because there was little obvious technical difficulty so there was no excuse for the voice not to be smooth perfection or the words tellingly put across.

Giles had never got over the disparity between the voice he heard in his head and the voice picked up by a microphone. To his ears, it invariably sounded thinner and sadder than he expected it would. With some music he had to affect a conviction that wasn't there. Dowland spoke to him, however. It was one of the enthusiasms, along with Pergolesi, that he had been able to share with Eliza. These songs would never be in demand in the concert hall – they were far too small, far too quiet – but hearing them sung back at him he was fired up afresh with amazement that they were not more celebrated.

He soon gave himself up to the nerdish pleasure of comparing one take with another and of discussing the order in which the pieces – all of them miniatures – might best be placed on the finished disc. Time melted. For all his effort in producing them and alertness to their minutiae, the songs cast their spell on him, a kind of decorously erotic melancholy. His troubled thoughts, his personal preoccupations, were ironed as smooth as he was trying to iron the phrases of the songs.

When they broke for lunch he found he had forgotten to worry about Dido and when they were finally through he found he was thinking only of the pleasure of a quiet night at home with Julia. No performance, no company, just civilised peace with a civilised woman.

Giles did not love Julia. He had never sighed for her as Dowland sighed or been thrown by her into a jealous rage. But she had become such a part of his existence that he could no more imagine life without her than he dared envisage a future in which he could not sing for a living.

She worked for the agency who managed his career. She was still a junior there when they met, but was briefly assigned to him while Selina, the agency's head, took compassionate leave for a death. Poor Julia. She thought it was an easy assignment: escort not particularly important countertenor to meeting at opera company's publicity department then sit in on photo shoot to ensure all runs smoothly. Had the agency known his life had fallen apart that week and that an important personality at the opera company was partly to blame, they would never have entrusted him to someone so inexperienced.

She made the mistake of starting a conversation with a bright, safe, 'So. How are you today?' and he told the truth. Most of it. He did not whitewash himself.

'I neglected her,' he eventually admitted. 'I was so self-obsessed. A career's just a career but a marriage . . .'

'You *have* to think of your career,' she said with unexpected force. 'It's your life! You *have* to be self-obsessed sometimes. We all do. Don't blame yourself so much.'

She watched him closely all through the photo shoot, craning her neck whenever the photographer or stylist blocked her view, as though only her concern were keeping him from breaking down there and then. The shoot took a long time, most of an afternoon, and when it was through she would not hear of his travelling home alone.

'I can't imagine what you're going through,' she said as they settled back into another cab and he found himself telling her.

By the time they reached Islington, he had talked himself out of the relatively secure position he had been in when she picked him up and into a vulnerability so thin-skinned that he suddenly couldn't bear her to leave just then. So when she looked out of the window at his overflowing dustbins and, spinning conversation, said, 'Pretty house,' it was easy to ask her in for coffee. And a glass of wine.

She rang the agency to update them and, in the mess by the phone, found a French tax indemnity form he was meant to have signed and posted back. 'I'll take it in tomorrow.'

He was going to suggest ordering in a takeaway. He had been living off takeaways since Eliza left and their litter of greasy foil about the place was a satisfying testament to his despondency. But she had a better idea. With the firm insistence of a kind nanny, she sent him upstairs to bathe and change while she rustled up supper. When he began to protest that she had done far too much already she said, 'Don't try to assert yourself. You're in no state right now to do more than maintain just you,' in a way that comforted as it compelled. Refreshed, he came downstairs to find the kitchen tidied, a store cupboard risotto of pancetta and porcini waiting on the stove and no sign of Julia.

Riding home through scorching rush hour traffic snarls, exhilarated by what felt like a good day's work, Giles felt a pang at taking Julia for granted. Why should they have a quiet night in like an old married couple simply because he was tired? He should make more of an effort. He should have learnt from the mistakes he made with Eliza.

Before reaching Starcross Road, he rang a newish restaurant he knew had caught her eye to make them a booking. But when he let himself in he found the air full of cooking smells and the table laid for eight. He had forgotten it was Selina's birthday – Julia's boss – and they were to entertain her and her girlfriend, a famous Australian film director and his boyfriend and an oboe player the agency had recently signed and her much younger husband.

'Food's all under control,' Julia said as she stepped into the shower. 'All you have to do is dress. How'd it go today?'

'Fine,' he said and slipped downstairs so she wouldn't hear him cancel the reservation.

So, instead of a quiet night in or a romantic night out, he would spend the evening remembering; not to ask Selina's girlfriend yet again what an actuary actually did, not to talk about the director's boyfriend's notorious piercings, and to draw out the painfully shy oboist.

A further blight on the evening was that instead of the young husband the oboe player brought Villiers Yates. When they had first met, Villiers had been the most intent of all Giles' student circle on becoming a professional musician. Never one to confess personal disappointment, he now held down a nominal academic position but made his money hunting down musical treasures for an American collector. Villiers was one of those old friends who was not really a friend but would have been far too risky a proposition as an enemy and so was best kept sweet. Wildly gay when they were students, he had reinvented himself as a heterosexual heartbreaker, attracting women in the same way he then wounded them, by being fundamentally uninterested in their welfare. Perhaps the oboist was the latest of his victims. Certainly she was looking more than usually pained when they arrived.

Once, and once only, when they were both very drunk at an Oxford party, he had let Villiers kiss him. If only for this reason he had done his best to drop him since but for the same reason Villiers proved a burr and had befriended first Eliza then Julia as insurance.

Villiers was almost entirely driven by a hunger for compromising knowledge about people. Whether he ever did anything with it was not the point; he simply liked to *know* things and to remind one occasionally just what he knew. Had he not found an opening as a scout for the billionaire collector he discreetly referred to as Mr Mister, he would have made an excellent spymaster for Walsingham.

'Of course!' Giles heard him telling Selina with a glance across at Giles that had a penknife's twinkle. 'Giles and I go back longer than anyone cares to remember . . .'

Irritated, Giles decided to punish him by ignoring his presence entirely. 'Selina,' he told his agent, 'you never look any older. It's quite sinister. Happy birthday.' He kissed her and turned his back on Villiers as he drew her aside to give her the present Julia had remembered to buy from them both.

It was a black velvet scarf. Very Selina. While the oboist and director's boyfriend came over to admire it too, he noted with satisfaction that Villiers had slunk off to pester Julia in the kitchen. He could sit with her for dinner, that way Giles might even get through the whole evening without addressing a word to him. He had the perfect moral excuse: disapproval of Villiers' meddling in the oboist's delicate marriage. Like anyone who has ever been dumped, he retained a reserve of righteous indignation easily drawn on. One did not stand by while a child pulled the legs off a spider.

Giles sat at one end of the dining table, Julia at the other. Their eyes met repeatedly, even as her mouth was chatting to Villiers and to Grover, the film director. She had not changed much since he first met her but she had acquired an extra layer, a sort of imposing quality she could pull over herself like an elegant shroud. She was not beautiful but she made a great deal of what she had, did it largely by presenting the world with this shrouded impressiveness. Those it did not repulse, it flattered.

Watching her at work – and to give her credit she was working as hard as he was – he wondered if he had spoiled her, if he should never have taught her how to smooth herself out so. He had found early on in life that if he did nothing, said nothing in particular but merely held up his face like a mirror to whoever was talking to him, people assumed of him whatever made them happiest. They looked at his golden hair, blue eyes, smooth complexion and assumed that he liked them, that he was interested, that he understood them. Woman after woman, some men too, had read love into his silence.

The oboist suddenly looked far less pained, touched the back of his hand and gave it a little squeeze. 'My God, that's so *true*!' she exclaimed with a toothy smile.

Giles wondered what he had just said and felt lonely behind his face.

7

Her dinner party was going awry and Julia found she was powerless to save it. It was always a bad idea to drink when you were entertaining, at least until all the food was safely served. It was just that people made her so nervous so she drank to calm her nerves then said something stupid which made her more nervous still and so down it spiralled.

It was hard to imagine a more frightening gathering. She could handle Selina or Villiers on their own but in company they were toxic – social sadists both. Selina would flatter her in a way that made her gibber and Villiers always drew a group's attention to her as though she were cleverly playing a part.

'Look at you. Miss Perfect Host,' he would say or, 'You made this? You, Julia, actually put your hands inside a dead animal and made this?'

This time tomorrow it will all be over she told herself, drawing Grover's attention to the cheese which had stalled in front of him. *Sooner than that. In two hours it will all be over.*

This was a bad habit learned in childhood. Rather than face a torment head on she would think herself forwards to the time when it would be over, tune out mentally then find she could not get back in. At school they accused her of being tone deaf.

She wasn't, actually, she simply had a naturally deep singing voice like all the women in her family and would have been quite all right if allowed to slip back a row to sing tenor. The music mistress sang the tenor line at pitch all the time to demonstrate things and nobody thought it odd.

'Just mime,' Julia was told crossly.

Mime. Not leave the choir, which would have been bearable, but stay there and mime. She would get through the torment of boys pinching her bum or tweaking her hair or girls around her pointedly leaning over to hear her not singing by tuning out. *This time tomorrow the concert will be over. This time next week we'll be on holiday. Eight years from now I won't be at school any more.* Then she would forget to turn a page or leave her mouth open a fraction too late and the mime would be exposed.

She was miming now, opening and shutting her mouth, laughing at jokes, looking intelligent, making all the right noises when she was actually on the other side of the room or somewhere up by the light fittings, watching the dinner party go down in slow motion flames like the amaretto wrappers Grover's wretched boyfriend kept igniting on the candles.

She had been like this all day. It was not just the wine. She had been late for work. She was never late. She had fluffed her French idioms when speaking to someone at the Aix Festival office. She had spent the day muddling the Czech clients' names, misdialling numbers, slopping coffee. Normally any one of these would have jolted her back into awareness and efficiency, been no more than a momentary glitch but what was so frightening was that today she could not seem to care.

It was as though someone had pumped her full of tranquillisers. She felt well – really, deliciously, toe-flexingly well. Perhaps she was going down with some benign virus, hence the sensation of unworldliness? She had been sick again this morning but then she was sick so often, usually when she felt she had eaten too much, that it was hard to gauge its significance.

'Darling?' Villiers brushed the back of her hand with a celery leaf.

'What?'

'Is Giles angry with me about something? He hasn't said a word all evening.'

'Oh you know Giles. He's hopeless. He's probably exhausted because of the recording.'

'You're sure?'

'Positive. He came straight from Kilburn to this without drawing breath.'

'He turned his back on me.'

'Villiers, he's fine. He'd have said. I love that shirt on you. Brings out your eyes.'

She cursed Liana Barton for bringing him. Villiers was such a gossip. It was amusing when one was safely alone with him, on neutral territory, but to bring him into one's house and set him loose on friends and colleagues was to court trouble. He missed nothing. It was exhausting merely shielding oneself let alone protecting guests.

Liana was sleeping with him presumably, or fixated and hoping to. Julia had slept with him. Just once. Years ago, when she had only recently arrived in London and was too inexperienced not to realise he was basically gay. Publicly Villiers slept with women. Privately he only slept with women when he wanted something, and got his real pleasure in some unobserved elsewhere. The astonishing part was that he could still find women who were grateful. He had slept with her because she was working for Selina and he wanted Selina to hear the vocal consort he had been trying to launch beyond the amateur circuit. She had felt such a fool when she had realised the truth about him. Soon after she moved in with

Giles she had discovered Villiers was an old friend of his so, on the principle that a snake in the hand was dangerous but at least you knew what it was up to, she had swallowed her pride and went through the motions of befriending him too. She guessed he had always fancied Giles so gained a measure of satisfaction in confronting him regularly with the fact that she had something he wanted.

She forced herself to tune back into the conversation and found they were discussing a court case in the day's news. The headmaster of a prominent boarding school was on trial for sexual offences against the boys in his care. His accusers were now grown men and had found one another on the Internet and managed to pool their similarly damaging experiences.

'It's all very well, all this guff about outraged innocence,' Villiers said, 'but I was a filthy little boy at nine or ten and gagging for it.'

'Perhaps these little boys weren't,' Selina suggested, stubbing out a cigarette and taking a fresh one from the packet her well-trained partner passed her.

'Oh of course they were, Selina,' Villiers said. 'Only they're married with children and Retrievers now and can't square that with their sexy memories of fun and games with Sir.'

'You weren't abused, were you Villiers?' Giles had been so quiet for a while, content, apparently, to rest his voice and listen, that Julia was startled.

'No,' Villiers admitted. 'Unless you count genteel neglect.' He was playing to the gallery but nobody laughed.

'Nobody held you down and raped you?'

Selina's girlfriend tutted. Uneasiness fluttered around the table.

'No one took your little hand and rubbed it inside their knickers?'

'Oh for Christ's sake,' Selina said. 'We're eating cheese here.'

'No,' Villiers said again. 'They didn't.'

'Fine,' Giles said. 'I just wanted to establish that, as usual, you're talking for effect and have no idea of the facts of the matter. As usual your attitudinising is puerile and offensive.'

Nobody said anything. Julia had thought someone would drunkenly lurch to Villiers' defence but perhaps they all agreed with Giles. Even Liana was pushing her wineglass around, not meeting his eye. Villiers had two little heat spots in his cheeks and was plainly mortified.

'You like chocolate ginger, don't you?' Julia told him softly.

'I love it,' he said.

'Thought so.' She opened the box and pushed it towards him. 'Does anyone not want coffee?'

He looked almost sweet now the wind was out of his conversational sails but all she could think was how glad she was that he would never be returning there and how brave Giles was to face up to him. She never wanted Villiers in the house again and keenly wanted Giles to make love to her the moment everyone could be persuaded to leave. Perhaps even down here, with her perched on the sideboard or stretched across the half-cleared dining table where splashes of gravy and hot wax and wine would be ground into her hair.

But that was out of the question naturally. That wasn't the Julia Giles had chosen to live with. He was drawn to a high maintenance, rather cool version of herself she had originally projected out of nerves and now struggled to keep in the foreground of her personality so as not to unnerve him.

Her feelings were beyond control today, her carapace thin. If somebody said something tender to her she might break down and cry just for the sensation of it.

She brought in coffee and fresh ashtrays and a plate of Medjool dates and walnuts and touched Giles' shoulder reassuringly as she set a fresh bottle of water at his elbow.

Giles apart, nobody was sober and no one could even remember what the little outburst had been about. Despite Liana's protests, Selina had put on her new CD of the Strauss concerto. With the bubbling phrases to inspire them, conversation welled up again, about recording studios, and session musicians and why so many of the best acoustics were in places like Enfield and Kilburn, never anywhere one wanted to shop or do lunch.

And, with the conversation, welled up the possibility that Julia might be pregnant.

8

Pearce knew beef cattle pretty well. He had grown up around them, as had generations of the family's men before him. But for all his expertise, his father had always relied on Billy Pender for advice and so did he. Nearly eighty now, with a shock of white hair and matching tufts at either ear, Billy was an old purist with a herd of pedigree South Devons on his farm near Helston. He rarely saw anything he wanted himself at the auctions but he enjoyed the chance to gossip with other farmers and displayed a touching loyalty to Pearce since Pearce's father's death. He also made most of his money not from his herd but from running a livestock haulage business. It was part of the unspoken deal that any animals Pearce bought at auction or sent to the abattoir would travel in one of Billy's three lorries.

The auctions used to happen in Camelford, where the banks and lawyers were, but the noise and the lorries became too much for the locals, and with buyers and sellers coming from all over Devon and Cornwall there was too little space. So the cattle market had moved to Hallworthy, near a crossroads where there was little more than a pub, a letter box, a branch of the NFU Mutual and a handful of bungalows on the edge of a gloomy plantation of pines. There was a big car park, a steamy cafeteria, then yard upon yard of covered pens and walkways where animals could be viewed and talked over before being herded into the ring. When not in use, the ring must have looked like the dank arena for some particularly brutal gladiatorial sport. Surprisingly intimate, it was surrounded by a tiered, seatless concrete viewing area where the buyers stood about or leant on the railings in guarded conference. The auctioneer looked down on the ring from a kind of pulpit, close enough to exchange friendly words and glances with buyers between lots.

Pearce met Billy in the car park and took him for a bacon sandwich washed down by a cup of strong tea. Billy had already walked round the pens exchanging greetings and news while eyeing up stock and advised Pearce to reject two of the five lots he was considering as being too small in the face.

They crossed to the ring in good time for the remaining ones because it was always amusing and informative simply to watch.

For all the joshing that went on in between lots, bidding and selling was serious business. Breeders often drove their own animals about the ring rather than trust them to an auctioneer's handler, tapping them this way and that, keeping them in constant, nervous motion while the auctioneer kept up his burbled numbers and bidders variously raised their catalogues, tapped their noses or nodded to him to commit to a price. It was rare he had to ask for a buyer's name when the gavel came down on a deal.

During the last foot and mouth crisis, which by some miracle had not crossed the Tamar, rumour had been rife because some of the first infected cattle had been traced to a farmer who regularly sold stock through this ring. With cattle movement strictly limited to those under specially issued licences, the auctioneers had visited individual farms with a camera then mounted a sale by video. The effect had been sad and surreal. No lorries in the car park, only eerily clean cars, the pens empty, buyers and sellers wading through disinfectant to stand around the ring to bid on the basis of what was shown on a screen. The camera angles had rarely been steady and there was an abiding suspicion that the inevitable dodgy animals in each lot were being kept conveniently out of focus.

Many farmers desperate to sell young steers and heifers or to restock had fallen back on their grandfathers' techniques; calling up old friends or acquaintances, passing the time of day on one another's farms and occasionally rounding off the visit with a gentlemanly bargain or two.

This was the first auction since movement restrictions were lifted and there was a powerful sense of the auctioneers re-establishing their position in the chain of commerce after a period in which they risked being cut out of countless deals and thousands of pounds worth of commission. There was a sense too of a community relieved at a return to what felt like normality. There was much back-slapping and there-but-for-the-grace relating of terrible news from Dartmoor, where so many animals had been culled and cremated. There was envious, silly talk too of timely compensation payments, early retirements and wilful cross-infecting of herds and flocks.

It always surprised Pearce how few women were here. Women served you in the cafeteria or took your cheques in the offices in return for cattle passports if you made a purchase but, considering how many women were directly involved in farming, there were few ever present at the ringside. It was as though bartering beasts was still man's business. When there were women, he had noticed they often brought along a man – husband, son or brother – to do any bidding on their behalf.

In today's sale there was just one woman who appeared as a breeder. He had spotted her before. She was unmistakable.

A moorland farmer with a brood of burly sons who were as cowed and twitchy before her muttered instruction as the shaggy-coated steers she drove around the ring with her stick. The sight of her, something in her impatience perhaps, and refusal to waste money on her hair, filled him with a powerful nostalgia for his mother.

'How's Molly?' Billy asked, reading his mind. Molly had become engaged to Morris largely to gratify their mother and had married him in a spirit of desperation after her death.

'She's fine, thanks. Still at the library.'

'And Morris?'

Pearce pulled a face. Little needed saying on this subject because so much went understood. 'Surviving,' he said.

'Sad business,' Billy said, scribbling on his catalogue with a stub of pencil. 'Very sad.'

Molly had met Morris on this very spot. When she had moaned once too often that it was impossible to meet anyone new, Pearce and his father brought her along, largely as a sort of joke to cheer her up. Morris had been bidding against their father for the same lot, then, having outbid him, offered to go halves, four heifers each. The cheek of it amused Pearce's father and a conversation began and a deal was struck, although such behaviour was strictly against his father's code of practice.

Nobody could recall Molly saying anything so it came as a shock when Morris appeared the next night to take her out.

'I take it back,' Billy muttered quickly as a lot he had rejected, Belgian Blue cross, were herded in. 'They're okay. Thought one had a bad leg but he's fine, look.'

Pearce duly bid for and bought them for slightly more than his budget allowed. He wished he could consult Billy's instincts about Janet.

'I'm taking a complete stranger on a date tomorrow night,' he wanted to say to him. 'I know she's got a thing about men with dirty hands but . . . is she all right? Is she the one? How will I know?'

Or the moorland farmwoman, who was back in the ring, smacking at the rump of a frisky heifer with a cut above its eye; he was sure she'd be a quick and trustworthy judge of character. There again, perhaps it was fear of that judgement that kept her lumpen sons single and at her oily apron strings.

9

When Dido began to walk, everything changed. She could no longer be fitted in around the interstices of a fragile academic life but burst demandingly into its centre. Forced to move out to a bedsit in Oxney, desperate for time alone to read in silence, fighting the impulse to let everything slide, Eliza leaned more and more heavily on the good nature of friends, librarians and her landlady until she could sense cracks of strain appearing in her every relationship.

Then came a day of unseasonal warmth. She had escaped the claustrophobia and sweet, nappyish fug of her bedsit and staked out a pleasant territory in Christchurch Meadow with rug, books and a large bag of fruit. Dido was at the stage of hating to have her hand held and battling confinement in her pushchair unless she was ready for sleep. She would consent, however, to wear a harness and reins and if Eliza fixed the reins to the ground with a meat skewer, she could read in peace while Dido played with her toys and whatever beetlish delights she found in the grass.

Eliza was so deep in thought, struggling to bring her tourist's Italian to bear on a new article on Monteverdi, that she did not hear his approach. Books had always offered her a refuge as deep and rapidly accessed as sleep and she emerged from them as reluctantly and in a similar fog. Still reading, she became distantly aware that Dido was being very easy and affable, then that someone had crouched down to play with her. The soft shaking of a tambourine finally drew her full attention.

'Giles?'

A severe haircut had diminished the halo effect of his golden hair. He looked up briefly to smile then fell back to shaking his tambourine for Dido who laughed in her efforts to seize it from him.

'She's so sweet,' he said. 'Very funny. *What* a funny girl!'

Eliza registered a momentary chill that after such an interval he should prove less interested in her than in a toddler. The moment had an odd flavour, intriguing, unplaceable.

But then he looked up again and held her gaze and every thought went out of her mind but how to keep him near her. When she felt he was growing tired of sitting, she suggested a walk and when Dido grew fractious after dozing in her pushchair, she suggested tea and cake. And when Dido's nappy needed changing, he suggested they go back to his flat because it was closer than her place.

Eliza could not help exclaiming at the flat's size. Compared to her bedsit, anything with a sitting room and a spare room felt palatial. He had no sooner heard her description of where they were living than he insisted they move in.

'But we . . . I couldn't possibly,' she said, thinking suddenly that she barely knew him, knew nothing about him.

'Why on earth not?' he asked. 'There's bags of room and I've been looking for lodgers in any case. Don't be silly. I can help you move with my car.'

She hated feeling coerced and this and a crying jag from Dido, who was tired of socialising, brought on a wave of panic. But he calmed Dido so expertly that she fell asleep in his arms after eating half a mashed banana and Eliza accepted his offer. She stilled any qualms that she might be taking advantage by agreeing not to let her bedsit go just yet and to treat the change of address as a trial period, a sort of sabbatical from squalor. Similarly she insisted on paying him a fair rent, although it would cut deep into her scant finances.

He was comparatively rich, however, having come into a trust fund and waved aside her rent cheques. He told her to buy food occasionally instead, something she did less and less because he was such a good cook and she always seemed to buy the wrong things, things he put on one side to gather dust or mould.

She only kept on the bedsit for a month. She revisited it a few times to collect post or clothes or books they were missing, until she had effectively moved out anyway and it seemed both sad and profligate to continue paying rent on a dank, uninhabited space from which someone else would profit.

People assumed they were lovers. Even her tutor, Dr Goldhammer, who was rectitude personified, implied in an offhand remark that she had *fallen on her feet*. But the situation was stranger than that and it embarrassed Eliza so much to discuss it that she preferred to let people continue in their misconstruction. The truth was that she and Dido were Giles' pets. He housed and fed them, was solicitous of their welfare and sought them out whenever his mood needed lifting. Eliza had never in her life felt so cherished. He was intensely methodical, exercising his voice and rehearsing on his own every morning, singing Evensong with his college choir every afternoon and rehearsing or performing with various early music or opera groups on perhaps three evenings out of seven.

He had a gift for entertaining Dido, who was transfixed and lulled by his singing, and he encouraged Eliza to leave her in his care while she spent the morning in the library or worked in her room. When he had an evening in, he would bring back booty salvaged from the covered market at closing time and conjure up elaborate meals. When he entertained, Eliza was simply there too, one of the party, less as consort than sister.

Apparently he was oblivious to how she felt for him. Whatever interest he might once have had in her had been dispelled by familiarity, and perhaps by seeing her as a mother, so he paraded his beauty before her with heedless cruelty. Padding around the flat making phone calls in nothing but a towel, lolling on her bed to gossip when he came in after she had retired for the night, even on several occasions asking her to rub painkilling gel into one of his shoulder blades.

Daily proximity only stoked her desire for him however. She did all she could to feel for him as a sister might and made herself dwell on his least pleasing aspects – his fastidiousness, his vanity, a vein that pulsed disturbingly on his temple when he was agitated – only to turn them into the flaws that heightened his attractiveness. She even tried to find something creepily effeminate in the eagerness with which he took on the burden of babysitting Dido but could muster only gratitude.

If only the rumours which so often irrationally arose about counter-tenors were true, if only he had been gay or sexually incapable, but he regularly negated both possibilities by bringing home women. He bedded them with as little noise or drama as if he had been sleeping alone, and despatched them so promptly that Eliza only once encountered one at breakfast. When she tentatively suggested that there was no need to dismiss them quite so cavalierly, he shrugged and changed the subject as though dwelling on the idea were distasteful.

She tried in vain to find another man to focus on but they all seemed less evolved creatures beside him, with larger helpings of testosterone perhaps, but not in a good way. More than ever she threw herself on the dusty mercies of study. Her doctorate grew and, as the year wore on, she found herself entirely consumed by the romance of two men, one oblivious, the other long dead. A confidante would have helped, some feminine voice of sound and mocking reason, but her long habit of secrecy had hobbled her capacity for making friends.

Then her mother announced she was coming on a visit. Eliza had been careful to take regular trips home to Cornwall since Dido came to live with her, to give her a grandmother's due and forestall such a crisis but her mother had suddenly got it into her head that it was time to repay the compliment. Nothing Eliza said would forestall her, no number of spontaneous lies about having a cold or a heavy burden of teaching.

'I'll treat myself,' her mother calmly insisted. 'I'll stay in the Randolph. I'll be no bother. I'll go shopping and visit the museums and take Dido out in her pram. You won't even have to come to church with me. Don't fret so. It would be reassuring for me to see where you're living.'

So that was it. Perhaps a spy had told her. Some friend of a friend's envious daughter? Either that or maternal curiosity simply could not be baffled indefinitely. And here was an end of Eliza's painstakingly constructed normality. She was not worried about protecting her mother – any assumption that Eliza was living in sin would be inaccurate after all; it was Giles she wanted to shield. If only he had been due to spend time out of town all might have stayed as it was but a meeting was inevitable, if not between Giles and her mother then between her mother and someone else who knew him, and with Dido an ever present prompt. The ugly truth was bound to come slithering out.

The least she could do, she reasoned, was forestall a wounding revelation. So she told Giles everything: about Hannah and her problem and her death and Eliza's fear of the repercussions for both Dido and herself, the blight it cast on their futures.

He was startled and appalled, but compassionately so. He actually came around the table and put an arm across her shoulder, and at his unexpected kindness she broke down. It was as though only now, with someone to bear her up, could she admit how unbearably heavy a burden she had been carrying. Voicing it all at last, she saw with stark clarity how cruel a sentence she and Dido lived under, what careful pariahs fate had made them.

'You mustn't tell her. Not till you have to,' he said. 'She must have as normal and happy a childhood as possible. We'll tell nobody. When did Hannah first . . . ?'

'Oh.' She thought back. It was so strange to be talking about this that she shuddered. 'I don't know for certain. Nine or ten? Unusually late, apparently.'

'Do you have pictures of her?'

Of course she had. As though to balance out her daily disloyalty, she kept a small stash of photographs hidden behind ones of Hannah as a child in a folding leather frame. She showed them to him with a kind of pride. Hannah as a teenager, as a young woman, in mountaineering gear. She watched his lovely face as he pored over them and saw not the slightest flicker of feeling. He showed only curiosity so that she half-expected his next words to be *she looked like you*.

'Could she sing too?' was all he asked and she found herself describing Hannah in detail – her extraordinary courage, her anarchic sense of humour and terrible instinct for justice. She felt grief afresh and with it a keen sense of how profoundly she had missed her and missed her still.

As she talked she gradually became aware that he was looking at her, watching her talk rather than listening to her words. He was sitting close, unbearably close. She broke off, tried to break the moment's intensity with a joke, and he kissed her. When he asked her to marry him she thought she had misheard and he had to repeat the question.

She protested, astonished, but now it was his turn to talk and it emerged that he had wanted her ever since they first sang together, could not believe his luck in persuading her to move in but had despaired of ever winning her interest.

'I couldn't even make you jealous,' he said. 'I've been steeling myself to accept you as a sort of sister but if you'd met someone else I think I'd have had to ask you to move out. It's been torture. I was beginning to tell myself you must be gay.'

Even as the vanity of this piqued her, she accepted. Just as she had first held back the truth about Hannah, so now she held back the truth that their passion was mutual. He was so very good-looking, made her feel so very mousy by comparison, that she felt a need to retain at least a tactical upper hand.

She was still a virgin when they married, with her delighted mother a witness and Dido a bridesmaid-in-arms, at the Oxford Register Office.

'Do you mind?' he had asked after a clamorous pause on the night she accepted him. 'But I'd rather wait. I don't want you to be just another, you know.'

To her surprise she had not minded in the least. Why not? Why not wait, withhold herself and be special?

'Why are you laughing?' he asked.

'My mother would be so proud of us,' she explained.

Her mother moved from her hotel to their flat so as to babysit while they took a short honeymoon in Paris.

Sex was at once startling and a disappointment. After such a wait and months of hunger for him, the intimacy of the act was so extreme she was shocked not to feel more altered by it. As he explored her and ploughed into her she felt none of the pain she had read about and feared, only a scorching heat as though she were burning from the inside. Amazed at finally finding his smooth, hard body next to hers, she wanted to explore it in turn but he was quite firm. Using no words, only gestures and a repeated pressure on her wrists, he made it plain that he preferred her to do nothing, not to speak, not to cry out, not even to laugh. Apparently he liked her as a sort of statue, or rather a doll, for he would move her about into different positions but it was always he that did the moving and if she showed initiative and moved an arm or a leg he might frown slightly and rearrange her as before.

Though inexperienced, she was not ignorant. She went to films and read books. She knew his tastes were not normal and that the impulse behind them was repressive and should fill her with womanly indignation. But just as some music and poetry were the more intensely emotional for being formally rigid, so she found her pleasure in his lovemaking wound up in pitch by being constrained to so narrow an outlet.

'You're happy,' her mother said when they returned to England. She had seemed worried before they left, Eliza felt, concerned perhaps at the disparity in their looks and worldly ability. Now she examined Eliza almost with satisfaction, as she might the crust of a baking pie. 'You've got that – what do they call it? – that *certain glow*.' She returned to Cornwall with the hurtful air of a woman whose account was settled in full.

And they were happy, both of them, intensely so. Giles pressed her to continue with her doctorate. Her room became Dido's room. They sang together. They entertained. They acquired a local standing as a couple, he for being beautiful, she for being enigmatic, to the point where his beauty spilled over onto her a little and her air of mystery onto him, so that each was enhanced by the other.

The early music group he sang with made some recordings for which she was asked to write the sleeve notes. She acquired enough teaching in the music faculty to feel she was paying her way. Dido grew and blossomed into bumptious infancy. They made initial enquiries of a solicitor friend as to what steps they might take for Giles to become Dido's father officially but took the matter no further because there seemed no point and, as with the drawing up of wills, neither felt ready yet to deal with the possibility of the other's dying. Although Eliza had explained, and he had accepted, that there was no question of her having children of her own, they felt the need to spread their happiness over a larger area, to have a garden, a spare room, a study. They began to look at larger houses, in cheaper parts of town where married people lived and pushchairs outnumbered student bicycles. They even, once or twice, discussed adopting a child as company for Dido.

Then he was signed up by an agent and everything changed. Selina Bryant met him by chance at a BBC broadcast of *Judith* from one of the college chapels and locked onto him with the quiet efficiency of a virus so that Eliza came to doubt that *chance* had played any part in the process. Eliza found her terrifying. A white Zimbabwean with long, very dry, grey hair that always shadowed two thirds of her face, she was so soft spoken that one was forced to lean close enough to feel the little explosions of her consonants against one's cheek and was then surprised at the ruthlessness of whatever she was saying. Selina Bryant seemed too mundane a name for her so Eliza used to madden Giles by calling her Carabosse. Behind her back, of course. In her expensive, black-draped presence, Eliza barely dared speak. When she once leant over Dido's cot so that the shadow of her hair fell across the child sleeping within, Eliza was tempted to wake Dido at once to make sure she was unharmed.

Convincing Giles his future lay as a soloist and that his looks were wasted in a nerdishly authentic consort, Selina paid for some glamorous photographs, sent him to auditions and landed him a supporting role in a modish revival of *Giulio Cesare* in a disused London church. He commuted, spending occasional nights in town, which made them both wretched. He was singled out in reviews. He was approached by ENO, offered a contract for more Handel and the Voice of Apollo in *Death in Venice*. He needed a voice coach now to help him increase his volume and cope with the added strain and the best coaches were all in London. So they moved and, as he earned more money, moved again.

The idea, supported by Dr Goldhammer, was that she should complete her doctorate long distance. The university, Royal College of Music and British libraries would answer most of her needs and it was easy enough to slip up to Oxford for the odd consultation. London was vibrant compared to Oxford, full of cultural distractions; and Trevescan, the composer who for so long had been the only man in her life, came to resemble a discarded lover, inspiring guilt and therefore irritation by his long-faced persistence.

She maintained a study, but her Trevescan files slowly slid round from the shelf above her desk to an unregarded dusty corner. Uprooted from the world where her research was valid currency, she dared to wonder aloud what possible use it could be, a blasphemy which proved devastating. She took on more entertaining work that bore more immediate fruit. Through Giles' widening circle of contacts she met someone who asked her to write more sleeve notes for recordings, someone else who asked her to write short essays for opera programmes. Detective work into the finer points of Elizabethan polyphony gave way to accessible pieces on the sexiness of Monteverdi or self-borrowings in Handel. She was called onto the radio a few times, though never asked back for a live broadcast because her nerves made the experience a torture for everyone involved.

Dido was growing into more of a person which made Eliza feel more of a mother. It was a short step to relaxing into becoming nothing more than a wife.

She could date the start of this process to a Sunday lunch party. Up to this point most of his friends had treated her well, been friendly enough. On this day however so little of the conversation was directed towards her that she found herself enumerating it obsessively, counting off the gobbets of small talk afterwards.

'Hello.'

'Hi.'

'How are you?'

'Hello.'

'Hello.'

'Hello, er . . .'

'Do you sing too, Eliza? Oh.'

'Goodbye.'

'Goodbye.'

'See you.'

'Bye!'

She could perhaps have survived the experience had she not been cooking for once, or had Giles noticed, but his saying what an enjoyable party it had been stunned her into wounded silence. Stripped of status, she yielded. As when answering, 'Do you sing too, Eliza?' with 'No. Actually I'm a . . . no. I don't.' She consciously abandoned Trevescan, abandoned writing even sleeve notes, and tried instead becoming nothing in particular.

Innocent of or oblivious to its cause, Giles was disconcerted at the alteration in her. Many opera singers had partners in the business, rarely of equal stature, whose relationships were slowly embalmed if not entirely poisoned by a drip feed of resentment and insecurity. He liked the idea, he often said, that they had broken that pattern, and that, as an academic

Eliza belonged to a kinder, cooler world than the performing seals of opera. As Dr Eliza Hosken, she could have been a status symbol. As a mere wife and mother she was rather less. He had fallen in love with her as one thing and now she was turning into something else, princess into frog, self-contained, mysterious bookworm into sprawling, lazy, needy wife. On his days off he would cook, clean, take Dido to and from school, all in a not so very discreet effort to leave Eliza free to study. When he found her filling out a crossword, watching an old film or curled up with an undemanding novel, he would make some light comment and she would hear the strain in his voice.

Ostensibly he bought the dog because Dido wanted one and because he worried that he was putting on weight and would benefit from walks. The covert purpose, she sensed, was to jolt her out of the despondent slough into which she was sliding. It was a chocolate brown standard poodle, big, athletic, intelligent to the brink of neurosis, in desperate need of occupation. Fastidious and principled, Giles persuaded Dido it was better to rescue an adult dog than go to a breeder.

Curly's owner had bought him out of sentimentality, but was far too old to give him the exercise he needed, and had driven the dog half-mad by confining him to a small back garden of an even smaller terraced cottage. His liberation came when his mistress was confined to a nursing home after a bad fall – a fall he had surely caused in his bumptiousness.

He was Curly for only a week, then Giles took Dido to an organ recital by Carlo Curley and the dog promptly became Carlo.

He was an impossible animal. Relentless. Asleep or exhausted he was docile, healthy and beautiful. The rest of the time he was a constant source of stress. For some reason Venetian blinds drove him into a tail-chasing, cushion-shredding frenzy, as did the doorbell. Anything that came through the letter box was eaten, any food left within reach – and Carlo's reach was long – was stolen. If he heard Giles pissing standing up, he had a tendency to piss in sympathy wherever he was, so Giles had to learn to sit down like the women of the household. He barked at cats on the television, and birds, and one particular newscaster. He dug up flower beds then made gritty, muddy nests for himself by jumping on one of the beds and turning in circles until sheets and duvets were wound comfortably to his satisfaction. He hated to be left, so babysitters had to be found who were not afraid of him.

Worst of all, there was something about the pitch of a counter-tenor voice that made him throw back his head and howl, which Giles couldn't help but find wounding, try as he might to laugh at the dog's lack of tact.

Dido had only ever really wanted a puppy, for all her polite acceptance of the rescue dog option, and soon began regarding Carlo less as a pet than as an irritating brother, best ignored. Giles, for all his protestations of wanting to get fit, was rarely available at the appropriate times. Eliza knew she was being manipulated, that this was a clumsy attempt at a cure, but found she had no choice in the matter. She dealt with the mess, the chewed shoes, the shredded cheques, the unexpected puddles because she was most often the one to find them. Carlo learned to come to her with his lead in his mouth because he knew she was the one most likely to take him out.

Once again Eliza found herself unintentionally an adoptive parent.

10

Sleep eluded him. Anxious for his voice, Giles had long since got out of the habit of drinking much. While the rest of the party had got ever merrier and less and less discreet, he had become more and more buttoned up, aware of being the only sober one at the table. He had consoled himself with coffee and several pieces of ginger in bitter chocolate and now his head was buzzing with the early warning signs of a migraine and his heart was on fire.

Alcohol made Julia very sweet and clumsy. It gave him a glimpse of the bolshie student she must once have been, or typist, or whatever. It made it easy to imagine her a ball of bad-tempered envy with no manners at all. Powerfully amorous when he came to bed, she had fallen asleep mid-kiss as suddenly as if he had pulled out her plug. Her hair flopped, cool across his chest, one of her thighs was flung across his.

It saddened him that something in his personality, his need to control, or whatever, usually inhibited what might have proved a counterbalancing exuberance in hers. It saddened him too that it took wine to bring out this less guarded side of her nature because he found it immensely attractive. Familiar with alcohol's dangers, he knew better than to make her aware that he liked what it did to her.

She had been unconscious for nearly forty minutes while

he lay there ever more alert and uncomfortable. As always she radiated heat in her sleep. He slid out from under her in careful stages, anxious not to wake her but when he was sitting on the edge of the bed fumbling in the dark for his dressing gown she said very clearly, 'What?'

'Headache,' he muttered but perhaps she had only been dreaming for she did not stir but carried on breathing into her pillow as deeply as she had been breathing into his shoulder minutes before.

Down in the kitchen, surrounded by the dirty plates she insisted on leaving for the cleaning lady, overriding his protestant guilt as pathetically middle class, he drank a pint of tepid water and knocked back a mega dose of feverfew, which usually did the trick. The air down there remained sour from Selina's and Villiers' cigarettes. ('You don't mind, do you, darling?' 'Don't ask, Selina. Light up, then we all can!') Because they were now the only people in his circle who smoked, the smell conjured up their personalities in a single inhalation.

He retreated upstairs to his study. They called it his study but the only work he ever seemed to do in there was write cheques to pay bills. It was actually what an American might have called a den, a snug room with a desk and filing cabinet, certainly, but also a messy leather sofa and an ancient carpet. This was the one room spared Julia's retouching and into which the possessions had retreated which she scorned but would never be allowed to throw out. The threadbare carpet, long since stained and chewed by Carlo, dated from the first weeks of his marriage and the sofa was even older. They had travelled with him from address to address like old retainers.

Not bothering to turn on the light, he flopped onto the sofa and stared out at a lime tree lit up, by happy accident, by the street lamp its foliage had grown to cloak. Sometimes he could sleep here when sleep eluded him in bed. He moved down here if Julia or he had a cold. What Julia could not know was that this room had been Eliza's study, where she failed to write her thesis.

What had possessed him to become so heated tonight and sound off so foolishly? Villiers knew which buttons to press to get a rise out of him. He should never come to the house again. Never. Luckily Julia had said nothing so perhaps they were all too drunk or failed to notice Giles was not drinking with them and put his little outburst down to alcohol.

He swung off the sofa, clicked on the desk lamp and looked in the hiding place between his old school Bible and a 1972 *Roy of the Rovers* annual. The prints of Dido were still there. Presumably Dido stumbled on them when her pulling out one of the photo albums caused the other books to tumble sideways.

It was a wonder she had not found them before. Perhaps because Eliza and he had granted her so sketchy a background, the few old photographs that confirmed the little she knew had never lost their fascination for her. Occasionally she would startle him with a question like, 'So Joyce and Nigel . . . are they still together?' or 'Why did your mother suddenly change her hair?' and he would know she had again been poring over these colourful, patchily annotated records that left out as much as they appeared to chronicle.

So now she had chanced on a less edited record of family life.

He imagined Julia's reaction if she came across the prints too, during one of her outbreaks of efficiency. He thought about giving one to Eliza who, being an innocent herself, would surely see it as nothing worse than sweet. But no, it was impossible. He took a pair of scissors and sliced them up like a fraudster destroying evidence.

So now, naturally, he really felt smutty.

He flicked off the light again and flopped back on the sofa, defensively facing the half-lit stairs this time.

The cruel joke was that, if he was honest, Dido had always had a hold over him. But not in that way. At least, not directly. Not at first.

When they first met to sing together, he had pursued Eliza automatically because her apparent nonchalance piqued his vanity; she seemed immune to the looks that worked so easily on other women. But it was only when he saw her with Dido, so miraculously turned into a cross, slovenly, impatient mother, that he fell in love with her.

Eliza was always so hopeless, ill-equipped for interacting with the world of things, defeated by the cellophane on a CD box or the padlock on her bicycle, but Giles might have dismissed this as a pose; plenty of academics affected unworldliness and it usually irritated him. But somehow she woke in him a wish to protect and guide her which was only intensified by there suddenly being a defenceless baby thrust into her unsuitable care.

This probably took hold so completely because it was utterly out of character for him. His mother's toxic combination of dependency and predatoriness had left him able only to think of women in a limited and sexual light. The sexual feeling for Eliza had always been there, ever since Villiers had invited her to share the solos with him in that candlelit concert. She was a wafty blonde with absolutely no idea of how attractive she was. This was a potent combination even before her baby broke through his cynical defences.

When they lived together merely as unmarried friends, he had been wooed by baby Dido as efficiently as he had first planned on wooing her mother. Solely for the baby's benefit he had turned on the full panoply of his impressive bachelor tactics – cooking, cleaning, vivacity – with no calculation at all as to their wider effect. By the time he had asked

Eliza to marry him — he who had never given marriage a second thought — he was already vowing that protecting and nurturing and entertaining Dido would be his One Good Thing in life. Hearing the full horrific story of Hannah only made him the more determined that helping to raise this child should be the one entry in his spiritual ledger over which he need feel nothing but pride.

He would surely have fallen in love with Eliza anyway — she was so unlike the others, so not set on pleasing — but it was Dido who saved him from himself. Whenever he felt tempted to sneer at his mother's talk of how little things set her on the slow path to recovery from alcoholism, he remembered that and was chastened.

And how had he repaid Dido? By failing to love Eliza as he ought, by fantasising, even, about wresting the child from her protection and now by betraying Dido's trust.

For some time he had been tormented by erotic dreams about her; purely symbolic ones at first and then ever more appalling in their physical frankness. He tried to ignore them as meaningless. People dreamed about sex with the Queen. That did not mean they wanted it any more than dreams about talking cats, flying or being able to breathe underwater were meaningful reflections of waking life. But the dreams about Dido took hold. They were affecting his relationship with Julia because he felt he must keep them secret from her and they affected his relationship with Dido because he remembered them whenever she was near him. And now, of course, she would tell Eliza about the photograph and . . . and sitting on his lap and that would be that. Eliza was unlikely to take any direct action — nothing had really happened, after all, and aggression, legal or otherwise, was not in her armoury — but he had given her the little reason she would need to call a halt to the precious, pseudo-parental visits.

This would set Eliza free. She could divorce him, at long

last, take a proper share of his house and his money and move far away, taking Dido with her. Then he would be honour bound to marry Julia. And then what?

Unbidden, the perky refrain of an especially cruel Sondheim song popped into his head: *Love will see us through till something better comes along!*

He lost consciousness at last only to dream of Dido. Dido crouched in his lap, arms round his neck. Dido breathing, 'I was a bit scared at first, but it's nice really.' Then she started to take long, slow licks across his impassive face until he melted like a human lolly. He woke to find the street lamp off and the room monochrome with pre-dawn light. He forced himself off the sofa and walked upstairs, feet aching from cold, to slide back into bed with Julia.

She barely stirred but he clung to her as to a life raft.

11

Apart from Selina, who had her suspicions, and Villiers, who trusted nobody entirely, everyone at the dinner party assumed Julia had an upper-middle-class background. Her slightly imperious manner and hints of a childhood in the west country overrun with animals, her knowledge of the better ski resorts, wine, and flower-arranging, her accent, her reluctance to smile, all pointed to it. She never mentioned a university and often referred to herself as *thick* but she had the social and cultural confidence of someone sent to a good all-girl boarding school, Cheltenham Ladies, say, or Wycombe Abbey, followed by a little polish acquired at a Swiss cookery school or Florentine academy.

The truth was more interesting. Her father was a laid-off miner scraping a living through odd-jobs and she went to the state school where her mother was a part-time dinner lady. They lived in a shoddily built 1960s house where there was barely room for a family of five (she had two older brothers from her father's first marriage), still less for the animal waifs and strays her mother was forever taking in. Julia was not maltreated but she spent most of her childhood fantasising that she had only been placed with this family to learn humility. It showed and, chilled, her family stopped a little short of cherishing her.

She left school at sixteen and escaped, mapping her path steadily away from home in a series of jobs and addresses. She was a waitress, a live-in child minder, a department store demonstrator of little kitchen devices, a caterer's skivvy, a secretary. She had no firm ambition beyond attaining financial independence and social liberty; if she had done she would have stayed in school longer. She was not academic but she was far from stupid and approached each job hungry for whatever she could learn from it. Employers liked her because her curiosity flattered them but she was always restless to move on once she had taken in whatever they had to teach.

None of this was conscious, none of it calculated. She could not help it if even as she was told how to make a sponge without burning its edges or how to answer a certain type of letter she was also learning how to wear make-up without it showing or how to pronounce *really*.

She learned from boys too, and men, but resisted the easy temptation of using sex as a means to an end and tended only to become involved with men who were not strictly available. Her parents had so clearly made a mistake picking one another that she was determined not to settle for anything permanent until she could be sure it was right.

On a succession of depressing Christmas trips home it dawned on her how much she had changed and how little she now had in common with her parents and stepbrothers. When her older stepbrother moved to Malaga and persuaded her parents to follow him, Julia took it as a convenient pretext for letting her family ties shrivel and now barely kept in touch. Perhaps the reaction was mutual for there was a similar lack of overtures on their side.

She had been living in London for a few years, temping, sharing a flat with people she could rub along with but did not particularly know or like, when her agency sent her for a week to Selina Bryant Management.

Selina liked her and offered to hire her permanently as her assistant, on the understanding that she was being trained and might eventually acquire clients of her own. Julia had been made such offers before but she sensed Selina would never make the mistake of trying to mother or control her. And she was growing tired of constantly changing jobs and being unable to answer simply when people asked her what she did.

'We're not just a booking service,' Selina would say. 'We mould and nurture careers here, yadda yadda yadda, but at rock bottom we're not about art. We provide the same management and support that other firms might to ventriloquists and dancing poodles but the bottom line, as far as you and I are concerned, is the deal and the commission.' Selina did not care that Julia was unmusical. 'I like it that you don't know anything. Nerves'll make you learn the faster.'

And they did. Julia became an adept at bluffing, at peppering her dialogue with just the right phraseology, much of it picked up from reading concert and record reviews every morning. She was good at telling people they were wonderful. She was even better at telling would-be clients they weren't quite up to Selina's mark. With clients performing all over London every night in the opera houses, in churches and concert halls, even in rich people's houses, there was no lack of complimentary tickets and these and programme notes became Julia's musical education. She learnt music the way one best learns any language, by total immersion. And she began to specialize in singers. Selina's dark secret was that she hated opera. Julia had seen her sleep through entire performances. The CDs in Selina's Mercedes tended to be middle-of-the-road rock. She kept a radio button tuned to Radio 3 in case a client ever needed a lift.

Julia's early bad experiences in the school choir made her especially good at describing the niceties of a technique she would never master. Like a blind woman mastering ways of describing the visual arts she absorbed the full vocabulary of singing. Where her colleagues spent as long as possible gossiping in the Floral Hall and as little as possible in their seats, Julia would always find time to read her programme notes. A second-hand *Kobbé's Opera Guide* became her bedtime reading. The convoluted opera plots of Handel and Verdi's librettists soon made up for the fairytales her mother had never found time to tell her. She still mimed to the hymns at weddings and funerals but now she was as fluent in *facher* as a football nerd in league tables. She only had to hear a few bars of a demo disc to know a *hochdramatische Sopran* from a *Zwischenfachsangerin* and needed minimal research to remind herself whether a role being cast required a *tenore di grazia* or a *tenore robusto*. That these terms were increasingly regarded as quaint and old-fashioned by people who had never grasped their nice distinctions only made her use them with greater confidence.

The job kept her so busy and fulfilled that it came as a shock to realise she had been in it a year and not developed her usual restlessness. Here at last was a subject she could never know entirely. By degrees music had become her life.

Most music lovers could pinpoint a breakthrough moment when a Stravinsky ballet made the hair on their neck prickle or a particular violinist brought tears to their eyes. Julia's was hearing her first counter-tenor. She had heard sniggers about them, heard that – as if castration were still practised on promising choirboys – they were less than virile. Selina confessed it was a sound that invariably made her want to giggle. Julia heard David Daniels as Rinaldo, however, and was captivated.

Ordinary male voices, tenor, baritone and bass, rarely moved her. Tenors were so often short and/or unprepossessing, putting so much obvious effort into the production of their sound. The bass voice, she feared to admit, registered in her ears as a sort of tuneless growl.

The only Lawrence novel she had read, as a set text at school, was *The Rainbow* and she had never understood the heroine's subversive delight at taking her beau to church and hearing him sing higher and louder than anyone else. She had always projected onto the passage the squally high tenor Cs of the male voice choir her father sang with. Now she understood. Here was a sound that was heroic, entirely and athletically male and yet with all the clarity of a *soprano spinto*.

When Giles was taken on by Selina, Julia became an ardent, secret fan, attending his performances wherever possible. By the time she was asked to look after him for a few days, she had done all her homework thoroughly.

12

Pearce had never intended to be a farmer. Or rather, he had done when he was small, trailing around after his father or grandfather at every opportunity, riding on trailers, adopting calves, wearing outsize gauntlets obediently to heave on one end of some barbed wire while his father nailed it tight to a fence post. But as soon as he was old enough to pick up even an inkling of farm economics he saw that the real money and comfortable living earned around farms was made by vets.

He made a pact with Molly, who was clever enough but hopeless at science, that when they grew up he would be a vet and she could marry a neighbouring farmer and thus double the size of the family's holding.

'You can't be a vet,' people told him. 'It's twice as hard as being a doctor even. The training's years longer so it costs more *and* there's even more competition for fewer places.'

Which naturally made him all the more determined. He loved the farm, land as well as house, loved it more each day and even longed for a brother so there might be less expectation that he would take it on. He became genealogically territorial, hating the thought of anyone living there who wasn't a relative. But he saw how his father worried, especially once Pearce's paternal grandfather died, how the rules and regulations hemmed him in, how the paperwork mounted in his office until his mother was forced to learn how to deal with it herself rather than face an inspection by Customs and Excise or the Inland Revenue.

He was tactful. He allowed people who did not know him well to assume he would be next in line in the tractor seat, but his mind was made up and he pursued his chosen course with the advantage of a boy whose mind was fixed on a goal years before his contemporaries had progressed beyond wanting to play rugger for the Pirates or be the first Cornish astronaut.

He met with no opposition from his father. Mild to a fault, Polglaze Senior had suffered too much at the bullying hands of duty and chapel ever to hold his own children back. He did not make an issue of it because he knew his wife would fret about how they would survive in old age, or some such. His way around the problem was to joke, say things like, 'Oh well. When you're qualified, we can get all these injections half-price, can't we? And there'll be no call-out fee!'

Undereducated themselves, both parents had bottomless faith in education and homework always had to be finished before either child might volunteer for chores. Whereas his father had thought nothing of hooking the boy out of school mid-term to help plant daffodils or harvest potatoes, Pearce's father thought money well spent if hiring extra labour would help the children focus on exam revision.

So Pearce had stayed at school into the sixth form while friends of his dropped out to follow fathers into field or fishing boat. He showed willing and enjoyed helping on the farm when his studies allowed. But he also took on holiday jobs as a dogsbody in the Penzance vet's where the farm held an account, clocking up as much valuable experience as they let him. And in due course, despite all the nay-sayers, he slogged his way onto the veterinary course at Bristol.

He loved it there, for all that he was bitterly homesick, and he worked harder and played harder than he would have thought possible. There were girls but nobody significant. There were new friends but no soulmates, no one outside the family to dissuade or encourage him.

During his second year of preclinical studies, his mother became seriously ill. She had developed angina then had a heart attack. It was agreed that no one was to tell Pearce because he was about to sit crucial second-year exams. Molly worried he ought to know and told him anyway. He respected his mother's wish not to have a fuss made, so stayed on and sat the exams but he was worrying so much he failed them.

His tutors were understanding, suggested he take a term out to be with his mother then sit the exams again and, if he failed them a second time, repeat his second year with a fresh intake of students.

His mother might have been holding on for his return, or it might have been anger at realising Molly had told him, or dismay at his flunking the exams, but she had a second heart attack the night after he came home. She was dead a week later, at just fifty-six.

With both Pearce and Molly home for the holidays, the family could hole up together in a tight knot of grief. His mother had been a mainstay of the St Just Chapel and the congregation rallied round and were almost unbearably kind. There was no question of either Molly or Pearce taking a holiday job. There was more than enough to keep them busy at home. On farms, as in gardens, there was an implacability to the season's demands and there could be little observed mourning. The tasks that would not wait were a welcome distraction.

But at the summer's end Pearce had to admit that he could not leave again to return to Bristol. His widowed father was a lost soul and could not be abandoned. That he had never learnt to cook or run a household was a minor detail — it would have been easy enough to bring someone in to help him – but grief seemed to have sapped his ability to make decisions in his working life. Where once one of his more maddening habits was plunging on in some course without consultation, digging out a new ditch, demolishing a shed, building a hideous lean-to on the first spot to catch his eye, he now consulted Pearce about everything.

'Should we bale the straw today or not?'

'Is this barley dry enough to store, do you think?'

'I can't make head nor tail of this fungicide label. How much should I put in the sprayer, do you reckon?'

It was as though Pearce's mother had secretly been advising him all these years, protecting his dignity with feminine discretion in public but privately proving an oracle of agricultural lore. Molly's marrying Morris and moving away to his farm up by Nancledra was the deciding factor. His father looked so utterly wretched that Pearce concocted a merciful lie. He pretended to have received a letter from the university.

'Turns out they haven't room in this year's intake on the course,' he said. 'So I'll have to wait another year before starting again. Not to worry. We've stuff enough to sort out here, haven't we?'

In fact he had written to the veterinary faculty explaining the situation and they had written back suggesting that he take a year out but warning him they could not hold a place for him indefinitely.

So he moved back into his boyhood room and, when Molly married and moved out, took over her room for a farm office. He broke his father's lifetime practice of doing all farm business at the kitchen table and stuffing receipts and bills in its crumby drawer with the napkin rings and old birthday candles. He took on the farm's financial work, bought them a computer for the accounts and the cropping, spray and animal treatment records, acquainted himself with the regulations about correct use of chemicals and fertiliser, even went on a locally-run course or two. Many of these things were now legal requirements his father had been blithely flaunting. Tired of them living off chops and sausages, he taught himself to cook.

At first his father paid lip service to the idea of Pearce still training as a vet but by tactful degrees the subject was dropped and instead, as months turned to years, he began instead to drop hints about children.

'Something for your boys to be proud of one day,' he said, when they had rebuilt a hedge the rabbits and cattle had brought down or laid new tin on an outhouse roof. 'That should last till your lad takes it on.'

It was a harmless enough fantasy but a foolish one because it saddened them both. They rubbed along well enough in their strange, bachelor existence. They had Sunday lunch with Molly and Morris every other week, there was an occasional trip to the cattle market or into Truro. Otherwise labour saw to it that their mornings were too early for conversation and the sociable part of their evenings shortened by the need to sleep.

At the end of an especially grim February day of harvesting broccoli in the driving rain and wind from eight until it was nearly dark, his father made one remark too many about sons. He said something like, ''Spect it'll all be done by machines when your boy's turn comes.'

'Dad, I don't have a boy. I don't have a wife. How the hell am I going to meet one? Where? I never go anywhere and if I do it's with people I know, women I've known since they were girls, women like sisters. Big-hipped, apple-cheeked sisters. I'm only doing this for you. I never wanted to do this. You know that. And I don't mind because it's for you and it's a beautiful place but no kid of mine will grow up here, even if I have any. I wouldn't wish that on them.'

'You'd *sell* if I died?' His father looked stricken.

'No. Probably not. But I'd let it and move away somewhere, or give it to Molly and Morris. They'll have others besides Lucy. They'll have a boy soon enough.'

'But . . . I thought you liked it here now.'

'I do, Dad. But . . . it's not what I want. It was never what I wanted. You always knew that.'

'I thought . . . I thought you'd *changed*.'

'No,' Pearce sighed. 'I just took a leaf out of Mum's book and never complained. Sorry. I'm sorry, Dad, that was . . . sorry. Forget I said anything. I'm tired. We're both tired. I'm turning in, okay?'

The next day was Saturday, traditionally his father's day for tinkering about the place, not working precisely but doing the small, niggling tasks it was easy to put off, like oiling padlocks or fixing dripping taps.

It was sunny, windless, a day full of false spring before the March storms arrived and Pearce took the Land Rover into Penzance to buy food, a weekend paper, a few essentials at Cornwall Farmers. He liked his Saturday mornings in town, liked the holiday atmosphere, the rampaging schoolgirls in inexpert make-up, the optimistic Jelbert's ice cream trolley by the bank, the mad preacher on the corner of Causewayhead, the olive stall with its Provençal soap, thumb-stuck focaccia – the nearest he would come to the Mediterranean. He took his time as he always did.

When he drove home the first thing he saw was the ladder, because it was blocking his route across the yard. He assumed his father had dropped it there while he ran in to answer the telephone. But the back door was shut and his father always answered the phone leaning in from outside, rain or shine, because he had been trained not to walk mud into the kitchen on his boots.

With the winter rains, springs began to flow all over the farm. One of the more useful sprang up in a bank in the field immediately above the yard then ran across it, past the Dutch barn and into a concrete-lined ditch near the house. When sweeping or scraping needed to be done, this stream could be relied on to carry much of the fertile muck away into the seaward fields. Crossing back to the Land Rover to fetch a second box of food after finding the back door shut and no sign of life inside, Pearce saw blood streaking the flow of water where it entered the ditch.

In seconds he had traced it to where his father lay crumpled over in the mud. He was dead and already turning cold, the front of his head staved in on the concrete. Pearce was always on at him about positioning the big, two-part ladder properly so that the grooved side of the rungs was uppermost and the rubber grips on the ends were firmly hugging the ground. Yet again his father must have set it up the wrong way round, only this time losing his step when too high to jump safely clear. There was a hammer stuck in his loose leather belt, a bag of roofing tacks in his jacket pocket. He was wearing his weekend tie.

Pearce rang Molly first, then the ambulance. He knew the ambulance crew could do nothing and that it was irresponsible to summon them but it was an automatic response, boyhood-bred. It was Molly, trained in womanly practicality, who knew to call the GP to register the death and the village joiner, who was also the undertaker, to take away the body.

Pearce assumed it was an accident, a stupid, avoidable one. Year after year farmers were sent Government or union warnings about the dangers of farm life. The commonest cause of death on farms, discounting suicides by gun or weedkiller, and accidents to children, was falling. Many farmers apparently died in a farcically short but deadly tumble when they stepped, exhausted, out of their tractor cabs, slipped and fell headfirst onto concrete. Many others fell when making cheap, inexpert repairs to gutters or roofing.

The life assurance assessor visited a decorous fortnight after the funeral. He had been at school with Pearce's father. His brother was the area's main grain merchant. He had sung in the choir at the funeral. He hated having to look into the death of a man he respected, he said, but needs must. Pearce had no idea there had even been a policy. It was all he could do to persuade his father to shift idling capital from his current account into a building society.

He showed the assessor where he found the body, where the ladder was, described the task he assumed his father was on his way to do. It was dry that day and windless, he said, a safe day for the job, a perfect day, only his father had a tendency to misplace the big ladder and, because it was heavy, could rarely be bothered to take it down and reposition it even if he noticed his mistake.

'My guess is he had reached the top when he slipped,' he told the assessor. 'And he grabbed hold of the edge of the roof to steady himself a second, which was how he came to kick the ladder away.'

'And if you don't mind my asking, where were his hands when you found him?' The assessor was pained, taking notes, but now he looked up and Pearce could tell he needed to read his expression as he answered.

'Out,' he said.

'Spread out?'

'Not exactly. Er. Out but underneath him.'

This was a lie. The assessor accepted it almost gratefully however and made one last note.

As they walked back to his car, he said, 'Your solicitor knew of no major debts or money worries.'

'No. We're pretty lucky,' Pearce explained. 'No rent. Means

we can keep the overheads down and pull our horns in when we need to.'

'I can't see any problem, Pearce. Even if I could, I wouldn't, if you see what I mean.'

'That's very kind.'

'You should receive a cheque from us in the next few weeks.' He paused. 'I thought you were going to be a vet, young man.'

'I was. I still might.' Pearce was touched this near stranger should have remembered such a detail.

The cheque was not life-changing but it was made out to Pearce and it would be enough to pay tuition fees and living expenses for his remaining years at Bristol. Only he never went. Shocked at his duplicity, he sought to cleanse the money of bad associations by sinking it in a very long-term savings bond for Lucy.

For, in turning his father's body over and then in feeling for a pulse, he had disturbed hands thrust, with unthinkable bravery, deep in trouser pockets. Time and again he replayed in his mind what must have happened minutes after he drove into town. His father kitted himself out for a task he never intended to do, set the ladder up the wrong way, climbed onto the roof, kicked the ladder away, then, hands deep in pockets to ensure nothing broke his fall or delayed his end, dived headfirst off the roof.

He had learnt to dive as a boy, taught how to plunge neatly off a rock in the cove below the seaward fields by an American airman billeted with the family. He had taught both Molly and Pearce in his turn. He would have fallen as straight as an arrow.

The actions intended to set him free to pursue his lifetime's ambition had prevented Pearce ever doing so. He could not touch the money and had to stay and continue his father's work. How could he not? He never told Molly what he knew. She took the death very badly, worse than she had their mother's, and he suspected it was as much to blame as Morris' hopelessness with money for the eventual breakdown of her marriage. A hefty dose of suicide guilt on top was the last thing she needed as she tried to straighten out her life.

He remembered his father's secret whenever circumstances forced him to use a ladder. He did not clean the gutters nearly as often as he should.

13

Post clattered through the door, reminding Eliza that she ought to get up, get dressed, get out, buy food and pay for the telephone to be reconnected. The sound of the flimsy metal flap bouncing against cheap woodwork was one she associated only with bills and demands, with the oughts of life. She received few letters – those that came stuck in her mind and were apt to seem as threatening as the reminders to test Dido's eyes or revisit her dentist.

This was a proper letter, however, with a stamp instead of a franking mark, its address waveringly written by hand in a turquoise shade that spoke to Eliza of schooldays, thank you letters and tentative experimentation.

She left the letter on the edge of the table, showered, dressed and came back to it feeling a little stronger.

It had a Cornwall postmark.

Dear Eliza, she read. *I tried ringing you a few times but there was an unavailable tone and when I checked the lady said you'd been disconnected. Oh dear. I hope this has found you. There were so many addresses for you in your mother's book, I wasn't sure which to write to and seriously thought about writing to them all. But then I thought that might cause trouble so plumped for this one.*

I won't beat about the bush. She's not well, Eliza. Not well at all. She had a nasty fall in Wesley Street. Didn't break her hip, thank God, but Dr Pengelly suspects a stroke so they're keeping her in for observation. Treliske Hospital. Trevithick Ward.

Don't worry about her house and things. I'm near enough, as you know, to keep an eye. But frankly I think you and little Dodie should come back for a bit.

Do come soon, Eliza. She misses you both, I know, and it would go hard on you if she went suddenly.

I don't know if there's anyone else I should write to?

If money's short, let me know. Silly to let a thing like that stop you coming at such a time. If not for your sake then for Dodie's.

Perhaps you'd better ring me when (if!!) you get this so I can know and stop worrying!

All good wishes,

Auntie Kitty (Mrs Barnicoat)

These two names, the one all playful, bun-baking sweetness, the other as severe as judgement itself, threw Eliza into a panic. There was a cruel sense that one was the woman she had known in childhood, the other the woman she had become, disappointed and dauntless. Eliza hurried from the flat as though Mrs Barnicoat might appear in person at any moment. She pushed the letter back in its envelope, tore it into several pieces and let them fly from her grasp in the dusty wind which always whipped around the skirts of the tower.

She cashed a benefit cheque, paid the phone bill then rang from a call box to have her number reconnected. She made herself buy a bag of fruit instead of cake, and potatoes to bake for supper. Then she hid in the reference library, reading scholarly reviews of books she couldn't afford and which the library would never stock. Slowly she was soothed by the presence of other lost souls, the slow turning of pages and the sour odour of disappointment which hung about the periodicals section.

She lost track of time and was late home, which meant she was late putting the potatoes in the oven. Patient, Dido volunteered to bathe before supper instead of after. This meant that she did not hear the telephone ring or, if she did, almost certainly could not have made out Eliza's hastily murmured,

'I'm sorry. I think you must have the wrong number.'

Eliza suddenly lost all appetite and retreated to her darkened room leaving Dido to fend for herself. She heard Dido emerge from her bath and deal with the potatoes, heard her boil the kettle for tea. When Dido appeared in the doorway to ask if she was hungry still, Eliza pretended to be asleep but then she lay awake for hours worrying.

With no Carlo there to wake her at intervals through the night, she slept deeply when she finally lost consciousness and must have slept through her alarm. (Keeping the alarm set was one of her last concessions to leading a responsible life, even though she usually woke only to turn it off again before rolling over.)

In the morning she woke instead to the telephone and heard Dido answer it and say,

'She's still asleep. Who's that?'

The conversation continued but Eliza could make out no more because Dido had closed a door between them. Then Dido slipped out and Eliza fell back into merciful senselessness.

Dido woke her later with tea and toast. Far from climbing into bed to breakfast with her, she was busy packing two large nylon laundry bags.

'Shouldn't you be in school?' Eliza asked, peering at the clock.

'Not going,' Dido said, holding up a frock for closely critical inspection. 'You just sent them a letter to explain. I checked and there's a coach to Redruth at eleven. Auntie Kitty says she'll meet us off that and drive us the rest of the way. She sounds nice. You never said you had an aunt.'

Eliza sat up to take this in.

'Because I don't,' she said at last. 'She just calls herself that because she's a meddlesome old cow with no children. We can't go, Dido. We can't afford it. Most of my benefit went on the phone bill.'

'Giles is paying. I just went round there and told him.'

'He shouldn't have to pay.'

'He doesn't *have* to. He wanted to. He's sad about Granny. If there's going to be a funeral, shouldn't we have black?'

'Who said anything about funerals?' Eliza retrieved a fallen pillow to prop herself up better. She took a piece of toast.

'No one, but Auntie Kitty dropped hints so I guessed.'

'Where did you learn how to fold dresses like that?'

'I watched Julia once, when they were getting ready to go on tour. And if you fold shirts and blouses like this and then roll them up really tight, you don't have to iron them again at the other end.'

'Sounds most unlikely. Julia never looks as though she rolls anything.'

'Drink your tea. We have to leave in half an hour. We can get a train straight through to Victoria but the man said the bus station's quite a walk beyond that.'

The journey across London then along two motorways and a chain of increasingly empty dual carriageways took six hours but seemed to take twice that time. Eliza found it impossible to stay awake for long. The sun in her eyes as they headed west, alternately frazzled by the greenhouse effect of unopenable windows and blasted by ache-inducing jets of cold, stale air when Dido fiddled with the overhead 'air conditioning' system, Eliza found herself lulled into a state beyond speech in which she lolled, stared, slept, woke or obediently ate whatever fruit or homemade sandwich Dido passed her.

Dido, by contrast, was all attention, feasting her eyes on the unaccustomed sights, enjoying the novelty of the on-board lavatory and taking in the other passengers and the professional insincerities of the two uniformed attendants. Eliza felt guilty that she was not turning this into an educational opportunity, not explaining things, which in turn made her all the sleepier. Dido didn't care. She was enjoying herself. Apparently she was on holiday.

Invariably, when Eliza mentioned that she came from Cornwall, people responded with fatuous cries of how lovely that must be, how romantic. What lovely holidays they had spent there, they would say, and how could she bear to leave it?

Eliza's roots in stony-faced Camborne, however, lay in the other Cornwall, some might argue the *real* one. An industrialised heartland of miners and quarrying, devastated by the twin forces of recession and market pressure. In the eyes of the all-important tourism operators, Camborne was best airbrushed out of the olde worlde picture. Ironically it retained the Royal School of Mines, the distant outpost of Prince Albert's Imperial College, which continued to attract student engineers from those counties for whom mining remained a viable industry.

Eliza and Hannah's father had been a lecturer there, specialising in seismology or, as their mother liked to put it sourly, *the detection of shocks*. The assumption had always been that he had left the country. Eliza had taken to imagining that he was not driven away by the trauma caused by Hannah but that he had fallen helplessly in love with one of the rare female students, from Cape Town or Buenos Aires perhaps, and had followed her home, a helpless slave to passion. Seeing the area again now she wondered if it had simply been an attack of geographical abhorrence.

Dido's imagination was untroubled by pictures of kindly farmers' wives and stout-hearted fishermen, of rugged coastline and golden beaches. She had never been further afield than Kent. All of Cornwall might have been like this for all she knew. Perhaps she even found the mixture of gaunt, shabby and bleak reassuringly like home.

'There are no tower blocks,' she said as they pulled into the bus station at Redruth.

'No need,' Eliza sighed. 'Not enough people. Look. There's Auntie Kitty. See? In the yellow fleece. Remember, she's very religious so you mustn't swear.'

The childish naming was automatic. She could not think of the woman who had been Auntie Kitty for so long as Mrs Barnicoat. Even without the canary yellow fleece, Kitty was easily spotted in a crowd for she was spectacularly fat.

As a child, Eliza had longed to take a tape measure to her, convinced she would turn out to be basically spherical, as wide as she was squat as she was deep. In most of her memories, Auntie Kitty and her mother were only a kitchen table top apart, anchored by a teapot and open biscuit tin. A true Cornishwoman, Kitty excelled at the various combinations of flour, lard and sugar that were the cornerstones of Cornish baking; heavy cake, saffron buns and pasties.

Disappointed in her husband, who was long gone and had left no traces, she disapproved of most things except the consolations of her particularly judicial brand of Christianity, and wild birds, either of which she would have died defending. Her garden was a welcoming thicket entirely given over to her feathered friends – bird baths, bird tables, bird nesting boxes – and the ferocious exclusion of cats.

Their father's side of the bed was barely cool from his defection when Kitty homed in on their mother with her cake and homilies. They were all girls together now. Men were not to be trusted and boys, being only men in the making, were bad until proved otherwise by good works or an ability to hold down a steady job. Girls were weak by nature, prone to sin and, as likely as not, to being corrupted by the wrong sort of boy. You were better off with Jesus and a slab of cake and the simple delights of watching pied wagtails on the fence and wrens in the hedge. Most offensively, Kitty had always implied that Hannah was a stigma inflicted to save the family from sin. The arrival of cheerfully fatherless Dido had silenced her on that score, her only revenge a flat refusal ever to remember the child's name.

'Well look who it isn't!' Kitty exclaimed, firmly holding Dido before her as she planted a kiss on her cheek. 'Last time I saw you, Dodie, you were a miserable babe in arms.' She was so short they were nearly eye to eye.

'My name's Dido,' said Dido. 'She was Queen of Carthage but she died.'

'Because of a man who abandoned her. Mind you remember that,' Kitty told her sharply. 'And Eliza.'

'Hello, Kitty.'

Surprised by warmth, it was Eliza who did the kissing. Kitty smelled just as she had always done, of lily of the valley soap and an essential sugariness that might have been a lifetime of sweet things seeping through her pores.

'I expect you'll be wanting to unwind a little before going to the hospital,' Kitty said.

There was nothing Eliza would have liked more but she feared she might crawl into bed and not be able to leave it.

'Oh, I think we'd rather go straight there,' she said. 'If you wouldn't mind, Kitty. Before we collapse for the evening.'

The hospital was barely half an hour's distance, on the outskirts of Truro. On the way, Kitty filled them in. The doctors now believed Eliza's mother had lost her balance and fallen on the kerbstones of Wesley Street because of a stroke. She had suffered a second stroke since, which had all but paralysed her. The prognosis was not good.

Eliza glanced across at Dido as they took the lift up to the ward, recalling her own dread of hospitals at that age, but Dido seemed fearless, covertly examining a young, scantily gowned man attached to a mobile drip.

Perhaps because of the way the woman loomed in her conscience and dreams, Eliza had forgotten how small her mother was; not a towering witch but a little old lady. She looked lost in the bed, barely disturbing the sheets and baby blue blanket that covered her skinny frame. Her fine hair was brushed off her face in a style not quite her own. Her mouth was slightly open. She did not stir against her bank of pillows as they approached. All her strength, all her character, had retreated into her dark-brown eyes, which stared as unreadably as ever, and into her fingers, which twitched and skittered on the blanket counting invisible banknotes or feeling some unseen stuff for quality.

'Annie? Annie? Look who I've brought to see you! I said they'd come if we prayed hard enough.'

Holding Dido for security, Eliza had positioned herself in what seemed to be her mother's line of vision, but her mother's dark eyes appeared to strain away to look at Kitty.

'You see? She's so *glad*!' Kitty said. 'I told you, Annie. I said they'd come.'

It seemed to Eliza, though, that the eyes were demanding *Why have you brought them here? Take them away at once!*

'I'll leave you three in peace,' Kitty murmured to Eliza. 'It's been so long since you saw each other. I'll be out in the corridor by the drinks machines.' She all but tiptoed away.

Stranded, Eliza stared. Her mother stared back.

'Hello, Mum,' Eliza said at last then fell silent, oppressed by

117

her mother's stare and the triteness of everything it occurred to her to say next. The hands continued to twitch and fumble. Eliza thought of frogs' legs attached to batteries.

Dido came to the rescue, breaking free of Eliza's nervous grip and, entirely unprompted, moving forward to give her grandmother's cheek a fulsome kiss.

'Hello, Granny,' she said. 'Can you hear me? It's Dido. We took hours to get here. We left after breakfast and crossed London on the Tube. Then we got a coach and then Auntie Kitty brought us here in her car. We're going to stay in your house, I think. I hope that's okay. I should call her Great Auntie Kitty really, shouldn't I?' She took one of the twitching hands and held it in hers. 'Take the other,' she told Eliza. 'I don't think she can see us but she knows we're here.'

Eliza pulled up a chair on the other side of the bed. Her mother's bony hand was surprisingly hot. Feeling it twitch between her palms then lie still, she thought of wounded birds and their unfeasibly rapid heartbeats.

'Here I am, Mum,' she said and gave the hand a little experimental squeeze. No squeeze came in return. She looked inside the bedside locker and found a wash bag. She took out the hairbrush and gently brushed her mother's hair back into an approximation of what she remembered as her unvarying style.

'How about lipstick?' Dido asked.

Along with a cracked tortoiseshell powder compact, there was a stick of her mother's trademark dusty pink, adopted when an article in *Good Housekeeping* assured her that red lips made pale faces look ill.

'Her mouth's too slack,' Eliza said. 'I'd only make a mess.'

'Here. Let me.' Dido took it from her and rubbed some of the colour onto a fingertip before gently transferring it to her grandmother's lips where it looked like the last molten traces of a strawberry ice cream.

118

'Come on,' Eliza said at last. 'I think she's asleep. We should let her rest.'

'Ohh!' Dido whined, like a child with someone else's puppy. 'But she looks so *sweet* now!'

Sweet was the last thing this woman had ever been.

'Come on, Dido. We can see her again tomorrow.'

As they crossed the ward, Eliza glanced back. The dark eyes were still staring, wide in horror or judgement. It struck her that Dido was almost entirely untouched by her blood family. Setting aside herself and some early photographs of Hannah, she had little idea who they were or what they were like.

'Now,' Kitty said as they walked the short distance from her house to Eliza's childhood home next door. 'I made up beds for you both and there's some food in the fridge and the larder.'

'Oh, Kitty, you shouldn't have.'

'It's all right, dear. Your mother had only just collected her pension so I used that. Here we are. That's your mother's key. I'd better hang on to the spare in case of emergencies. Shall we go and see her again tomorrow morning? Say at about ten?'

'Yes,' Eliza said, suddenly weary. 'Thanks Kitty. Thanks for everything.' She unlocked the front door, letting an eager Dido in and releasing a smell — furniture polish, full Hoover bags and an undertone of kipper — that returned her to childhood so sharply she fought for a reason, any reason at all, to delay stepping across the threshold. 'Kitty?' she called out sharply.

'Yes, dear?' Kitty turned on the weedy gravel.

'She didn't actually *say* she wanted me here. Did she?'

Kitty dithered. Eliza had remembered and gambled on her inability to lie out loud even when it would certainly be kinder to do so.

'I . . . I knew she'd want you,' Kitty said. 'Especially when Dr Pengelly said how poorly she was.'

'Yes, but she didn't actually *say*, did she?'

Kitty glanced away at some teenage boys mooching noisily by, eating from paper bags. When she looked back it was with an aggrieved, you-made-me-do-this air.

'No, Eliza,' she said. 'No. She didn't. I'll call round for you tomorrow at ten.'

Eliza followed Dido into the house. Dido had already put the kettle on and found a packet of chocolate biscuits and now was exploring.

'Which was your room when you were little?' she called out.

'Up the stairs and turn left,' Eliza called back without needing a moment's thought.

'Show me.'

'Don't you remember?'

'I was a baby,' Dido reminded her. 'Granny's always come to us. I don't remember any of this. It's scary.'

'It isn't really. It's just dark. We always told Mum to cut down those sycamores but she wouldn't and now they take all the light.'

It was a gaunt Victorian villa in a once pretentious district left behind by even Camborne's fashions and now marooned on the wrong end of town for shops, buses, everything. It was far too large a house for an old woman on her own, had been on the large side for a middle-aged one with two children. Once it was clear their father was not coming back they had begged her to move to somewhere more practical, nearer the centre of things, but their mother had held out for the same reason she had stayed on all these years without them, because hers was a life in need of a grudge.

Cursed with excellent health, she had to look to external causes for a source of regular complaint and this dingy house with its stained-glass panels that rattled as they let in draughts, its superfluity of awkward sized rooms, its dank, red-tiled kitchen, cavernous bathroom and increasing lack of neighbourhood proved a reliable supply. The garden was a jungle of bindweed and bramble, a haven for the cats that made war on Kitty. A host of sycamore saplings, spawn of the larger ones, thickened the unhealthy, fly-dirtied shade.

With no lodgers and no other visitors to displace things, Hannah and Eliza's rooms had been preserved as if in aspic. Fading teenage posters hung on the walls. Sinister dolls watched from the corners where each girl had banished them. In either room a pitifully inadequate bookcase stood crammed with every book the girl had owned from birth to university.

While Dido fell gleefully on the stack of laughably anti-quated *Bunty* annuals, Eliza moved on, opening cupboard doors, appalled at the clothes hoarded there, musty dresses, long contorted by wire hangers, lank shades of social failure. Hoarded to what end? To prove that she loved her daughters more than they loved her and continued to care once they had moved on? Or to stoke the fire of condemnation when it threatened to die down into forgiveness?

Leaving Dido to 'The Four Marys', she pushed open the door to her mother's room. The big, ugly bed had been a wedding present and must have been of the highest quality for it barely sagged to this day. There was a hideous wardrobe to match, and a dressing table at which the girls had once sat to preen and play at princesses. A wedding photograph was still defiantly displayed. Eliza saw for the first time that her mother had married late and been considerably older than her dapper father. A small triple frame showed Hannah, Eliza and Dido, each of them pictured in blameless babyhood. She took the pictures to show Dido – for the image of her grandpa and the proof that Granny loved them all. Then she showed her the bathroom and the spare room whose window looked directly onto a brick wall and which had a vast mahogany wardrobe

121

stretched across the wall at the foot of the twin beds. She did not confess that she had always thought the room haunted; the house was forbidding enough as it was.

Kitty had tactfully made up the two daughters' beds and draped antique, sandpapery towels across each of them.

'You can sleep in Hannah's old room,' Eliza said. 'See the view your mum used to wake up to. Now let's have that cup of tea.'

The shade cast across the ground floor windows was so deep and so green that returning downstairs was like descending into a basement or a sunless tarn. Most childhood homes surely threw up one or two things the returning prodigal would clasp to their heart. Eliza could find nothing in hers to please or charm her. She would have happily seen everything consigned to a skip; most of it was too tatty for charity shops.

The piano, which was the one object in the house for which she had felt any affection, was long since gone. She remembered afresh the shock of coming home during the weeks before starting university to find only four indentations in the carpet where the instrument had stood.

'Well you'll not need it where you're going and I certainly won't need it here now you're gone,' her mother had said.

Looking around now, taking in the lack of television or radio, it occurred to her that her mother might have hated music. Eliza's conscientious hours of practice on the woolly-toned Bösendorfer might have been torture to her. Eliza had always felt bad counting off the weeks until her escape but perhaps, all along, her mother had been counting off the years to be shot of those hesitant clunkings and fumbled chords.

'It's funny,' Dido said as they drank their tea at the kitchen table and ate their way through a saffron cake Kitty had baked for them. 'I can't imagine you here.'

'Neither can I,' Eliza told her.

'Were you happy?'

'Not very,' Eliza said after thinking a moment. 'I mean, I wasn't miserable. Granny didn't abuse us or anything nasty. And she must have earned a bit as a teacher because we were never hungry. It's just I was always wanting to be older than I was. I always wanted to grow up and leave. Some people seem to have these amazing childhoods and they spend their life comparing backwards. And for some people childhood's just a stage to get through, like having chicken pox or . . . or being a sort of larva. And Granny wasn't very happy most of the time so . . . she wasn't very good at making life fun. But she wanted you very much, you know. When your mum died I think she sort of hoped she'd get to keep you. To bring you up.'

'What? *Granny* did?' Dido pulled a face, the very idea of her being raised here comical to her.

'Maybe,' Eliza said, 'she thought she could make a better job of it second time around. But I wasn't going to leave you behind. Not my precious bundle. You were so *sweet*!'

'Eli-za!'

'Sorry. More cake?'

'No thanks. It tastes too yellow.'

'You know, don't you, Granny's probably going to die. She's very ill.'

'I know,' Dido said, fingering the buttery crumbs on her plate. Then a thought occurred to her. 'Would we have to live here then?'

'You must be joking!'

'Oh. So Granny rents all this house from the council?'

'No,' Eliza told her. 'She owns it. If she died it would become ours and we could sell it and buy somewhere else.' But this thought was novel and disturbing so she put it from her. Dido sensed her discomfort and lapsed into thoughtfulness.

They walked into town after their tea and cake, Dido having expressed a wish to see Camborne before night fell and Eliza itching to escape the house's oppressive atmosphere. The place had altered little apart from the inevitable supermarket or two in optimistically large car parks.

'Everything's closed,' Dido said.

'It tends to be in the country,' Eliza told her.

'But this isn't country. It's a town, isn't it?'

'I think it counts as country if you can see fields in the distance. There are fewer people so the shops can't afford to stay open so late and everyone goes home instead.'

Merely saying this conjured up the deserts of aimless bike rides and uniformly uneventful evenings that were Eliza's school holidays.

'I thought Cornwall was on the sea.'

'Most of it is. Just this bit isn't. Look! Seagulls. The sea isn't so far.'

'Could we go? Giles' mum said the beaches are much better here than in Kent.'

'Maybe. Let's see,' Eliza said, cursing her mother-in-law.

They paused to examine a war memorial and made a detour into the churchyard so that Dido could see a handful of plain ancestral gravestones. She found Hannah's grave without being shown. Its marble was still shockingly pale amid all the polished granite. They looked at it in silence for a minute or so. It was Dido who led them away. As they continued their walk, past more sad shop windows and secretive pubs, Eliza wondered if it disturbed Dido to remember so little of her mother. Had she stared at the grave and felt nothing?

'Everybody's white here,' Dido said.

'That's another way of telling you're in the country.'

The walk into town was further than Eliza had remembered so they treated themselves to fish and chips by way of compensation for Camborne not having a beach.

While Dido was enjoying a long soak in Granny's peculiarly deep and narrow bath there was a knock on the front door.

'Oh dear,' Kitty said, her big face so awash with tears it seemed to be melting.

Eliza found herself staring, unable to say more than, 'When?'

'Just now. They just rang. Oh dear. You must be brave, Eliza. I . . . I'll call round in the morning.'

Eliza knew she ought to have offered some comfort. As an old and dear friend, Kitty's grief was so plainly going to be deeper than her own. She could feel the strange coolness in her repelling the older woman but could make no move towards her. She was still unsettled by the sudden confrontation with Hannah's gravestone. Had they touched, she might have caught Kitty's grief and been unable to check it. She could not face telling Dido right away. Her reaction was likely to be strong. This was, after all, the death of one of only two blood relatives. Eliza would need all her strength to sustain them both.

It did not occur to her until Kitty had left to ask her for a lift to the hospital. Not that she felt any great desire to look upon so pitiful a body but she knew Kitty might have liked to pay her last respects and would not have felt able to go on her own, being a non-relative. For a few minutes Eliza was frozen in indecision and when she did decide to go round to ask, she opened the front door only to see Kitty's house and path in uninviting darkness.

There was no alcohol in the place. Her mother was strictly teetotal. By investigating the old hiding places, however, the mending box, the plate warmer, Eliza found the remains of a small box of Old Master chocolate liqueurs. There was still a ticket number stuck to the lid from a tombola stall. They were so old it was quite feasible that her mother had not eaten one of them but had been solemnly offering the box to her rare, less principled visitors over the years.

'I'm going to bed,' she called through the bathroom door and retreated with the chocolates to her room.

Bundled into bed, horizontal at long last, she lay trying not to choke on the unpleasantly sweetened gush of Drambuie as she munched, waiting for emotion to steal up on her. She felt nothing. Blood singing from sugar, she leaned from the bed to tug her wallet from the back pocket of her discarded jeans.

There was a photo pocket filled with the roughly trimmed shot of Dido powdering her nose in Giles' dressing room. Behind it was a letter, much read and refolded so often it had the practised creases of a map. There was a date, of several years ago.

Dear Eliza, she read, *I continue well and hope you do too. I tried to ring you just now and poor Giles told me what you have done. I don't know what to say beyond expressing shock that a child of mine should fall so low. How can you face yourself? How can you face Dido? Her mother was so strong and principled; why can't you be more like her?*

I know you are not (no longer, that is) a Christian and probably never were in your heart; but you have to accept that I am. And for that reason I can no longer have anything to do with you. A relief for you, perhaps. An ageing mother is hardly a joy forever.

Being outside time, God knows us instantly at every stage of our lives, so he knows that I shall always love you as you were and that I shall continue to pray for you, as I do for Dido and that I shall always be
   Your Mother.

14

At first Carlo could not believe his luck in being given the whole of Hampstead Heath to run around on and each time Eliza let him off the lead he would vanish in search of rabbits, squirrels and other dogs to chase. She routinely lost entire mornings wandering around in search of him until she learnt that he was more likely to find her if she remained in one place. So she would let him off near the café in Parliament Hill Fields then sit at a table in the warmth, completing a crossword or reading a novel until he came back.

It was while sitting there on one particularly protracted morning that she met Paul. She had met him before, apparently, at one of Giles' first nights but she had forgotten that and had just decided she must recognise him from the television when he walked over from buying his coffee, sat at her table and said hello.

He saw at once how she failed to remember him and was hugely amused. He took further pleasure in discomforting her with a precise recollection of what she had been wearing the night they met and what she had said.

'It was *Agrippina*,' he said. 'The first night, October before last and you were all in brown with a sort of furry collar and gold shoes, like a rather glamorous mouse.'

'Paul,' she said at once. 'You're Paul Lessing the director. This is so embarrassing. Giles would kill me.'

'I've got one of those faces,' he said. 'Instantly forgettable.'

But he didn't at all. His features were rugged, ravaged even. He had smoker's skin and an unruly shock of greying brown hair. He must have been in his fifties. He was a mess. However, he wore a faintly theatrical leather coat with a purple velvet collar and carried himself and his plainness with a beguilingly misplaced swagger, as though he were an ex-beauty, at least, or an ageing rock star who could afford not to care.

He was waiting for his ex-wife to drop off their boy for half term. The news that he was a veteran of a marriage war lent him extra interest, like a scar on a face with no other suggestion of violence.

He complimented her on an essay on seventeenth century performing practice that she had written for a recent *King Arthur* programme and was just starting to quiz her on the topic of Trevescan when his wife and child arrived.

The wife peered at Eliza through the steamed up windows with sharp eyes then vanished. The child was a sullen, hulking fourteen-year-old who said nothing to her beyond hi and answered his father's eager questions with short answers that had to be prised from him. He was at once aggressively shy and oppressively the centre of attention and it was with relief that she saw Carlo loitering sheepishly by the litter bin and was able to make her farewells.

'I ran into Paul Lessing on the Heath today,' she told Giles and thought nothing more of it.

But then Paul invited them out to dinner, a small, intense dinner party in a restaurant, at which Giles was the only singer and was conversationally out of his depth. Paul contrived to be on the Heath the next day and walked with her. He took to ringing when she was alone in the house.

Had she told Giles about every walk and conversation, the relationship might have developed into that chimaera, the sexless friendship of man and woman. Something silenced her however and her silence lent their encounters a charge of riskily transgressive excitement. Giles had secrets after all, she assured herself. There were many things in his working day – conversations, flirtations, interests – that he told her nothing about. She was sure of it.

Once she admitted to herself that she wanted more than a passing liaison from Paul, there was no reversing the thought, no unfeeling the feeling. He made her feel special, like more than a mother, true, but also like more than an unfinished thesis. Had she enjoyed a confidante, someone to grill her about what she was embarking on and why, she might have come to her senses. She might however have admitted aloud that she was drawn to Paul because, unlike Giles, he did not handle her with care. He was frank, impolite and gave the impression that any woman throwing in her lot with him would be living on her wits and risking everything for . . . for what?

She had to know. So one day, as they finished walking Carlo – who Paul had trained to stay in close calling distance, apparently by simple alpha male presence and an ability to whistle – she said, 'Show me where you live. I don't have to pick Dido up for two hours yet.'

Sex with Paul was like conversation with him; no artifice, no leaving off of lights or drawing of merciful curtains. He was entirely without shame. It didn't seem to be about emotions at all but entirely about sex; a sort of athletic contest as to which of them could get the most out of it. It was dirty and untender and utterly addictive. Far from making Eliza feel bad or guilty, it left her whole and healthy. And hungry for more.

For two weeks Carlo's walks all ended at the foot of Paul's huge bed. The fact that they were now having sex went undiscussed. The fizzing, stimulating conversations – about music, art, politics, people, history – bubbled up within minutes of sex being over. The combination of words and bodies was intoxicating.

It need have gone no further. She had heard how such affairs had a way of burning out in their own heat.

Paul began to voice regrets, however, not that he had slept with her but that he had slept with her *first*.

'How do you mean *first*?' she asked.

'There are so many people I wanted you to meet,' he said. 'Places I could take you. New York. Santa Fe. Sydney. Buenos Aires.'

'And now you can't?' she began.

'I can't get involved. You have Giles. You have a life already. I swore I wouldn't do this.'

'Are you saying you can't respect me because I slept with you too easily?'

'I'm saying I want you here, in my life, want you even more than before, and I know it's not fair to ask that of you.'

He showed her the room she could have as a study and the room Dido could have as a bedroom. Warming to his theme, he painted a picture of their life together. Giles was a lovely man, a superb singer, but like so many performers he was, Paul implied, a kind of child, trapped in a kind of distorting immaturity by the necessity of putting his technique and welfare and career before anything else. She could never reach her full potential with him because his childlike demands would always be holding her back. With Paul, by implication, she would blossom.

She had never thought of Giles in this way before. Perhaps because she saw him in the dim light of her truncated career and uncompleted doctorate, he had always seemed the dauntingly capable one, the more adult of the pair, the achiever, the star. This new image of him as the infant

130

destroyer checking her growth took root. Before long she had convinced herself that she would be Dr Hosken by now if Giles had not lured her from her chosen path. Most insidiously, Giles had convinced her she was weaker than she was. She did not need his protection. Quite the reverse!

As soon as she dared entertain the possibility of leaving him it became a reality she could plot. She gave him no inkling of what was in her mind but regularly caught herself setting him tests. *If he comes home from rehearsals and asks how my work's going before he tells me about his, then he loves me and I won't leave him. If he stays facing me as we fall asleep, I won't leave him.* Test after test was failed in all innocence.

He took her to a party to celebrate the anniversary of Selina Bryant Management. It was a typical agency gathering – the agents and their staff infinitely spanglier and wittier than the talent they represented, Russian tenors with little English and no manners, quiet pianists eaten up by insecurity, wind players painfully aware the agency could not afford to represent more than one exponent on each instrument so might drop them at any moment. On the Tube over she listened to Giles chatter about the new production of Edward Pepper's *Job*, noticed the irrational distaste she had developed for his extremely clean and tidy fingernails and told herself that if he took the trouble to introduce her to five or more people, she would break off with Paul and make an effort to save their marriage.

He left her side as they were handing in their coats and introduced her to nobody. She spent the evening walled in by people's backs in a quiet corner with a viol player with no dress sense and smelly hair.

She walked out on the marriage the next day. She was conscious of leaving in a hurry, of wilfully simplifying her thoughts to block out reasoning. She left him a letter, which was cowardly, but she took pains to write the truth.

Your love was based on pity, she wrote. *Paul has shown me that I'm worth a little more than that.*

She gave Carlo one last rampage on the Heath, for old time's sake, but felt she must leave him behind. He was Giles' dog and it would be too cruel for Giles to come back to an empty house. Then she imagined how traumatised Dido might be to lose him without warning so took him too. She settled the latest phone bill, which she could ill afford, crammed her belongings into one case, Dido's into another and picked Dido up from playgroup on the way. She rang Paul moments before leaving saying merely, 'It's me. I'm coming.'

It only occurred to her as she was hastily giving Dido a simplified version of events in the taxi that he might have misinterpreted this and greet them naked and, as he liked to put it, *with a full head of steam.*

If he was expecting merely another assignation, Paul hid his surprise masterfully. He laughed. He kissed her. Then he kissed Dido, kissed Carlo, lugged their cases inside and whirled them out for a celebration meal.

Dido had no idea who he was but was charmed and christened him The Party Man. She cried that night, however, as it dawned on her that Giles was not joining them and they were not returning home. She decided Paul's bathroom was frightening and would not sleep in her new bed unless Eliza lay down beside her. Unerring instinct told her to exploit Eliza's guilt as fully as she could. Lulling her to fretful sleep then curling up with Paul on the Chesterfield at one end of his huge, barely furnished sitting room, Eliza was on edge for a phone call that never came.

All that first weekend Paul was charm personified, considerate, playful, supportive. On the Sunday night he warned her he was about to start a rehearsal period on a new play and so would be absent a lot and abstracted when he was around.

'I'll cope,' she said.

'Good,' he said, 'because I'm glad you're here. Truly I am.' But she had underestimated how absent and abstracted he meant.

Rehearsing the play was more than a nine-to-five job. Routinely rehearsals spilled over into trips to the pub or on to a restaurant. The actors and playwright, he explained, were like insecure teenagers needing constant reassurance. He had to be there for them and it was vital to the production's cogency that he forge a temporary sense of family with them. She wondered how many social groups Paul thought of as children besides opera singers, actors and playwrights. Ex-wives? Mistresses? All women? But this was a passing cynicism only.

With Dido away at playgroup Eliza drifted around his big house, not snooping exactly but piecing together pieces of his life from photographs, postcards, carelessly discarded letters. When Dido was there, Eliza worked hard at making the strange house feel like a home for them both.

Paul had lived there for years – before, during and after his failed marriage – and seemed oddly oblivious to his surroundings. Occasionally seeing it all through her eyes, he would say,

'It's terrible. We should get someone in. What do you think? Move the kitchen? Make this an upstairs sitting room?'

But he would soon lose interest and nothing would be done.

There were stacks of ill-assorted paintings against walls, unhung because he had not got around to changing their frames or could not muster the focus to decide where to hang them. Everywhere were the traces of things his wife had taken when she set up home elsewhere – the ghost of a picture in a square of less faded paintwork, the memory of a chest of drawers in a quartet of compressions on a carpet, even, in one room, light fittings she had removed leaving naked bulbs on dangerous-looking naked wires. He saw no reason to hide these traces. Dusty shelves were crammed with books in so little order that browsing for even a novel was oddly dispiriting and finding anything as useful as a map or a dictionary a near impossibility.

He had never learned to cook, so the kitchen cupboards were haunted by ancient rice and time-faded spices; gestural offerings left by long departed guests. He was a hypochondriac so the bathroom cabinet spewed patent medicines. Marie, a young woman from an estate near Giles' house, came twice a week to swab hard surfaces with bleach and walk the Hoover around but Paul did not like her to dust because it made him sneeze and aerosol propellant gave him sore eyelids.

There was the sense, the smell, of neglect everywhere, particularly as one sank into a chair or lay on a bed. Had Eliza been a different kind of woman, she would have taken advantage of Paul's long absences to make improvements, replace dead light bulbs and moribund houseplants, hang some pictures, rearrange some furniture. She did try, if only to help Dido settle in, but the effort overwhelmed her and invoked a lingering sense that she lacked sufficient influence to impose herself.

She had a dream in which she showed her father around the place and he turned to her in the last room, astonished, and exclaimed,

'But this is a house of death!'

At last a letter arrived from Giles in response to her departing note.

He did not rage. There were no exclamation marks, not even trails of angry dots. He was fairness itself. Her letter came as a surprise, he said, although he was aware things had not been brilliant between them lately. He did love her, he said, whatever she might think, but perhaps he could never love her enough or in the way she needed. He was happy she had found happiness. He would not stand in her way if she wanted a divorce. He was sure Paul would make a great father figure to Dido. To help him adjust, he had accepted an invitation to sing in Lyon and Paris but would be back in six weeks if she needed to discuss anything.

His failure to send love to Dido wounded Eliza more than the passionless ease with which he gave her up. She lied. She had to. *Giles sends you his love*. It helped that he had gone away, however. It gave a ready answer if Dido asked to see him, and would ease her through the domestic upheaval. After the first night's tearfulness, Dido had showed remarkably little upset over the change in her life; she was already a level-headed child.

Eliza did her best. She reassured Paul by setting up an office in the room he suggested, arranged her files and took on some CD booklet commissions. Reviving her Trevescan research was unthinkable however, in a house of unexecuted plans and neglected wishes. She took Carlo to the Heath less and less, not because it had associations with her meeting Paul but because it now reminded her of Giles. Instead they made do with a toxic little park beside the defunct neighbourhood church.

Carlo disliked the new house. He would not settle in his bed but would follow Eliza around the house, flopping on the floor when she sat at last and watching her reproachfully until she moved again. He irritated Paul by demanding to sleep in their bedroom, where he had so often lain panting and muddy while they made love, then punished them for his banishment by repeatedly shitting on the already murky bathroom carpet.

With astonishing confidence and no warning, Paul returned

the dog to Giles after a man to man chat and bought Dido a teddy as replacement.

'The dog'll be happier there,' he said, 'And he'll cheer Giles up.'

She could not rid herself of the sense that she had made a huge mistake and that her presence in this great, dusty house was only provisional, like the placing of the unhung paintings. This was confirmed, it seemed, by the people – many of them glamorous, household names – who rang for him when he was out and showed neither surprise nor curiosity at her answering the phone. When an especially famous actress did pause to ask, in her famously smoky tones, 'So who *are* you, dear?', Eliza found she could only say, 'I'm Eliza. I . . . I live here.'

To which the actress said, 'Oh. I see,' in a bored way, evidently taking her for some sort of pushy lodger, a poor relation, perhaps, or impoverished drama student.

Paul's excited talk of working trips to Sydney and New York did not become a reality any more than his initial suggestion she research play texts for him or meet his host of famous friends. Some of the famous friends came back with him one night, an unheard of event, after an awards ceremony. Eliza was upstairs spooning Tixylix into Dido – they both had streaming colds – and felt obliged to stay upstairs in hiding until there were loud farewells and the front door thudded an all-clear.

Every third weekend the ex-wife, who was an Antonia, called round to drop off Paul's son, Simon. Having looked her fill the once, she showed no more curiosity than the actresses. The son was sweet enough to Dido but relapsed into adolescent silence if Eliza tried to draw him out. Still, she came to look forward to his visits since they were a guarantee that Paul would be present and keen for them all to do things 'as a family'.

As the day for the play's opening drew near, she began to worry that she had nothing good enough to wear. She went to the hairdresser, at least, and fixed up a babysitter for Dido. Then it became plain that he had no more thought of involving her in the first night than he would an au pair.

'We'll all be talking shop,' he told her. 'And everyone will be neurotic as hell. You know what actors are like. But no, of course you must come. I'll have them leave you a ticket with front of house. Do you want to bring a friend?'

She cried off at the last minute, nerves failing her, blaming a no-show from the babysitter. He came home rather drunk, for him. His snoring woke her soon after dawn and she lay there in the grey light and it was as though a cruel fairy, or Selina Bryant no less, had waved her blighting wand. Instead of her beautiful, gold haired prince, she was in bed with an old man who smelled of red wine, was balding, not in a good way, and had patches of grey fur on his shoulder blades.

From there it got rapidly worse. She began to dwell obsessively on unflattering details. He began each day by pissing with the door open and invariably produced a sad little mew of a fart halfway through. He never used soap in the shower, either, but seemed to think it enough that he let the foam from his (hair-thickening formula) shampoo trickle over the rest of him.

Heart racing, she rang Giles when she knew he'd be in. But a woman answered and said he was practising and should she fetch him. Not recognising the voice – his mother stayed very occasionally but this certainly was not her – Eliza echoed the famous actress. She forced a little woman of the world chuckle that actually came out rather squeakily and piped,

'Sorry, but who *are* you?'

'I'm his girlfriend,' the woman said sharply. 'Who are you?'

'Oh . . .' Eliza crumbled. 'It was just Eliza, tell him,' and she left a number.

Giles never rang, so perhaps she had caused a row.

This time she did not leave in an impulsive hurry. For Dido's sake she planned the move with military precision and forethought. She presented herself at the council housing offices, explaining that it was impossible for her and her daughter to remain with her husband, that they had a temporary arrangement but that it wasn't clean and it couldn't last. A flat was found on the same estate as Marie, Paul's cleaner. (When they passed on the stairs, Marie looked straight through her, not recognising her so violently torn from context.)

Eliza took possession of the keys and, for the next fortnight, after dropping Dido off, spent the morning decorating. She had next to no money but she wanted it to be perfect. She had seen enough of dinginess. She was quite new to decorating but found the most cheerful colours on the reduced price shelf and slapped them up with grim determination. She made Dido a proper bedroom – a little girl's room – with matching (slightly short) curtains and bedspread. She shopped with Paul's occasional handouts then squirrelled food away in the fridge and cupboards. She would have felt like a murderer if only he had cared but he blithely set off for a working weekend in Paris leaving her free to move out as openly as she chose.

Dido liked her new bedroom and, with a child's wisdom, edited out the social disadvantages of their new address and saw only that it meant they had a balcony and lived higher than the birds. She enjoyed riding in the lift.

'Paul was only temporary, wasn't he?' she said with devastating accuracy. The only reassurance she required was that they would not be moving again, for it transpired she had a box containing a complicated arrangement of things she called her treasures which she did not care to unpack lightly and which had remained packed up all their time at Paul's house.

Eliza had intended to leave Paul a note or write him a letter after the move but when she sat down with pen and paper she found there was nothing to say beyond what he could see for himself, that they had gone. She did not feel sorry for him since she could not see how he would miss her presence. Short of hiring a private detective, he had no way of tracing her. Her new phone number was ex-directory and, for all that he occasionally directed plays that were strenuously grim in their social outlook, his colonial childhood had left him with a cheerful trust in a constant supply of people to service his needs and a complacent mental ability to edit out vast sections of society about which he had no curiosity. He would assume she had left him for another man's protection. A lone mother's bolt-hole in a council estate was the last place he would think of looking for her.

15

Giles was doing sit-ups. The house had a couple of fairly dingy basement rooms whose barred windows afforded a squint at the paved area on either side of the steps to the front door. One housed Giles' music library and an old upright on which he could stab out notes where necessary. The other was a utility room to which Julia had banished the rowing machine and abdominal board which had once cluttered a spare bedroom.

Time was when Giles had quite unfairly managed to maintain a flat, even washboardish stomach simply by leaning back from the knees for two minutes whenever he used his electric toothbrush.

Loading the washing machine that morning, however, he had noticed a slackness in the waistbands of his underwear that spoke of strain on the elastic as much as age of material. He had observed, too, a worrying tendency Julia and others had developed of letting a hand linger above his hips when they hugged him, as though comforted by a cosy sleekness there.

So he was resolved on performing a hundred sit-ups before breakfast. He had found that these were most effective inflicted on an empty stomach. Legs locked around the abdominal board's cushioned supports, he had done fifty straightforward ones and was just starting fifty twisty ones, touching, or aiming to touch, alternate elbows to their opposite knees.

He recognised Dido's legs, black socks beneath the navy-blue skirt of her uniform, and broke off, hurrying upstairs. Julia was still preparing to leave for work and he wanted to intercept Dido before she did.

'I'll get it,' he shouted up the stairs as the doorbell jangled. He heard the hairdryer switch off.

'What?' Julia called.

'Don't worry. I'm there.'

The hairdryer started again. Giles opened the door.

'Hi. This is a nice surprise.'

'Yeah, well, sorry to bother you,' Dido said. She headed past him into the kitchen where she finally met his eye. 'I need some money.' Her expression was deadly serious.

'Sure.' He had reached for his wallet before he started wondering why. He imagined playground protection rackets, alcopops, drugs.

'Are you in trouble?' he asked.

'No!' she said indignantly. 'It's . . .' She paused and he saw that whatever came next was a lie. 'It's the phone bill again. We've been cut off.'

The cash would go on food, probably. He knew that, with a child's acuity to the niceties of poverty, Dido sensed there was bravado in a cut-off phone but shame in an empty fridge. Giles sighed and counted out the notes for her quickly, grateful he had been to the cashpoint recently and happy Julia was not there to witness the quick transaction. His maintaining an estranged wife's chaotic household was a bone of contention between them. She did not care that it was cheaper this way than involving lawyers and being saddled with an officially fixed maintenance level. Julia only saw the galling, continuing link between them and wanted it severed. She could not begin to believe that someone could be

141

so unworldly, so unaware of her legal due as Eliza was and so looked for darker motives.

'Thanks.' Dido stuffed the notes in her breast pocket.

Julia came swiftly through the hall, picking up her bag and the newspaper she would glance over on the train into town. 'Hi,' she said, seeing who it was. 'Everything all right?'

'Fine, thanks,' Dido told her.

'We missed seeing you yesterday morning.'

'Sorry. I had stuff to do at the flat before school.'

'Thought you might.'

He noticed how diplomatically Dido never used the word *home*.

Julia's perfume reached him – *Arpège*. He loved those old-fashioned touches in her. She would never have worn a scent one saw advertised. And *Arpège* was unofficey. It spoke of indolence and mistresses which, had she more sense of humour, he might have taken as a witticism on her part. Addicted to heels, she was clutching her shoes in one hand to save damaging their floors.

'I'm late,' she said. 'Bye both. Walk you to school, Dido?'

'Er. No thanks,' Dido said, so untactfully that Julia smiled.

'Fine,' she said. 'Giles. Don't forget.'

'I know. Selina at eleven.'

They listened as Julia opened the front door, paused to step into her shoes on the doorstep then closed it behind her.

'Is everything okay really?' Giles asked.

'Fine.'

'Breakfast?'

'No thanks. Better go. I'll take a banana. Look.'

'What?'

'I won't be round next weekend.'

'Oh.' He knew better than to show he was hurt. 'Okay.'

She said nothing further but went out to the hall where Livia had just let herself in to start the washing up. Dido took advantage of this to slip away. 'Hi. Bye,' she called, and was gone.

'Morning, Giles,' said Livia, her Bajan combination of lilt and dignity making him think of church and all the things he had left undone.

He realised he had given Dido only what she had asked for and thought of running after her with another twenty pounds, then realised he now had too little cash to pay Livia so would have to go to the cashpoint anyway.

'Sorry about the mess, Livia,' he said. 'But you know how it is. I'll get out of your way.'

It was only as the cashpoint at Highbury Corner drooled out notes into his hand that it occurred to him that the sudden, almost defiant demand for money might have no bearing on Eliza's hopelessness at budgeting and everything to do with the photographs he had cut up last night.

'Giles, come in. Sit down. That was such a ball last night. So sweet of you both. I won't be a second. Sorry. Sit.'

Selina waved him over to her little leather sofa and indicated the jug of coffee, bottle of chilled water and plate of buttery cookies. Selina never smelled of anything, unless steel or paper had a smell. Hot contracts, perhaps, or a whiff of boot leather. She sat back behind her desk and clicked a call she was taking back off the mute setting.

'Jemima? What can I say, darling? I don't believe it. You *can't* be that old! Good grief! But look, I can't be there. It's crazy and my values are fucked but there it is. I can't. Forgive me? You'd better, but we'll talk soon, sweetness and I'll see what I can do about Nimbus and bloody Rita . . . You think? Hmm. Okay. I love you. Bye.'

Selina always said she loved you at the end of her calls but in a completely flat, nearly ferocious way. It was one of the few times her Zimbabwean heritage showed beneath its London overlay. That, and the way she pronounced *okay*. And her manner when placing any kind of order anywhere.

Giles had glimpsed Julia on his way in but had not greeted her. They had established long ago that the best way of avoiding any awkwardness in his being at once her lover and her boss' client was for her to ignore him when she was working. She would be going out soon, to grab a sandwich in Marylebone.

In much the same spirit they had both learnt never to refer to Selina's girlfriend during working hours. It was nothing to do with lesbianism, simply that, when she was working, Selina regarded any allusion to her domestic life as undermining and the air would crackle with unvoiced displeasure for half an hour afterwards.

'So, sweetness.' She was all attention now. She swept her long, dry hair back off her face. Giles always expected to see sparks in it. 'First you need to sign these. There, there and there.' As he signed each form, she slung it in the out-tray by her door. From time to time during any meeting with Selina, the door would open slightly without anyone knocking and a hand would reach in to whisk away whatever papers lay in the tray. 'Bad news and good news. And possibly excellent news. Depending.'

'Bad first?' Giles suggested.

'Sure? Okay. Nothing at ENO in next year's season. Nada. I'd hoped they were reviving *Ariodante* but they're not. Not yet, because Georgia isn't free for it and they want you both. But what really pisses me off is that they're reviving *JC* without you.'

He shrugged, wounded, as she knew he would be. Worse than wounded. He immediately wondered who they had hired for the revival of what he had come to think of as *his* production, an old hand or a threatening new talent? A pit seemed to open in his stomach and the room felt far too small and everything too close for comfort. Selina included. 'Good news?' he prompted her.

'Good for you, this is. It makes me next to nothing, of course, but no ENO season leaves you free to tour the lute songs with Douglas, which'll tie in with the CD's release. It's looking quite good, actually. Aix is a definite date and Edinburgh and some festival in Leiden. We'll see. Early days.'

Selina hated him doing anything like chamber music because it didn't tally with her view of who he should be. Secretly Giles was quite pleased to have a chance to establish a different, quieter side to his career. He had no illusions about the brutal shortness of many counter-tenors' operatic shelf lives. He might be lucky and stay the course as long as Bowman but as insurance he needed to keep other avenues open, especially on the Continent, where the baroque music scene remained in robust good health.

'Now,' Selina went on. 'The possibly excellent news is that you did a better job last night than you realised.'

'I didn't know I was doing any job last night.'

She dismissed his disingenuity like so much smoke from in front of her face. She never lit up when her singers were present (unless drunk) but there was always a clean Hermès ashtray on her desk, always with one of the little gold devices in it she liked for easing stubbing out when one had nails to think of. She tapped the ashtray now, nail tips tinkling softly against the porcelain until it was neatly squared off with the desk's corner. One half expected the hand of another spectral minion to fly out of one of the drawers to replace it with a fresher one.

'Grover didn't say a word about it last night but he has a *Midsummer Night's Dream* crisis.'

Giles' mind darted back to the previous evening and the few things he remembered Grover saying. A film director who had only recently broken into opera production in his native Sydney, Grover was about to make his London debut in the field with a production of Britten's *A Midsummer Night's Dream*. Giles had registered this much, but only enough to feel piqued at not being considered for the lead role, one of the few such for counter-tenors in the twentieth century repertoire.

'But he said they were about to start rehearsing!' he said.

'They are. And Robby's dropped out at the last minute.'

Robby Wilson was Giles' principal rival, of the same vintage and training but Robby had recently found a truly international audience with an extraordinarily bold CD on which he sang romantic mezzo soprano songs by Schubert, Chausson, Fauré and Brahms which underwent a subtle chemical change when sung at pitch by a man. The CD was still riding high in the classical charts and Giles was beginning to worry that Selina felt she had backed the wrong man. Bookings for counter-tenors were so rare compared to ones for tenors and baritones that there was only room for one on her books. The only advantage Giles had was castability; Robby Wilson was chubby, pasty, short and not even an artfully trained beard could conjure planes from a face of lard. He looked, as Selina once pointed out, like the screechy eunuch of Handel's nightmares.

Giles' heart was light again. 'Is he sick?'

Selina fell back to tapping the ashtray. 'Let's just say there were personal differences. Anyway, Giles, it's you Grover would like to see for a director's meeting this afternoon.'

'But I –'

She held up a hand. 'It's not an audition. He knows your voice, as does Simon.'

'Simon's conducting?'

'Sure. Besides, we all know you'd be doing them a favour

this close to rehearsals starting. But Grover wants to try you out alongside his Puck and he has, well, certain *physical* priorities.'

'How d'you mean?'

'Grover's not a musician, sweetness. We both know that. He made his name in rock videos and multiplex-packers. His values are a bit leftfield. This will be a wild production.'

'He's kept it very quiet.'

'Hasn't he. Because it's going to be huge. Well. As huge as Britten's managed to be for a few decades. And it would be your Garden debut, my darling, and there's an extremely lucky precedent for last minute replacements there.'

'Who else is he seeing?'

'He plays a tidy game but as far as I can make out, just you. Do you need a score? We could pick yours up on the way.'

'It's fine,' he said, tapping his head. 'That's one of the few that went in here and stuck.'

As the cab drove them along Marylebone High Street, Giles spotted Julia. As he thought, she was doing a sandwich lunch. The surprise was that Villiers Yates was doing it with her.

'Is everything okay between you and her?' Selina never missed a thing.

'Yes. Everything's fine,' he said. 'Why?'

'No reason, really. She's a special girl.'

'Amazing.'

'It's just that, if ever there were difficulties between you for some reason . . .' Her voice trailed off suggestively. 'I mean, these things happen in this business, especially if you have to travel a lot. If there *were* difficulties, I'd hate you, either of you, to feel you had to stick together simply because of the agency. It wouldn't be the first time. We could weather it.'

'Everything's fine, Selina.'

But she was suddenly calling out to the cabbie. 'You'll need to take the next right or we'll get snarled up in the roadworks on the next block. Please don't argue with me. I've been taking this route all week. Thank you.' She shut the window between them and the cabbie then grinned at Giles. 'Good,' she said, 'because I love you both.'

There was a growing crowd outside the stage door; girls mainly, who should have been in school, and a sprinkling of adult men perhaps unwittingly dressed like teenagers.

'What the hell?' Giles wondered aloud as they pushed through. There was much withering talk about classical artists crossing over into more popular forms but this was ridiculous. 'Who's this in aid of?'

'Not an opera singer.' Selina cast a faintly hungry eye over the eager crowd. 'Grover's Puck. There must have been a leak.' She had a quick word with the men on the reception desk. 'I'll wait for you here afterwards,' she told Giles. 'I won't cramp your style. You'll be swell. He'll be through for you in a second. Just remember he's a wild child and go with whatever he suggests, okay?'

She kissed him dryly for luck then slipped outside for a smoke and another analytical look at the fans.

Giles sat on a sofa, watching men and women, impossibly thin dancers, beer-bellied stage crew passing in and out of some swing doors kept in near constant motion. The old backstage sensation took hold of him, half-thrill, half-nausea. His teeth chattered slightly as adrenalin began to course through his system and he forced himself to yawn then repeated the movement a few times with his mouth shut, feeling the muscles in his throat stretch and relax as his soft palate shifted. Luckily he had fitted in at least forty minutes' warm-up and practice before leaving the house for the agency.

Suddenly Grover was there, big-pawed, stubbled, his shaven head and leather jacket less startling in this setting than he might have hoped. 'Hey! My fucking saviour!'

He kissed Giles' cheek and pulled him into an entirely unaffectionate hug before leading him through a warren of
corridors and steps to the rehearsal space. 'This is so great
of you. I didn't like to say anything last night. Didn't want
to put you on the spot. I mean, you have your pride, yeah?'

Giles simply smiled.

Grover froze a moment, examining his face closely. 'Fuck,'
he muttered. 'I wish we were filming this. Hey! Maybe we
can! You're gonna be perfect. It's that . . . that chilly Pom
thing. Fucking A. Sorry. Okay, Giles. Have you warmed
up?'

'Yup. Earlier on. I'm fine.'

'Okay. So what I want is for you just to sing yourself into
it a bit. Lose Giles, right, and get into fairy mode. And look,
this isn't pretty. No gossamer. These guys are primal; our fears
and cravings, okay? Sing whatever bit you like. Charlie Boy
there's got the score. Whenever you're ready, okay?'

He took a few bounding steps to the back of the rehearsal
space and threw himself into a chair which skidded slightly.

Giles approached the *répétiteur* at the piano. 'What do you
think?' he murmured.

'Let's be obvious,' the *répétiteur* suggested.

'Wild thyme?'

'Uh-huh.'

Giles walked to the middle of the taped-out stage area,
nodded to the *répétiteur* who played the few transitional
bars before Oberon's one big solo. Taking his cue from what
Grover had hinted at, Giles thought Englishness, thought
frost, thought C S Lewis' Snow Queen. 'I know a bank,' he
sang, 'Where the wild thyme grows.'

Grover jumped up, running forward, interrupting. 'Look!'
he shouted, holding out his beefy forearm. 'Gooseflesh. I've
got gooseflesh already! This is gonna be great. Now Giles, are
you feeling brave?'

'Er. Fairly,' Giles said uncertainly.

'Okay. Shirt off, shoes off, everything off and sing it again. Only kidding. The shirt'll do. Everyone! Shirts off. Keep the poor guy company!' He tore off his shirt and rubbed his hairy chest with relish. The *répétiteur* muttered mutinously but carefully unbuttoned to reveal monastically pale flesh. Giles peeled off his shirt and tossed it to one side. Luckily the room was warmed by the summer sun burning in at high windows or he might have felt shivery to the point of throwing up. Unasked, he kicked off his shoes and socks.

He felt surprisingly good. Like many singers, he had always relished the chance to perform in bare feet; a sense of being rooted, earthed, was always inexplicably helpful.

'Thank you,' Grover said, staring. 'Thanks very much. Now. Take it from the top again and Giles?'

'Yes?'

'Remember how pissed off you got last night when we got talking about paedophiles. Think of yourself not as you – nice, normal, beautiful Giles – but as a guy whose idea of love is to control and whose idea of sex is being allowed to watch. Now go.'

Giles began to sing again. Outside there was a sudden burst of cheering and screaming. A few minutes later the rehearsal room door opened and Giles saw who all the fuss was over. Dewi Evans.

Once the self-consciously 'bad' member of a million-selling, all-Welsh boy band, Dewi was now a ridiculously popular solo artist. He made a great play of flirting aggressively with his gay following while Grover was one of those gay men who assumed that all men were vain enough to be persuadable; they were made for each other. This was casting genius.

'Keep going keep going!' Grover shouted as the *répétiteur* broke off at the piano.

'There sleeps Titania,' Giles sang on as the piano came

in again, 'Sometime in the night, lulled in her dreams with dances and delight.'

Grinning from ear to ear, Dewi Evans tore off most of his clothes too and sank to the floor at Giles' feet. He was as dark and ferally hairy as Giles was pale and smooth. He winked broadly as he put a tattooed hand on Giles' calf and stared up in obedient adoration. He held the pose as Giles sang to the end of the aria. Then they looked expectantly out to Grover, who was staring from his perch on a seat back. Slowly a smile broke over Grover's craggy face.

'This turns out better than I could devise.' he said. 'Dewi, Giles. Giles, Dewi.'

Dewi took his grasp off Giles' leg to jump up and shake hands. Even standing, he barely reached Giles' shoulder. 'Wish I could sing like that,' he said in his lilting Rhonda accent.

'Wish I had your sales figures,' Giles said.

'I won't mess with the music,' Grover assured Giles as he saw him back to the stage door area while Dewi slipped out another way, 'but visually this is not going to be Britten as you lot are used to it. Are you in?'

'I'm in.'

Another kiss. Another unaffectionate hug.

16

The agency occupied the first floor of a house off Marylebone High Street. The building belonged to Selina's girlfriend, Peggy, who was said also to own several former slums in areas like Southwark and Clerkenwell. She let out the ground floor to Tobit Hart, the couturier. The upper floors of the house were her and Selina's home. Early arrivals at work would occasionally catch whiffs of their mysterious domesticity, grinding coffee beans, a cat's paws scrabbling in a litter tray, a simmering tiff, before Peggy left for the City and Selina came down and closed the door to their realm firmly behind her.

The site was cleverly chosen. With good shops and restaurants on the doorstep, plentiful taxis and the Tube an easy walk away, it ensured a happy workforce who were thus less likely to demand unfeasible pay rises.

Trainees who proved their mettle and were made associates of the firm were then placed on a performance-related bonus system; the better and more numerous the deals they brokered for their clients, the better their annual bonus.

Julia loved her work. When Selina first took her on she used to dawdle on her way from the Tube, ogling shop windows and estate agents' details, fantasising about living in the area like Selina, but in a tiny attic flat. Now she was comfortably established elsewhere, she still felt a buzz of pleasure that she was working in this street and not somewhere noisier like Hammersmith or Holborn. Pausing to buy a bunch of flowers for her desk, exchanging a smile with Tobit Hart on the doorstep or overhearing colleagues' Russian or German phone calls, she would see herself vividly, as in the film of her life, and be gratifyingly reminded of how far she had progressed.

Like any nunnery or girls' boarding school, the agency soon drew new arrivals into the same ovular cycle. Julia had never stayed long enough in any other office to experience this. Intensely private, she had been aghast at first but she soon came to see it as a relief. There was no overt discussion, nothing tasteless, but as the cramped little bathroom beside the stationery cupboard took on a distinctive mineral tang and the communal jar of painkillers was set out beside the kettle there was a comforting sense that one had companions in indignity and did not need to explain oneself.

The painkillers were out that morning, and the air was lightly coloured by one of Selina's Canovas scented candles and there was a certain amount of unnecessary crossness. All of which made Julia keenly aware that for once she was excluded from the monthly ritual. She tried to feel uncomfortable about this, even guilty, but had difficulty in repressing her sense of well-being. The secret kept bubbling up within her. Only Selina's grouchily accusing, 'You look well,' and the superstitious fear of premature disclosure kept her from confessing. Her sense of smell, too, had become unusually sharp so that the smell of Selina's candle brought on sudden waves of nausea, so she did not look or act well for long.

She had a full day but behind all the talk and negotiations lay a quivering anticipation that tonight she would tell Giles. All that remained was to confirm her suspicions with a pregnancy testing kit. With everyone spending longer than usual in the bathroom, it would be easy enough to smuggle one back to the office and use it before going home. She bought one in her lunch hour.

She had meant to buy some sandwiches to eat at her desk because the problem with the Israeli Philharmonic remained unsolved and she had little time left to fit everything in. Villiers was in the sandwich bar too – he had been examining something in a Wigmore Street violin dealer's for Mr Mister, apparently – and insisted she join him for a post-mortem of the dinner party. She tried to plead work pressures but he was adamant and she knew it was safer to placate him. So she sat at his table. She could eat as swiftly there as at her desk, after all.

Again he grilled her about Giles. What had Giles said about him? What had he done to offend him? Giles was such an old friend and so on. She did not like to say that the cruel fact was that Giles never spoke of Villiers from one week to the next and that last night he had said no more about him behind his back than he had to his face. As a diversionary tactic, she left the table to buy them each an espresso.

When she came back Villiers was looking more than usually mischievous and she saw that the pregnancy testing kit was visible at the top of her bag.

'There's something you're not telling me, Girl,' he teased.

'Oh don't be silly,' she laughed, pushing it back out of sight. 'I bought it for Shawna, at work. She's on reception and couldn't get out.'

'Balls. No one buys these for other people, any more than blokes buy each other condoms.'

'How would you know?' she protested. 'Drink your coffee. I'm late already. I must gulp and go.'

But she could not fool Villiers. No one could. His relentless teasing made her smile and her smile connected through to the happiness she was trying so hard to tamp down and it all came welling out.

'How sure are you?' he asked.

'Ninety percent,' she said. 'I've been being sick and everything. I've even got a heightened sense of smell, like a werewolf. I only bought the tester to be sure.'

'What are you going to do?'

This struck her as an odd question in the circumstances and only then did she realise that Villiers had not said how wonderful or well done. He was looking quite grave, as though she had confessed to a lump in her breast or a growing blind spot in her field of vision. Of course, she reminded herself, Villiers was basically gay; he might lure the odd girl into bed but he was never going to fool one of them into marrying him. Excluded from parenthood, he probably found the whole business mildly offensive.

'I thought I'd tell Giles tonight,' she told him gently. 'He adores children. He's going to be so happy.'

'Is he? Giles? Are you sure?'

'Well I think I know him pretty well,' she said, half-offended in her turn.

'And what about your career? I thought you were doing so well.'

'I am. Pretty well. But it'll keep. Selina will understand. She can't sack me for taking maternity leave. Then I . . . I haven't really thought about it much yet but I suppose after a bit I'd do what everyone else does.'

'What? Find a childminder or one of those park-and-pay places while you come back to work?'

'Yeah. Why not? It's pretty much the norm, now.'

'Suppose so.'

'The thing is I'm not really career-minded,' she said.

He mimed incredulity.

'I'm not,' she said and realised the truth of the declaration as she voiced it. 'I've been making the best of it because sooner or later you have to or you'd crack up but . . . if I gave it all up tomorrow and became a full-time mother, I think I'd love it.'

'You?'

'Yes. Me. I think first reactions are very telling and my first reaction hasn't been panic. I've spent most of the last two days feeling blissed out, natural. Maybe motherhood was my destiny all along?'

Villiers drained his coffee, pulling a little face as the dregs hit his tongue. 'Sorry. I'm being a pig. It's wonderful news. It'll be a stunner. What do you want, boy or girl?'

'I don't care so long as it's got all its bits in the right place.' She shivered uncontrollably. *Someone stepping on my grave* she thought. 'A boy would be fun,' she went on. 'After all, we get a girl fix with Dido on a regular basis.'

'Hmm. It's just that . . .'

'What?'

'Oh. Nothing. I'm being silly.'

'No, what?' she insisted.

'Well.' Villiers unwrapped his sugar lumps and munched one judiciously. 'It's simply that you're so different from Eliza. Different in every way.'

'Thank Christ.'

'Quite. And it always struck me that, quite apart from your looks, it was your unElizaishness that attracted Giles to you.'

'Meaning?'

'Oh I don't know. I'm being a prat. Ignore me. I've made you late and I'm late too now. I'm thrilled, darling. Honestly.' He kissed her on the lips rather ostentatiously as he stood and retrieved his briefcase.

'Villiers?'

'What?'

'You don't mind not telling anyone. Not just yet?'

'Of course I don't,' he said. 'I know how it is. Early days. You don't even know your own mind yet. You and Giles might not even decide to keep it. I won't tell a soul. Bye.'

Julia knew she should go too but felt pinned to the little table by the shock of what he had just said. She had grown used to the image of herself as practical and unflinching. A Pill-taker. She had been obliged to have dealings with an abortion clinic just once. That had been experience enough, however, to prevent her ever again viewing the process as a simple choice in which her emotions could remain unengaged. Even if she was an earth-mother in the making, happy to abandon her career, perhaps a baby would be a disaster for Giles?

One of the more senior associate agents had started a family four years ago and had barely had a grasp on her desk diary since. She was forever cancelling things or rescheduling them so as to fly out of the office on the tail of some child-related crisis and several of her more important clients had asked to be reassigned as a result. Then there was Gideon Stone, four years ago their most promising new signing and all set to become a star baritone after a famously good and daringly young Don Giovanni at Cardiff. He had started a family with his longstanding girlfriend – marriage, mortgage, the works – then he had started turning down important offers, saying he needed to spend time with the children. Then his looks went sort of puffy and his hair thinned and his voice started to seem less than extraordinary. Selina had not dropped him – she had a heart in there somewhere – but she had signed another, brighter, more ambitious baritone and it tended to be Julia who returned Gideon's plaintive calls about work prospects.

Yes, Giles loved Dido, but she was not a permanent fixture in the household. And she was a growing girl and a tidy one at that. Perhaps he would be disgusted as Julia morphed from neat professional into blowsy maternity and appalled as their domestic order was thrown into noisy chaos by a baby. No amount of careful advance planning could forestall broken nights, nappies or a sea of hideous plastic objects. Fight them as she might, circumstances would conspire to turn Julia into another Eliza, housebound, exhausted, depressed and needy. Before she knew it another woman, sharper-eyed, wiser to his needs, would be luring Giles away.

As if confirming this grim prophecy, Tobit Hart ignored her as she smiled at him on her way back into the office. Such was the fate of all cow-minded mothers: invisibility and social demotion.

She performed the test the moment the office bathroom came free. Selina had taken Giles to a director's meeting and half her other colleagues were out as well; nobody who mattered was there to notice. It was positive. The instructions suggested that she visit her GP for confirmation but every organ in her altering body told her the little plastic wand in her fingers was only confirming what she already knew. What more could a GP add but a referral for a termination?

She hid the tester back in its box, wrapped the whole in a plastic bag then thrust it to the depths of the rubbish bin in the office kitchen, amidst the mess of empty yoghurt pots, half-eaten salads and used teabags. She would take no action just yet. She would not even risk telling Giles and letting his reaction dictate the baby's future. She would wait and watch, a practice that had never failed her in the past.

She lost herself in work all afternoon. When Selina returned and gleefully announced the good news about Giles and Covent Garden it felt like the first bitter shoots growing from the doubts Villiers had planted. In fantasy, swimming on her hormonal sea all that morning, she had told Giles the glad news and he had taken her in his arms, kissed her over and over again and told her how happy he was. And he had said how much he loved her.

But Giles had never said he loved her, she reminded herself now. Not even in the abandon of sex had he ever gasped, 'I love you,' in the meaningless way some men did.

She resolved to say nothing just yet but to watch and wait.

17

Pearce so rarely had appointments to keep that he had to make a great effort both to remember them and not to be late. His timetable usually had little to do with clocks; he rose when the sun woke him, stopped for lunch when he was hungry then worked on until there was no more light. Molly was forever teasing him or rebuking him about his tardiness. It was amazing how fast she had adjusted to worldly timekeeping after leaving Morris' farm.

But there was little risk of his forgetting this date the way he did appointments with dentist or bank manager. He had thought of little else since Sunday night yet still he had a horror of being late. He had calculated and recalculated how much time he should leave for washing, dressing and driving and as a result drew up on the outskirts of Hayle far too early. Even using a town plan to find it, he arrived on Janet's street at a quarter to eight.

Feeling inept, he parked well away from her house and made himself listen to a radio programme on skin disorders to pass the time. Battered and muddy, his old car felt as out of place here as a Sherman tank.

Portreath Way was not a smart address but a row of council or ex-council semis. He wondered how long she had lived here. Strung out along sand dunes on one side and a partially silted-up harbour on the other, Hayle had always depressed him because it seemed to lack a centre and the social cohesion that implied. But perhaps Janet had been born here. Perhaps there were things about it she loved. Perhaps she would lead him to see its hidden charms. He forced himself to stay in the car until five past then had to double back to it from halfway down the street when he remembered the wine he had left tucked in a box of grease canisters in the rear.

34 Portreath Way. He had repeated it to himself so often there had been no need to write it down. Still a council house, he guessed, judging from the standardised cream paint and blue door. The grass needed cutting but perhaps the children preferred it long. There was a football, an inflated paddling pool, a framework with a tiny swing on one half and a truncated slide on the other, both in orange plastic.

A child answered his ring, a dark, mop-haired boy who stared.

'Hi,' Pearce said. 'I'm Pearce. Is your mum in?'

The boy stared a second longer then half shut the door and ran into the depths of the house yelling, 'Mum?'

Pearce heard Janet shouting, 'Bed, you. Now!' He imagined her quick glance in the looking glass before she opened the door afresh.

'Hi,' he said.

'Well. Come in, then.'

She hurried him in off the doorstep before he had time to take much in. She was a brunette but had used some kind of purplish rinse in her hair that made it look dead, too uniform. Her face was tired and rather sharp. Like him she had made an effort though. As he followed her to the living room, he saw she had on a sexy, very revealing dress that showed off a mother's full chest to advantage and was wearing a richly suggestive scent. Her tanned legs were bare and she had on a pair of heels that gave her trouble. She wobbled nervously on them and soon kicked them off.

Two much smaller children were peering through a baby gate at the top of the stairs.

'Bed!' she hissed at them and they vanished, giggling. A bedroom door banged and there was the rhythmic squeaking of beds being manically bounced on. The house smelled powerfully lived-in: lamb chops, cigarettes and air freshener.

The boy had retreated to the huge sofa where he was defiantly watching *The Jungle Book*.

'Lance? Bed!' Janet said.

'You said I could watch this.'

'Bed.'

'You said.'

'I don't mind,' Pearce said. 'Honestly.'

They both looked at him. Perhaps Lance was unused to having his cause defended.

'You sure?' she asked.

'Yeah. Haven't seen this for ages. It's funny. I . . . I er bought you this.' He offered the bottle.

'Red gives me migraines,' she said, sitting by the boy. 'But help yourself. I've got one on the go.'

'I want one,' Lance said.

'Don't push it,' she told him.

Pearce saw the bottle opener she had used on the Riesling she had started. Perhaps it was rude not to drink the same as her? What the hell – he hated Riesling. He poured himself a glass of the madly expensive Brouilly he had bought on the way home from the cattle auction.

The chairs in the room were both at the wrong angle for watching the television and he did not know her well enough to go moving her furniture, so he sat on the other end of the sofa, the cross little boy as effective as any bolster between him and Janet.

Mowgli was dancing with the monkeys. *King of the Swingers*. He struggled to recollect how much of the film that meant there was still to run. He remembered seeing it when he was this age, he and Molly wedged between chuckling parents in the Savoy in Penzance.

He saw the computer on a cluttered table in the corner. An abandoned computer game was playing with itself, nervously roaming a repeating sequence of torchlit Gothic halls, looking for demons. He wondered if she used it when the children were still in the room, tapping in lascivious chat while they sat on the sofa watching cartoons. No. He had only ever met her in the chat room after their bedtime.

'You found us all right then?' she said.

'Oh. Yes. I used the map but –'

'Ssh!' Lance hissed.

Janet tutted and reached for cigarettes and an ashtray which had been modestly tucked beneath the sofa. She offered one to Pearce behind Lance's back. He shook his head. She lit up, inhaled deeply, then lay back and fired a plume of smoke at the ceiling.

Softened by life in a smokeless world, Pearce's eyes began to itch almost at once. He fought the urge to cough.

'Where's the . . . er?' he asked.

'Next door to the kitchen,' she said, still staring at the ceiling.

The lavatory walls were a shrine to the children's father. There were school groups – he had gone to the same school as her in Hayle, so perhaps they had been childhood sweethearts – then football team shots, then pictures of him in Navy uniform. There was a picture of an aircraft carrier and a group shot of him and some mates posing on a dockside, ridiculously young, hair cropped brutally short. Pictures of him clutching babies. He was the image of the kid on the sofa. Then Pearce saw the shot of the war memorial on Plymouth

Hoe with fresh wreaths about it. When could he have died? The children were so young. Not the Falklands. Gulf War? Bosnia? Surely no ships went there? Iraq? Perhaps he had died in a training exercise. Perhaps he merely died? Perhaps he merely abandoned her?

The lavatory window was far too small to climb out of so he flushed, returned to the sofa and watched *The Jungle Book*. The smoke was not so troubling now it had overcome the air freshener.

Her hand slid along the sofa back after a minute or two and began to massage his neck. He felt he should return the favour but it was impossible while her arm was still in place. After a while her hand dropped down onto the sofa back as if exhausted. Then, when Mowgli risked the scorn of a million little boys by catching sight of a giant-eyed village maiden gathering water, she tapped his shoulder and indicated that Lance had fallen fast asleep.

'You mind doing the honours?' she whispered. 'I've got a bad back.'

'Oh. Sure.'

'His room's straight ahead, at the top of the stairs.'

Perturbed that she did not think to come too, he scooped the sleeping boy up in his arms and carried him upstairs. The light from the landing spilled into the little room revealing a bed littered with toys and comics. Pearce managed to clear some space by pushing the duvet aside with his foot then laid Lance on the bed. The kid was still fully dressed but it did not feel proper to remove more than his trainers before pulling the duvet over him.

When he came back downstairs she had turned off the television and dimmed the lights. The pulsing glow from the computer screen revealed her stretched out on the sofa, hands behind her head. She stood as he came in.

'Should I . . . er?' he began.

'No,' she said quietly. 'Shut the door.'

There was a rustling sound as he turned from shutting it and he found she had slid the dress down around her waist. Her breasts were bare. They looked full and sore.

'Get over here,' she said, 'And do me. No foreplay.'

She pulled him into a furious, smoky kiss as soon as he stepped towards her then began to tear his shirt off him. They fell on each other, scattering the ashtray, cushions and empty Riesling bottle.

It was horrible, all-consuming. They were like starving people bereft of all humanity by the urge to take what they needed from each other. As he came with embarrassing swiftness he was appalled to hear the bed-bouncing noises starting up again from upstairs.

She rolled away from him, slid her dress back over her shoulders then fumbled for a cigarette. In the flare of the match she looked so desolate he felt something like tenderness, felt he should hold her, but she was standing apart, making herself unholdable.

'Can I see you again?' he asked. 'Maybe I could take you out somewhere next time.'

'What do you think?' she asked.

He had absolutely no idea how to answer that so stooped to relace his boots.

'You'd better go,' she said. 'We've woken the girls.'

She walked out of the room, clutching her shoes in one hand, and disappeared upstairs.

He drove home with the windows wide open until his teeth began to chatter. The house seemed unimaginably remote and cool and dark. He went straight to bed but found he couldn't sleep. Despising himself as the worst kind of hypocritical puritan, he got up again to take a shower in an effort to wash the evening off him.

18

Kitty was unexpectedly amazing. Perhaps she was striving to fill a maternal void. She dealt with the undertakers – a local firm who ran up kitchens and bookcases as well as coffins – and rallied the scant group of mourners back to her house for a funeral tea. Eliza was dimly aware of being an object of pious curiosity – the daughter who had survived but was a disappointment – but people were kind and there were a few faces she recognised.

Never one to trust others to get things right, her mother had paid for her obsequies long in advance, so much so that there was actually some money left over from interest earned. Her solicitor was a member of her church's congregation. He attended the service then lingered on afterwards so as to broach the delicate matter of the will.

'You could call at the office during the week if you prefer,' he said, but Eliza wanted the business out of the way so they risked farce by going through the will while sitting on her mother's bed, joined by the murmur of voices, the flushing of the lavatory, the regular thump of footsteps up and down the stairs.

She had left everything to Dido. She had even slipped in a little pointed reference to 'my granddaughter, who has no father to support her.' She was not a rich woman and had long made a habit of giving much of what she possessed to charity. There was the house, however, whose deeds were in her name, not her husband's.

If they decided it was best, the solicitor murmured, they might sell the house and invest the funds in a trust he could administer on Dido's behalf, paying out a monthly allowance until she was eighteen.

Knowing nothing of the letter, apparently, Kitty was mildly indignant on Eliza's behalf. It was some relief to learn that the surviving daughter had been cast off in respectable privacy; Eliza had occasionally pictured a ritual anathema being pronounced on her by the assembled congregation. She had even fed the fancy by looking up the Service of Commination in the Prayer Book. *For now is the axe put unto the root of the trees, so that every tree that bringeth not forth good fruit is hewn down, and cast into the fire . . . His fan is in his hand, and he will purge his floor, and gather his wheat into the barn; but he will burn the chaff with unquenchable fire.*

'She can't have been thinking straight,' Kitty said, when they rejoined her downstairs and Eliza told her the news.

'I can assure you she was quite cogent,' the solicitor insisted. 'I went over the implications of this with her several times.'

Eliza was relieved. For Dido to have her own allowance, a blessed pool that could not be dipped into for electricity bills or trips to the supermarket, but which could cover the cost of her clothes and shoes, music or driving lessons, all the things Eliza could not always afford, was far more reassuring than a sudden legacy of her own would have been. As was having that pool administered by a professional.

'It's okay,' she interrupted Kitty's insistence that she contest the will as unfair. 'It lets me off the hook.' She spoke without thinking and Kitty and the solicitor both looked

so appalled that she backed off and let them argue themselves out.

'There's just one thing I don't understand,' the solicitor
said, 'and as her daughter you might be able to shed some
light on it so we can speed up probate. I've got the details of
the house and her building society account – which has six
thousand in it we can transfer into Dido's name immediately
– but I can find no trace of a bank account.'

'She didn't like banks,' Eliza said simply. 'She thought they
charged too much.' She remembered her mother's fury, her
shame as she put it, that Hannah died leaving behind a small
overdraft.

'So the building society was all she had, so far as you
know?'

'That and her pension, yes. That's right, isn't it, Kitty?'

'Yes,' Kitty said sadly. 'She was always a very careful
woman.'

Eliza's mother had evidently been careful enough not
to tell her best friend about her *running away fund*. This
stash of money she held back from both bank and building
society, along with a handful of family jewels she was
too quiet to wear and too sentimental to sell, she kept
tucked in the lining and pinned inside the sleeves of her
second best dressing gown. *The first thing I'd throw on in
a fire. The last thing a burglar would think of touching.* Eliza
had instinctively checked on it the night her mother died.
Naturally, because it was the second best dressing gown,
Kitty had not dreamed of packing it to take to her friend
in hospital.

That night, when everyone had gone at last, Eliza slipped
into Dido's room to make sure she stopped reading and got
some sleep, although she knew the bedside light would be
turned on again and the novel retrieved the moment she had
closed the door behind her. She sat on the edge of the bed

and, while they brushed each other's hair, she explained about the legacy.

Dido was a fiercely pragmatic girl but poverty had not made her remotely acquisitive. Where other children in her position fantasized about new trainers or clothes, the latest technology or holiday destination, she carried no mental shopping list and found the need to come up with suggestions at Christmas and birthdays stressful.

'Does that mean I'm rich?' she asked as the news sank in.

'Not exactly,' Eliza told her. 'I mean, it's relative. You couldn't buy a damp bedsit in London for what this place is probably worth. I suppose it means you're middle class though, property-owning.'

Dido smiled faintly at this. 'Like a landlord?' she asked.

'Yes. In a way. But you're not to worry about it. The solicitor can look after everything and nothing in our life has to change unless you want it to. Okay? Lights out when you finish that chapter.'

Disturbed at the pin-sharp image that came to her suddenly of Dido demanding rent, Eliza retrieved the jewellery-studded dressing gown from the back of her mother's bedroom door and took it into her own room. Either the old woman had been buying lottery tickets on the sly or become more than usually distrustful of the building society in her last years. Eliza counted out enough to keep her and Dido fed and amused for three months. She counted and recounted it as she drank from the bottle of wine she had bought in the Co-op and smuggled upstairs. She wore no jewellery and had a horror of pierced ears, but the brooches, clips and rings she retrieved from inside the dressing gown's sleeves spoke to her directly in a way no words in the funeral service had done and aroused a feral instinct to hoard up and survive.

For two whole days Kitty drove them onwards, helping Eliza sort out the contents of every cupboard and drawer.

While Eliza sorted and folded, bagging the wearable and burning the stained or overly private, Dido helped Kitty ferry sacks of clothing to the numerous charity shops in the town.

Then there was all the junk. Lamps made from converted rosé bottles. A whole cupboard of cleaned and delabelled jam jars. A drawer of string. Another of carefully folded brown paper. Another of plastic carrier bags. A terrible, greasy drawer of skewers, knives, old corks and mysterious, rusting utensils.

'I had no idea about all this,' Kitty said. 'She let me into the house but she never let me help.'

The solicitor sent several estate agents round to value the house and Kitty called in an auctioneer from the congregation, who specialised in house clearances to set a price on the moveable furniture. She could no more understand that Eliza had no use for any of it than she could conceive that the two laundry bags they had brought on the coach from London contained most of their wearable clothes. So the better bits of furniture went, most of it hideous, heavy 1930s stuff with a walnut veneer. A dining table and chairs which, in Eliza's memory, had only ever been used at Christmas. A sideboard. The suite (what else could one call it?) of furniture from the master bedroom. A nest of tables. A melancholy spinney of standard lamps. The Art Deco piano stool, which had outlived the piano because her mother kept knitting needles in it. The sight of her mother's huge bed being borne out into the full gaze of the sunshiny street was as startling as her tiny coffin's progress down the aisle of St Dunstan's, if not more so, coffins maintaining, after all, a rigorous privacy.

Eliza had made no plans. She assumed that, once probate released it, the house would be put on the market and she and Dido would return to London. Kitty had something else in mind, however.

'Now you need a holiday.'

'We can't possibly afford it,' Eliza said automatically.

'You can if you don't mind staying in Cornwall. There's my caravan in St Just. It's all fitted out for the summer because I was down there birding only the weekend before your mother's fall. You'll have to catch the train, I suppose, then another bus but once you're there you can get about easily enough on the two bikes.'

'Kitty, that's very kind but we ought to get home.'

'Dodie needs a holiday.'

'Dido.'

'Needs a holiday. When did you last take her anywhere?'

Eliza thought and pictured only occasional excursions within London, usually inspired by school projects. She had come to rely on the weekends Dido spent with Giles to provide anything in the way of actual trips.

'I dunno,' she admitted.

'Exactly. Anyone can see it, poor mite. She's been excited about just being here, and this is Camborne, for pity's sake.'

'But don't you let the caravan out?'

'Not any more. No point. It's too basic – I couldn't compete with the proper sites at Kelynack and Sennen. They lay on pools and shops and all I provided was a field, a view and a chemical lavvy.'

'Kitty I –'

'Just think about it, okay?'

But Kitty slyly worked on Dido, telling her all about it and all the things they could do there and Dido was able to point out that term time was about to finish in any case. So the laundry bags were packed again, slightly plumper this time because Dido had been coming back from the charity shops with whatever clothes caught her eye.

At the last minute, Kitty spared them the train and bus ride by electing to drop them off herself. Eliza suspected this was because Kitty had noticed how little interest she took in shopping for proper food or even cooking, and wanted to be sure they stopped off at a supermarket to load up with supplies on the way. Food shopping, with money, ample money, was an unfamiliar pleasure. While Kitty waited in the car reading a paper, Eliza enjoyed going around the supermarket saying yes to Dido's every suggestion for once, so that they ended up with a trolley-load that was not entirely nutritious and certainly made little economic sense.

Back on the road, as they rounded a bend and the magnificent sweep of Mount's Bay opened before them, Eliza exclaimed as loudly as Dido. She was on holiday too, now. She must have been this far west at least once on a school trip but it seemed familiar only from pictures. They skirted Penzance – Eliza having promised Dido that yes, they would come back to see the Egyptian House and St Michael's Mount and to swim in the salt water lido – then climbed high, away from the bay, over Mount Misery, where fishwives used to watch in dread after a storm and onto the St Just road.

'Not long now,' Kitty told Dido as they passed through Newbridge, 'and you'll see the sea again but this time it'll be the North coast, just above Land's End. We're on the toe of England now.' She pointed out unchanged views of fields and farmsteads they could see in the Newlyn School paintings in a Penzance gallery. She slowed to let them admire a buzzard watching from a gatepost then speeded up again as Dido spotted the remains of a run-over badger. 'Any minute now. There it is!'

They passed a water-filled quarry and gravel pit and quite suddenly the land fell steeply away before them down to St Just – a huddle of houses around a pretty church and a looming chapel – and the Atlantic beyond it.

'The end of the world,' Kitty announced cheerfully and Eliza became aware that Dido was singing to herself; Dido who never sang unless she thought no one could hear her. 'And down here,' Kitty swung off the road and onto a dirt track, 'your palace awaits.'

The mobile home had not been mobile for years. It was already on this site, resting on breeze blocks, when Kitty bought it off a woman in her bird-watching club. Painted dark green by its former owner and camouflaged still further by Kitty, who had encouraged ivy, clematis and rambling courgette and squash plants to smother it, it could not have looked less like the glaringly white caravans they had passed in a campsite near Penzance. Tucked into a tiny parcel of land on the edge of a farm, it was all but invisible until the car drew close.

'Wow, Kitty!' Dido breathed.

'It's very basic, as I said,' Kitty explained as she panted across the grass. 'It's a hide, really, with some plumbing and a bed.' A hose ran from a sacking-lagged standpipe to somewhere on the leafy roof. Kitty turned on the tap and there was a distant gurgling which disturbed some chattering squabbling sparrows. 'That'll feed the shower and the sink,' she explained. 'Turn it off again when you leave. The waste water runs into a tank on the other side I use to water the plants. There's no WC, as such, just a chemical lavvy in that garden shed, and that's where the bikes are too. They'll need pumping up and oiling probably, 'cause my nieces haven't been down for a year.'

She unlocked the door and showed them how the key was concealed behind a ceramic tile of St Francis and the birds. There were two low-ceilinged rooms, one with a bed and a chest of drawers, one with a sofa, table and chairs and what Kitty called a kitchenette. There was also a gas cooker and a fridge.

'How does a fridge run on gas?' Dido asked.

'Search me,' Kitty said, opening the valve on a gas canister and clicking an ignition button to set the fridge cooling. 'Just praise the Lord for Science. Bedding's in the chest of drawers and St Just's down the hill. Well, you saw it, didn't you? Buses to Penzance go by the top of the lane every two hours just about – you can flag them down. There's a baker and a bank and a library in the town. Everything, really, but it's more fun if I leave you to find out for yourselves.' She paused. No one said anything. They were too dazed taking it all in. 'So I'll be off and leave you to unpack, then,' Kitty added.

'Don't go,' Dido said. 'Stay too.'

'I wouldn't fit, poppet. Have fun, now, Dodie. Stay as long as you like. You've got my phone number, haven't you? Just in case.'

'Right here.' Dido patted her pocket.

'Good. There are phones down the hill. Are you all right, Eliza? You've been ever so quiet.'

'I'm fine, Kitty. This is so kind of you. I don't know what to say.' As when they first arrived at the bus station, Eliza felt a keen need to hug Kitty but this time she held back.

'Best say nothing, then,' Kitty said. 'Bye all.'

Dido ran out to wave her off. Eliza made an effort to be less dreamily passive and stayed inside to unpack their shopping onto one end of the kitchen table. The table was topped with shiny red melamine, worn through to the wood in patches. Very Festival of Britain. And when she opened the cupboard over the tiny sink, she found black and white plates and cups of the same vintage. Three of everything. Like a doll's house. She made a mental note not to break anything; things like the plates would be impossible to replace. She loaded bacon, pizzas, eggs, milk and toffee yoghurts into the fridge which, mysteriously, was already getting cold. Obediently she praised the Lord for Science.

Dido wanted them to ride into the town but both bikes had flat tyres and there was no sign of a pump so they walked in, trusting in the hardware store to sell them one. The sky was blue and cloudless, the distant sea millpond smooth and a fresh breeze was sending waves through fields of some green crop. Dido was in high spirits, even without a bicycle. She continued to sing under her breath, timing her strides to the rhythm of a song playing in her head.

'Someone's happy,' Eliza said then wished she hadn't because Dido immediately stopped singing.

'What's that then?' Dido asked, pointing at the waving green crop. 'It's not just grass, is it?'

'No. Barley maybe? Or wheat? It's hard to tell when it's so young and the ears are only just showing through.'

'I thought you grew up in the country.'

'You saw what Camborne's like. Not proper country.'

They arrived at a field of pigs. Delighted, because she had never encountered them in the flesh before, Dido stood on a gate to watch. A vast sow nosed for roots, oblivious to the piglets which clustered, squeaking, around her trailing dugs. When a younger female came over to the gate, Eliza won back a few country wisdom points by showing Dido how to scratch its back with a stick. Dido laughed as the beast grunted with pleasure.

'Eliza?' she asked cautiously.

'Yes?'

'When were *you* last happy?'

'Ooh . . .' Eliza pretended to think. 'You mean apart from now?'

'Yes. When were you last really, truly happy?'

It was a challenge.

'About ten minutes ago, when Kitty finally left and I had you all to myself again.'

Dido looked at her, assessing this for a moment then said with devastating simplicity, 'Huh,' then jumped off the gate to keep walking into St Just.

Eliza was deeply unsettled. Dido's simple question had summoned up a university room, open books in a pool of sunlight on an uncluttered desk and no trace of a baby or its plastic paraphernalia. It was a scene she had not thought about for years but it sprang into her mind with such immediate clarity she knew it for a truthful answer.

She had last been really, truly happy before Hannah's death had thrust motherhood upon her or vanity and weakness had led her to muddle her life with any men other than long dead composers. Try as she might to believe otherwise, her life had been a falling-off from there onwards and, as they continued down the hill, she let Dido lead the way, feeling unable to meet her eye and feeling the guilt burn scarlet on her face.

The unfamiliar little town soon provided distraction enough for them to talk of other things. Lanes radiated out from the church and main square with its memorial clock tower, its rival bakeries, fish and chip shop and newsagents. There were the inevitable galleries, with a few surprisingly good paintings whose prices seemed at odds with the humble housing surrounding them. There was a shop – or a party headquarters, it could have been either – devoted to all things Cornish and the promulgation of the Cornish language.

This was a small victory for Eliza because Dido had thought she and Kitty were fibbing when they talked of Cornish nationalism as they passed huge graffiti on the road bridges near Hayle which declared *You Are No Longer In England!* and *Kernow Bys Vykken!*

They found an Aladdin's cave of a hardware store, whose owner was proud to produce a rather dusty bicycle pump and assured them that his son could mend punctures if they got home to find the pump did not solve the problem.

Surprised by hunger, Dido insisted they visit one of the bakeries to buy pasties and was presented with a free piece of heavy cake by the sales assistant when she heard it was her first time west of Penzance.

'Well, you're in proper Cornwall now,' the woman told her. 'The rest don't count. Not really.'

'I like it here,' Dido declared as they walked into an unexpected grassy arena surrounded by cottages and sat on a bank to eat.

'The sun's shining,' Eliza reminded her. 'And everyone's being nice. Wait for an off day. I bet it drizzles here even more than in Camborne or Islington.' Drizzle was one of Dido's reliable hates.

'Why do we live in London?'

'It's where everything happens. Work and things. And Giles has to live there.'

'But he's not my father.'

'No, but . . .'

'And you don't work. You haven't worked for ages.'

'I try. My contacts sort of dried up.'

'You could not work here much more cheaply than you don't work in London.'

'Dido I —'

'And I could go to school down the road there. They've got council flats. We could do a swap with someone. There's a list you can go on — that's how Nitin's family moved to Brighton. Or we could buy somewhere now. Property's cheap here. Kitty said so.'

'Hold your . . . Your money's to be held in that trust until you're eighteen.'

'The solicitor'd let me buy a house. It's an investment. Kitty said I could buy a cottage. You could grow vegetables instead of just sitting around.'

'I don't just *sit around*!'

'But you do. It's all you've done for years. And now you're scared of change. So we're just going to be stuck in that stinky flat till we rot. I really like it here. You could be happy here only you're scared.'

'No I'm not.' Eliza realised she was shouting now.

'You didn't even want to come here for a holiday.' Suddenly Dido was on her feet.

'Where are you going?'

'For a walk. I can find my own way home.'

'Don't be cross. Dido. Please?'

'Oh piss off. Just piss off! And leave me alone or I'll tell Social Services you're unfit.'

Eliza sat, helpless, as Dido stamped off.

They had argued furiously before and often. Dido displayed more of Hannah's strength of will every week. But this was new. It had felt like a full-blown teenage strop. As always the thought of Dido in relation to the looming storm clouds of puberty was unsettling.

Eliza followed at a cautious distance and watched in admiration as Dido crossed to the main car park, approached a gang of boys who were gathered around the recycling bins and traded her slice of heavy cake for a turn on a skateboard.

Eliza became aware that the whole little scene had been witnessed by a big boned, black-haired woman eating her lunch in the sunshine on the low wall just outside the library. Ashamed, she began to come closer, thinking to call Dido back, but halted near the woman, excluded by youth and still weakened by the guilty vision of academic independence that had troubled her earlier and now lingered like the troubling puzzle of a dream.

'Difficult age,' the woman sympathised and Eliza noticed once again how it was the teasing, ironic Cornish accent as much as the scenery, that made her feel she had come home.

'She's only nine. Ten in a couple of months.'

'Yeah . . . like mine, though. Ten going on forty seems to be the norm these days.'

'I should get her back. They'll be wanting that skateboard. She can be awfully bossy.'

'She'll be fine. See that tough-looking lad in the red baseball cap? That's my Lucy. She'll look after her.'

'Oh. Thanks,' said Eliza, bewildered.

'Library's officially shut for lunch but you're welcome to look around. But I can't make you out a card if you're only visiting.'

'Oh. Are you the . . . ?'

'That's right. My little empire. Help yourself.'

It was a featureless single storey modern building, little lifted by a brave school of Hepworth sculpture beside the wheelchair ramp. It was comfortably cool and shady inside after the outdoors glare, however, and Eliza had always found libraries soothing, even their hectic, underfunded local on the Holloway Road.

Some things were the same the country over, it seemed; a bank of computers and shelves of videos and CDs took up yards of space where bookshelves might have been and the children's library sprawled to take over a third of what was left. There was a bay titled Novels Of Particular Interest to Women, however, a magnificent collection of dictionaries, including the longer Oxford, and a well-endowed local studies section.

From idle force of habit, Eliza scoured the local studies and the music shelves but saw nothing on Trevescan so was dimly reassured that no one else, not even a local historian, had ploughed her particular furrow ahead of her. In a display devoted to farming and farmhouse bed and breakfast accommodation in the area, there was a well-indexed map of Cornwall's tip. Every farmstead was listed by name. She scanned past the mass of names beginning with Tre to find Vingoe, Trevescan's family farm, and was amazed. Not only was it still in existence – she had assumed that the name, if not the farm, would have been long lost since he left no heirs – but it was not far from Kitty's caravan. Because of it having been famously raided and torched by the Spanish, she had always assumed it must lie nearer Mousehole, on the more accessible southerly side, yet here it was, in all probability visible from the hill she and Dido had just walked from. There again, names changed and moved and the romantic house names in Cornwall were as frequently copied and repeated as the Dunroamins and Hillcrests of elsewhere. But she looked again at the map and saw how this Vingoe had a sheltered cove below it where a Spanish boat might well have been forced ashore, driven by fierce winds.

She was just turning from the noticeboards, distracted by the librarian who had come back in and was fiddling with the cash register behind her desk, when she spotted a small sign among the merry posters for amateur shows, open gardens and charity sales.

FANCY SINGING SOMETHING QUIET FOR ONCE?
MADRIGAL GROUP MEETS WEDNESDAY AT 7
MUST READ MUSIC – NOT SOL-FA
TENORS ESPECIALLY WELCOME.
RING MOLLY ON 788669

'Tempted? We could do with another soprano.'

'You're Molly?'

'I am. Well?' From her speaking voice, the librarian was plainly a contralto.

Eliza smiled wistfully. 'I haven't sung in years. Not since I was a student. There are probably crows nesting in there.' She rubbed her throat instinctively.

'Naa. You can still talk, you can still sing.'

'I'm only on holiday.'

'So? Come just the once. Where are you staying?'

'A friend's caravan. Up on the hill.'

'Oh. Kitty's place.'

'You *know* it?'

'Everyone knows Kitty's place. Before she bought it it was very popular with courting couples on colder nights. Probably still is. Does she still keep the key behind St Francis?'

Eliza nodded and felt herself grin. This woman's warmth was infectious. 'Anyway, I couldn't come. I've got Dido and I can hardly leave her up there on her own.'

'Your kid?'

'Sort of. My niece, actually.'

'Oh. That's nice. Well bring her. If she hasn't had a strop with Lucy by then, they can hang out upstairs and kill things on the computer.'

Eliza pulled a face. 'I don't know. I'm so rusty.'

'It's my cottage in St Just we're talking about, not the Wigmore Hall . . . Look. Here's the address. Just follow the signs to Cape Cornwall and you can't miss it. A long terrace with front gardens gone mad. Just round the corner from here.'

'Oh God. It's tonight, isn't it?'

'Yes. Go on. Come. Lots of sexy men.'

'Really? Singing madrigals?' It sounded most unlikely.

Molly shrugged, stifling a mischievous smile. 'Sure. If you go for camel coloured cardies and beige socks . . .'

19

Caught on his way to the shower, Giles stumbled through the house cursing because the bedroom phone was not on its base unit. He lunged for the kitchen one just as the answering machine was cutting in, then took refuge in the hall where his nakedness felt less vulnerable.

'Mr Easton?'

'Yes?'

'It's Sue Stokes. Secretary at St Saviour's.'

'Ah. Hello.' Giles instinctively fastened the towel more securely at his waist then sat down on the stairs. 'What can I do for you?'

The unmistakable sawdusty smell of vomit drifted from the downstairs lavatory unmasked by orange and cinnamon room spray. Giles frowned and went to shut the lavatory door. A bad smell was as unexpected in Julia as a loud colour.

'Well Dido hasn't been in to school for a week. We haven't registered her since last Monday, a whole week ago. And since I haven't been able to get hold of her mum, and she hasn't responded to my letter, I wondered if you could explain.'

Giles stopped himself saying that Eliza's phone had been disconnected, tempting though such disloyalty might be. 'I last saw Dido on Tuesday morning,' he said. 'I've not heard from either her or her mother since.'

'It's only it's most unlike Mrs Easton. She's normally very efficient about sending sick notes or getting permission in advance but an unexplained absence of this length would normally get Dido on the truancy register and I wouldn't have bothered you but you are down here as the number two contact for Dido and –'

'Don't worry,' Giles said affecting calm. 'Mrs Easton hasn't been very well, that's all. It's probably nothing to fuss about but I'll call round there this morning, if you like. To check?'

Bemused at the thought of Eliza as a paragon of efficiency, worried at the trouble in which she was landing Dido he showered quickly, dressed and skipped his morning exercises. He registered a grim amusement too that Eliza should see fit to have the school call her by her married name when in all correspondence she remained Ms Eliza Hosken.

He had time on his hands. The Mechanicals were rehearsing all morning. He was not called until after lunch, for what was ominously billed as a *movement session*, with Titania, Puck, Fairies and non-singing extras.

He kept a key in his sock drawer, copied from Dido's without her mother's knowledge, for just such an emergency. He had never used it. He had never called at the flat before. The rule seemed to be that he stayed in his world, Eliza stayed in hers and Dido shuttled at will between them.

There were three towers, Shakespeare, Jonson and Dekker, placed with a view to their forming a pleasing sculptural whole rather than with any thought of how their proximity would affect their tenants. They shaded one another and set up tremendous eddies of dusty air in the intervening space. Sometimes one would see a discarded carrier bag whirling twenty or so floors high.

If Dido were playing truant, she would not be alone. Seven or eight children were clustered, arguing, around a bench near the entrance to Dekker and ignored him as he passed. The towers had been improved in recent years, with security coded entrances and a new playground. Giles had the security code written on the key's paper label but had no need of it because the postman held the door open for him as he approached. He summoned the lift but its interior – stainless steel virtually obliterated by layer upon layer of dazzlingly sprayed on tags – sapped his confidence in the thing and he took the stairs by way of an exercise substitute. He knew himself for a lily-livered, middle-class snob. There was no more to be scared of in the lift than there was in the shouting children outside but still he felt marked as an intruder and at risk.

It was not so bad as he imagined. Yes, the tags and graffitti continued up the stairs like crazed wallpaper but the stairwell smelled of toast and bacon, not piss, and he heard cultured snatches of Radio 4 as he climbed, not the territorial blast of hip-hop he had expected. The people he passed as he climbed – a Sikh in an old brown suit, a pink-faced young father and matching baby, a woman with clanking bags of recycling – shamed him by greeting him when he had not considered speaking to them.

Eliza's door was no different from the others on her floor. Its cheerful paintwork was undamaged, its number was not missing, but it felt weak, somehow, provisional compared to his own. He pressed the doorbell but heard nothing so knocked on the door rather feebly then flapped the letter box a few times.

Silence.

He crouched to call through the slot, 'Eliza? Dido? It's me,' doing this as much to reassure anyone who heard him letting himself in as from any hope they were there. 'It's okay,' he added. 'I've got my key.'

He felt relief at closing the door behind him, then shame at feeling relief.

'Hello?'

Even before he called out there was a stillness to the flat that told him it was empty. People changed an atmosphere by their presence. Dido had let slip how often Eliza slept during the day and he had half-expected to find her sleeping now, but he knew at once she was out. Then he noticed a handful of letters and the free paper which must have skittered across the floor when slung through the letter box. He was about to pick them up, tidy them into a heap, when a burglarish impulse stayed his hand and he let them lie. He walked around the place.

It was so untidy it would have been hard to tell if there had just been a police raid, still less if any tell-tale thing were missing. There were small piles of things everywhere, evidence, he imagined, of Dido's spasmodic efforts to impose some kind of order, but there was no guiding principle beyond clearing a space on which to sit or eat. Unopened letters, many of them official, old newspapers, library books, photocopied articles and, perhaps most poignant in a household without a cook, recipes torn from magazines, littered every surface. The only spots of order were the untouched spice rack and the small collection of CDs for which Eliza must have written sleeve notes but which she could not play, having no CD player.

Then there was Dido's bedroom, of course, her other bedroom, just as small and orderly as the one he already knew. He opened the wardrobe. It was half-empty but then she possessed so few clothes that maybe it was never full. He crossed to Eliza's room but was driven back by the intimacy of its tumbled, unmade bed and sweet, hairbrushy smell which brought her back to him as shockingly as if he had suddenly heard her voice at his elbow.

He was a feeble detective. What would Julia have done? Look in the bathroom. He looked and saw at once the lack of toothbrushes. And Carlo had gone. Of course he had. He

185

was dense not to have noticed at once. Typically disorganised, Eliza had taken the dog but forgotten his lead, so would be having to improvise with a belt or a piece of rope. He paced from room to cramped room once more and saw that other things were missing – the novel Dido was currently devouring, the denim jacket she all but slept in.

Hands shaking, he pulled out his diary and rang the school. 'There's no sign of them here,' he told the secretary, 'but please don't worry. I'd have heard if there was anything seriously wrong. They may be visiting family or . . . or Mrs Easton may be attending a conference.'

Where did that unlikelihood spring from? The secretary accepted it, so perhaps it was of a piece with her version of a highly efficient, note-sending Eliza.

'I'll be sure to let you know as soon as I hear anything,' he said. 'I'm so sorry you weren't warned. As you say, entirely out of character.'

He hung up before he blurted out any other craziness then slumped on the nearest piece of furniture, a cheap and nasty sofa so down-in-the-mouth it might have spent time in a skip before being dragged up here. It reeked of Carlo however which was more comforting than repellent.

He had been bluffing on the telephone. He had no idea where they might have gone. Eliza had no relatives beyond her mother with whom she might have contact. As for friends, one of his abiding memories of the sad, last months of their living together was of his helplessness at watching her slide into depression while realising she had no close friend he could call to her aid.

It came home to him how little he knew about her now. Everything – messages, complaints, requests – was filtered through Dido. He never saw Eliza because there was no need; Dido handled everything, controlled it even. Quite possibly Dido had been feeding him and Julia a pack of lies for months.

And not just them but the school, even social workers. Eliza might be insane, dangerous even, and he would be none the wiser. It would take very little to push her over the edge. Dido would certainly underestimate the strength of the emotions she stirred up.

He looked about him at the terrible little flat, where the attempts at cheerfulness − a bright, too short curtain, a dog-eared Italian film poster, one wall painted an uneven yellow − only emphasized how low Eliza had sunk. She was still his wife. Whatever his resentment, whatever Julia said, he should never have let this happen. In her absence from his daily existence he had, for ease of mind, turned her into a kind of destroyer but this was no monster's lair, merely the hiding place of a woman who was failing to cope.

Giles was not a religious man but, like many performers and public men, he was a superstitious believer in pacts and promises. There was no Jesus in his private pantheon but there were fates and furies. Things could be bargained for and bad omens diverted. So he did not pray now but he made a pledge that if he found out where Dido was, where they both were, he would make restitution. He would restore the child's faith in him and, if she would let him, set her aunt free of him with her dignity and independence restored.

All afternoon his concentration was shot and he drew sighs of vexation from his colleagues as he repeatedly forgot the blockings and choreography even as they walked him through them. Again and again he thought of Dido's bald demand for money, which he had so crudely read as blackmail. It was not for herself at all but for train money or, God help him, plane money. They might not even be in England any more.

'Sorry, Grover. Sorry guys. Miles away. Sorry. Can we start again?'

20

Julia had barely hung up the phone from talking to a flautist about a problem with the VAT on some session work he had been doing when it rang again on the internal system.

'Are you busy?' Selina asked.

'Not especially.'

'Good. Pour us both coffee and come in for a chat.'

Selina's office looked out over the street. She had chosen it over the calmer room at the back because she liked to look out and see people busy. It spurred her on, she claimed, as a quiet view of rooftops or a little garden could never do. Julia had never witnessed the trick but it was said that Selina also made a habit of thrusting open the windows when she wanted to pretend she was calling someone on her mobile from outside; a useful ploy when dealing with clients who felt she should be wearing out more shoe leather on their behalf.

The windows were open now, filling the small room with sounds of hectic activity and making it feel strangely public.

'Bless you.' Selina took a cup of coffee and closed the door behind them. 'Sit,' she said.

Julia sat on the little sofa. Being on the short side Selina preferred to lean on the front of her desk when addressing staff.

'So how are things?'

'Fine.'

'You get on top of that Decca nonsense all right?'

'Yup. Contracts came back signed this morning. Dieter's stopped worrying.'

'Good.'

Things were not fine at all. In a week Julia had said nothing to Giles beyond making small talk and administrative chitchat. She was throwing up every morning and felt sure she must be losing weight rather than gaining any. It was a wonder Giles had not noticed but then he had never said anything about her ambivalent relationship with food; too well-bred or self-occupied to take her slimness as anything but a natural blessing.

She had been to see a clinic about an abortion. They had offered to book her in the next day but she had panicked, truthfully claiming pressures at work, and made a reservation for Friday week. The receptionist had been very kind and understanding; she must see indecisive, hormonally addled women all the time.

Selina's little sofa was unexpectedly comfortable, like a capacious armchair. Julia had to resist the impulse to slide her legs up onto it. If Selina, bathed in dusty sunlight, said anything sisterly, she would dissolve. Luckily Selina was reliably not the type.

'How are things with Giles?' Selina asked.

'Great,' Julia said.

'How long has it been now? Two years?'

'Four.'

'He really ought to divorce Eliza.'

'Oh well. It couldn't matter less to me, you know.'

Selina played her trick of leaving a comment hanging until its coating of deceit withered and fell off under her scrutiny.

'How are his rehearsals going?'

Caution aside, Julia was finding it hard to bring up the subject of her pregnancy with Giles because they had argued. It was a pointless argument really and Giles had probably forgiven her but there was still a fallout from it between them, a kind of static which was stopping her from revealing her defenceless state.

'All right. Fine, apparently.'

'They'll appreciate his coming to the rescue. *I* appreciate it. But you would say, wouldn't you?'

'What? You mean if —'

'If things weren't okay. The point is, Julia, I value Giles but to be brutally frank he's not first flight and if he were going to be, he'd be there by now. I mean Grover could do it for him. Possibly. He could do for him too, though, if the production's a stinker. But in many ways I value you more. In the long term.'

'Don't!' Julia wanted to tell her. 'I'm only fit for breeding now. I'm a fraud.'

Giles was worrying about Dido. She had not appeared for her usual weekend visit and nobody was answering Eliza's phone. She had been strange when he last saw her, he said. Then he had asked if Julia had argued with her about something or upset her in some way. Defensively Julia had said no. They never argued. She liked Dido. But she had reminded him the girl was growing up and had a choice about what she did. He was not actually her father and perhaps he should start to let go of her a little. After all he hadn't lived with Eliza for years now. Perhaps Eliza was asserting herself. Perhaps she had taken her away for once. And quite right too.

'You're both always so discreet about each other when you're dealing with me,' Selina went on, 'and I understand that but I just wanted you to know that *if* something went wrong, there'd still be a job for you. Just because he's a client, I wouldn't . . . He's *only* a client. I think that's what I mean.'

'Oh. Right. Good.'

'But things are okay, you said.'

'Yes. Things are fine.'

'Good. Now. Business. I've got an almighty fucking favour to ask you.'

'Fire away.'

'Jemima's playing her swansong at the Trenellion Festival. The Walton. And I can't possibly go because it clashes with Kimiko's Barbican gig.'

'But we never bother with Trenellion. It's hardly Aldeburgh. I thought there was an understanding about no agents going there.'

'Yes but this is different. It's Jemima. My oldest client, for God's sake. She's being all very stiff upper lip about it but I know she's pissed off and if I sent someone down there it would avoid leaving bad blood between us. And since you'd be doing me such a favour, you could fly to Newquay and charge it.'

'Oh. Right.'

'And I already took the precaution of booking a room down there for you because it's high season.'

Giles had been furious. Julia had no right, he had said. This was not her affair. 'And you're always trying to change the way Dido looks,' he had said. 'Trying to make her prettier. She doesn't like it. It makes her self-conscious.'

And so on, in yes she does no she doesn't mode. Until, as usual, Julia apologized, although it was he who had given offence.

'When is it?' Julia opened her diary. Apart from steering Alexy, her Georgian bass around, and a couple of tricky phone calls to slippery promoters, the week was fairly empty. Once he had gone, there was nothing she could not cancel, but a trip to Cornwall was the last thing she felt like. 'Do me good to get out of town.'

'I knew I could count on you.'

A pneumatic drill started up. Selina shut the windows.

21

In a spirit of atonement, Pearce spent Monday on tasks
he had been avoiding. The first of these was waking the
combine harvester from its long winter slumber. *Farmer's
Weekly* always advised servicing a combine before putting
it away at the end of the harvest each autumn. The harvest
tended to overlap with other equally urgent jobs however,
especially if there was any hint that the grain was not
quite dry enough to store yet. So invariably the combine
went into its shed still hot from its last day's work and
did not emerge until days before it would be needed. This
year, he thought, he would at least service it a few weeks
in advance and save himself the usual last minute panics
and delays involving journeys across the county in search of
drive belts to replace the ones time or field mice had gnawed
through.

It was a fairly old machine, having seen some twenty sum-
mers. He was debating whether it would be better economics
to replace it when it finally gave up the ghost or to take
to using a contractor. The problem with contractors was
that every farmer tended to need them at the same time
so they could charge through the nose, but new combines
were becoming insanely expensive. Perhaps he would have
to hold out for the grim chance of picking up a used one at

auction when yet another of the region's farmers went out of business. Or killed himself.

Naturally it did not start first time. First the battery was flat, so he switched it with one from the tractor and put the combine's one on to recharge. Now when he turned the key the starter motor groaned into life but the engine failed to fire. Cursing his slackness at not servicing the thing when he had the chance before last year's broccoli harvest started, Pearce set about taking out the fuel filter.

Like most farm machinery, the combine was beautifully designed for doing its job and hopelessly designed when anything needed fixing on it. Few parts that needed regular access were easily accessible and could only be reached by loosening or removing other parts, all of which would then need precise readjustment afterwards. While removing the fuel filter, he noticed that the hydraulic pump's drive belt was about to break. None of the belts was a joy to replace but this was his *bête noire* because so much fine tuning was needed to see that the new one was correctly aligned for the system to work properly afterwards.

Then he banged his skull painfully on a piece of jagged metal where the access had rusted through and been crudely repaired in a hurry. Then he rounded off the perfect morning by placing his hand squarely on a mound of fresh shit Simkin had daintily tucked beneath a thin thatch of barley straw.

In the spirit of doing all his least favourite jobs in one grim batch, he did not head off to buy spares as he was but cleaned himself up and changed into more presentable clothes. His maternal grandfather was in a home at Gulval – he could stop off on the way. Molly was forever on at him to visit more. 'He always asks after you,' she would say. 'It's so awkward. I have to explain that you're still alive.'

He found this hard to believe since, whenever he visited, his grandfather barely spoke. He was ninety-six and had relieved everyone by taking himself into a home when his wife died. He was not particularly confused but he was physically frail, plagued by arthritic knees and, like many men of his generation, incapable of looking after himself. At first his time in the home had been like a return to childhood in the best sense, reunited as he was with people he had not spent time with since they were in Gulval's village school together. But he had outlived nearly all of them then been all but silenced by a stroke. Now he was one of those vacant old men who haunted such places, gravitating away from the sun room to a sunless brown area beneath the staircase, where lay the unofficial 'boys' bit', less chatty and optimistic, where the long pauses in conversation were filled by the jabber of the sports channel or the gurgle of someone's restless gut.

Pearce hated going there with a passion, hated the brisk niceness of the staff which seemed designed to make visitors feel even guiltier for not taking family burdens on themselves, hated the way it made him long for his grandfather's death. The men on both sides of the family seemed cursed with confused longevity. It remained the one consolation of his parents' early deaths that at least this was a fate they had been spared.

Today Pearce caught Grandpa in the sun room, by arriving soon enough after lunch to find the residents still trapped in their chairs by their tray tables. As always everyone except his grandfather gave him a lovely welcome.

'Well look who it isn't!' one of the old ladies said. 'A nice young man to see you, Tommy. You missed lunch, Percy.'

'Had a pasty in the car,' Pearce told her and pulled up a stool. 'Hello Grandpa.' Grandpa stared at him a moment, then went back to chasing crumbs on his tray with skeletal fingers.

'You found a wife yet?' one of the other women asked, a bold-faced old thing given to conducting one-way flirtations with the old men.

'Er, no. Not yet,' he told her, smiling gamely. 'No time.'

The women laughed.

'Hear that, Joyce?'

'What?'

'He says he's no time. No time to find a wife.'

'We'll have to see who we can find you here. Bessie's available, aren't you, Bess?'

Bessie, a sweet orderly, blushed deeply and hurried away with an armful of tray tables.

'Anyway,' he told the bold-faced one, 'I thought I was going steady with you.'

They cracked up at that. They always did. Grandpa swatted another crumb. Bessie came back in and handed Pearce a cup of tea and some biscuits.

'Thanks,' he said.

'See?' someone else said. 'She's available!'

As Bessie left in confusion, Pearce caught his grandfather watching him and nodding. Perhaps this was how he had found his grandmother, by doing nothing while the women around him arranged things to their romantic and practical satisfaction. His father had always joked about finding a wife at the one and only hunt ball he had ever attended.

'So I said to myself, *No need to go to one of those again.*'

But what if his image of himself as a marital Viking carrying off a prize woman on one shoulder and her dowry of conveniently placed fields on the other was one carefully engendered by a team of skilful women? Adept at the handling of male vanity, aunts, neighbours and mothers might have placed Pearce's mother just so, knowing his father would catch sight of her just so. Cattle tracks. The men of the family had all been on cattle tracks, their belief in their freedom of direction a kind illusion. Was that so very bad if the end result was a kind of happiness? Pearce was not given to nostalgia but the thought of having his future sort of happiness lined up for him in the next room by a troupe of benevolent busybodies all at once seemed quite appealing. He never went to church or chapel however, fête or village disco.

He smiled back at his nodding grandfather and dutifully munched one of the pink wafers Bessie had given him with his tea. Even when he was a boy their papery texture and rosy taste had seemed to him desolation in biscuit form.

22

Molly's house was at one end of an isolated terrace on the edge of St Just. Perhaps if the mines at Pendeen, Truthwall and Geevor had continued to thrive, the town would have continued to expand towards them along the coast and grown to the size of Penzance. As it was, this terrace faced only open fields and the distant sea. A donkey watched Eliza and Dido cycle up but slipped off to stand with a pair of fat ponies before Dido could stroke its nose. The front gardens were as eccentric as Molly had suggested, and seemed to be egging one another on. So where one contented itself with a cottagey look, all tumbling herbs and soft colours, its neighbour strove to suggest the subtropics with a spiky flourish of cabbage palms, yuccas and phormiums. One house might have belonged to a sculptor, for its garden was littered with lumps of stone and twists of metal all in the process of becoming something else while another was merely piled high with junk on which a pack of Jack Russells were basking in the last of the sun. Molly's garden spoke of good intentions and strong impulses, for its balding grass and concrete path were littered with plants still in their plastic pots. Where most of the row contented themselves with ramshackle porches, one improvised from an old dinghy, Molly's sported a spanking new plastic conservatory, its windows open to the evening air.

Eliza arrived on time but the conservatory was already crowded with people greeting one another and choosing their seats from the broken-down assortment on offer. Eliza noticed the piano to one side of the front door and was startled to realise they were going to sing out there, effectively in the lane.

Lucy was lying in wait for Dido, red cap still firmly on head. She claimed her at once and the two of them stomped upstairs.

There were ten singers, including Eliza, four men and six women, aged between Molly's mid-thirties to a quaking old man with dazzlingly false teeth. Assuming that new members were unusual in such a society and transient ones even more so, Eliza had been fearing Molly would make a performance of introducing her to the group. Molly was either careless or the soul of tact however, for she merely said a kind but entirely unsurprised hello, handed Eliza a glass of chilled plonk and found her a copy of the standard madrigal collection Eliza's first tutor had edited.

Then Molly closed the door into the house – the one from conservatory into garden was left wide because the space was still quite warm – and sat at the sun-bleached old upright. After some muttering it was agreed that it was Toby's turn that week.

Toby, the old man with the shaking hands and the teeth, reached for a list tucked into the back of his book, and announced with a smile, '*April is in my Mistress' Face.*' Evidently they took turns to select the week's songs. Molly thumped out a split chord, raised a hand to bring them in and seconds later they were singing.

Eliza need not have feared the rustiness of her voice. The sound the choir made was full-throated and often way-ward. Welcomed rather than auditioned, the singers were ill-matched, the men far louder than the women, the altos beefier than the sopranos. The woman beside Eliza was moving her lips and following the notes in the top line with a sharpened pencil but making no discernible sound at all.

It was probably more authentic than the politely bloodless sounds produced by more gifted groups in her student days, an approximation of the noise heard around many a Tudor table of an evening. Hearing it in such close confinement put Eliza in mind of a Sacred Harp choir she had once heard on tour from Pennsylvania. Sacred Harp singers were proud of an uninterrupted tradition reaching back to early English polyphony and regarded full-throated song as an act of both divine worship and neighbourly friendship.

Merely to be singing again, after more years than she cared to count, felt extraordinary. For all that her muscles were out of condition, her voice was still there enough to gain her glances from Molly and the silent one. But she was so out of practice she had forgotten how to breathe or support her breathing with her diaphragm and so the euphoria induced by music-making was compounded with dizziness and a pleasurable sense of her blood buzzing.

The group had no thought of public performance. Unlike most such amateur gatherings, it had the admirably modest purpose of meeting solely for the pleasure of singing. The session was more observance than rehearsal. Only if a madrigal broke down entirely – as did some of the less familiar or florid ones Toby had chosen, such as *Sweet Suffolk Owl* – would a passage be taken apart or Molly called upon to thump out some notes on the piano. Usually when a piece finished it would be agreed at once to sing it a second time. Always there would be a comment. *Well, that was good* or *Lovely cadence.* Very occasionally a piece would fail to impress, the comments would be polite but lukewarm and the madrigal would go unrepeated.

Sometimes a chosen madrigal would go unperformed entirely,

deferred until the reappearance of some absent singer who was the lone holder of certain high or low notes in a part, or because a composer called for more voice lines than the group could confidently fill out that night.

As the sun set on Molly's garden and the Jack Russells took themselves indoors, Eliza found the ninety minutes flew by, reunited as she was with old and intimate friends. She knew these pieces so well it startled her to realise how many of them she had never actually sung. Conscious of her outsider status, she kept her learning hidden and frequently bit her tongue rather than correct the stiflingly slow speeds at which some madrigals were taken or the mistaken pronunciation of certain words like July, heart and honey.

Only once, when there was needless consternation that a bar suddenly contained six beats where its neighbours had all contained four was she unable to restrain herself.

'The bar lines were added later, by the editor,' she said, aware as she did so that it was the first time she had spoken and that all eyes were on her. 'Elizabethans didn't use a bar line system. I used to study this stuff,' she added apologetically, appalled at how entirely unCornish her accent sounded in such company.

'However did they keep together?' the silent woman asked her.

'They counted, unlike us,' a man said and everyone laughed. He was older than Molly but a bit younger than the other men, a weather-beaten early-forties, Eliza guessed. He had said nothing until now and seemed abashed of the attention his words commanded. He dropped his gaze to his lap where his hands were so broad his book seemed smaller than everyone else's.

'No, but how?' Molly asked her, gently smacking his leg by way of reproof.

'You really want to know?'

'Yes.'

'Well . . .' Eliza thought. 'A lot of this is conjecture but judging from contemporary pictures and how things were done in Italy – the madrigal came here from Italy – er . . . they didn't have more than one singer a line and they sat close together. A bit like a string quartet or a viol consort. It was more like chamber music too in that each singer only had their line of music, in a separate book, which would have forced them to listen hard to what the others were singing.'

'She's saying we're too loud, lads,' Toby said and all the men laughed.

'Well you *are*!' Molly put in, at which the women joined in.

One of the men joked that he had learned to sing with the Sally Army on street corners and *didn't do quiet*.

'Time you chose one,' Molly told Eliza. 'Visitor's privilege,' and everyone murmured assent and looked at Eliza expectantly.

'Number thirty-two,' she said. She did not need to look in the book to check. 'Roger Trevescan: *Go, Dissembler, I Care Not.*'

'Now there's a lady with taste,' said Toby and they found their places and sang.

It was a diplomatic choice; she had already heard two of the men enthusing about an entire evening of Thomas Merritt at a Redruth Chapel so knew they would favour a Cornish composer, however minor. But it was also a personal experiment. It had struck her afresh how amazing much of this music was, how daring its harmonies and sophisticated its texts. Now she wanted to see if Trevescan's lone surviving madrigal, having once been familiar to the point where she could have penned its six lines out from memory, would sound commonplace or stale after such an absence from her life and mind.

Certainly she had never heard it sung so slowly or so loud but it had lost none of its arresting force.

The text – assuredly Trevescan's own, for it had been used nowhere else – was a derivative piece of Elizabethan erotic fatalism. Stung by a betrayal, the poet bade his uncaring lover to leave him to die of his spiritual wounds. The charm of the piece lay in its second verse, complete with startling key change, where the poet dropped his pretence of sang-froid to say that, of course, if the lover could bring themselves to remain at his side just a little longer, to die in their arms were infinitely preferable to dying alone, for the one led straight to 'Hell's hotte caverne' but the other afforded 'a verie glimpse of Heavene'.

As Eliza had expected, some of the women sighed afterwards about how sad the song was. She did not think it her place to point out that the death sung of was, in all likelihood, a poetic euphemism like *le petit mort* and that the madrigal was a sly comparison of solitarily to mutually induced orgasms.

Hearing and singing the little piece again, she wondered at how she had allowed her thesis to drag on for so long unfinished. Not only did the fascination of Trevescan and his story present itself afresh before her with the notes but, as was often the case, the perfect logic of music, its notation and dissolving and mutating harmonies, created the sensation of a perfectly cogent argument in her mind.

Perhaps, she thought, as Toby announced number seventeen and they all turned their pages and waited for another chord from Molly, the problem was that she had begun to cast the net of her thesis too wide? With the insecurity bred by delay, insecurity which in turn engendered further prevarication, she had felt the need to research deeper and deeper into her chosen period and to include more and more musical comparisons and historical context, until the slender proposal with which she had set out was quite bowed by a freight of citations. Perhaps, she thought, as they began to sing again, it would have been both wiser and bolder to answer a miniature with a miniature and instead of spreading her argument wider and wider to move in as close as possible to the madrigal in question and make its scant nine hundred notes the whole world of a revealingly myopic enquiry.

'Well,' Molly said, glancing at her watch. 'Better make that it for a week. Peggy's got to drive all the way back to Marazion.'

As books were closed and pushed into bags or jacket pockets, Eliza reluctantly closed hers and began to stand but Molly played another chord, a G major triad. Then everyone breathed and sang from memory.

Because of the opening chord, Eliza had assumed that someone's birthday was being honoured but she realised at once it was another madrigal, one she had never heard before yet one whose style seemed instantly familiar to her. Was it a translation from the Italian? Something by Monteverdi or Arcadelt, perhaps? But no, the cadences were as English as clipped yew. Again she thought or the Sacred Harp choir she had heard. She remembered an interview with its director in which he described how their singers took it in turns to sit out in the middle of the great circle in which they rehearsed, to be sung at and to bathe in the notes. Were they singing anything else, Eliza would have been profoundly uncomfortable at being so singled out and sung to. But she too was bathing now. No matter that some of the singing was off-key or that this group was so poorly balanced; her mind raced as she tried to take in every detail of the familiar yet unfamiliar piece.

The words, insofar as she could make them out, spoke of exile in the country when one's heart lay with an absent lover in the town. What was so startling a reminder of Trevescan's madrigal was the second verse. There, far from offering to pine away or die quietly, the poet announced that 'country goodness and a second, quieter love' had provided balm for his wounded spirits and that he was schooling himself to the enjoyment of 'softer pleasures and a sweet obscurity'.

'You all right?'

They had finished and people were saying their goodnights and walking through the garden. Eliza tuned back to reality to find Molly staring at her.

'It wasn't *that* bad!' Molly joked.

'No, no,' Eliza said. 'Not at all. That last piece, though. What was it?'

'*Country Goodness*. That's what we call it. We always end our sessions with it now. It used to be *The Silver Swan* but *Country Goodness* sort of took over. I think the old boys like the fact that it goes so low for a change. Don't you, old boy?'

Once more she flapped a hand against the knee of the only remaining man, the younger one with the big, calloused hands.

'I like the words,' he said sheepishly and pushed Molly gently in return. Eliza heard that they had the same voice – a low, patient murmuring version of Cornish without the querulousness the accent so often carried with it.

Before Molly said, 'This is my brother, Pearce,' Eliza had guessed they were related.

'I'm Eliza,' she said and he shook her hand with unexpected gentleness.

'Eliza's staying up at Thorpe's Lane. In the caravan.'

'Kitty's place? What's that like, then?' he asked.

'Er . . . I don't know yet,' Eliza said. 'We only got here this afternoon.'

She was going to ask again about the mystery madrigal but he looked at her in a way that momentarily addled her brains and then the girls came racing down from upstairs, Lucy loudly relieved that the *awful noise* was over, Dido trailing in her wake, girlish by comparison. Dido was wearing the red cap now so they must have made friends. Lucy punched her uncle in the stomach, failing to wind him, and told Dido,

'This is Pearce. He sings, but he's all right.'

'How d'you do?' Pearce held out his hand for Dido to shake but she was overcome by a yawn.

'Long day. We'd better ride home,' Eliza said, but Molly insisted Pearce drive them.

'He can sling the bikes in the back. Can't you, Pearce?'

'No worries,' he said. He slipped outside and when they joined him he was leaning into his Land Rover thrusting fertiliser bags and bales of barbed wire aside to make room. He lifted the bikes inside like a couple of toys then held open the passenger door so Dido could scramble up and Eliza get in beside her.

'So how long are you down for?' Molly asked through the open window.

Eliza shrugged but Dido shouted, 'Two weeks!' over the sound of the engine.

'Good,' Molly said. 'We'll see you next week then, if not before.'

Even in such an old vehicle it was a short drive, Eliza knew, through the little town and up the steep hill to their track, and the labouring engine was too loud to speak over without shouting. Having Dido placed between them was also somehow inhibiting. Still smarting from their spat that afternoon, perhaps, she could not afford to let slip even a hint that her old enthusiasm was reviving.

'Tell me about that last madrigal,' she wanted to ask him. 'Why wasn't there any printed music? Who wrote it? Why haven't I heard it before? Sing me the last line! Tell me the words!' But instead she stared out at the passing cottage windows and hedges and enjoyed the rare pleasure of Dido leaning in heavy contentment on her shoulder. Evidently their spat had been forgotten and forgiven.

'Just here's fine,' she called out as she suddenly recognised their turning but he had already swung the Land Rover onto the heavily pitted track and was soon bumping them to a halt in Kitty's little field.

Ask him now, she thought. *Just ask him*. But he had already climbed out, leaving the engine running while he retrieved their bikes as carefully as if they had been so much Fabergé. Dido called out, 'Night' to him and hurried to find the hidden key and let herself in.

'Thanks,' Eliza said, unable to shake hands now because hers were full of handlebar. 'We could have ridden home all right but . . .'

'You don't have any lights,' he pointed out. 'People drive like maniacs over that hill at night.'

'Oh?'

'Would you . . . ?' he started then fell silent.

'What?' she asked.

'Dinner,' he managed. 'Would you come out for dinner?'

'With you and your wife?'

'Er. No. Just me. Tomorrow. But she could come too.' She saw him work to remember the name. 'Dido.'

'Oh. Yes. Yes, please.'

'Good.' He smiled for the first time since he had dared to crack a joke in the madrigal group. 'How about tomorrow at about seven?'

'That would be lovely.'

'Good.' He smiled again. 'I'll pick you up about seven, then.'

A date. She had just been asked out on a proper, old-fashioned date. And said yes! Bewildered, she watched him climb in and start to drive off. He leant over to shout something through the passenger window which she had left open but the engine noise was too great so she simply smiled in reply.

It was only as he drove off that she realised they had been talking in moonlight. His headlamp beams had bounced off into the darkness but the night was barely darker without them. There were stars too. Hundreds of them. She shivered as though the lights were points of ice.

'Look,' she pointed out to Dido, who had come to see if she wanted cocoa. 'It's night but we're still casting shadows!'

23

A reprieve of sorts was waiting on Giles and Julia's answering machine when he came in, shattered, from the day's rehearsal.

'Mr Easton? Sue Stokes again from St Saviour's and I owe you a huge apology. I've only just been handed the note Mrs . . . your wife wrote me last week. Dido gave it to a friend to hand in and it had gone in the wrong pigeon-hole. Anyway it says they've had to go to Cornwall because her granny's ill in hospital. So sorry to have caused you unnecessary anxiety.' She laughed nervously. 'Just thought you'd like to know. Bye.'

Perhaps she was used to such poor communication in the many divided and realigned families she had to deal with. Perhaps not. But she conveyed a certain gossipy satisfaction in knowing more of his wife's movements than he did. He noted her sensitivity in backing off from calling Eliza Mrs Easton at least.

Giles had only met his mother-in-law a few times, when she came to babysit Dido during the honeymoon and during the few brief visits she paid after their move to London. When Eliza described her as a Latin teacher he pictured a Classics don, dry of wit, essentially unshockable, the begetter, presumably, of Eliza's bookish detachment from worldly affairs. It was a shock to meet, therefore, a tight-buttoned, rather shy churchgoer whose strict views were all the more startling for being shyly presented. Mrs Hosken was the sort of person his mother would cattily have described as *a funny little woman* but Giles found himself charmed by her, perhaps because she made no attempt to please unless it could be done while telling the truth.

She admitted to finding opera *unsettling* and counter-tenor voices *not right, somehow*. Whenever she stayed he made a point of escorting her to the church her advance researches had deemed suitable. He even wore a suit for her. She opened out to him a little. Confessing she thought his looks *wasted on a man*, she claimed to understand perfectly why Eliza never revisited Camborne. Their hometown was culturally limited, she said, unable even to support a Latin teacher any more. He suspected he touched on her real motive the one time he tried to draw her out, apropos Dido, on the subject of Hannah. She said, with characteristic soft-voiced firmness, 'Oh no. I'd rather not talk about that. Not really', the conversational equivalent of a handbag clasp clicking shut. Giles understood secret torments so pried no further.

Eliza hated her mother's visits. 'She looks at me as if she's just waiting for me to fail in some way. She does it to Dido too. She hates women. Her church hates women. She actually refers to us as the Weaker Sex — I've heard her!'

Hearing Mrs Hosken talk when Eliza was not around to goad her, however, Giles gained the contrary impression, that she loved Eliza deeply and would do all she could to keep her in the wealthy south, which she regarded as the sphere of fulfilment as well as sin, rather than back in Cornwall, which she spoke of as the land of failure, even if she had to make her hate her to do it.

Just once he thought Eliza might have been right. He and Mrs Hosken had taken Dido to a local playground and were watching her play boldly on the slide with other children when quite suddenly Mrs Hosken sighed, 'The sins of the mother. That little girl is a time bomb,' and he caught something like grim relish in her expression before she resumed her customary respectable blankness.

He did not love the woman, but his relief that Eliza had a good, unthreatening reason for removing Dido so suddenly was such that he felt a corresponding rush of nostalgic concern. He kept a list of names and addresses in an old desk diary of all the people who ever sent him Christmas cards, many of them, like Mrs Hosken, people he rarely saw.

Mrs Hosken was predictably upset when Eliza left him. He had to break the news to her when she made one of her rare phone calls and, being upset himself, probably furnished her with more details than was kind. He was at a loss to understand, certainly, but he blamed himself and did not mean to sound vindictive. He felt terrible when she said, 'If she doesn't come to her senses, I shall have nothing more to do with her,' because were he to plead Eliza's case it would only make him rise the higher in her mother's esteem.

She sent Christmas and birthday cards, usually with a short letter tucked into them. He assumed these would stop once she heard about Julia, but she must not have heard because the cards continued to come, addressed only to him, and made no mention of his wilful plunge into sin after her daughter. Secretly he reciprocated, even remembering her birthdays, which Eliza almost certainly forgot or ignored, and guiltily penned her little reassuring notes about his news and Dido's progress from which Julia was carefully excised. Challenged, he might have said he did it for Dido's sake, keeping open a channel of untroubled communication with her grandmother in case the child should ever have need of it but actually he did it because he loved the idea that there was someone out there, someone of stern judgement and high morals, who believed he was good and sinned against and who prayed for his welfare.

Mrs Hosken's address was near the beginning of his Christmas card list because she had never moved house. Presumably Eliza and Dido were staying there. He glanced at his watch and rang the number but reached only the number unobtainable tone. He dialled again. Same response. It was certain Mrs Hosken was not as feckless as Eliza about remembering to pay bills. This was a remote woman who despised the world, however, who saw no need for a car or a television and in all probability no longer bothered with a telephone when she had neighbours who could ring people for her in an emergency. He tried to imagine life without a telephone, imagined Julia's reaction if he had theirs disconnected out of moral principles.

Warmed by admiration, he reached for the phone again and his credit card and ordered a generous bouquet she would probably think immoral as well as vulgar. It was easier this way, saving him the awkwardness of a conversation with Eliza. His Christmas and birthday cards normally restrained themselves to *with all good wishes, Giles* but, dictating the florist's greetings card, he signed off with *much love, as ever, Giles*. He imagined the small blush the words might rouse on her cheeks before she set the card aside and dutifully decried his extravagance.

24

Of all Julia's clients, Alexy was the most demanding. But he was also the most prestigious and the least reliable so she had learned to keep her diary free on his visit to London so as to shadow his every move and see his every whim catered to. He was a bass, a fabulously Slavic bass who actually looked like the noble warriors he played whereas most of the competition resembled defrocked priests or upturned turtles, and accepted any number of free flights, penthouse hotel suites and tremulously accommodating mezzos as his due. One went along with him because Alexy was deservedly a star but also because he accepted all these blessings not with a star's arrogance but with the sweet, comfortable nature of an adored youngest son. Julia went along with him because he had only to smile, dimpling his chin, and rumble, 'Zzank you, Yoolia,' to fill her with a desire to cook him dumplings and make his bed.

Which was how she came to find herself skipping after work drinks for the receptionist's birthday to accompany him to a psychic's house in World's End.

'It always leave me so very *tender*, Yoolia,' he explained. 'I need you there afterwards.'

He swore by Barney Swift and consulted him whenever work brought him to England. Julia had been a little nervy when she first accompanied him but now knew what to expect. It was a perfectly nice house and one could have taken Barney for a friendly wine merchant or estate agent. It was no seedier or stranger than a visit to a dentist or chiropractor.

Barney ushered them into his tiny house and, avoiding shaking hands, led them upstairs and told Alexy to make himself comfortable in the sitting room, 'In any chair but the blue one.' He then took Julia to sit in the kitchen where he made her a cup of tea and offered the day's papers and some excellent shortbread on a rather pretty plate.

He did not go into a trance. There was nothing embarrassing or untoward. He simply faced the kitchen window in silence for a few minutes, hands on the edge of the sink, and breathed deeply. Then he walked into the sitting room and shut the door. Through the wall she heard him start to talk almost at once and keep up a stream of words for nearly twenty minutes.

Apparently this was why consultations with him were so exciting; there were none of the tell-tale am-I-on-the-right-track questions, just a confident unburdening of thoughts, much of it disturbingly to the point. Alexy had once refused to sign a contract when warned off by something Barney had said, which maddened Selina until the opera production he had thus avoided turned out to be notoriously unlucky, plagued by ill health, bad reviews, union action and the violent, onstage death of a scene shifter. Intrigued, forgiving, Selina made an appointment for herself, from which she returned grey-faced and refusing all questions.

When it was over, Barney usually returned to the kitchen looking impressively tired. He would merely nod at Julia with a little smile then take himself off to another room leaving her to retrieve Alexy, who was usually left wildly keyed up by the experience.

Today's consultation took a little longer than usual. As she sat at the table drinking her tea, she heard more questions and answers than usual as it neared its end and sensed all had not gone quite smoothly. Then Barney came in, looked at her and said, 'Of course! Stupid of me. It's you they were talking about. I know you're worried but don't be. It's going to be fine. There's a cross and a star, a beautiful healthy child and a handsome man. It's all going to be fine. They say you're not to worry.' And he slipped out as suddenly as he had come in.

She was astonished for only a moment, then angry that he should stoop to trying to recruit her so crudely. It could not have taken him much research – a phone call to one of the office gossips perhaps – to find that she lived with Giles on Starcross Road. The rest was just guesswork and intuition.

She fetched Alexy with some impatience, to find him similarly displeased.

'It not go so well, Yoolia. He think I get married soon.'

Which at least meant that he was not so excited as usual and could be dropped at his hotel without a lengthy winding down drink.

Julia and Giles had a routine when he was rehearsing an opera. They went overnight from gadding about to living with the single-minded simplicity of a farmer and his wife. All socialising stopped. They ate well but carefully, at home, and were early to bed every night. Julia enjoyed the change. It was like visiting a health farm each evening only without the tedious exercising. In bed she would massage his back and shoulders to relieve the tension that built up there and, as often as not, he would then fall asleep and she would slip downstairs to watch television quietly until she felt tired too. He had no footballers' superstitions about sex having a malign effect on performance but if they made love during a rehearsal period it tended to be without ingenuity or great enthusiasm, a physical release rather than an emotional outpouring.

Tonight Giles was already home when she let herself in. He was in a good mood, full of gossip about Dewi Evans but also relieved because he had solved the mystery of Dido's non-appearance at the weekend. Hearing they had simply gone to visit her sick grandmother, Julia too was relieved. Despite her realism, she must have borne the psychic's words home with her because she sensed Giles' improved mood and the house's warmer atmosphere with a kind of recognition.

Typically Giles did not apologize in so many words for his accusation that she had driven Dido away but he did so in gestures, cooking her favourite supper – pasta with lemon and chicken – complimenting her on her hair, which had been trimmed in her lunch hour, and being generally charming. Chattering about the afternoon's rehearsal he told her he now had a few days off. 'Dewi's shooting his new video and Grover's directing it. We've done my first and last duets to death and the two dances, which leaves all the scenes with just me and Dewi. Shame you can't take time off mid-week. We could have a little jaunt somewhere.'

'Damn,' she said, remembering.

'Tell.'

'Lousy timing. Selina's sending me down to your favourite Cornish music festival tomorrow to fly the flag for her at Jemima Beale's farewell concerto there.'

'So? I could come too. Take Friday off and we could make a little holiday of it and come back on Monday morning.'

She pulled a face.

'But *Cornwall*,' she said. 'It's a bit . . . It'll be heaving.'

'It's different if you don't have children in tow. No buckets and spades and crowded beaches. We could stay somewhere nice, eat in some of those famously good restaurants they have down there now, unwind.'

'Selina's already booked me in at the Porth Keverne.'

'Great. I'll just call ahead and make sure it's a double.'

'Oh it's a double. Selina doesn't believe in singles. And I'm flying. You might not get a seat at short notice.'

He grinned. 'Don't you want me to come?'

'Of course, but –'

'You think I'll cramp your style!'

'No.'

'Good. I'm coming. More pasta?'

'I'm not hungry any more.'

'So now you can eat for pure pleasure.'

'Oh go on, then. Giles?'

'Mmm?'

'Did you have a spat with Villiers the other night? Apart from the paedophile thing?'

'No. Why?'

'Nothing really.'

'Oh god. Has he taken umbrage at something? I probably forgot to admire his shoes or pat his bum. He's so fucking thin-skinned. I just wish he'd relax and admit he's gay; go the whole hog and stop being so prickly and sour.'

'Yes,' she said. 'It's not as though anyone would be remotely surprised.'

'He's probably a perfectly nice person underneath.'

'Hmm,' she said. 'Possibly. For a snake.'

As the evening wound on she felt a great weight of worry lifting. Of course Villiers was against her having a baby. Villiers was against anyone having babies, against happiness, against family, against anything that did not involve subterfuge and pain and Villiers.

But now it did not matter. She could tell Giles this evening. She could tell him in Cornwall. It no longer bothered her. Whenever she told him, Giles would be happy. He was so much simpler than her, emotionally. So lacking in Villiers' deviousness. When he was hungry he reached for a skillet and cooked a steak. When he was happy, he said so. Perhaps Barney Swift was right after all.

I'm happy, she thought. *Here. Now. Stars and crosses. A healthy, beautiful baby. A handsome man. It'll be all right.*

25

It was one of those occasions when Pearce wished he had a dog. If a dog had come bounding up to greet him as he came in at the back door or lay, sleepily tail-wagging on the kitchen sofa, he could have shared his excitement with it by taking it for a moonlit walk to hunt rabbits or at least rolled and played with it on the hall rug. As it was, Simkin being out mousing, he had to content himself with a glass of Scotch and a Women's Institute rock bun.

He had so nearly not gone this evening. Molly's madrigal evenings had been born when she hectored a group of them into coming carol singing with her to raise money for a campaign to save West Cornwall Hospital. It had been unexpectedly enjoyable rehearsing so she then had the idea of a repeat performance the following summer, only singing madrigals instead of carols. They began to rehearse but could never agree on which to perform or when to walk around local pubs and houses performing them, so rehearsing was established as an end in itself.

Pearce had begun to tire of the group however. He liked the fact that they never performed but they were pretty awful and it depressed him that, despite all the practice, they never seemed to get any better.

He knew Molly had a sentimental attachment to music-making of this particularly Cornish kind. It reminded her of their mother, who had always an alarming ability to pressgang the most unlikely gathering into clustering about the harmonium to sing *Goliath of Gath, Trelawney* or *The Hymn of Saint Buriana* or something raucous and thigh-slapping by Merritt, and maintained a small sheet music library for no other purpose.

Whenever he had gently tried to hint to Molly that he might not always be relied on to turn up, she would either make him feel he was hurtfully reneging on some long established family tradition or go for his sensitive spot in turn by saying he was never going to meet anyone if he never came out. She never specified a gender, never said girlfriend or wife, but he knew what she was getting at. In any case there was never anyone new in her conservatory, despite the little notes she kept pinned up in the library and the more musical of St Just's pubs.

The men who came were regulars from any number of local choirs or euchre drives and tended to greet him with wearisome jokes about cauliflowers and potatoes, even when neither was in season.

The few women not married or old enough to have played hopscotch with his aunts, were made as unromantic for him by familiarity and too much of the wrong sort of knowledge, as he felt sure he must be for them. Pauline was embittered from living with her sick mother. Ruth was perfectly nice but seemed the last person in St Just to have realised that she was a lesbian, which left Bet. Bet was actually very pretty and, unlike him, had completed her veterinary training and specialised in small animals at the Penzance firm which looked after the livestock on the farm. He had occasionally caught her looking at him with something like wistfulness when he went in to pay a bill or pick up an antibiotic injection for one of the steers. But he had never asked her out because he had never been able to forget the rumour, probably quite untrue, which had circulated at school to the effect that, when aroused, she smelt like a swamp.

The heat in the old people's home in Gulval had left him drained of energy, then he had spent an extremely bad-tempered afternoon fitting the new fuel filter and hydraulic pump belt on the combine. And once he had finally sprung the engine into life at about six, he felt ready for nothing but a long hot soak followed by a drive down to Sennen Cove for a pasty and a pint of Doom Bar.

He had just decided to pretend to have forgotten what night of the week it was when Lucy rang to say she didn't understand algebra and Mum didn't understand it either and he was coming tonight wasn't he. So, guiltily, he had said yes, of course he was and had grabbed a pasty and pint on his way through the town and arrived early enough to help her with her homework and to put up a shelf of Molly's which kept falling down because she was too proud to ask Morris to rehang it.

So he was sitting in the conservatory with the others, already well into a second pint, thanks to Mervyn the tenor, who always brought a couple of jugfuls down from The Star, when she walked in with her funny little girl and sat shyly among the sopranos directly across from him. She sat by Bet, in fact, which meant he couldn't look at her as much as he liked because every time he did, Bet intercepted his gaze and looked wistfully back.

Eliza. She was the most beautiful thing he had ever seen. In the flesh, at least. Like a girl in a shampoo advert, only serious, tremendously serious, like a small girl having to read the lesson or recite something from memory. Above her rather worn moleskin jeans she had on a funny, floaty top that didn't really match, which he liked, as though she had her mind on other things when dressing. And when she sang she took on a faraway look so that she reminded him of the dreamy, rather hippyish girls he had seen on the arms of artists when Molly dragged him along to private views at local galleries.

He had never studied music. His mother had taught him to read it at the same time as she taught him to read words, sitting on her lap at the harmonium while she played and sang to nursery rhymes and folk songs in an old book with illustrations by Walter Crane. Or was it Kate Greenaway? Pretty girls in bonnets with watering cans or baskets of cherries. *There was a lady loved a swine. 'Honey,' said she. There was a lady loved a swine. 'Oink!' said he.* To read the words now was to hear his mother's voice, cushioned on the supportive swaying of her bosom and feel again her bony arms safely pinning him from either side as she played the simple harmonies.

He sang bass because that was what Molly told him his voice was. Beyond that he understood little. He had a good memory for notes, however, and knew chunks at a time of the bass lines off by heart because they had sung them so often. So he was able to look up occasionally as he sang, unlike the others, unlike poor, swampy Bet. So he saw, as they did not, that Eliza sang every madrigal from memory. She kept the book politely opened at whatever page old Toby had them turn to, but once she had seen the title, she read no further, merely sang.

He loved Molly with a strong, true, brotherly love which he never questioned or doubted. But he felt a new, warm surge of affection for her when she insisted he run Eliza and the girl back to the caravan. He knew as she waved them off she was mischievously trying to catch his eye but he dared not look back for fear of laughing then having to explain himself.

Where had he found the courage to ask her out? Perhaps it was because he knew she was not staying long and knew no one. Nobody would hear about her refusal or make a fool of him. It was not like asking out Bet or sad, frowning Pauline. But perhaps his encounter with Janet had something to do with it? Perhaps she had made some kind of adjustment in him, tightened a drive belt or whatever, and now he knew such things were possible he knew no restraint.

Driving home down Carn Bosavern towards Kelynack, he had counted the sequence of distant lighthouse flashes and felt a rush of feeling so intense that he swung the Land Rover drunkenly from side to side in a way that always made Lucy scream and Molly furious.

He took a second rock bun to bed with him, and a recipe book.

26

'So what do you feel like doing?' Dido asked after their holiday breakfast of muffins, coffee, strawberries and chocolate. For the first time in weeks, Eliza felt entirely rested, despite the damp, the lumpiness of the bed and a dawn chorus in which the honks and screams of pigs had joined with birds.

'You're on holiday too,' she told Dido. 'You decide. Beach? Penzance? St Ives? Coast path?'

Dido glanced out of the creeper-framed window; the day was cloudlessly sunny but with a crisp breeze.

'Bike ride?' she suggested.

'Okay. But not too far. It's hilly around here and I just sit around all day, remember?'

Dido scowled at this reference to yesterday's row. They pored over the battered map left with the bird and flower guides and well-thumbed paperbacks on the mobile home's solitary bookshelf.

Dido had recently been studying how to read Ordnance Survey symbols so Eliza encouraged her to plot them a circular route. Dido's initial circuit – taking in both Penzance and St Ives – would have challenged a professional racer. They opted instead for a round trip to Land's End, returning around Chapel Carn Brea, the country's westernmost hill. Eliza was fairly sure that this was too ambitious as well but she held her peace. She had resolved, in light of yesterday's altercation, to be more venturesome.

So instead of riding down into St Just they turned left out of their track then down the hill in the other direction, past the cemetery, drinking in the magnificent view across the fields towards Sennen and Land's End.

Entirely without caution, Dido flew on ahead while Eliza found she could not quite surrender to sensation and kept spoiling her own wild pleasure by applying the squeaky brakes. Watching the wind whirling Dido's pigtails she wondered whether they should be wearing safety helmets. And they should surely have tightened the wheels, checked the brake blocks, oiled things. There were few cars however; this was hardly like riding down Blackstock Road or Archway Hill in a welter of London traffic. Then she went over a bump and tensed her hands on the handlebars, unable to stop herself imagining the front wheel parted from the plummeting frame and the sudden contact of ankle with tarmac.

But the road was levelling out and with it her fears. She was also distracted by a single word on a sign at the road's edge. There was a cluster of old houses where the road swung sharply to the left as the road rose again. The sign stood some way beyond them, leaning into a hedge where a lane plunged down towards the sea. All she glimpsed was a bright yellow background, a cartoon of a tent and the word Vingoe. As they rode on, Eliza growing breathless in her effort to keep Dido at least in view, on their route past a little airfield, round several tight bends, across a T-junction and onto the stretched out village of Sennen, the word took hold and with it, like an unscratchable itch, the need to hear the mysterious madrigal again.

The night before, lying in bed in the moonlight, lulled by the comforting sound of Dido's snores, she had convinced herself that she was mistaken, that the piece was simply one she had never heard and that the suggestion of a common author sprang simply from hearing the two compositions side by side. Though there were not many English madrigals she had not heard – she was specialising within an already specialised field after all – she suspected there were many so minor they had never been republished even by enthusiasts.

One of the 'old boys' in Molly's group had probably stumbled on the music in some Victorian album of his grandmother's, some mildewed collection of *Glees For the Fireside* or bowdlerised *Catches and Rounds of Merrie England*. The few nineteenth-century editors to have taken an interest in Elizabethan or Tudor song had invariably felt they must 'correct' the daring harmonies and more suggestive words or impose key or time signatures which made more 'sense'. Given that they would then misread the originals and have the pieces performed at funereal paces, it was a wonder the revival of interest ever came at all.

Land's End was a disappointment. The first impression was of a huge clifftop car park abutting the film set for a cheaply made historical epic; the second, as one drew nearer, of an already undistinguished hotel inflated into a baldly whitewashed, blank-walled cinema or prison. The extension was a theme park, thrown up in an effort to make money from crowds that would otherwise have come merely to view a geographical feature. With such a view to either side, it seemed perverse to have built a structure with no windows but of course the view might have distracted visitors from parting with money.

Skirting the aimless crowds, gift shops and amusement arcade, they wheeled their bikes around the side to recover their energy while looking at the view. Eliza fantasised about flattening all the buildings and planting the headland out as a forest instead.

'You'd still need a car park,' Dido told her.

The view of the Longships rocks and their lighthouse, set in a meringue of surf was fine enough but the famous headland was not nearly so dramatically sharp in rocky reality as it looked on the map. The more exciting cliff scenery of the north and south coasts was plainly visible farther off. As Dido and Eliza sat and gazed, anticlimax settled about them like so much slackening sail.

'I thought it'd be like the prow of a ship,' Dido said. 'And it isn't at all. How do we *know* Land's End's really this bit? It could be there. Or over there, say.' And she looked disdainfully at a couple from Ottawa posing for photographs beneath an artificial crossroads sign pointing to London one way and to the hometown of one's choice in the other, complete with preposterous mileage.

They consoled themselves with ice creams – which were not even Cornish – then Eliza sat and stared at the view while Dido fired off a salvo of postcards to classmates and neighbours. It amazed Eliza to see she not only knew so many people but remembered their addresses and postcodes.

'Who's that?' she asked, seeing one addressed to someone called Naz who lived in their building. (At least Dido had forgotten his surname.)

'Naz,' Dido said simply. 'He lives on the floor below us, opposite corner. He's quite old. He's got a little dog with a funny eye. I help him carry things sometimes when the lift's not working. He's very serious but he's nice.'

It was like catching Dido in unfamiliar clothes or emerging from an unfamiliar house. Eliza knew she ought to be reassured that she had a social life but the glimpse of her niece's independence only made her feel somehow under fire.

Dido coerced her into co-authoring a cheery missive to Kitty then began to stick stamps on the little pile of cards.

'Aren't you writing one to Giles?' Eliza asked.

Dido shrugged and raised her eyebrows to avoid frowning. 'No,' she said. 'Later maybe.'

'Are you two getting on okay?'

'Fine.'

'You did tell him we were coming away?'

'Of course I did,' Dido said with a quick glare. 'He gave me the money, remember?'

'Oh yes.'

'It's just that . . .' Dido looked down at the cards and flicked their edges across her fingertips. She clamped her teeth together and pouted crossly so that her jaw stood out and the obstinate ghost of her mother was only thinly masked.

'What?' Eliza asked, disturbed, anxious to change her expression.

'Stop!' she wanted to say. 'Stop that or the wind might change!'

'Well he's not my father, is he? But sometimes he tries too hard to . . .' Dido frowned again, looked away. 'He's not as nice as he thinks he is.'

'What do you mean? What's he been saying to you?'

'It's okay, Mum. Nothing.'

She only ever called Eliza Mum when she wanted to calm her. Used so rarely, the tiny word was doubly efficacious. It was her elephant dart, capable of flooring the wildest temper. Eliza was always so startled by it that she forgot everything but the momentary pride of being claimed as a parent.

'To hear him go on,' Dido continued, 'you'd think all he did was give but in fact he's quite needy.'

'I thought he had everything,' Eliza said honestly. 'What does he need?'

Dido slid off the bench clutching her cards. 'Oh, you know,' she said casually. 'Stuff. Love. Better post these. Then we can set off again.'

Eliza watched her walk to the postbox and solemnly scrutinise the details of collection times before trusting it with the postcards and was confronted with a brief, terrible vision of her as a kind of child labourer, staggering under a burden of adult wishes.

I should shield her more, she thought. *It's good that we had to come away.*

But then Dido turned from the postbox and strode back, confidently plain, skittish even, robustly putting a clutch of herring gulls to flight, and Eliza saw there was no cause for alarm.

On the way home Dido demanded they break off to climb Chapel Carn Brea, which their route closely circled. The small car park at the hill's foot was deserted but they hid their bikes behind a farm wall to keep them safe. Eliza was far from fit – even cycling on the level had left her breathless – but the path lay up the hill's shallowest side. They climbed gently, breathing the coconut scent of gorse blossom and the butcher's shop whiff of warm bracken.

There was a charred metal beacon at the top, a leftover from the millennium eve celebrations, Dido said, and the land around was so low lying that the summit seemed gratifyingly higher than it probably was. West Cornwall was spread around them like a map; the north and south coasts, Land's End, Penzance and the graceful sweep of Mount's Bay towards the Lizard. Turning the other way they watched a small plane taking off for the Scillies from the grass runway of the tiny airfield then stared beyond it at the sheepy moorland which led down to Zennor and St Ives. The hamlets around each farm or church seemed distributed with perfect evenness among the ancient field patterns. Dido exclaimed at the number of churches. There weren't so many more than in London,

Eliza explained. It was just that the fields between London's villages had all been built on, which blurred the view and hid the towers.

'What's this?' Dido pointed to a stumpy concrete pillar with a brass insert.

'A trig point,' Eliza told her.

'What's it for?'

'Oh God. Erm. To tell you how high you are? To join up with other trig points? O-level Geography. Sorry. I've failed you.'

'That's all right.' Dido looked back at the view. 'You know other things.'

'Down there,' Eliza told her, pointing to the seaward valley beyond the airfield, 'is where Roger Trevescan lived.'

'Your Trevescan? Old Trevescan?'

Eliza nodded.

Dido looked back towards the valley and frowned. 'I thought he lived with Elizabeth I.'

'Well, he spent time at court, yes, and there's even a theory that he was a spy for Walsingham. There were lots of Cornishmen there. Elizabeth said they were 'all born courtiers and with a becoming confidence' which of course, in those days, meant as much that they were trustworthy as that they were brave. But then Trevescan had to leave, under a cloud. So he came home, to the family manor down there, and died protecting his brother's wife in a Spanish raid. I'd always thought they lived nearer Mousehole but then I saw it on the library map yesterday. Where's Kitty's map? Yes. Look. There it is. Vingoe. I suppose Spanish ships could have set down a boatful of men in a little hidden valley like that far more easily than they could sail into Mount's Bay. Or perhaps they were driven apart from the rest and forced to land there so they had to fight their way back to join the others.'

They sat together on a rock, staring towards Trevescan's

heroic last stand. Dido breathed deeply, as she always seemed to when pondering.

'What cloud was he under?' she asked.

Eliza paused only a moment, wondering whether Dido was old enough to know of such things then dismissing her qualms; the girl watched plenty of soap operas at Giles' house.

'He was accused of being gay. Well, they didn't call it that then. They called it effeminacy or sodomy or something. The nobleman who accused him was embarrassed because Trevescan was in love with his brother. So he took the sneaky, patriotic way out by accusing him of being involved with a Spanish envoy instead. People have always had a way of linking gayness with treason. Anyway Trevescan was a good courtier and knew it was also treason to draw a sword in court except in the Queen's defence, so he chose to respect the Queen and be thought a coward and he came back to Cornwall. But of course he proved himself not a coward or a traitor at all, by dying defending his brother's fiancée from the Spanish. It's a good story but it could all be nothing more than gossip.'

'What about the boyfriend?'

'History doesn't relate. I expect he married and settled down. Most men did then. Life tended to be short and dangerous so it was important to have children. Love was a sort of extra. Marriage was about securing property and heirs.'

Dido yawned. Eliza feared she was boring her but Dido jumped up saying, 'Let's go and have a look.'

'There'll be nothing there. I'm not even sure it's the right place; Cornish names tend to repeat themselves. For all we know Vingoe just means *rocky valley* or *vineyard*.'

'No harm in looking, though.'

So they continued their ride around the base of the hill and back past the airfield to where the lane branched off down into the seaward valley. The yellow sign was more clearly visible than when they had been riding from St Just. *Vingoe* it said. And in smaller letters: *Campsite. Showers. Shop. WCs. Pony trekking. No dogs sorry.*

Dipping out of the salt-laden prevailing wind, the valley drew them down to proper, fairly straight trees, ferny banks, the sound of a stream. Two of the cottages they passed had ad hoc plant stalls at their gates, as if the spot had lushness to spare.

Promisingly ancient granite gateposts gave onto a short drive to what had once been a farm. They passed a line of pony trekkers on the way down. The tents and caravans were scattered across one field, mobile homes, smarter, less camouflaged versions of Kitty's retreat, stood in strict order across another. There was a view of a rocky inlet.

Vingoe. Like Manderley, the name had always conjured for Eliza imagery of old, ivy-draped charm, a pillared porch, mullioned windows, the doomy calls of rooks. Instead here was an entirely ordinary house, its walls smoothly rendered and painted white, its sash windows replaced with white plastic ones which added insult to injury by having pseudo glazing bars in the right places while opening the wrong way. There was a proud modern conservatory, a patio marked out in potted pelargoniums, a tidy lack of overshadowing trees. The outbuildings were old, or had been once, but had all been put to new use as communal shower rooms, a WC block, a shop. Only the stable was still a stable. Vingoe proved more of an anticlimax than Land's End had done.

A man emerged, whistling, trailing terriers, from a door marked Reception.

'Can I help you?' he asked.

'Erm. I don't think so,' Eliza began, already turning her front wheel, but Dido chipped in.

'We're looking for Vingoe. My mother's writing a book about Roger Trevescan.'

'Bull's eye,' the man said. 'Not much of it left, though.'
He said they did not normally show people the house but,
since Eliza was writing a book, he would make an exception
for her.

He summoned his wife, a well-maintained woman evidently
adept at delegating, who proudly showed them around. Traces
of the old house remained, all but swallowed by later building:
an exposed granite lintel, an inglenook fireplace, a cramped
back staircase. There was a well in what had once been a
courtyard but was now roofed over as a ping-pong and pool
room. The well was glazed in and the wife smartly flicked a
switch to turn on a green spotlight in its dank and mossy
interior.

'And this is the Betrothal Window. It's all old glass,
see?'

It was an old mullion window but its glass wasn't old at all.
It was nearly all Victorian, to judge by the intense colouring of
the stained panels and olde worlde leading but Eliza feigned
interest out of politeness.

'Why *betrothal*?' she asked and the woman drew attention
to one pane, probably once obscure but now repositioned at
the window's gaudy centre.

It was a diamond lozenge of clear glass whose drippy
inconsistencies would have marked it out as older than the
rest even without the scratches made on it: *RT&MS1595*. Eliza
leaned closer so that her breath misted the glass.

'Did Roger Trevescan write that, then?' Dido asked.

'No, my beauty,' the woman said. 'He was dead by then.
Died fighting off the Spanish. This was Robert, his brother
and Mary Semmens, who married that year.'

Eliza had seen such initials and graffiti many times before,
carved in glass with diamond rings or in stone pillars or choir
stalls with patient penknives. As in other cases, this one had
doubtless been gone over with more professional tools in later

years but the original could only be gone over afresh, not erased, so there was no reason to doubt that the design, the letters and date were a tracing at least of the sixteenth-century original.

Dido was restlessly unimpressed and the woman wanted her house back so Eliza pulled herself back to the present and followed them out to the front door.

Within, however, she felt the way she had in the Bodleian Library once when a librarian handed her a small box tied with grubby ribbon, as casually as he might have passed over last week's Sunday papers. And she had sat at her desk and opened the box and taken out a drably bound first edition of Byrd's *Songs and Sonets*. It was, she told herself, only paper, just as the carved window pane was only glass, paper not so very different from that used today. But it was paper made in the sixteenth century, printed in the 1590s and fingered and sung over if not by Byrd himself then quite possibly by a member of Elizabeth's court. Stone was different. One thought little of climbing steps or walking courtyards climbed and walked centuries before by legendary figures but paper was so very vulnerable, so apt to soak up sweat, grease, blood, wine splashes, that each reader left behind their own impression on it.

'Is anybody there? Hello?'

'Sorry,' Eliza said. She had ridden home in a silent daze and had still been miles away as they ate the pasties bought at the Vingoe campsite shop. And now she was sun-dazed as well and Dido was staring at her expectantly. 'Did you say something?'

'What are you going to wear?' Dido said.

'When?'

'For your date this evening.'

'God, I'd clean forgotten! It's not a date anyway. You'll be there.'

'It's still a date. What have you got that's nice?'

'Nothing. I dunno. Nothing probably. It's not a date, Dido, honestly. We're just going there for supper.'

'You don't remember his name, even. Do you?'

'*Pearce did dance with Petronella*. He's called Pearce.'

'You're hopeless.'

'So you choose, if it matters so much.'

Dido stared for a moment then thought better of what she was going to say and went inside to riffle with judicious scorn through Eliza's clothes.

Overcome by the sun, the bike ride, the weight of pasty in her belly and the sense that her life was undergoing one of its periodic convulsions, Eliza fell deeply asleep.

She had no vivid sense of his face. Giles and Paul had left immediate, strong impressions, the one of angelic perfection the other of ugly sexiness. She had noted that he had dark, curly hair and a labourer's deep tan but when Dido woke her saying it was time to get ready, Eliza felt a mounting fear that all she could recall with any clarity were his big, battered hands and rumble of a voice.

While she was sleeping Dido had cycled to St Just's chemist shop and returned with fancy shampoo. She had also bought some cunning tape which one pressed to one's dampened nose and forehead for a few minutes then peeled off to find it peppered with tiny stalagmites of gunk from every dirt-clogged pore. Eliza stated once more that this was simple socialising, not a romantic fixture, then gave in and allowed Eliza to fuss and minister like an ambitious duenna, washing her hair at the sink and peeling off the blackhead tape with little squeals of disgusted delight.

Dido made her dress as soberly as a governess, in a not very crisp white blouse and a navy blue, ankle length skirt. The strict effect was softened by the skirt being light and swishy and having tiny mirrors sewn into the embroidery around its hem.

'I don't remember this,' Eliza said. 'I haven't worn skirts for years. When did I buy this?'

'Kitty and I did. We found it in a hippy shop in Camborne while you were sorting the house out. Put it on. It'll suit you. You wear jeans too often. Men don't like it.'

'How do *you* know what men don't like? And who says I have to please them?'

'Just try it on.'

'And I haven't shaved my legs in ages.'

'Why not?'

Freshly aware of them, Eliza rubbed a big toe on the fine blonde hairs that she wore like a pair of footless tights. Dido giggled.

'Well . . . I dunno. I didn't see the need.'

'There's no time for that now. Or is there?'

'No!'

'The skirt's long anyway so it doesn't matter.'

Eliza obliged her. She felt naked with the sudden draughtiness about her legs but Dido was right. The skirt did suit her. She had always thought long skirts made her look like a pepper pot but this one seemed to make her tall and slim.

'Are you sure, though?' she asked, craning her neck in a clumsy effort to see the effect reflected in the soap-spattered fragment of mirror.

But then there was the sudden booming of a Land Rover turning off onto their track and it was too late to change again.

He was taller and broader than Eliza had remembered and his accent more bluntly Cornish. His hair, which she remembered as Byronically dark, was shot through with reassuring silver. His eyes wrinkled as he said hello and she saw the way they quickly took in her clean but still damp hair and the unfamiliar line of her skirt.

She had read once that it was important to keep one's appearance consistent when getting to know someone new and not to bewilder them with shifting colour schemes, worrying variations of heel height or changing perfume, as though blurred early impressions could never coalesce into a unified and adorable whole. If that were so then they had both flouted the advice.

He seemed wonderfully clean. His thick hair, which he had evidently tried to tame with a comb, was still damp at the ends, like hers. His nails had been clipped almost to the quick. A few tiny drops of blood in his beard-line betrayed the thoroughness with which he had just shaved. As they shook hands, it was not the subtle stink of some aftershave Eliza breathed off him but the sinless white tang of soap.

'It's bigger than it looks from the outside,' he said, looking about him at Kitty's den.

'Did you come up here in your misspent teens?'

He stared a moment then caught her meaning and smiled to himself. 'Molly was the wild one,' he admitted. 'Not me. But I had mates who came here sometimes.'

They fell silent and Eliza watched as he stooped to shyly read the titles on the bookshelf. It was left to Dido to chip in. 'Shall we go, then?'

They climbed into the Land Rover. (Perhaps reassuringly, this had not been cleaned.) Dido, who had clambered into the rear, immediately hung forward between the adults to ask questions. Having her daughter along on a date was an entirely new experience for Eliza. If asked cold, she would have said it was a lousy idea, bound to cause everyone involved discomfort. Something about him made her shy, however. The scent of soap, maybe. Soap seemed to suggest a hope of getting close, which in turn made her conscious that she rather liked the idea, which in turn froze her with self-consciousness. Did she smell funny? Were her fuzzy legs showing? She felt her skin had a Londoner's sickly pallor, that her voice, if she spoke, would sound over-cultured and silly. So she was grateful for Dido's inquisitive chatter.

With no understanding of what she was doing beyond satisfying her own curiosity, Dido played the role of a mother with daughters of marriageable age, asking the questions that might have seemed too forward in Eliza's mouth. Thus on the short drive down the hill to his farm Eliza was able passively to learn that he was younger than his weather-beaten face – forty-two – that the farm had two hundred and fifty acres, which was just small enough for him to manage with only seasonal assistance and that it had been in his family for at least two centuries. And no, his herd had suffered no foot and mouth or BSE.

They turned off sharply at Kelynack down Cot Valley along a lane which, like the one to Vingoe, seemed to enjoy a microclimate. Sheltered, sycamore and Cornish elm thrived on either side and the few cottages they passed had gardens lush with tender foliage. Then the road became a dirt track which crossed a stream, affording a brief glimpse of the sea before crossing a cattle grid and climbing the valley to a point where it levelled out into a farmyard.

The house, whose walls were thickly carpeted with some creeper that fluttered in the breeze, was long and low, as though the builder were used to the idiom of stables and sties and saw no reason to adapt his style for humans. The only unbarnlike detail was the way one end turned a sharp corner so as to capture enough shelter and warmth for a small, low-walled garden.

'How old is it?' Dido asked.

'Two or three hundred probably,' Pearce said. 'Before that the house was over there, where I store the corn.' He gestured across the yard to a small, two storey building with a flight of stone steps up its outside, dwarfed by the grain silo which was linked to it by a length of pipe.

'It's so quiet,' Eliza said.

'Except when the auger's going,' he said. 'Or one of the tractors. Or the planes to the Scillies . . . And on sunny days all the amateurs are up there too in their microlites and what have yous.'

But it was quiet now. Despite the proximity of the sea, the air seemed still and expectant and the only sounds were the urgent conversation of swallows on a telephone wire that crossed the yard and the confidential murmurs of two brown hens scratching in the grass beneath a laden apple tree. The tree dominated one side of the little garden, which was otherwise given over to unkempt and sprawling lavender bushes.

Dido was wary of the hens until Pearce showed her how to lure them up the ramp into their little hutch for the night with a handful of corn.

The interior of the house was dark after the dazzle of outside. As her eyes adjusted, Eliza made out quantities of heavy mahogany furniture, which were surely inherited rather than chosen, and a scattering of watercolours in chipped gilt frames. Rather than fight the shadiness, he had perversely courted it with rich dark colours on the walls, a tobaccoey red, olive green.

'Typical farmers,' he said, seeing her eyes trailing round. 'They only thought of how it would be when they came in after dark. No thought for the poor souls stuck inside in the gloom all day.'

'So do hens lay eggs out of their backsides or where?' Dido asked. She had never been brought to make the connection between egg and chicken before and Eliza foresaw months of squeamish abstinence from one of their cheaper staples.

'Not exactly,' Pearce told her, grinning. 'I'll find you a

book.' And he left Dido poring over a fowl husbandry manual while he went to open a bottle of wine.

They ate almost immediately. He clearly was unused to entertaining and gave Eliza the impression that it was something he wanted out of the way as soon as possible. In his apprehension that they might run out of food, he had cooked far too much. Everything had been made in advance and left in the warming oven of the range so that it might be served with bewildering speed. It was good food – carrot soup, a simply roast chicken with salad and potatoes, a cherry crumble with clotted cream – but his nervousness left little room to enjoy it. Eliza was aghast that he had unwittingly cooked two of the things – carrots and cherries – that Dido could not abide and was amazed to see her eat both without demur and even politely accept his offer of seconds. But perhaps she was helped in her politeness by his failure to provide anything softer than watered red wine for her to drink.

The night was still young and the sky not quite dark when they left the table for coffee in the ochre-coloured sitting room but Dido was soon fast asleep on a little sofa below the open window. For a few minutes a pregnant silence descended on them. Without Dido single-handedly keeping the conversation going, the two adults became painfully shy. But then a huge, white cat came through the open window and settled on Dido's stomach, purring loudly.

'Sorry. Is she allergic?' Pearce asked.

'No. I don't think so, anyway.'

'She's an amazing kid. Is she ever short of something to say?'

'Only when reading or asleep. Or sulking.'

'Could I ask . . .' he asked then. 'Does she take after her mother or her father?'

'Oh, well, we never knew who her father was,' Eliza began then found she could not check herself. His face was so wholesome and unjudging and the wine had so relaxed her that she began to tell him about Hannah's death and that somehow flowed quite naturally into a description of Giles and her marriage. The only thing she held back was any real depiction of Hannah; with the natural egotism of the drunk, she made a narrative entirely about herself.

Pearce kept her wine topped up and said nothing beyond the occasional, encouraging, 'What was he thinking of?' or 'How did you manage?' And his eyes were so very kind and his tone of voice so very comfortable and his accent so like the best sort of homecoming that she found herself leading the way to the other sofa where she was so relaxed, so utterly herself, that not content with telling him about the affair with Paul and the better, sadder, more sorry part of her life's story, she started to cry.

27

The timing could not have been better. Giles had one more morning of rehearsal then the *répétiteur* and choreographer were to be forced to work for a week only on the scenes for the Mechanicals and the lovers, giving the three principal fairies a week off while Dewi Evans and Grover flew to Jamaica to shoot a video for Dewi's new single. Being freed for this was a condition of Grover's accepting the commission. Plainly his ability to make Dewi part of the production was what induced the opera management to accept what would normally have been unacceptable.

It was an oddly placid opera for Giles to work on. While the lovers scurried about and fought and wept he had little to do but glide in and out and look powerful. Even when enraged, Oberon was essentially static. Compared to the spite, heroics and vocal acrobatics of so many baroque roles, it was a breeze to sing. He had a superb Titania – a voluptuous young Frenchwoman whom he suspected was out of his league or would be within a couple of seasons. He had become used to Dewi's omnivorous flirtatiousness and the conductor was entirely trustworthy.

He was trying not to think about the costumes, or lack of them, and suspected the clamorous rumours were planted by Grover's team to whip up a frenzy of anticipation among jaded punters for whom a glimpse of a pop star's buttocks was more exciting than one of musical paradise. As insurance, however, he had doubled his daily abdominal workout to the point where it sometimes hurt when he breathed.

Selina was beside herself with pleasure, apparently, though being Selina her pleasure manifested itself as a kind of threat. 'This is going to be huge, Giles,' she kept saying. 'Huge. Up there with Miller's *Rigoletto* and Hockney's *Rake*. Just so long as nobody loses their nerve again and buggers it up.'

He did not like to point out that the productions she cited were all about a certain look or a certain director and that nobody now could name their original casts.

Julia put in a morning's work too then he picked her up in a taxi with their bags. They had not taken a holiday in months. They both worked hard, certainly, and then there was Dido to consider, since he did not feel he could whisk her away from Eliza for longer than a weekend. But he worried sometimes that their official line, that they much preferred a pampering long weekend here and there to a prolonged stay in one place masked their fear at what fault-lines a longer holiday without company might expose. Even this trip was not truly a holiday, of course, but work for her and duty for him with a pampering weekend attached.

Subsidised by the agency, they were able to fly most of the way on the little plane that shuttled a day long triangle between Gatwick, Plymouth and Newquay. Their fellow passengers seemed to be a strange mixture of business people calling on concerns in the south-west and south-westerners wealthy enough to use a plane service for an indulgent trip to the capital. At Newquay they hired a car and were skirting the beach at Polteath and heading up the north coast to Trenellion within the hour.

Poor Julia had been sick while they were waiting and again during the flight. She said nothing of it and insisted she was fine when he asked, although he could tell she was anything but. The effort of appearing fine left her tense. It was so like her. Whereas he knew he made heavy weather of even the lightest cold, she could not bear to be ill and treated even food poisoning or travel sickness as admissions of weakness. He took the sharp corners more slowly than if driving alone. When he pressed the button to wind down her window a little, he saw how she drew in lungfuls of sea air.

On the recommendation of Jemima Beale, the violist Julia was looking after, they had reservations in a small, isolated hotel one bay around from St Jacobs at Porth Keverne. It must once have been a tiny inn for fishermen but had grown a room or two at a time up the hillside and back towards the valley behind it. In place of fishermen the bar was hearty with people in fishermen's jerseys, naval blazers or quaintly nautical smocks. A late cancellation meant that they had a perfect room, up a narrow flight of stairs off the bar, lined with grisly photographs of shipwrecks. The bed was soft and squeaky and sounds of merriment would certainly rise through the floor at night, but there was a wide open window with a window seat and the walls were dazzling with light off the sand and water.

Julia emerged from the bathroom smelling freshly of Arpège and collapsed onto the bed, an arm across her eyes. 'Sorry,' she said. 'I'm never normally sick. I think it's because it was so small. The plane. I'll be fine in a while. Don't mind me. Go for a walk on the coast path or something.'

'Ssh,' he told her. He lifted her feet onto his lap and slipped off her shoes.

'I should unpack,' she said. 'My dress'll get crumpled.'

'Ssh. It's not a remotely dressy festival.' He began to rub her feet slowly between the palms of his hands.

He kissed them one at a time. They were warm but dry. She moaned faintly. She had an unvoiced passion for having her toes very gently parted and sucked. She was still in her work clothes. He reached up and began to slide off her tights as the room filled with an outburst of gull cries.

The forty-seven women he had slept with – and he prided himself on knowing precisely how many of them there were, if not on recalling all their names or faces – fell into two camps. One lot had not been able to arouse him immediately. Not that drunkenly snogging Villiers Yates once made him remotely gay but he had needed some trigger, their kiss, their tears, or merely, reprehensively, the thought of himself having sex with them. The second, much smaller group was his proof that there was such a thing as body chemistry, for he had only to be near them, close enough to breathe the warm air off their skin, to be aroused beyond recall.

Eliza, whom he had loved deeply and felt as protective towards as of his own flesh and blood, was in the crowded first group. Julia was in the exclusive second. He felt little emotional engagement with her when he was elsewhere but he had only to be sitting like this, her bare feet in his lap, her dress sliding back off her crazily smooth legs, to be her single-minded slave.

28

The restaurant at The Porth Keverne Hotel prided itself on an immunity to fashion. Wood-fired ovens, cuisine minceur, nouvelle cuisine, Pacific Rim, coriander, lemon grass, even the sun-dried tomato went unmentioned on its menu. Brandy and cream were much in evidence as were flambéed dishes, Cona coffee machines and red napkins. Loyal diners could rest assured they would be offered favourites long lost elsewhere; Steak Diane, Beef Stroganoff and Sole Veronique were served unseasoned by irony.

The local resorts, like Polteath, were intimidatingly youthful these days, slick with twenty-something surfers whose idea of dining was a tortilla wrap and a fruit smoothie in the beach car park. But here, Julia saw as soon as they came in, she and Giles were the youngest in the room by at least a decade.

They were nearly late for last orders so she had no time for more than a quick wash before they dressed and hurried down. She had dabbed on some scent but felt the whole room could tell they had just made love.

'Everyone's staring,' she murmured to Giles, scanning the menu in vain for a simple piece of grilled fish.

'That's because you're better than TV,' he said, tapping his knee between hers. 'You've got a glow.'

She touched her cheeks. 'Don't,' she said. 'You'll make it worse. It's a vampire's ball.'

'Vee can't help it,' he murmured, 'if you taste zo gut.' And he discreetly sniffed two of his fingers then slid them into his mouth.

'Stop it!' she laughed. 'We should order. It's late.'

'Shall I order for you?' he asked.

'Why?'

'I want the lobster and it's for two.'

'But it's so . . . oh okay. Why not?'

'Yes, we'd like to order please,' Giles said. The passing waitress, who had not even been looking their way was immediately all attention. It was an old trick of his, a trick of the voice or merely the self-belief of good looks, which always got him served as soon as he stepped up to a bar or looked for a waiter.

'We'll drink a bottle of number twenty-seven, the Pouilly Fuissé. And we'll have the lobster Thermidor.'

He wasn't paying for this, Selina was, but he made it feel as though the money were his and she liked that; travelling for work tended to be so unsexy. She was naturally so much more controlling than he was that she loved it when he took the whip hand for a change.

'So tell me your plans,' he said. 'What happens tomorrow?'

'Jemima's rehearsing with the orchestra late in the morning,' she said, 'so I ought to sit in on that. Give me a chance to say hello. Then Selina told me to take her and Peter Grenfell and his wife out for lunch if they're free. They've got nothing on until the concert. You could come.'

He pulled a face, reminding her that his experience of the festival had not left a happy taste.

'Or you could take yourself off to be a tourist,' she suggested. 'Just hook up with me in the evening.'

'Would you mind?'

'Not at all.'

'It's only I really should head over to Camborne to see how Annie's doing.'

'Who?'

'Eliza's mum. I thought I told you.'

'Oh yes.'

'You don't mind?'

'Why should I? No. I mean I really don't. I won't need the car again if you drop me at the church on your way. There'll be plenty of other drivers.'

This was true. Whatever the busman's holiday ethos of the festival, she preferred to keep business and home life separate and she knew she could not pay Jemima her full attention if Giles – a client too – was fretting about issues of his own. It would be a relief not to have to split herself in two.

'We should do this more often,' he said a little later, watching her eat the meat he had retrieved for her from one of the lobster's last unplundered crevices. 'I love coming away with you. Hotels get me horny.'

'What, again?'

'Especially when I can look around and know we're the only ones here who are getting it. And you know how seafood affects me.'

'Giles . . .'

'Oh please, Babe.' He lowered his voice. 'You could just lie there. You could pretend to be asleep. You could slip upstairs first and leave the door on the latch and then I could come up in half an hour or so and pretend to break into your room. You pretend to be asleep and I'll be a complete stranger.'

'What if I want crème brulée?'

He knew calling her Babe always weakened her. Under cover of the layers of heavy red tablecloth he had slipped off one of his deck shoes and now slid his foot between her legs, resting his heel on the front of her chair and flexing his toes where it mattered. Playfully and no less surreptitiously, she closed her thighs, trapping his foot there as their waitress returned to the table.

'Would you like any coffee, at all?' she asked with the upward inflexion Giles found so maddening when Dido used it. 'Or a brandy perhaps?'

Watching Giles' face, Julia clutched and relaxed her thighs then clutched again.

'Yes, please,' Giles said. 'I'll have both. But my wife's a little tired so . . .'

'I'm a little tired,' she told the waitress.

'I'll take them in the bar,' Giles said and the waitress left them.

'What'll it be?' Julia asked, tweaking down her skirt as she stood. A few of the other diners had fallen to playing bridge at their cleared tables, she noticed. 'Nightdress, dressing gown, towel or nothing?'

'Surprise me,' he told her. 'You're not expecting me, remember?'

She returned to their room. A chambermaid had been in to remake the disordered bed and had closed the window and drawn the curtains. The room felt stifling again so Julia opened both.

. She knew that he liked to think himself smutty but that he was in practice quite fastidious. She had a hot shower, using no soap, then turned out the light and arranged herself on the bed on her front, covered only in a cold sheet. His rape fantasies were wholly unrealistic for he liked her as prone and unassertive as a corpse. It would have been quite wrong to have put up a fight. She pictured his face if he came in to find her sitting up in bed as she normally slept when staying in a hotel on her own, buttoned into her flannel nightie, face slicked with night cream, reading a trashy novel and enjoying a nightcap and a bar of Toblerone from the minibar. She pictured his face if she told him they were going to become parents.

She heard his nervous throat-clearing on the stairs and tweaked the sheet down off her buttocks then shut her eyes and pretended to sleep. She tried to still her thoughts but they kept rampaging off into anti-erotic territory. She tried to imagine herself as a lovely statue, marble cool, but all that came to mind was that Giles had never seen Eliza pregnant, never had her press his hand on her belly and whisper, 'Feel! He's kicking!' For all she knew, Eliza had married him as a virgin mother.

The door opened, causing a rush of sea air through the window which made her shiver. The sheet sliding further off her thighs tickled and raised goose pimples. With no preamble he was pressing her face hard down into the pillows and thrusting into her from behind.

29

It was a disaster. Pearce had made her cry. Her child had done all the talking while she got drunk and now she was crying. The date could not have gone worse if she had turned out to be vegetarian or he had fed the child something that sent her into anaphylactic shock.

He glanced across nervously as Eliza blew her nose but was relieved to see the girl still sound asleep, gently kneaded by Simkin. No one should see their mother like this.

'Don't cry,' he told her ineffectually. He held out her wine glass. 'Have something to drink.'

She took it with a little, absent-minded moan, handing back his sodden handkerchief, and gulped the wine as if it were water. Then she covered her face with one hand and looked as though she were about to drop the empty glass with the other, so he took it from her. Both hands covered her face now and she took deep, slow breaths. The storm of tears had subsided.

He had seen the moment he stopped off to collect them that this evening meant something to her because she had made an effort. Compared to how it had been the night before, her hair was brushed into sleekness and tied back with a rag of blue velvet that matched her long, witchy skirt with the glittery hem. Then, by the time they reached the house, he had realised she wasn't interested in him at all but was merely being polite. She came from another world, a clever, bookish one, and he was a sort of anthropological specimen, nothing more. She had listened as she might to a garrulous Greek fisherman or a *Big Issue* seller or a mad old lady on a bus. The child had picked up on this clearly, which was why she kept up her nervous patter of questions.

And he had cooked too much. Far too much. Cooked enough to feed four hungry labourers, not a skinny woman and child. And seeing the groaning table, the child had politely accepted second helpings she must have had to force down. And he had forgotten to buy anything non-alcoholic for her so had probably made her sick with unaccustomed wine.

But then Eliza had quite unexpectedly come out with all this . . . this *stuff* about her dead mother and her wayward sister and her marriage and her infidelity; a dreadful story. It horrified him that she should come out with it in front of the child who, thank God, was asleep. It disturbed him even more than Janet smoking all over her little boy the other night. And the rest. But worse was his anticipation of how much she would regret telling him all this, undoing in minutes her careful show of distant poise. He had thought she was a sort of nymph, a lovely, clever alien when in fact she was a mess, what Molly would call *a human bomb*.

So now he felt protective towards her, not that he would ever have a chance to tell her, as well as embarrassed at how he had misread her, and angry too. Not that he could tell her that either.

Before she started crying, she had spoken casually about how she had come to be raising her sister's child and made it sound like a burden rather than a blessing and he wanted to say, 'Careful! She might be listening.'

The angle of her head changed, slumping forward slightly.

'Eliza?' he said. 'Hello?'

She was asleep.

'Eliza?' he said a little louder. She breathed deeply then made a comfortable, settling sound, like Simkin when stroked in his sleep. 'Dido?' The child did not stir either. Only the cat looked up, with a startled chirrup, and ever hopeful of food, dashed, purring, to the kitchen. Pearce remembered they had been for a bike ride. Sea air and exercise then food and red wine was a powerfully narcotic combination.

Pearce slipped upstairs to check on the bedrooms. Three were chaotic with displaced furniture but his old bedroom and the spare room he still thought of as his grandmother's room were usable and had been aired last month after he repainted them. He quickly made up the beds, cursing Simkin for having slept in the airing cupboard at some stage leaving white hair all over one of the sheets.

When he came down, Eliza had drawn her feet up onto her chair so it was easy to slip his arms around her back and under her knees to lift her. She was not heavy but she flopped disconcertingly with the total relaxation of a sleeping child and he worried she was going to bang her head on something. It was like carrying a dead person. His grandmother's bedsprings twanged as he lowered her onto the mattress and Eliza murmured peacefully. He slid off her shoes then pulled the sheet and blanket over her, adding the quilt as an afterthought because she was not used to the country and it might feel cold after London. Then he could not resist untying the velvet that held her hair back. He held the fabric to his face but it smelled of nothing. Nothing human. Shampoo perhaps. The temptation to kiss her was intense so he pulled her curtains, backed out and quietly shut the door.

Dido was not where he left her. He found her in the kitchen, watching Simkin drink a saucer of cream. 'Where's Eliza?' she asked.

'I put her to bed. She's a bit tired.'

'Oh. Are we staying here, then?'

'Looks like it. For tonight. I didn't like to drive her home like that.'

'Was she drunk?'

'No. Not really. Tired.'

'Was she sad?'

'A bit.'

Dido yawned, leaning against a table leg. 'Don't worry,' she said. 'She'll be fine in the morning.'

'Oh. Good. Time you were in bed too.'

'Suppose so.'

'Come on.' He held out a hand to heave herself up on.

'Your hands are huge,' she said.

He laughed. 'That's just farming. The more heavy things you lift, the bigger they get. They sort of flatten out, like pastry.' He looked at them.

Unabashed, she took one and spread her own palm against it to compare. Her hand was hot and damp. 'If I farmed, would mine get like yours?'

'Maybe. Come on. Bedtime.'

'Can Simkin come too?'

'Oh, he goes where he likes. He's in and out most of the night hunting but leave your door ajar and he'll probably find you before morning. He's a bit heavy on a single bed though.'

'I don't mind. Do you mind us staying?'

'No.'

'But you weren't expecting it.'

He smiled. 'No. But it's a nice surprise.'

'Good. Do I have to brush my teeth?'

'Have you got a brush?'

'Course not.'

'No, then.'

She went to the bathroom then he showed her to her room. His old room. He offered her his one-eared rabbit to sleep with until Simkin appeared but she shamed him by asking if she could borrow a book instead and read for a bit. So he left her reading *Finn Family Moomintroll*.

Putting away uneaten food, turning out lights and locking front and back doors, he was startled to find that it felt entirely normal. This was a house that required more than one person in it. He never had people to stay. Now that he had, he found he was already dreading having the house to himself again.

30

Eliza woke with a start to find herself lying on a strange bed. She was still dressed but someone had slipped off her sandals and drawn a soft old patchwork quilt over her. Morning sun shone through the thin floral curtains revealing the shadow of the cat, who was chattering through his teeth in impotent rage as he watched swallows on the wire outside.

She dimly recalled Pearce's blunt words of comfort but nothing of him putting her to bed. Had he carried her? She pictured his tender concentration as he manoeuvred her snoring body through doorways and staircase, careful not to bump her head or bark her knuckles. Was this his mother's room?

She took in the faded chintz armchair, the dressing table mirror speckled with age, the pair of green glass candlesticks, the framed sampler carefully hung where the hot morning sun could not fade it. *Tell me where I can find a friend both good and true, who tastes my joys but shares my burdens too. Ruth Dorcas Pender. 10 yrs. 1949.*

There was a sudden thundering sound and the cat jumped off the windowsill and hurried through the open door with a mew. Eliza peered through the crack in the curtains to see the yard briefly fill with creamy coloured cattle. Pearce was walking behind them, driving them placidly out the other side with low murmurs and an occasional hissing between his teeth. He looked up as he passed but she stood back from the window, forgetting she was dressed.

She followed the cat out onto a long, sunny landing that ran the length of the house, lit by a double height window on the stairs. In search of the bathroom and Dido, she found three cluttered spare bedrooms, their striped mattresses bare, their air so undisturbed that entering felt intrusive. Then she found his room, its window open to birdsong and the rustling of creeper leaves.

The first impression was of tidiness but there was a reassuring heap of discarded clothes – the clean ones he had on last night – flung across a chair and the toe of a boot protruded from a walk-in cupboard in the corner in a way that suggested disorder hastily contained. He had somehow made the bed look like a single, perhaps by having only one bedside table. There was no looking glass, either here or in the bathroom, where she washed her face awake and attempted to brush her teeth with borrowed toothpaste and a finger.

There was a note for her on the kitchen table, propped up between bread and butter dish. The handwriting was cramped and forward sloping.

Dido said she wanted to go to the last day of school with Lucy so I dropped her off. She said you could amuse yourself. Didn't wake you – thought a lie in might do you good! Will be in and out of the yard all morning for when you want a lift back up the hill. Pearce.

Amused at Dido's electing to return to school, any school, rather than prolong her unofficial holiday a day further, Eliza buttered a thick slice of floury white bread and poured herself a mug of the stewed tea from the pot. Glancing around the kitchen, she wondered for a moment what it reminded her of, then realised it was Mrs Tiggywinkle's house, complete with range, cluttered mantelshelf and dresser that came so close to the ceiling it might have been built in situ. Mrs Tiggywinkle, however, did not have old copies of CLA newsletters and *Farmer's Weekly* displacing her tea service or a filthy Ivomec wormer-dispenser rubbing shoulders with her cereal packets.

Eliza relaxed back on her chair, chewing, as she flicked through a copy of *Farmer's Weekly*. As in any specialist magazine there were countless niche-market advertisements, these ones being astonishingly crude and to the point. There was an amazing number of photographs of people crouching on grass or among plants, awkwardly posed with one arm gesturing towards an offending weed or prized new crop. The pictures varied little when an animal not a plant was included. Even in a picture of a farmer who had taken to breeding alpacas the pose was the same. She wondered if perhaps the same busy photographer took all the pictures and gave out the same patient instructions. *Yes. That's it. On one knee. Now one arm out, please. Just the job!*

The vast majority of the pictures were of men although, judging from the letters page, many of the readers were women. Was this, perhaps, an unofficial way of finding wives? She looked more closely and, sure enough, the farmers described as *farming with his parents* or *farming in partnership with his brother* and making no mention of wives or children were often in cleaner clothes than the rest or had taken obvious pains with their hair or backdrop. Some pictures carried a subtle subtext; *fond of small animals, likes flowers* or simply *has a good head of hair like his father*. Read in this light, what had seemed dry became strangely moving.

She stood and walked around the ground floor trying to work out why this house felt so different from other men's houses she had known, most obviously Giles' slightly controlling elegance and Paul's no less contrived intellectual shabbiness. Unlike them, she realised, Pearce had not felt the need to leave his mark or erase those of predecessors. It was a family home in the truest sense. He had not even spoken of it with any great sense of ownership. When, in the course of her interrogation, Dido had asked him the farm's precise acreage he humoured her, giving a precise answer broken down into pasture, rough and cultivated hectares.

'And you own all that?' she had asked. 'Does that make you rich?'

'Not really,' he had said. 'It's not as though I paid for it. I certainly couldn't afford it if I had to. It's more that I'm holding it in trust. Looking after it.'

'Who for?'

'Whoever comes next.'

When Dido had fearlessly pointed out that he had no children, he had laughed shyly to himself and looked away to pour more wine by way of changing the subject.

There was a harmonium at the foot of the stairs. The *Oxford Madrigal Book* lay on top of a heap of music that included *Hymns Ancient and Modern, The Methodist Hymnal* and a dusty volume that was surely the same age as the harmonium called *Songs That Will Live Forever.*

Eliza pulled up a chair, opened the keyboard and began to pump the pedals. She started to play one of the few Bach preludes she had from heart, a slow, minor key one. But the technique of pumping the pedals regardless of the beat, to keep the bellows full, while producing a legato action with her fingers was beyond her and she broke off.

'Don't stop,' he said. He was leaning in the front door-way.

'I'm hopeless,' she said. 'It needs the coordination of a chimp.'

'You're better than me.'

'Don't you play it then?'

'Only with one finger. I pick out the bass lines on it when Molly wants us to sing something new. Mum played. She was deputy organist up in St Just. That's where Molly got her music from. She taught us our letters with one hand and how to read music with the other. Sleep all right?'

'Yes. Fine, thanks.' Suddenly the embarrassment of the previous night loomed up but Pearce seemed cheerfully oblivious.

'Hope you didn't mind me taking the little one off like that but she was determined. Wouldn't let me wake you, either.'

'No. That was fine. Is it legal, though?'

'Doesn't matter if it isn't. Lucy's form teacher's a sort of cousin. She won't mind one extra. It'll make up for all the truants she gets among the farm kids at this time of year. Do you want to see that song, then? Seeing as Dido says you're an expert.'

'Oh, Dido'll say anything.'

'Well you know more about it than anyone else round here.'

'All right then.'

'You'd better take it down. My hands are a bit dirty. It's up there. In the Bible.' He indicated a large Bible with a handsome leather and gilt binding, much eaten by time and worms.

Eliza set it down at one end of the dining table and opened it at random. It was a handsome thing, eighteenth-century, to judge from the typesetting. She looked up, frowning.

'It's at the back,' he explained, going into the kitchen to wash the grime off his hands.

The weight of the pages was such that turning the entire text over at once threatened to tear the binding even further. She fetched a cushion from the sofa and set the book's spine on that before opening it out again, turning to the back more gently.

There were several unprinted pages at either end of this edition, possibly placed there at the request of whoever first had the Bible bound as a wedding or baptism gift. Eliza was so shocked by what she saw there that she had to sit down. There were five sheets of paper pasted onto five consecutive blank pages. This was much older paper than that in the Bible, thick and yellowed. She swiftly recognised the five handwritten voice parts of the untitled, anonymous madrigal Molly's group called *Country Goodness*. The notes and text were minute but electrifying.

There were only two surviving documents in Trevescan's hand that Eliza knew of. One, in Trinity College, Dublin, was a lute song setting, *As Night from Daye, As Moonlight from the Sunne*. The other, in the Bodleian, was a letter written from court to his brother. Everything else, all the other music, was known only in published form. Along with his rumoured homosexuality, one of the reasons for the assumption that Trevescan had been trained up as one of Walsingham's spies was his habit of destroying evidence. In the first year of her research, Eliza had flown to Dublin and studied the lute song manuscript at length. (Although she was too poverty-stricken at the time to stay overnight in Dublin and had dozed in airports in either direction.) She had pored over the letter in the Bodleian times without number. There was so little to them that it was easy to know both intimately. The provenance of each was both credible and minutely detailed. Trevescan's handwriting had few tics but he favoured a Greek E, which was rare enough at the time, and wrote his Qs in a unique fashion, like an astrologer's Venus symbol without its horizontal line. The two tics together were as clamorous as any signature and even more trustworthy. And here they were, combined in a single word, *quieter*, towards the end of

261

the second verse whose text, as was customary, was written at the bottom of the page, without notes, as in a hymn book or Psalter. *A second, quieter love.*

'We had no idea it was there.'

She was so absorbed, she had not sensed his approach. 'Where . . .' She was threatening to squeak in her excitement. She swallowed, controlled herself, withdrew her hands in case they left sweat stains on the precious pages. 'Where did they come from?'

Pearce shrugged. 'Lord knows. It's full of stuff people used to stick in there. Locks of baby's hair. Pressed flowers. Birth certificates. Even a recipe or two. But not glued in like those. I suppose whoever put those in didn't want to lose them.'

Glue. She had not thought. She looked back at the precious pages. Sure enough, each was firmly glued in place. Depending on how long ago the pages were fixed in, this might be anything from flour and water to boiled cow hoof. She ran her fingertips round the rough, torn edge of the cantus part. Glue was so useful and so swiftly destructive.

'How did you know how to transcribe it all?' she asked Pearce. 'If you can only play one-fingered? I mean these are alto and tenor clefs! Many professionals can't read these without some practice.'

'Neither could I,' he said. 'I just used trial and error, kept shifting it up and down a tone or two until I found a good fit. It's over here, look.'

He went to the pile of music on the harmonium and retrieved a clutch of manuscript paper on which he had laboriously made out a fair copy, five parts joined together in miraculous harmony by as blunt a process as experiment.

'You can borrow that if you like.'

She was going to ask if she could borrow the original for photocopying but shame silenced her. No reputable library, she knew, would subject such valuable manuscript to the glare of some high street photocopier and even photographers would need a licence.

'The book can't leave the house,' he added, and she blushed as though he had read her thoughts.

'Why not?' she asked nonetheless.

'Superstition, really. It's never left here, you see. It's part of the farm.'

'How come?'

'It's a family Bible. See?' He reached across her to turn to the front of the volume. Again, the binder had left several blank pages. And there, as if echoing the solemnity of the genealogies at the start of the Book of Matthew, was a sort of family tree. Generation upon generation of Polglazes had signed the book, with their wives, on returning from church on their wedding days and recorded the safe delivery of each union's children. She saw the latest entries – first Molly, then her younger brother Pearce, then Molly's husband Morris and their Lucy.

'I don't think I met him the other night,' Eliza said.

'No,' Pearce said. 'They get on well enough but not when they're under the same roof. Molly's got a temper on her and Morris is, well . . . he hasn't had much luck. Lost his farm.'

'But that's awful!'

'A lot of it about. He still farms but for other people. Bit of this, bit of that. You know. I get him in when I can. He'll be helping with the broccoli planting tomorrow. Sad, though. The little house is all Molly's. She said she couldn't face living somewhere thinking she might lose it any day. Said it wasn't fair on Lucy.'

His expression clouded so Eliza did not like to ask further. She turned back to the list, where suddenly Pearce's isolation, his lack of comforting additions seemed glaring. Her eye drifted up the page, marvelling at the repeated homages to ancestors in the naming of babies so that Johns and Michaels, as well as Pearces, abounded. There had once been a Raleigh, however and there was a cluster of magnificently biblical women – Micahs, Rebeccas, Keziahs and Sarahs. She turned back a page to where the ink browned with age and the lettering became smaller and less confident. When the Bible was first purchased or given, some Polglaze had written back the family line as far as anyone living could remember so that the list began with several generations in the same handwriting and with few dates.

The name jumped out at her. In circa 1615 a Michael Polglaze married a Rose Trevescan who bore him an astonishing eight children, John, Michael, Robert, Pearce, Lucy, Mary, Rebekkah and Shem before dying, presumably of exhaustion.

'Are there many Trevescans around here?' she asked.

'No. Used to be. Used to still be a whole clutch of them around Sennen in my grandparents' time but not now. Why?'

She turned back to the madrigal. All her training taught her to accept only the facts and not to twist the evidence to suit subjective hopes, but it was hard to resist. As she turned the pages back and forth, taking in every detail of the familiar script, comparing sheet with sheet, she noticed that one of them had worked looser than the rest. There was printing on the other side.

'Could I?' she asked Pearce.

He shrugged, caring only about the Bible, perhaps. 'If you can do it without tearing.'

She used an old trick, lifting the page as far as she dared then leaning in close to breathe slowly and warmly into the weakening join, keeping up a gentle pressure with her fingertip. In lucky cases it worked the same way as a steaming kettle, only without the excessive moisture and heat. And she was lucky. The old adhesive gave out with only a slight furring of fibres drawn from the newer paper below. Flour and water paste, perhaps, not cow hoof . . .

She turned the page and stared. Printed music. Another madrigal. Another unhelpful bass line. It showed the last few lines of music. *Fie no, no, no, no, no!*

'Shall I a virgin die?' she said.

'What's that?'

'How the line starts. Damn! That's all I can remember. Can't think who wrote it, either. Brains are so weird and stupid. Damn! Pearce, could I take this to the library? Just this sheet? If I guard it with my life.'

He smiled. 'Sure. Want me to run you into St Just now? Molly will have opened up.'

'No, I mean to London. The British Library. I'd have to go up overnight. Do you think Molly could put Dido up?'

'Course she could. Or I could. Lucy was going to help with the broccoli tomorrow. Maybe Dido could join in too? Earn some pocket money.'

'Are you sure?' Eliza's mind raced. She had money up at the caravan. She could call at the flat to pick up more clothes and her files. The thought of the long, tedious coach trip gave her pause.

'Run you to the station if you like,' Pearce said. He was smiling slyly.

'You're laughing at me.'

'No no,' he said. 'I'm not. Sorry.' And he stopped smiling. 'It's just that you were so limp and sad earlier and it's like someone just gave you fresh batteries.'

31

Camborne was a dreadful place. Giles was startled. Despite the mixture of duty and love that had brought him over there from the north coast, he found himself resenting the incursion of such ugliness into his little holiday. It was grim in the way some parts of Wales or the Midlands could be. There seemed to be no planning, just sprawl, mess and a sense of a community without purpose.

He rebuked himself for such a patronising attitude as he drove into town, balancing a small red book of Cornish town plans open on his lap. Quite possibly Camborne kept its charms hidden and was wonderful in ways that could not strike one on first encounter.

He found himself thinking of Eliza as powerfully as he had done in her poky flat, imagining her in such a dispiriting context and wondering how she had survived. When he first met her at university, surrounded by fine trees and ancient buildings, immersed in studious stillness and the incense of high culture, he had invested her with some of the spirit of the place. Had he first encountered her on a cramped Camborne pavement, pushing Dido past rows of wretched shops, would she even have caught his eye?

Mrs Hosken might despise this place but she had stayed here long after she might have moved away and she belonged here absolutely. But Eliza? Even without what he knew about Hannah and the long shadow she cast, he realised Eliza's youth must have been one long bitter straining at the leash.

He found the street. It was leafier and less grim than the industrial side of the town through which he had just driven. He found a parking space and left the car, wrinkling his eyes behind his sunglasses to read house numbers in the glaring sunlight.

He passed number eight at first because he thought it was derelict. The number was obscured, as was much of the house, by a stand of sycamore trees. The paintwork was flaking. A piece of gutter had come adrift. There was also a For Sale sign stuck through the moss of what had once been a flowerbed.

He let himself in at the rusting sunrise gate and approached the door, mentally preparing a greeting for Eliza, in case she should be the one to open.

He knocked. There was no sound of life from inside. He tried peering through a window but the glass was too grimy to make much out. This did not tally at all with his image of Mrs Hosken, always neat, handbag always to hand. Perhaps, left alone, she was closer in spirit to poor Eliza and spent her days not polishing church brass and regimenting her jam cupboard but mired in slovenly listlessness.

'Hello?'

He turned round. The voice seemed to have come from behind one of the thorny shrubs that swamped the neighbouring garden.

'Viewing's by appointment only. You'll have to call at the agents on Fore Street.'

'I'm looking for Mrs Hosken, actually,' he told the bush. 'Or her daughter Eliza. Eliza Easton . . . Hosken? I'm Giles. Giles Easton. Her son-in-law.'

'Of course you are. I should have recognised you from the photograph. Hang on.'

There was a rustling, then one of the roundest women he had ever seen — and opera companies offered a generous selection — appeared at the gate and waved him over.

'I'm afraid she died,' she said and for a moment he thought she meant Eliza. 'But it was very quick and peaceful. In her sleep, they said. And Eliza and Dodie have gone for a little holiday to my caravan.'

'Oh,' he said, his mental scenery readjusting around him. 'Oh! I see. Well . . .' and he must have looked even more pathetic than he felt because she introduced herself as Mrs Barnicoat and led him next door for a restorative coffee and slice of heavy cake. It was the sort of confection — all weight and sugar crystals — he had not eaten since the days when fellow students would produce slabs of cold, parsimonious pudding made from stale bread and raisins.

'That better?' she asked and he nodded, licking sugar from the corners of his lips and tempted to accept a second slice. 'The secret's in the lard,' she said. 'That and keeping a vanilla pod in the sugar jar. We're no different from birds, really. We all need a bit of fat from time to time. You need a bit of feeding, Giles Easton. Does that girlfriend of yours not bake?' She must have seen surprise on his face. 'Mrs Hosken never knew,' she assured him. 'She died not knowing. It was Dodie told me.'

'Dido?'

'That's right. I don't disapprove. Not really. A man has to live and Eliza's a sweet thing but she's no sense. No sense at all, really. I made them buy plenty of food in Penzance so the child won't go hungry up there at least.'

His eyes were caught by an enormous display of white lilies and baby's breath studied with carnations the exact shade of apricot lavatory paper.

'They were lovely flowers,' she said. 'I'm sure even where she is Mrs Hosken is most appreciative. I thought about taking

them to her grave but flowers get stolen if you leave them
there. People have no shame.'

'I'm glad they're not going to waste,' he said and they
sat in silence for a while, except for the ticking of a dripping tap in the steel sink and Mrs Barnicoat's great wheezy
sighs.

The clock struck twelve. It did not strike, precisely, but
released a burst of recorded bird song.

'Thrush,' she said with satisfaction. 'One o'clock's a wren
and two's a blackbird.'

'A different bird for every hour? How clever!'

Julia had gleefully pointed the thing out to him in a
catalogue once and they had laughed, imagining the daunting
bird cries one could use for a true country flavour. Buzzard.
Seagull. Bittern. Crow.

He could not have failed to notice the collection of bird
baths, feeders and nesting boxes as they came through the
jungly garden but now he saw how the house's interior was
devoted to birds too. Savage beaks and sharp little eyes were
everywhere, on calendars, tea towels, wall-mounted plates.
He recognised the syndrome from his mother and stepfather.
Bird love was the refuge of people for whom intimacy was
perilous and personal loss too traumatic to be risked. Reptiles
in feathered disguise, birds would never come close enough
to break a person's heart or upset their equilibrium the
way a dog or daughter might. Unless collecting porcelain
thimbles illustrating *Finches of the World* constituted a loss
of equilibrium . . .

'That girl needs a father's love,' Mrs Barnicoat said abruptly
and he felt rebuked for his secret sneer.

'I love her as well as I can,' he said. 'It's not easy only seeing
her every other weekend and the odd weekday, though.'

'And your girlfriend —'

'Julia.'

'Yes. She can't find that easy either. She'll be wanting children of her own.'

'Oh, I don't think so. Not really her style. But she loves Dido. She's like a big sister to her. I think sometimes a stepmother can help a girl in ways a mother never can.'

Mrs Barnicoat cut another wodge of heavy cake for him and waved this aside as so much sophistry.

'The thing you young people don't realise, because you don't want to, is that sometimes when you have no choice, when you have to make do with something, you end up making a better job of it. Would you have her back?'

'Dido? I think we'd adopt her like a shot.'

'Eliza. If your . . . Julia wasn't around, muddying the waters, would you have her back?'

'I don't know.' He laughed, unsettled at such direct questioning from a stranger. 'I haven't thought about it.'

'Of course you have. She's still your wife. If you're so sure you don't want her back, why haven't you divorced her and set her free to start her life again?'

'I'd divorce her if she asked me. But she hasn't. So it would seem a bit . . .'

'She'd have you, you know. If there weren't Julie.'

'Julia.'

'Yes. She'd have you. She'd come back with the girl if you asked her.'

'I'm not so sure . . .'

She shrugged with surprising brutality. 'Well. You should know. You're her husband.'

A tanned woman in a mauve sundress came up the garden path and rang the doorbell.

'Keep very still,' Mrs Barnicoat hissed, 'and she'll go away.'

Mrs Barnicoat was hidden in shadow but Giles was sitting in a pool of sunlight and could easily be seen. He froze and, sure enough, after lifting the letter box rather rudely to peer into the empty hall, the woman turned on her heel and retreated through the little jungle. When she heard the gate clang to again, Mrs Barnicoat relaxed but offered no explanation.

'Got a card from her this morning, little imp,' she said instead and fetched him down a postcard of Land's End. He saw Dido's spidery scrawl on the back. 'You can read it if you like.'

Dear Great Auntie Kitty, he read, *(Sorry!!) Your caravan is wicked especially the little shower and the pigs next door. We got the bikes pumped up and have ridden all the way to here. (See other side) But I think it looks more exciting on the map, don't you? How's my house? Hope you get good neighbours and no more cats. Love and ice cream, Dido xx*

Eliza's smaller, neater hand had inked in *Eliza, too* in the small space Dido had left.

'Sweet,' he said and handed it back. 'She's very polite sometimes. Quite formal compared to other kids. I worry she's a bit solemn.'

'She's got a lot to think about.'

'Yes,' he agreed. 'Have you known the family long?'

'Always,' she said with finality. 'Annie Hosken was like a sister to me. I took a mother's interest in the girls.'

'So you knew Hannah?'

'Of course.' But he saw the same buttoning up of the face, the same blanking out of the eyes he had seen when he had questioned the mother, so he stifled his curiosity. 'She was an amazing kid in her way,' Mrs Barnicoat volunteered. 'And Dido was a kind of blessing, whatever people might say.'

'Sad, really,' he said after a moment or two, 'that Dido never really knew her grandmother well. Was Eliza . . . ?

I know they hadn't been close these last few years but was she very cut up by the death?'

Mrs Barnicoat thought about this. 'I didn't see her cry,' she said, 'to be honest with you. Her eyes were dry at the graveside and I always think that's a bad sign.'

'You think she didn't love her?'

'*No*,' she said impatiently. 'But she needs to let it out. That's what funerals and wearing black is for. Grief gone bad is a poisonous thing and I'd worry for that child. That's why I told her to take a holiday. She can grieve more easily in a place with no associations. Is your mother still alive, Giles?'

'Oh yes,' he said. 'Very much so. But my father died when I was a boy. She took that very badly. I used to wish he'd left her for someone or somewhere else, the way Eliza's father did. I think that would have been easier . . .'

'She grieved hard, then?'

'She was . . . angry. Angry and very frightened to be on her own with only me to shield her. So she drank for courage and the drink made her angry.'

And then, perhaps because she was not just a stranger but a great fat cartoon of a woman; he told her everything. And each piece of the tale, how his mother drank, how she raged, how she took him into her bed for company then used his frightened hands to feed her hungry loneliness, how day after day her bright manners and lickety-spit smartness denied the pitiful disorder of the night before: each piece was like another piece of horror he could leave behind in this ridiculous, bird-infested house.

He cried a little as he talked to her, blew his nose on tissues she pushed across the table to him and when he was all talked out, even to the point of telling her about taking pictures of Dido as she slept and how dirty it made him feel, he felt light-bodied as well as light-headed, as though the secrets had been an actual load. He would never see her again, he sensed. Must never, if he were not to pollute himself with his own dark discharge.

'Dido is the one good, honest thing in my life,' he told her, sniffing so heavily she instinctively patted the tissues towards him. He helped himself, blowing loudly, and felt better. 'If I could only make things right with her and be the father to her I always . . . I think it would help everything else fall into place. Julia. Eliza. Everything.'

'Now *there*'s a rare thing,' she said. 'A man who knows his mission and isn't just stumbling about looking for one!'

She fetched him a map and showed him how to find her caravan. Bloated from cake, he declined her offer of a late lunch.

Since he was already two-thirds of the way there, he drove on past Hayle and Penzance and out towards St Just. After a few false passes, he found the caravan, but it was locked and deserted. He dozed in the stifling car, waited longer than he should, hoping perhaps they were merely out on a walk or bike ride. Then he panicked and drove back along the county's spine to Trenellion at a fool's pace.

It was an informal music festival whose attraction for many was as much the socialising over picnics before the concerts as the music which followed. In the fields around the church where cars were parked, people were folding away rugs and hurrying in as he arrived. Julia would be angry that he had not been there to socialise with her and Jemima.

He had been to the festival just once, as a soloist in a *St John Passion*. Musically it was fine; a little rough-edged at times but then at least half the performers were amateurs and their commitment and emotional involvement had been extraordinary. Socially it was another matter. Everyone had seemed to know everyone else and he had been a late replacement for someone more popular. Slightly too aware of his professional status, he had misread the cues for him to muck in and realised too late he was striking people as standoffish and snobbish. He left having resolved never to come again, only to have the festival pre-empt him by never again inviting him.

He was not too late to slip in and listen to the first half of the concert hidden in the porch or even in the ringing chamber, which had the best acoustic in the church. But then he saw a couple from the chorus whom he disliked and realised that in either hiding place he would still be running the risk of meeting people he knew and, worse, of meeting people he knew who then failed to recognise him.

Suddenly it was all too much. He lost his nerve and he slid low in his seat until the parking field was empty. Then he sent Julia an apologetic text message saying he must have caught whatever bug had afflicted her yesterday and had retreated to the hotel feeling queasy. *Party 4 2 tonite* he told her. *We can play together tomorrow. Later. Gxxx.*

32

The churchyard and the fields used as car parks were busy with concert-goers as Julia made her way to the old vicarage that now served as rehearsal space and dressing rooms. She had some good luck flowers for Jemima. In town she was spoilt for choice when buying agency tributes. At Trenellion choice was reduced to packets of fudge, Cornish fairings and a robust assortment of undistinguished flower bunches prepacked in spangly cellophane.

As she had feared, Jemima had not been overjoyed to see her. Although there were plenty of professionals among the performers, including conductor and soloists, part of the pleasure they took in the festival was the chance to make music while temporarily released from the pressures of contracts, union regulations and reviews, rehearsing and performing alongside people for whom music was purely an unpaid pleasure. The music business being relatively tiny, everyone knew how well (or not) everyone else's career was going. In the festival's unwritten constitution, the pulling of rank was outlawed and the only hierarchy that mattered was along festival lines; how long one had been coming, how well one knew the locals, how many generations of one's family were involved in some capacity. For two precious weeks, a trumpeter could be valued more for his surfing prowess and ability to mend the festival dishwasher than for playing with the Welsh National Opera.

Learning from Giles' bitter experience, Julia understood this as Selina had not. To have one's agent or even their proxy show up at a dress rehearsal here smacked of pulling rank.

Julia had undone the damage as best she could in several ways. She had dressed down with as much care as she might have dressed up. She had made no protest when a restaurant lunch for a client and her conductor turned into a pub lunch for the client, her conductor and five twenty-something music students. And she had joined them on the beach at Polteath afterwards for a choir-versus-orchestra rounders match.

Jemima had come down to the beach too — no diva-ish afternoon withdrawal for her — and watched the match from a vast, towel-draped rock with a covey of remarkably similarly bronzed, bare-shouldered old things. It was impossible to sit for long among a group so very like a clutch of matriarchs at a dance so Julia felt challenged to join the fray.

She had kicked off her shoes, the better to run on the sand, when a coltish girl with hair in plaits thrust the bat into her hand and shouted, 'Your turn! You're honorary orchestra!'

Quite suddenly she had found herself on holiday. When the match was over, choir beating orchestra by having more children in fielding positions, she was cajoled into somebody's baggy wetsuit and given a surfing lesson by somebody's non-musical but festival-loving brother. She declined the offer of high tea at the festival farmhouse but enjoyed a death defying lift back to Porth Keverne with a jeepful of gay tenors from the Hallé chorus.

Stepping into the shower to wash off the salt and sand she caught a glimpse of her reflection, a radiant, surprised stranger.

*   *   *

The back door of the vicarage was wide open. Julia wandered in and followed the sound of a viola tuning up, along the slate-floored corridor that linked back door to front. Jemima was warming up in the sitting room. Julia was about to let herself in when Jemima burst into one of her calling cards, a transposition of a gigue from one of the Bach partitas. She froze, listening.

Through a closed door it was hard to believe the player was in her seventies. It made her think, as she often did, of the unfairness that let instrumentalists continue to astound, even to improve on their ability, at ages by which most singers had no voice left to float on their years of acquired technique. It was something she had never dared discuss with Giles; what he would do when . . . It was impossible to imagine him without an audience but she supposed, like the loss of youth, it was something every singer must plan for and deal with.

A man in evening dress came downstairs, fruitily humming, and she felt she must interrupt or be thought an eavesdropper.

'Come,' Jemima called, hearing her knock, then continued playing a phrase from the Walton concerto. She played on, her back to the door, as Julia came in, repeating the phrase several times with slight changes in emphasis as though scouring it for any last crumbs of meaning.

The big window she faced looked out over a woody sprawl of old shrub roses, some vast old pines and a barley field that rolled down to the distant Atlantic. She was in bare feet and a black petticoat, the muscles in her shoulders and bowing arm undressed by fat.

'Wish I could play like this,' she said, breaking off to fine-tune a string. 'So much more comfortable. And ideally the audience should all be lying down with their heads in each others' laps. You brought flowers. You ninny.'

'Sorry. Boss-woman's orders. Just be glad she didn't send you one of her fruit baskets.'

'It arrived this afternoon while we were out.'

'Oh God. Sorry.'

'She must be feeling *very* guilty. Nice frock.'

Julia looked down at herself. All Giles had remembered of the festival dress code was *long floral* which wasn't really her, so she had opted for a dark purple cotton dress with an embroidered hem, the nearest she did to pretty and, defying the risks of mud, plum coloured slippers with tiny gold stars on them.

'Is it okay? Walking up from the hotel I saw everything from jeans to black tie.'

'Fuck, yes. And you see some of them in ancient velvet and others in Guernseys and shorts. It's a fashion nightmare.'

'What are you wearing?'

Jemima flicked her head towards a striking black silk affair with a black lace jacket. 'My Ida Händel number,' she said. She set down her viola and relieved Julia of the flowers.

'Very sweet of you,' she said. 'You've caught the sun.'

'Have I?'

'Suits you.'

'I should leave you in peace. I just wanted to check you had all you need and say good luck.'

'Thanks.'

'I can't believe it's your last concerto.'

'Oh, Christ. Believe me, girly, *I* can! Standing up in front of all those students in the band I feel like Methuselah's aunt. Still. It's nice to finish here rather than in London; this is where I started.'

'You're joking. At the festival?'

Jemima nodded. 'Aged fourteen. Back desk of the second fiddles. *Elijah.*' She paused. 'So. When's it due?'

'Sorry?'

'The baby.'

'Oh. Er. I'm not expecting.'

'Sorry. My mistake. I normally have a sort of sense for these things and you had that self-cherishing look. Sorry.' Jemima picked up her viola again. 'Everyone goes to the pub afterwards, if you're interested.'

'Okay. I'd er . . . I'd better go and find Giles.'

Disconcerted, Julia left the vicarage and slipped across to the church where Jemima had kindly reserved them a couple of seats. There was no sign of Giles yet. She glanced at her watch then began to read the eccentric notes in the programme.

'Excuse me. Sorry.' A woman with a very small boy in her arms was leaning past her to a man further along the pew. 'Colin, could you?'

He took the toddler off her.

'Just for the first piece,' she said. 'Crisis with the tea urn.'

'But —' he began to protest.

'Sorry,' she said. 'He's sleepy. He'll be fine.' Then she hurried off.

He sat down beside Julia again. The toddler sat side-saddle on his lap, leaning heavily into his chest, sucking its thumb and staring solemnly at Julia.

Abashed, Julia made an effort to go back to reading her programme but felt the dark-haired child's eyes boring into her and was compelled to look back at it and offer an appeasing smile. There was no smile in return. Its look was gravely judgemental.

'It's okay,' the father said with gentle irony. 'He's sleepy. He'll be fine. Actually he will. He eats like a little hog then falls fast asleep and not even barking dogs will wake him.' He stroked the boy's hair and the toddler gave a small whine of passing irritation then rearranged himself into his father's chest like a settling dog. 'What's before the Walton?'

She made a show of looking back at the programme, knowing the answer perfectly well but made shy by something in his face.

'More Walton,' she told him. '*Variations on a Theme by Britten.*'

'Is that quiet?'

'Fairly. I think. I don't really know.'

'Oh good. I'm always a bit out of my depth here.'

'Are you a regular?'

'My sister's involved. My mother has a cottage in Trelill.'

'Oh. Nice.'

'Hmm. But she has a way of buying more tickets than she needs then making us feel guilty if we don't use them.'

'Sorry.' She broke off to slip her mobile out of her pocket. There was a text message from Giles. 'Damn,' she muttered.

'Bad news?'

'I've been stood up,' she sighed. 'Boyfriend with bellyache.'

'Sounds like a song by The Smiths. About as welcome as Toddler with the Trots.'

'Does he?' she asked, alarmed.

'For once, no.' They both looked down at the child, who had fallen heavily asleep.

'He looks so comfortable,' she said, feeling a spasm of something like broodiness.

'Master Thomas is *always* comfortable.'

'Are you Cornish Thomases?'

'Yes,' he said. 'You must be Cornish too. Anyone else would assume we were Welsh.'

'My mother was a Rodda,' she admitted. 'But my dad came from St Helens. I grew up in Illogan.'

He held out the hand that wasn't holding his son in place.

'Colin,' he said as she shook. 'Colin Thomas.'

'Julie,' she told him. 'Julie Dixon.'

She couldn't tell what madness prompted her to give him her real name and to confess her origins. Perhaps it was because he was a safe repository, a concert-going Cornish dad was as unlikely to meet any of her acquaintance as a hairdresser or train passenger, other people to whom she had occasionally felt compelled to reveal herself.

The lie she lived was not a very large one, after all, more a matter of allowing people to jump to certain conclusions uncorrected than of actively telling lies. But like any untruth, it chafed a little more with each repetition and she occasionally felt the need to put it aside and remind herself of the reality that lay beneath it.

He smiled then remembered to let go of her hand.

'What?' she asked as there was shushing while the orchestra tuned.

'It's silly,' he whispered. 'Sorry.'

'But what?'

He was handsome, she saw. She had not noticed at first because of his messy hair, which seemed to be stiff with sea salt, the subtly wrong shirt and tie combination, bought as a pair for him by his wife she reckoned, and not least by the toddler. She had never understood the syndrome of going gooey over lone men with children – papoose fever, Shawna called it – but here she was harmlessly flirting with someone else's husband and loving it.

'You suddenly reminded me of a girl I had a hopeless crush on in the fifth form. Sorry. You're nothing like her really.'

He had stopped whispering and his voice carried dreadfully in the quietened crowd but she did not care. She pictured him a strapping sixteen-year-old in a uniform a year too small for him. She remembered such boys and how she had desired them even as she affected to despise them for desiring her so obviously. At that age Giles would have been too ethereal to have survived long in her school, unless he somehow won the protection of a beefy Colin Thomas.

His wife did not come back to relieve him of the toddler, who slept on as Peter Grenfell made his imposing entrance and conducted the first item.

As the variations reached their climax a trumpet blare woke the toddler who did not cry but became restless and threatened to start whining. Colin Thomas made to rise as the applause was dying down.

'Better find his mum,' he muttered. 'Lovely meeting you.'

But instead of rising, he crumpled across her feet and into the aisle. By some miraculous reflex, she reached out and grabbed the child on its way down, saving it from crunching its head on the tiles.

There was a fuss, inevitably.

'It's okay,' she told a man who had darted over. 'I think he just fainted. It's the heat.'

A cellist who doubled as a doctor loosened his tie and collar, granting Julia a glimpse of unschoolboyish chest hair, felt his pulse and concurred. More men got involved and bore him out to the church's lovely porch where the cellist-doctor bent Colin's knees slightly and slipped an old cushion under his head.

Duty done, the first-aiders returned to their seats and the concert continued, floating on a gentle tide of gossip. Julia could not very well leave him on his own out there. Besides, she was clutching his little boy. The boy had threatened to cry at first at being so jolted awake but had dozed off again now that Julia had sat on one of the porch benches. The acoustic was better in this spot than in the main body of the building, where too much exposed wood deadened all reverberation, so as the applause announced Peter Grenfell's reappearance with Jemima at his side, she sat on quite happily to enjoy the concerto in cool comfort.

It was a lovely, unsettling piece, full of youthful passion and restlessness and she was not surprised to read in the programme note that Walton had confessed it was almost indecently autobiographical in its depiction of an illicit love affair. It set Julia's mind racing, the way some music could, flickering through real and imagined scenes in her life as through publicity stills for a film.

The woman selling programmes and souvenirs from a card table on the porch's other side regarded Julia quite calmly.

She thinks I'm his wife, Julia thought with amusement. *The mother of his child.* Then she saw that her supposed husband had come round and that instead of giving the game away by sitting up, he continued to lie still, watching her from his slate bed as she cradled his child in her arms and listened dreamily to Jemima's hot-voiced swansong. He smiled when she saw him looking and watched her for a few seconds longer before he began to sit up.

Just then his wife came in at the churchyard gate, walking on the grass so as to avoid making noise on the gravel. She read the situation at once.

'He never eats enough and then he faints,' she whispered, taking the waking child from Julia's arms and shushing it.

Her husband stood and presented her to Julia.

'My sister, Sal,' he whispered. 'Julie Dixon.'

The programme-seller put a finger to her lips.

'You're a hopeless uncle and a worse babysitter,' Sal hissed, ignoring her. 'Thanks,' she mouthed at Julia with a grin and they left.

Julia sat on in the porch until the concerto finished, admiring the carved green man in its ceiling and enjoying the sense that the programme-seller was rapidly revising her assumptions about what she had just witnessed, failing to come up with a solution not suggestive of impropriety.

33

Parched from all the dust he had been breathing in while sweeping out the empty silo, Pearce came in for a glass of water and was startled to find Dido sitting expectantly at the kitchen table reading.

'Hello,' he said. 'How was the last day of school?'

'Oh. Okay. We had a quiz and Lucy and her mates took me to the chip shop for lunch. I messed around with Molly's computer for a bit then I thought I should come back so I rode my bike here. Where's Eliza?'

'She went to London for the night to look up some stuff in the library. That's my fault. Damn.'

'What?'

'I was meant to tell Molly. Sorry. So you could spend the night with Luce.'

'Couldn't I stay here?'

'Well . . . yes. Sure. If you like. You bored of playing with Luce already?'

'No. It's just . . . I didn't want to crowd her out. She didn't ask me to stay, after all. I can see her tomorrow.'

'Well, sure. You can help us plant broccoli. I'd pay you. Cash in hand.'

Her face lit up. 'Cool!'

'I didn't tell you that. It's completely illegal because you're a kid. But it's quite fun. They're cauliflower really. We just call them broccoli when we grow them in the winter.' He was getting better at anticipating her hunger for facts.

'Ah. What are you doing now?'

'You bored?'

'No. I'm reading.' She showed him. Done with Tove Jansson, she had found his old book of English fairytales in her room. 'I thought they'd be babyish,' she said, 'but some of them are really nasty.'

'Do you like scary stories, then?'

She nodded gravely. 'Usually.'

'Read this one, then, while I make us a cup of tea.' He found the place for her, with its picture of a little dog barking at an advancing shadow. 'But don't blame me if it gives you a sleepless night.'

'Huh,' she said scornfully then read while he put on the kettle, rinsed the barley dust out of his eyes under the tap and washed his hands. He took her a mug of tea and the last of the rock buns. She was a quick reader. Clever, he guessed. Like her aunt.

He sat sipping and watching her. He was so used to Lucy dressing like a boy that he tended to forget she was a girl underneath. It was novel to have a proper little girl about the place, with her hair in bunches and a cluster of rings and coloured bracelets on one hand.

'Oh!' she said as she finished.

He grinned, happy the story had hit its mark.

She looked at him in amazement. 'She doesn't get rescued or anything,' she said, then turned back to the first page, munching her bun. 'It's really *nasty*!'

'Yeah.'

'What are Hobbyars?'

'I don't know. I think that's why it's so scary. They just come at night and carry people off but it never says.'

'And poor Dog Turpie, having his legs chopped off just for being brave!' She laughed. 'It's really *nasty*! Are there any more like that?'

'Don't know. I don't remember. But that's the one that always got me. Molly used to scratch on the bedroom door like this.' He scratched his nails slowly on the rough underside of the table. 'Until I couldn't stand it anymore and said, 'Who is it?' Then she'd just scratch again and I'd say, 'Who is it?' again and there'd be a pause.' He dropped his voice for effect. 'And then she'd say '*HOBBYARRR!!*' and rattle the doorknob and I'd scream the house down.'

She didn't laugh. 'But you knew it was her.'

'Yes. But no too. If she kept it up long enough, I'd forget.' He remembered she was an only child. The idea of having a big sister to wind you up was completely alien to her. He scratched his nails on the underneath of the table again and looked totally serious suddenly. 'What was that?' he asked.

'What?'

He scratched again.

'Stop it,' he told her.

'I'm not doing anything,' she laughed. 'You stop it.'

He scratched with both nails. 'No. Come on now. What is that?' He jumped up and ran to the door to peer out into the hall.

'Stop it,' she said. 'All right? Stop it!'

The sun was low over the sea as they crossed the yard and walked out to the upper fields. The steers needed moving again. Dido was a game little thing and enjoyed scrambling over hedges and vaulting gates. He could see how she might get on well with Lucy. She was fascinated when he explained how every field had a name, some of them recording owners from hundreds of years ago. Gabriel's Piece. Lean Downs. Wedding Bells.

'So do you like Eliza?' she asked after a while.

'Course,' he said. 'She's lovely. Why?'

'No reason. What if the Hobbyars are really beautiful?'

'It doesn't say they are.'

'No. But they could be. Just because they kill the grand-parents and pull down the house and carry off the little girl in a bag we assume they're monsters but they might be beautiful.'

'Yes.'

'Pearce?'

'What?'

'Do you think it matters? Being beautiful?'

'I wouldn't know.' He tried to think of a more helpful answer. He was unused to this. 'I suppose it helps.'

'Because it makes people like you?'

'Suppose. But they'd find out pretty fast if you weren't worth liking. Handsome is as handsome does.'

'What's that mean?'

'You've got to be beautiful on the inside too. There are plenty of pretty people who are Hobbyars on the inside.'

'Hobbyar. It would be a good name for your next cat.'

'Old Simkin's got a while to go yet.'

'Well yes. But after that. Why don't you have a dog?'

'I don't know,' he said. 'Okay. Here we are. See them?'

'Yes. Hobbyars.'

'Steers.'

He called out to them and the herd started towards him in dribs and drabs. Dido held out her hand to the first ones who arrived at their side, and laughed when they sniffed and snorted and ducked away from her advances. She was not remotely nervous of them.

'I can see you're a natural,' he teased her. 'Now you want to open that gate for me and we can lead them into the next field.'

'Can't we chase them?'

'You could try but they're a darned sight easier to lead. Chase them and they go all over the shop.'

She grunted as she freed the bolt on the gate, then heaved it open so that it clanged against the stones on the hedge.

'Okay,' he said. 'Now sit on the hedge there out of the way till I say,' and he called the cattle again and walked through the gateway, encouraging them to follow him.

Without being asked she shut the gate behind the last one but had difficulty shooting its bolt. 'Seventy-two,' she said as he helped her. 'They're hard to count when they're moving aren't they? How'd you get to be a farmer?'

'Luck of the draw usually,' he said. 'Why? You after my job?'

'It looks fun.'

'Yeah, well, you can help plant broccoli for a morning then see how you feel about it.'

'What's for supper?' She jumped off a hedge then ran alongside him to catch up.

'Same as last night,' he told her. 'Only older.'

34

She was so out of touch. She had quite forgotten that the British Library had moved so she came as far as her first glimpse of the graceful new glass ceiling arching over the museum's freed-up inner courtyard before she remembered and had to walk up to St Pancras.

The new building seemed to have shed every vestige of the old one's ultra traditional inefficiency. Catalogues used to be cut and pasted into huge, unwieldy alphabetical albums and spread over yards of shelving around which readers jockeyed for space. Now they were entirely computerised and even available online.

Eliza knew her texts well enough to dismiss the most familiar composers. Not Byrd. Not Morley. Not Weelkes. Not Tallis. She scrolled down and up lists until she found a handful of lesser collections she thought might contain the crucial one while also matching Trevescan's dates. She bagged her seat and placed her order.

She had assumed she would have to call back for them in the afternoon and was astonished to hear she could be reading within the hour. She whiled away the interval in a stylish cafeteria tucked in beside a towering glass wall with shelf upon shelf of books backing onto it.

Returning to her seat with the day's paper, she revelled in

the soothing, familiar sounds of rustling paper, closing books, soft studious throat clearings. Scholars now took notes on laptops or electronic notebooks instead of dog-eared pads but still she did not need to look for long before spotting someone pretending to cough so as to slip in a forbidden toffee or surreptitiously gouging out ear-wax with a sharpened pencil.

Suddenly the little light on her desk lit up summoning her to the collection point. And there they were: eight first edition volumes of madrigals whisked across the centuries to her desk in less time than it took to get a cut and blow dry.

Nothing. She found nothing. The fragment was printed on a right-hand page, plainly the last in a collection because its reverse side had been blank until Trevescan, or, okay, yes, whoever, had scribbled in his neat addendum. So she turned to the last pages of each book in turn, doing her best not to be sidetracked by cherubs, prefaces and forgotten felicities of text.

A man might saile from Trent unto Danuby and yet not find so strange a peece as you be.

Were I a flea, in bed, I would not bite you but search some other way for to delight you.

Much delighted but nothing matched. Cursing her faulty memory, she turned to the last she had called up, Farnaby's *Canzonets*. She was sure the text she was hunting was not a Farnaby one but he was from Truro so it seemed possible his music would have found a favoured home in a Cornish manor of the time.

But no. Not Farnaby. And now it was too late to call up anything for consulting before the next day.

Cursing her giddy spontaneity too, she carefully slid the pack of slim Farnaby volumes back in their box. Then she looked up the catalogue numbers for several much later volumes, by Thomas Vautor, Michael East and John Ward. She wanted it to be none of them, of course, because Trevescan had died by the time their collections were published so could not have penned the mystery madrigal in the back of any of them. She knew she must remain dispassionate. To identify the fragment would give her a clear date on which to base her investigation. And merely because it was not the work of her pet composer did not make a previously unpublished madrigal by one of his near-contemporaries any less desirable a find.

'Mrs Easton!' someone whispered, tapping on her elbow as she waited in line. It was Villiers Yates. A contemporary of hers in the music department and very much part of Giles' coterie when she had first moved in with him.

'Villiers?'

'How stunning! How are you? You look so well.'

Disciplined and rigorous, he had received his second degree long ago. She had heard he was now attached to the Royal College in some honorary capacity while earning his money elsewhere. His sharp eyes looked her over with a critical disdain that gave the lie to his murmured speech. Villiers, as always, was as immaculate as any courtier.

He steered her to a corner where their whispers would disturb nobody. 'I thought you'd given all this up,' he hissed as though the library were some low haunt.

'Not really,' she said. 'But you know how it is; painfully slow.'

'And that bouncing baby of yours . . .'

'She's a galumphing nine-year-old!'

'Good lord. Is she really?'

'How's your book coming on, Villiers?'

'Which one?' he asked, quick as a blade.

'Last time I saw you it was the Gibbons thing.'

'Oh that. Well I *did* it but . . . you know what publishing's like now. So depressing. It came out in America. In a small, academic way.'

'And you're teaching now.'

'Only a bit. And a bit of consultancy for . . . for someone's collection. I seem to be doing more and more in America now.'

Somebody shushed them and got one of Villiers' lethal glares for their temerity. 'So what are *you* up to?' His gooseberry green eyes bored a hole in Eliza's bag.

'Oh. Still plugging on with Trevescan. A bit of consultancy too, actually. Villiers, you know the later stuff better than I do. I wonder if you'd recognise this.'

She took out the page Pearce had entrusted to her, which she had protected with a Ziploc sandwich bag as that was all she could find in his kitchen. Villiers' answers in seminars had always been demoralisingly swift and incisive. He did not disappoint her now.

'May I?' he asked, taking it from her, undoing the bag and sliding out the torn page. He handed back the bag off-handedly, as though she were some skivvy. 'East,' he said almost at once. '*The Fourth Set of Books*. Printed by John Browne? No. Thomas Snodham. That's Snodham's decoration at the end. Sixteen-ten. Sixteen-nineteen or so. *See The Declining Sun*. Where did you get this?'

'Oh . . . Cornwall. A friend's collection.' Even in her disappointment she noted Villiers' raised eyebrow.

He looked back at the page and flicked it over in his neat, white grasp. 'And what's this?'

'That's what I'm really interested in.'

'Yes. I can see why. One might take it for Trevescan, of course, with those Qs and the way he's drawn the clef but the dates are wrong, aren't they? Of course, it could always be a copy of a copy. Is it any good?'

'Charming,' she said, then bluffed frantically. 'A little group I sing with sometimes tried it out for me.'

'Why've you only got the bass part?'

She was hardly going to tell him the rest was still glued

in a family Bible. 'I didn't need the rest. Not yet. So you think East?'

'My dear, I know it. Don't run away.'

He crossed the room and approached a small woman in an unseasonably chunky jersey who was hunched over a laptop. They murmured together and Villiers returned with a blue box the woman had relinquished.

'Petra Huston,' he hissed to Eliza. 'Spotted her booking it out earlier. Wretched woman. No life. No colour sense. But obsessed with Tallis to the point of psychosis.'

Eliza glanced nervously across at Petra Huston. Professor Huston glowered back, watching jealously for the safe return of her loan from rival hands, emblematic as a warning sign with her bottle-bottom glasses and unloved hair.

Villiers had opened the box and was flicking through the contents. '1618,' he said. 'I stand corrected,' and he handed a kid-bound volume over for Eliza to inspect.

It was the bass part from *The Fourth Set of Books* by Michael East. She turned gently to the back of the last madrigal. It was a perfect match with Pearce's fragment and there were two blank pages following, inviting enough for any talented vandal wishing to pen in an extra song.

She tried to slip away while he was returning the books to Petra Huston, sensing he would sniff out her disappointment but Villiers was hard on her heels as she stepped off the escalator into the foyer.

'So this *friend* of yours, Eliza. Sorry. I didn't catch his name.'

There was something repellent in his unlooked for warmth, however, and something chilling in the hungry glances he repeatedly cast at her bag. When he said, 'I had lunch with poor dear Julia the other day,' waiting for her to ask him more, it made it all the easier to be rude to him.

She had let him keep her company as far as the Tube but

now gave him the slip, darting across from the Southbound to the Northbound platform just as a train was about to close its doors. Safe behind glass, she dared to wave at him and even mimed holding a telephone to her ear.

The train was stifling and the station where she got out was little cooler. It was one of those balmy summer evenings when even London's grimmer corners were lent a kind of honeyed softness. People leant on balconies and walkways chatting and drinking. Children played on the pavements. Music and food smells were everywhere. But still, returning to the estate was a shock.

A few days at St Just and already she was taking full horizons for granted, and green, well-fed grass and clean air. Here the grass was yellowed by drought and dogs and there was a sense of being hemmed in on every side. Except for days of especially bad pollution, she had never noticed the city's air before any more than she noticed herself breathing it. Passing swiftly from the train to museum to air-conditioned library, she had paid it little attention but now she was aware that she could taste it at the back of her tongue and imagined it leaving a sticky residue on her skin as she passed.

She must have swiftly become accustomed to silence too. Or, if not to silence, for the countryside was full of noises, then to a lack of background noise. Sitting beside Kitty's caravan or waking in Pearce's farmhouse, she found noises seemed to come singly and identifiably against a silent background. A pigeon's murmur, a tractor's ignition, the sudden, passing whizz and laughter of two cyclists, a pig, a helicopter, a cow; the sounds came as distinctly and definably as the consecutive images in a child's alphabet book. Here it was all blurred; bus into taxi into motorbike, car horn into dog bark into clattering shop front shutter. And behind it all lay traffic roar so constant as to be less sound than scenery.

She was shocked at the enforced intimacy. People's smells

and conversation and music spilled over and spilled again for lack of space. This was the buzz of the city, of course, a kind of obligatory communality true urbanites were expected to relish but riding the lift to the thirteenth floor and pushing back the door against the bunch of free papers and junk mail, she was as oppressed by it as any rustic newcomer.

She looked around her with cold eyes, listening to the insistent hum of the fridge and the competing television channels from the flats above her and below and smelling the ghosts of old, sick dog and her own depressed inactivity.

When she first moved into the flat it was in the full acknowledgement that she had made mistakes, both of them men. The price she had paid was the loss of a shallow toehold on the climb to an academic security. Relative security. Her independence now would have to be bravely willed where before it had come naturally. But she was determined and would survive. She wrote notes to her handful of contacts for freelance work, giving them her new number and address. She paid humiliating calls on the district's Citizens' Advice Bureau and the benefit office and claimed the financial help she was due by virtue of being both a mother and poor and effectively unemployed. Then, having received reassurance from Dr Goldhammer that she was not entirely written off her records and that, miraculously, she still had faith in her, she brought Roger Trevescan back into the centre of her desk and worked relentlessly towards finishing her long neglected thesis.

For a few months she rediscovered the rigorous pleasures of study and application. In the precious hours when Dido was at school or the unlooked for ones when schoolfriends' mothers took her off her hands, she made guerrilla raids on the British Library and Royal College reading rooms. She briefly acquired a bicycle and got used to lugging it in and out of the lift. She slipped back into the subculture of the industrious poor and became adept at feeding Dido and herself on economy brands, food just past its sell-by date and the produce discarded at a nearby street market. For a while a second-hand copy of a shameless paperback called *Poor Cook* became her Bible.

Then, playing with a friend one day, Dido found her way back to Giles' house. She burst into the flat, full of artless, unedited excitement. She and her friend had spotted a woman walking Carlo, followed her home and been asked in for tea by Giles.

Instinctively Eliza asked about the woman and had been at once reassured and unsettled to discover she was a paid dog walker who did not come inside.

'So it was just you and Savannah and Giles?'

'Yes,' Dido said. 'Julia works during the day.'

'What does she do?' Eliza tried to keep the squeak out of her voice.

'Dunno. Didn't ask. And Carlo was really good. The walker lady's been teaching him things. Can I go again, d'you think?'

'Well . . .' Eliza was at a loss. She was in no position to impose a ban but suddenly it was the last thing she wanted. She had a sudden fear that Giles and the mysterious Julia had the power to take Dido from her. 'We'd have to ask Giles,' she said, honourably.

'He said it was fine with him but I'd have to ask you. So can I go again? Can I? Carlo's so sweet now he's good!'

'We'll see. I . . . I don't see why not. But Giles is busy. Nearly as busy as Paul. He's often away. He won't always be there when you want to – oh all right.'

So Dido started to visit Giles at random but usually on weekday afternoons, when the mysterious Julia was at work.

There was no direct contact between the adults because there seemed to be no need. It was not as though Dido was staying the night or required maintenance. That is, she *did* require maintenance – it repeatedly shocked Eliza how much a child cost – but Eliza was determined to get by on her slender earnings and the assistance she had from the state.

At first the reason Dido gave for her visits was her desire to play with Carlo. But then she returned to the flat with the dog in tow, announcing that Julia was allergic to him so Giles had given him to her. Eliza had swallowed her outcry at the extra expense. She was pleased to see the dog. He was an old friend. And to take in any refugee from Julia gave satisfaction.

The visits continued, however, until Julia, not Giles, telephoned to say how very much they'd enjoy having Dido for the weekend occasionally, since Giles was *a kind of father to her*. Dido had been in the room at the time, filling in the blanks, so it had been impossible to resist the suggestion without seeming a monster.

The visits were never ratified, no more set out by law than was Giles and Eliza's separation. Extrapolating, perhaps, from the routines of schoolfriends, most of whom, it seemed, lived with only one parent at a time, Dido began to share herself out, edging both households into a routine whereby she alternated weekends with each – unless Giles was on tour – and spent Wednesday nights with him. Julia gradually assumed the characteristics of an edgy and then unpredictably nice stepmother. Giles and Eliza continued not to speak.

It would have been melodramatic to suggest that the failure of Eliza's resolve and her slow decline into what Dido called *just sitting around all day* dated from the afternoon Dido rediscovered Giles' house. Eliza only went to the British Library a few more times after that, however, and she wrote her last sleeve note two months later. She read less and less source material and more and more novels. She borrowed them by the greasy armful from the local library, often forgetting to return them on time and trusting Dido to slip them back for her with some winning childish fib. She ate less and less, saved on heating by staying in bed. It was hard to say whether she coped less and less because Dido coped more and more or vice versa but she fell out with one of her few remaining friends when he said nothing in her defence while his boyfriend accused her of punishing Dido for not having found one parent's love sufficient.

There was nothing to eat. Tea bags. A tin of pineapple rings. A bag of rice. The thought of going out again into the broiling blare of the street to buy overpriced food in a corner shop simply to bring it back and eat it in solitude galvanised her. She picked up the mound of papers and letters and sorted swiftly through them, throwing most back on the floor. What was left she thrust into a holdall, then carried the holdall with her round the flat adding things at random, a half-empty box of tampons, shampoo, clothes for them both, books. She also packed her Trevescan files.

She took one last look around. She could not answer for Dido, who was something of a hoarder, but there was nothing of hers left behind which she would not happily consign to oblivion. The flat, once a haven, no longer felt remotely safe. Even with the front door shut behind her she felt no more in a private space than she had in the lift.

She could not afford a berth on the sleeper but she was content to spend the night dozing on a seat. She would still sleep better than she could in her old rumpled bed.

Ravenous suddenly, she bought herself a portable supper in the station's supermarket. Sitting by a window munching grapes, listening to wealthier travellers chatter as they settled into their ingenious bedrooms off the corridor behind her, she felt again the unfamiliar stirrings of something like happiness.

She took out the sheet of music – she, too, was starting to think of the mystery madrigal as *Country Goodness* – and stared at its inky markings in minute detail. She felt a ghost of the pride she had felt when Villiers showed an unfeigned interest in what she was doing. When she held up her ticket for inspection, it was with a similar sense of vindication, of being, once again, a member of the world.

35

Giles had expected Julia to put up some resistance to his idea that they change hotels and move further west for a few days. She had once let slip something about the north coast of the county being the only bearable bit not spoiled by tourism. She was equable, however, even keen, and hurried to make their reservation in a good, small hotel in Penzance she had read about. She had not been remotely cross at his no-show at the church the night before, although she plainly saw through his lame excuse.

Her eagerness to move on and a briskness in her manner when she answered his enquiries with, 'Oh, fine. She played beautifully. It was great,' suggested that all had not gone according to her plans. Perhaps she had been a little too forward and been snubbed for it. Perhaps another of her players had been there and paid her no attention. He knew better than to pry.

'I don't know why Selina was so insistent on my being there, really,' she said as their car climbed the downs above Wadebridge and made for the faster road west.

'I'm sure Jemima was pleased someone from the agency was there,' he said.

'She was a bit embarrassed, actually. Oh well,' she sighed, kicked off her shoes and turned on the radio. 'Did my bit.'

He thought she had dozed off because she became so quiet and said nothing when he later changed stations but when they were passing the turn-offs for Redruth and Camborne he noticed she was both awake and tense, warily watching the housing estates and disused engine houses as they passed.

'So how did you get on yesterday?' she asked.

'Oh. Okay,' he said. 'Sorry. I should have told you earlier. I didn't think.'

'That's all right.'

'It's rather sad actually. Eliza's mother died. It was a stroke that sent her to hospital, then she had another one the night they got down here. She wasn't particularly old.'

'How are they?'

'Well I don't know. That's the thing. It was a neighbour I spoke to. Eliza's taken Dido off to the neighbour's caravan near St Just somewhere.' He heard how phoney his deliberate vagueness sounded.

'That's a bit off. I mean of her not to tell you.'

'You know what Eliza's like. Scatty at the best of times.'

'And why a *caravan*, for pity's sake?'

'I don't think she could afford much more,' he said gently.

'She could if she bothered to get a job,' Julia snorted. 'Shouldn't you tell St Saviour's? I bet she hasn't thought to.'

'They knew she was coming down. Schools must have broken up by now anyway, judging from this lot.' He braked and they both stared at the line of caravans and holiday-laden cars blocking both lanes of the carriageway up ahead of them. 'I'm just a bit worried about how Eliza takes it. Her relationship with her mother wasn't good and if she's going to slide into another depression . . .'

'*Another* depression? Is she out of the first?'

'You know what I mean. If she is, then a caravan at the back of beyond isn't the safest place to do it. And Dido's life's grim enough as it is.'

'So I suppose you'll want to go over and see them.' Julia was picking at some fluff on her toes.

'Oh, I dunno. Maybe. But we're on holiday. What do you fancy for lunch? Could we get lobster again, do you think? Is this hotel of yours up to it?'

It was a delightful hotel, perched above Penzance's little harbour with views across a small boatyard to St Michael's Mount. The owner, a legendary beauty, had furnished it like a private house so that each room had its own books, paintings and character.

They ordered two Newlyn crab for their supper then made do with a tapas and sherry lunch in a bar on the neighbouring street. For a moment Giles suspected that this admittedly pretty street was all that survived of old Penzance. German bombs had been discarded along the seafront, he had heard, by pilots turning round for home after raids along the South coast. The rest of the town, apart from a marvellously self-important domed bank, seemed to be bog-standard high street shops and substandard Victorian architecture.

But having strolled down Chapel Street, peering in at antique shop windows, passing a bizarre building in the 'Egyptian' style and the house where the Brontës' mother was born, they found delights hidden on the other, genteel side from the harbour. From the commanding church, with its views across both sides of the bay and subtropical graveyard planted with palms, eucalyptus and yuccas they were led on by curiosity and chance through a succession of pretty alleys, past lush gardens and nicely under-renovated Georgian townhouses, all with the constant keening of seagulls and occasional dazzling glimpses of the bay. They sat and sunned themselves amidst the fantastically unEnglish planting of Morrab Gardens, then wound on through another park to a small museum of Cornish life and a gallery of Newlyn School paintings. After a few minutes of paintings detailing the pilchard industry or with titles like *And Will He Ne'er Come Back To Me?*, fatigue, heat and sherry overcame them and they succumbed to a cream tea on the museum's little terrace.

'Well this is nice,' he said. And it was. He could not remember when he had last simply spent time with her for the fun of it. Apart from evenings, when they seemed to be either out, entertaining or exhausted or weekends, when time not dedicated to Dido would often be swallowed up in tedious domestic chores.

'Yes,' she said. 'It's a pretty town.'

'I can't think why it's less popular than St Ives.'

'No beach,' she said. 'No surfing.'

They sat on in companionable silence while he ate her second scone. A gang of girls came by, hot-cheeked and short-skirted from a tennis match. Flushed faces aside, they had Julia's rather Irish colouring.

'You'd fit right in here,' he said. 'Maybe we should sell up and move to Penzance, buy one of those nice houses with a big garden. We could live off the interest from the difference in value. I could give singing lessons and you could teach deportment and elocution.'

'Fuck off,' she said, only half-laughing. 'You'd die of boredom. No opera. No theatre. No half-way decent concerts. No Conran Shop. No Harvey Nicks. And half those little restaurants around Chapel Street will be closed out of season. And only one of *those* would be halfway decent. Fresh lobster for dinner's a treat, but it's not Granita.' She paused as if still contemplating the life change he had suggested. 'Shall we head back?'

'If you like.'

He put an arm on her shoulder as they walked, smelling

the tang of her fresh sweat, but she soon became too hot and adjusted her bag as a pretext for shrugging him off. He smiled to himself as they walked in silence. It was so true; things she rated as constituting *quality of life* were precisely the things dewy-eyed ex-Londoners gave up to pursue *quality of life* out of town. She had relaxed her look, at least, was wearing only lipstick and had her legs bare but he could be sure her bag contained mobile phone, address book, diary, vitamin tablets and Chanel lippy, that her tee shirt and linen trousers alone would have cost what most of the women they were passing spent on clothes in an entire year.

He had read her silence as placid, neutral and could not help hearing a certain sexual promise in her suggestion that they return to the hotel. But they were no sooner alone than she shook him off, prickly as a wet cat, and he realised her silence had been only a gathering storm.

'That's the only reason we've come here, isn't it? That was the only reason you came to Trenellion with me. You dressed it up as a romantic getaway but all you were thinking about was how to get away to check on Eliza! Well go. Just take the car and go over to see her. I can't *stand* seeing you pretending it's not the only thing you're thinking about.'

'Is that how it seems?' he said, wounded, despite his guilt.

'It's how it is, isn't it?'

'Not entirely.'

'Huh! That's even worse. Killing two birds with one stone – a romantic getaway *AND* a spot of marital maintenance . . .'

'It's not marital.'

'She's still your wife. Trust me. It's marital.'

'What's going on here? I thought everything was fine. What's up? This is so unlike you.'

'Please. Don't be nice to me.'

He had approached her again and laid a hand on the

small of her back, the spot that usually calmed her to melting point.

'Why not?' he asked, flattening his palm on her hot skin and amazed that he could be so turned on by her when she was furious enough to stab him. He saw fat tears squeezing out of her eyes. 'Hey!' he said, lifting the hair off her face. 'Don't cry. What's up? I don't need to check on Eliza or Dido or anyone. What's up, Babe?'

She clung to him now and began to cry so hard and so jaggedly that it took him a second or two to interpret the words she gasped into his shoulder.

36

'You heard,' she said.

Giles held her away from him. He looked shocked. He did not look happy. 'You're kidding.'

'I never kid,' she reminded him. 'I have no sense of humour.'

This was not what she had intended. When she realized why he had steered them down to Penzance, she had quietly accepted that Villiers was right. If she had any chance of winning him for good from Eliza, it was not as a mother. She had not meant to lose her temper and she certainly had not meant to cry and blurt out what she could never take back. Bloody hormones. As in the bathroom with Dido, it was as though the baby could read her mind and take desperate measures to guarantee its survival; throw open a gland, like a valve on a steam engine, and release another dose to course through her system and scupper her mood.

'I've got you pregnant,' he said, still holding her, still not looking happy.

'Yes. I guess we're one of those one-in-whatever couples the Pill lets down. But don't worry. I made the appointment as soon as I heard and it'll be sorted as soon as we get back. I wasn't going to tell you.'

'You'd have got rid of my baby without telling me?'

'It's not *your* baby, it's ours and it's not a baby yet, it's just a . . . a . . .'

Another blast on the steam valve. She tried to pull away, took the spotted handkerchief he offered and brought her mood to heel with a nose-blow.

'I know it's yours. I mean it's your body and your life and . . . Are you sure?'

'Villiers was so right.' She pulled away from him and sat on the bed's edge, reassembling herself from damp and sliding parts.

'What's he got to do with this?'

'He said you preferred me unencumbered, neat and tidy and *unElizaish*. Not a mother.'

'Fuck Villiers.' He knelt on the carpet, actually knelt before her, forcing himself into her downcast view. 'He's only right in that I'd never thought of you as a mother. You never seemed the, I dunno, the type. That sounds so stupid. Be honest. Look at me. Do you really not want it?'

'I hate it. I feel sick and when I'm not feeling sick I want to cry. It's making me soft in the head and then it'll make me gross. Then think of the chaos it's going to cause.'

'But Dido . . .'

'Dido's different. She's a grown-up in a kid's body half the time. And we give her back. This is . . .' Julia slapped her stomach wearily. 'This'll be full time. No excuses. No calling in sick. No *Eliza would you mind awfully.*'

'So you don't want it.'

'No. Really not.'

He sighed, stood up. 'Fine. Okay. Your body, your decision.'

'Why?' she asked. 'Villiers was right, wasn't he?'

'No. He . . . I . . . No. That's not fair. I'll take the day off if need be. Take you to the clinic.'

'You can't. It's on Friday. You've got the dress that afternoon. I'm a big girl. I can deal with it myself.'

'Have you done this before?'

She thought a moment, decided he had a right to the truth.

'Yes.'

'Since meeting me?'

'Just once. Yes.'

'When?' He sounded stunned.

'I don't know, Giles. Ages ago. I'd barely met you. I wasn't on the Pill when we met.' She remembered his relief and excitement when she let him stop using condoms. Condoms that had already failed them.

'Jesus.'

'What? I thought you just said it was my body.'

'It is. But I wish you'd told me.'

'Why? So you could beat your breast and wave your liberal credentials?'

'So I could have asked you to keep it.'

'But I thought you . . .'

He held her knees. 'Just because I never thought of you as, well, in *that* way, doesn't mean I don't want to be a father.'

'You?'

'I would *love* to be a father. I would love nothing more.'

'So you want me to keep it.'

'That's not fair. I can't make you.'

'No. But if I didn't go to the clinic, you'd be happy.'

Now *he* was getting teary. 'More than you'd ever know.'

'Oh,' she said. 'Don't cry or you'll set me off again.' She kissed his upturned face, kissed his wet eyes. 'You really want me to keep it? You're sure?'

'Yes. Yes. Sod your rights. I forbid you to do anything *but* keep it.'

'But what about work? We've got used to two incomes and children cost thousands a year.'

'We'll manage. Everyone else does. I'll just have to work harder, get Selina to work harder.'

'Oh,' she said.

'It'll be so beautiful.'

'Will it?'

'Of course.' He kissed her. 'And clever and musical and much loved. Fuck.'

'What?'

'I'm going to be a father.' He laughed. 'A proper father!'

She grinned, allowing herself to relax at last. 'Looks like it.'

He climbed up on the bed, pushed her backwards and undid the waistband on her linen trousers. 'Does it show yet?' He kissed her belly, tickling her. 'Can you feel it?'

'Only when I'm sick. It's still a tadpole.'

'Are you allowed to drink?'

'Now that I'm keeping it, not really. One glass won't hurt, I don't suppose. Oh God. Now I'll have to read up on it and everything. Go to fucking antenatal classes.'

'Me too.'

'Must you? It's not very sexy.'

'Oh, I dunno.' He kissed her belly again, tried to bite it. 'I want you to be huge.' He bit her hip. 'Immensely gravid.'

She ran her fingers into his curls and pressed so that his nose sank deep in her flesh. She let him make love to her in the slow, rather terrifyingly worshipful way he liked best, with her a kind of prone, inactive sacrifice.

He fetched them each a single glass of champagne. They spent the interval until dinner lolling on the bed alternately making playful plans or indulging in sweet, rare nostalgia about how they had met, how she had caught his attention, holidays they had taken, hotels they had stayed in, strange places where they'd had sex. As the languid afternoon folded into a woozy evening it was as though Villiers had never planted the doubts in her mind.

Giles reacted quite enchantingly in every way. He was supportive, sensuous, excited. They had gorged themselves on crab, creamy local cheese and strawberry shortbread and were finishing coffee beside the fire, bashful because of other guests, when it dawned on her that he had still not said he loved her, or mentioned the possibility of marriage.

37

The train pulled into Penzance at about eight in the morning. Her first impulse was to ring Pearce to ask for a lift but she checked herself. Not only had she just spent a night on a train in yesterday's clothes but she cherished dim hopes of not emphasizing the needy impression she must already have made on him. Instead she bought herself a hot chocolate at a greasy spoon then boarded the next St Just bus.

The bus was almost empty, but a smiling, confidential woman sat across the aisle from her and soon murmured that she was on her way to St Just to take up a new job in a butcher's there. Then she began to interrogate Eliza.

Perhaps because she was shattered, perhaps because the woman made her nostalgic for Kitty, she found herself opening up to her, not bridling as she would usually have done. She confessed she was married but separated, childless but a mother to her dead sister's girl, jobless, rootless but originally from Camborne.

'Ah, there! You see?' the woman said, brightening as though all were suddenly clear to her. 'That's it, then. You're too rackety by half! Chopping yourself into bits, a parcel of you here, a parcel over there. Not really a wife, not really a mother, not really anything at all. You need to settle down or you'll wear yourself out. Spread yourself less thin, my lover, and do it in one place. You're home now. That's the main thing. Find yourself a nice local man. They're stickers round here, if you choose carefully.'

'I'm not sure a man's the answer,' Eliza murmured.

'Well they're never the answer, true enough, but they're a step in the right direction.'

They were passing the quarry. Eliza wondered if she could persuade the driver to let her out early to save her the walk back up Bosavern.

'When I was a girl,' her companion went on, 'the best place to find the right man was St Just churchyard wall. Sit there of a morning, girls'd say, and see what you can see.'

St Just was coming into view. Eliza could already make out the defaced sign with *City Limits* painted under *St Just-in-Penwith*. She began to rise hesitantly.

'Robert, stop here. Young lady wants to get down.'

The bus squeaked to a halt and the doors opened.

'It's you that's in Kitty's caravan, isn't it?' the woman said.

Eliza nodded.

'Thought so. Bye then.'

Walking down the lane to the caravan, Eliza had an intense desire to curl up in sleep. She tossed her things on the table, took a bracing shower, then collapsed onto her bed still wrapped in a towel and fell into deep slumber.

She woke hearing Molly call her name.

'Thank God you're here!' Molly said, quite unabashed at Eliza's nakedness.

'What's happened?' Cold panic seized her. 'Where's Dido?'

Molly smiled. 'Don't fret. She's fine. It's just that she and Lucy can't plant broccoli all day – it'd wear them out – and we just had someone drop out. I was hoping you . . .'

'I'll get dressed. What time is it?' She found her watch and was amazed that the morning had melted away. 'Hang on.'

'Brilliant. Put on something old, 'cause you'll get covered in dust and spattered with rabbit repellent.' Molly sat at the little table glancing around her while Eliza tugged clothes from the mess spilling out of her holdall.

'Aren't you working in the library today?'

'Using up some of my leave,' said Molly wryly. 'That girl of yours is amazing. She's got Lucy keen to help out for once. Lucy never helps out. Mind you, Pearce is paying them something, so maybe that's it. How was your trip?'

'Tiring. It's good to be back.'

'Find out what you needed?'

Eliza shook her head. 'It was silly of me really. I wanted to be able to come home and tell you and Pearce that *Country Goodness* was definitely by Trevescan and that you could sell it for thousands of pounds to buy a new combine or something.'

'But it isn't?' Molly's face fell a little.

'Well. No. It can't be. It looks like his writing and sounds like his style but it was written after he died.'

'Ah well.' Molly shrugged as they got into her ancient Saab. 'It's still a nice piece.'

She drove like a fury over the brow of Bosavern and down to Cot Valley and up the lane to Pearce's farm. Only the potholes seemed to slow her.

'In case you're wondering,' she said, pulling sharply into a field, 'the Neanderthal driving the tractor is my husband. Morris. How's that? Perfect timing.'

The tractor had pulled up to a laden trailer while the planters reloaded the device behind it with blue plastic trays of sturdy seedlings.

'Hiya.' Dido was so muddy she was barely recognisable. Like Lucy's, her hair stuck up stiff with powdered earth. Her grin was startlingly white amidst the grime. 'How'd it go?'

'Thank God,' said Lucy. 'Come on. Let's go get lunch.'

'Now stick around at Pearce's, you two,' Molly said.

'We will.'

'Find something to eat and clean yourselves up. But no messing around on the silo or whatever.'

'Okay. See you later.'

The girls sauntered off back towards the farmhouse. Eliza felt a slight ache at seeing them go and feeling herself excluded.

'When you're ready.'

She turned back to find Pearce, Molly and another man no one thought to introduce sitting on the contraption waiting for her. There was a fourth seat left spare between brother and sister. She sat.

Pearce smiled kindly and gave her some bundled-up sacking to soften the metal seat. 'Thanks for helping us out,' he said. 'It's quite easy. You just take a handful of plants in your left hand. Don't worry. They don't break that easily. Then you click them, one at a time, into that wheel between your knees. Every other clicker. Roots uppermost. You'll soon get the hang of it. Ready?'

Comically nervous, Eliza grabbed a handful of seedlings from the tray before her. 'Ready,' she said.

'Okay, Morris!'

There were four metal seats fixed above four devices which simultaneously opened a shallow furrow, seized a seedling in a grip and tucked it into a furrow before pulling earth back around it. All the four humans had to do was keep the devices regularly fed and make sure the seedlings, which were some four or five inches tall, were seized at the right point on their stems to see them planted at the optimum depth.

It seemed impossibly hard to Eliza to click the seedlings into place fast enough while keeping her left hand supplied with fresh plants and without snapping their stems. The seedlings

313

were still moist with a white spraying of rabbit repellent, which splashed occasionally and soon began to make her lips feel hot and mustardy. Occasionally her planter's arms would click shut too soon and Pearce would halt the tractor, jump off, plant the one she had missed, then start them up again. It amazed her he had the time to keep an eye on her progress as well as his own.

The work became easier with surprising speed, however. She relaxed into its steady rhythm and began to enjoy the regular click-clicking of the four planting wheels. The sense of reaching, grasping and stooping in harmony with the others appealed to her, as did the simple pleasure of travelling with no effort across a sunny field while sitting on a bouncy seat with her feet hovering inches off the soil. She relaxed sufficiently to glance up now and then to enjoy the view of the nearby ocean. The repetitiveness of the task was more soothingly hypnotic than mind-numbing, and she realised she could think deeply of other things while doing it.

She felt strangely protected, with Molly on one side of her and Pearce on the other, each so much stronger and bigger boned than she was. They made her feel like a pale emissary from a less thriving tribe. Once it was established that she could cope, Morris gradually speeded up. They passed across the long field and back, pausing now and then to allow fresh trays of plants to be brought out from the storage rack or other ingenious stowing places around the tractor. The nameless man passed occasional boiled sweets and toffees and Molly offered up short bursts of gossip, or commentary on the state of someone's health or the behaviour of their children.

Pearce seemed entirely absorbed in the minutiae of the business at hand – whether Morris was keeping the lines quite straight, whether they had enough trays on board to see them back to the trailer or whether some new variety of broccoli they were planting was as sturdy as last year's equivalent. If anything, his silence made her more aware of his close presence than if he had been bantering with Molly and the pick'n'mix man. She noted his deep breathing and occasional unguarded sighs, the battered, antique watch he wore and the unfair advantage his wide grip gave him in enabling him to carry so many seedlings at once.

She thought about her sudden trip back to London and what it represented. Had the madrigal turned out to be penned in the rear pages of an edition that matched Trevescan's dates, she would have been unable to resist calling up Dr Goldhammer with the news. She would have come back fired up to complete her thesis and restart her life with a small spasm of labour and creativity. In her heart she knew, guiltily, that the unattributed madrigal was still exciting and entirely worthy of research – the brief, unsettling encounter with Villiers Yates had shown her that. But she was left seeing the trip to London as a last few sporadic steps up a blind alley, a last attempt to revive a life that no longer fitted her. The fact that she had reached the point where the madrigal only fired her interest if it could be made to fit in with the work she had already done on Trevescan was a measure of how poorly academic life now suited her. All the time she was with Giles (and indeed, for much of her insanely misjudged time with Paul) the thesis, neglected or no, had represented a kind of security pass, a voucher she had only to fill out to be readmitted to a world whose rules she understood and where she knew she could acquire a measure of public standing.

In a sense, though, yesterday's disappointment had invoked a curse only to break it and now she was at last free to begin any life she chose. Only now could she see just how oppressively guilt-inducing the incomplete thesis had been. And how entirely irrelevant to the wider scheme of things.

For years, she now saw, she had been drip-feeding a poisonous fantasy wherein her happy fulfilment rested solely on her being called Doctor and on her being quietly esteemed in a set of quiet university rooms by a succession of quiet people. Daring to step aside from all that was giddying. Dido was so simply happy talking with her new friend, muddied, tired and happy. Molly had her job in the library at a community's heart, her daughter, her funny madrigal group, her semi-detached marriage and the freedom to spend her paid leave getting filthy on her brother's farm. She radiated a quality that had nothing to do with status and everything to do with the uncomplicated acceptance of how life was. Giles and Paul were unhappy, unquiet souls it seemed to her because they would always be striving. They raised that strife into a kind of creed, mistaking it for the very sensation of life when its effect on their lives was the opposite of vivifying. Pearce, on the other hand, had perhaps learned not to strive. He had an inner life – one glance at his bookshelves told her that – but he was not forever troubled to change or improve his outer one.

Purely as an exercise in time-passing fantasy, Eliza tried on lives for size, lives that would enable her to stay in St Just rather than return to London. Piano teacher. History teacher. Singing teacher. Librarian. Sales assistant in a bookshop. Child minder. Village schoolmistress. None of the images she conjured up – with herself in settings and clothes to match – caused any revulsion.

'Do you ever need help in the library?' she asked Molly while they were discarding empty trays and taking on new ones from the vast crates she had learned to call stills.

'Sometimes,' Molly said. 'Especially when we have schools in. Why? Are you volunteering?'

Eliza only laughed by way of answer and carried on fantasising. She pictured a house, a modest cross between Pearce's farmhouse and Molly's cottage, a small garden, Dido leaving it for school, Dido leaving it on dates with nice, gruff local boys in borrowed cars.

As the afternoon drew on and several hundred cauliflower seedlings passed in and out of her grasp, the labour lost its novelty and charm and began to make her lower back ache. Molly showed her how to stretch backwards over a rounded rock in the hedge to relieve it between rows. But Eliza remained detached from both ache and labour in her private revelation. Her eyelids as well as her lips began to burn gently where she had unthinkingly wiped them with rabbit repellent but the sensation was cooler than that of the kindling possibility inside her.

The nameless man continued to dole out toffees but was never introduced.

She ended the day as she began it, swept along by others. When she refused payment, after Pearce had paid Dido, saying she owed him for the childminding, Molly in turn refused to let them go home to the caravan. Insisting Eliza stay, bathe, dress in clean, borrowed clothes, she softened her into staying for dinner.

Molly cooked while Pearce entered figures in the computer before joining her. Eliza lay in the bath amazed at the filth that floated off her and listening to the low buzz of brother and sister chatting in the room below her and the music and laughter from the television the girls were glued to elsewhere. Once again this house was claiming her – with food and clothes and comforts.

She had barely seen Dido that morning and enjoyed hearing her tales, how she had taken part in the last day of term activities and had helped Pearce round up cattle and helped Molly with a glitch in her e-mailing system.

'I really like it here,' Dido said artlessly as she finished. 'I think we should move.'

Lucy added her noisy support to this idea but Molly silenced them, saying, 'Yes, but Eliza needs to be in town for the libraries and concerts and, well, for her work.'

'Oh, I'm not so sure that any of that matters, really,' Eliza heard herself say. She had gorged herself on Molly's rabbit casserole and was finally understanding the sense of virtuous exhaustion Kitty had always referred to as *a good ache*. 'We could probably live here as easily as anywhere else.'

Perhaps she had imagined it but she thought she detected a distinct change in the atmosphere when she said this, a kind of realigning of attitudes. 'What?' she asked. 'What did I say?' and everybody laughed.

When Molly stood to go, Eliza did not stand to go with her but Dido did, saying she wanted to help Lucy to the next level of Queen of the Dead.

'I'll drop her off tomorrow,' Molly said and suddenly they were gone and Eliza was alone on a sofa with Pearce.

'Tell me about your parents,' she said, suddenly curious.

'She had a heart attack when she was, ooh, what, sixty-five and Dad died in an accident a little over a year ago,' Pearce said. 'Silly idiot fell off a barn roof.' He cleared his throat.

Then they both laughed because she had not meant how did they die but what were they like and quite suddenly Pearce was holding her hand, enveloping it in his which felt twice the size and very hot and dry and she could do nothing but stare at their interlocking fingers.

'They were lovely people,' she said, 'judging from you two.'

As answer he only squeezed her hand.

'I'm terribly drunk, Pearce. Drinking when you're tired's never a good idea.'

'Want me to drive you home?' he asked.

'Would you mind?'

'Come on, then.' He stood and held out a hand to pull her onto her feet. She noticed he had not had a chance to wash yet and realised this was because she had taken all the hot water.

The cold night air and the smells in the Land Rover sobered her quickly. She said nothing as he drove her up the lane and over the hill and neither did he. But he got out to see her to the caravan door and, when he stooped to kiss her goodnight, she found she could not let go. She fumbled behind her for the hidden key and, loath to stop kissing, they staggered into the tiny space and fell onto the bed.

They made love quickly, tearing at each other's clothes, barely undressing. She felt the grit between them, the earth thickening his hair, the druggy buzz of rabbit repellent as she kissed his face clean. When she began to come she felt tears on her cheeks and when he did, he swore, furiously and repeatedly, as though things had not gone at all according to plan. But then he mastered himself and laughed and wrapped his long legs tight about hers and she sensed that, if only she could see, he might have tears in his eyes too.

'Sorry,' he said at last. 'I was meant to drive you home.'

'I think you just did,' she said and they chuckled.

'This bed's a bit small,' he said.

'It's bloody tiny. I don't know how Kitty manages on it.'

'Where d'you want to wake up? Here or there?'

'Here,' she said without thinking. 'It's not that . . . oh God. Pearce, it's only because of Dido.'

He kissed her. 'I know.' He hugged her again and yawned deeply into her hair. 'I'd best go or I'll fall asleep on you,' he muttered. 'Can I . . . can I see you tomorrow, Eliza?'

'Yes,' she said. 'Yes please.'

When he extricated himself from around her, pulled his clothes back together in the darkness and stumbled out she felt suddenly cold and wretched so ran out after him.

'Pearce?'

'Yeah?'

'Just hang on, would you, while I grab some clothes.'

38

She was the first woman to sleep in this bed since his mother died. Pearce did not tell her that, naturally. He knew it would have disturbed her on several counts, not least the suggestion that he was a romantic failure.

Suddenly shy, because of the wash of light from the bedside lamp, she undressed quickly then slipped under the duvet with a giggle. And there she was, peeping up at him, a new woman in his parents' bed, tee shirt kept on for warmth and/or modesty.

He sat on the bed and touched her hair, amazed. She kissed his wrist then pulled him towards her so she could kiss him properly. But because she was still a new woman in his mother's bed, he felt unable to respond in kind and lay there for a while, making a play of being trapped on the wrong side of the duvet.

'Your hair's all earthy still,' she murmured.

'Oh yes,' he said, getting up, grateful. 'I'll take a shower. Can I get you anything?'

She merely looked and shook her head happily. Her eyes were heavy. He turned out the light. 'Won't be long,' he said.

But the shower and his excitement left him far too wakeful for sleep so he wandered into the office, wrapped in a couple of towels, and began sorting out paperwork into heaps. He wrote cheques for the most urgent bills then forced himself to go through the latest bank statement, ticking it off against cheque stubs, making sure there had been no mistakes.

The outlook was not dire but neither was it brilliant. The farm was standing still, financially. He flicked through leaflets and circulars he did not have the energy or will to deal with as he ought. There was a pot of Objective One funding earmarked for Cornwall by the EEC because it was so poor and many farmers were finding ways of tapping into it by diversifying, creating employment, opening farm shops, B&Bs, quad bike tracks and angling lakes, but none of it appealed. Pearce felt that if he wasn't to stay a farmer he had no business sitting on the farm.

He found a little drawing Dido had left him when she and Lucy were playing in here that afternoon, a surprisingly deft cartoon of the two of them swallowed up in a herd of steers, Dido visible only as a pair of legs. He smiled over it then pinned it on his board. There he found a circular from the Rural Payments Agency. He had pinned it up to keep it free of the mess as a reminder but had still taken no action on it. He knew he was eligible for more subsidies than he claimed. There was an Extensification Premium which required some complex calculations to compute but which certainly was not beyond him and would bring in several more thousand a year, as would his co-operating with the scheme hatched by a cunning neighbour and some local birding enthusiasts to half-flood some of their least productive inland acres to create a nesting and feeding site for waders near the existing footpath.

Even more than his father before him, who at least was old enough to remember the post-war conditions that brought them in, Pearce felt uncomfortable claiming subsidies when other farmers were so badly off. He was stung into doing so only by the knowledge that his under-claiming would make no difference and that there were corporate farms now who could afford to employ accountants to pursue such unearned income five days a week instead of on the odd rainy day reserved for paperwork. He suspected that the days of small family farms were numbered and felt that farming should not be kept alive artificially, any more than other industries had been. There was an irrefutable law of natural economics at work. More and more food was imported and less and less homegrown stuff required. He had stopped growing new potatoes because the supermarkets had created an expectation for year-round, washed ones, killing off the market for seasonal earthy ones. Farmers like him would soon have to retrain, become contract workers for corporate farms as Morris was trying to do, or expect to lose more and more money with less and less public sympathy.

As he reached to turn off the desk light and stop depressing himself, Pearce saw the answering machine was flashing at him.

He pressed play then hastily turned down the volume as the machine beeped, so as not to wake Eliza.

The voice was cultivated, plausible and made him immediately suspicious. 'Oh hello. My name is Villiers Yates. You don't know me but I'm an old friend of Eliza Easton. Eliza Hosken as was. Whom I believe knows you. Eliza led me to believe you have a music manuscript thought to be in the hand of Roger Trevescan. I don't know if she told you but I represent the Byatt Foundation in Texas, who are building up a valuable collection for the museum and university they expect to open in two or three years from now. I had an unofficial word with my contact there and, subject to its being at least reasonably authenticated by the British Library, for instance, they'd be extremely interested in making you an offer. I can't come up with anything off the top of my head but, to give you a rough idea, they've just acquired an incomplete and frankly I think rather dubious manuscript of a Morley part-song.'

He named a sum so startling, Pearce found himself writing it down on the top of a bank statement.

'Anyway. Enough of my waffle. You probably aren't remotely interested in selling but, given the cost of insuring things like that these days, I thought it only neighbourly to let you know. As I said, my name is Villiers Yates.'

Villiers Yates, Pearce wrote along with the sequence of phone numbers, home, work and mobile. This was not a casual enquiry, plainly. Nor a *neighbourly* one. He wiped off the message, stuck the details behind a corner of his noticeboard, then switched off the light. As he shut the office door, the draught knocked the bank statement down behind his desk but the smooth, suggestive voice and its message was wedged firmly in his mind.

Had Eliza been awake when he threw off the damp towels and slid in behind her, he would have asked her about it. But she wasn't. She stirred just sufficiently to take his arm and pull it around her as she nestled against him, with one of her small, feline noises, and the delicious smell of her and the novelty of climbing exhausted into a warmed bed and finding her in it drove all other cares from his mind.

39

Repeatedly through the night Eliza suffered variations on the same dream in which Dido was taken from her – by Kitty, by her mother, by the police, by Julia once and, most alarmingly, by her long dead sister – and she was given only the terse explanation: *it's because you're not fit*.

In each instance she woke doubly disoriented, slowly reassembling herself in an unfamiliar bed with an unfamiliar man. While she untensed, remembering where she was, he mumbled something, held her more tightly and fell asleep again. And the pressure of his arm and the faint, dog-beddish smell of the sheets (he clearly had not anticipated this visit) soothed her with their reality.

There was moonlight – he had no curtains in this room – and a spectral glow from an old electric clock-radio which softly creaked as it revolved its numerals. The house made sounds around them. A window thumped softly in its sashes rocked by a night breeze, boards creaked, mice – she hoped they were only mice – scuttled in the attic. The night was marked out for her in a series of these strange, wakeful interludes in each of which the room, the bed, the man, the house and its sounds grew less of a shock.

At last, when the boiler rumbled into early morning action and set the plumbing sighing and burbling to itself, she emerged from the dream without stirring, without causing him to wake too. She lay there, entirely awake. He was pressed in close behind her, his arm about her. She could feel his breath in her hair and, when she moved her head slightly, his stubbled chin pressed into the back of her neck. His knees had drawn up, following hers, so that she was effectively sitting on his lap. If she had woken with Giles or Paul this close, her instinct would have been to feel smothered and to roll free. Why, then, did she not feel trapped now?

Why not? she thought. *Dare to think it!*

The radio alarm clicked into life and Pearce stiffened against her, his morning glory nudging by degrees between her thighs while cultured voices urgently discussed terrible events in the other, larger world. A suicide bomb in Israel. An outrage against an Ulster school. He took advantage of a yawn and a stretch to press himself more completely against her and she slid a hand between her legs to guide him in. They made sleepy love during a heated discussion of the illegality of the continuing French boycott on British beef. It was all about him; Eliza felt herself watchful and unengaged. But she liked that occasionally. Controlling and giving pleasure could be as rewarding as abandonment to one's own.

Perhaps the thin sunlight made him shy, for he did not cry out or swear this time but only gasped and held her more tightly. Shameless because she could not see his face, she brought his hand down between her legs as he slipped out of her and, pressing down with both of hers, rubbed herself against his hot, hard palm until she reached what was at once a climax and a delicious return to sleep.

She opened her eyes at the soft chink of cup against saucer as he set some tea on the bedside table, then drifted off to sleep again. She woke once more as he started a tractor out in the yard. She sat up to drink cold tea and munch the buttered toast he must have brought up.

There was a deep recess in the wall behind the bed. An assortment of books was lined up there alongside a dented brass candlestick, a handful of rifle cartridges, a saucer spilling over with loose coppers and a very pretty Staffordshire greyhound. There was a photograph, too, in a cracked leather frame. She took it to peer more closely.

It was colour but only just. 1968? 1966? A version of Pearce but in a tweed suit and without the laughter lines, leaning against a granite stile. Two children, boy and girl, identically dressed in navy-blue Ladybird jerseys and camel-coloured cords perched on either side of him. His face was pained, hard even, but the way he had an arm wrapped round each child's legs and the way they were leaning into him spoke of kindness and protection. In the recess with candle and money offering, it looked like the icon in some informal country shrine. She replaced it carefully, recognising a precious, private relic.

She turned to the books and, from the little she had learnt of Pearce, was surprised to find a literary compost heap: some thrillers, a tractor maintenance manual, an unfamiliar Tolstoy, a guide to the footpaths of Madeira, Aubrey's *Brief Lives*, the Observer Book of British Insects, Elizabeth David's *Summer Cooking*, and both *Travels with My Aunt* and *Travels With A Donkey*. She reached for *Brief Lives* and, sipping cold tea, turned to fondly remembered stories; 'Sweet Sir Walter' becoming 'Swisser-Swatter' in the throes of passion and Queen Elizabeth's exquisite cruelty in welcoming the Earl of Oxford, returned after a seven-year embarrassed absence, 'My Lord, I had forgott the fart.' She read another potted biography, a sad one she had forgotten entirely or never read, then turned automatically to the brief entry on Trevescan.

There was more than one Cornish gentleman at court, for the Queen had it that they were all born courtiers and with a becoming confidence. Less generous spirits said it was more truly that she ruled such distant families by keeping their most favoured offspring by her side and still others, that men from such a remote and unruly county were the less likely to have formed dangerous and powerfull alliances close at hand. One such was Roger Trevescan, not a prized first son but a cunning Benjamin, skilled at languages, briefly a pet of Her Majesty's and most like to have proved himself a useful diplomat. He proved less a Benjamin than a Jonathan, however, for a friendship grew up between him and my Lord Beaufort's godlike younger brother, sighs, sonnets, madrigals and all, which set tongues wagging until My Lord must needs take action. To save the family honour while yet seeking to give a round offence and so inspire a duel, he took advantage of Trevescan's known excellence in Spanish and rumoured dealings for Walsingham among the enemie and penned a scurrilous unsubtle squib on the walls of the house of easement most frequented by the gentlemen of influence. The whole escapes me but I remember the opening couplet for its scurvy rhyme and libellous suggestion that he had whored himself to the enemy's emissary: 'Trevescan is Don Diego's Man, His Ladye, rather, or pute d'Espagne'. No mention of the godlike brother, for whom swift and manly business had been found elsewhere. The lines soon circulated, as such things are wont, and were even heard sung to the tune of one of Trevescan's more noted madrigals, until The Queen herself was heard to chuckle over them whereon it was assumed the Cornishman must fight. He fled home to his family's distant and fishy estates, however, proving his effeminacy.

Or so it seemed. Other Cornishmen came to replace him in time and he was quite forgot until word reached court that he had died a patriot and hero, defending the honour of his brother's betrothed during one of the Spanish raids then attempted in those less defended parts. For he was not a coward but rather preferred to seem so than to slay his friend's brother, as he surely would have had a duel been fought. Also a born courtier, as Her Majestie would have it, for an ancient law forbade the drawing of arms at court in any cause but Her own defence. My Lord Beaufort was distinguished only for the pox which cost him his nose. His brother may be assumed to have lapsed into virtue or plainnesse, for there came no further report of him.

Reading the familiar words, Eliza felt the old regretful twinge at Aubrey's casual scattering of references to Trevescan sonnets and songs since lost to posterity.

Showered, and dressed in her borrowed clothes, she followed the sound of the tractor out to a field above the sea where Pearce was cutting back the grass with a large, flat device that hung from the tractor's rear. Standing in a patch of yellow daisy-like flowers to watch his progress, she thought wryly that she should be holding a brimming jug of cider and a plate of bread, ham and onions.

He finished another pass across the field then paused and opened the cab door. As she approached, he offered her a hand then thought better, seeing how filthy it was, and turned it over to offer her his fist and wrist, with which she heaved herself up the high steps and into the cab. Stretching past her to tug the door to again he smelled so good she felt compelled to kiss him.

'Toothpaste,' he said.

'Grass,' she countered.

He set off again, glancing over his shoulder as he activated the cutting machine and lowered it. 'You'd better sit or you'll bang your head,' he said as they lurched away so she perched on a heap of old clothes, squashed in beside the armrest of his seat. He reached across her again to adjust a knob which made the noise from behind even louder. They nearly kissed again but he held back, said, 'You'll make me crash us,' and grinned.

He was heroically dirty as if he had rubbed earth between his hands then rubbed them on his cheeks. He seemed his own, wild, stiff-haired twin. Flecks of grass clung to his shirt, forearms, even eyebrows. The whites of his eyes, smile and a glimpse of relatively clean thigh through a rip in his oily jeans were the only vestiges of the outsize altar boy who had taken her on a date.

He saw her looking. 'Left the window open when I started on this,' he explained. 'Mind on other things, see.' He smiled to himself and she wondered for a moment what he meant.

'What are you doing?' she asked.

'What?' he said, turning down the radio.

'What are you doing?' she shouted for the noise was still intense even without *Woman's Hour* on full blast.

'Topping,' he said.

'Oh,' she said and he smiled again, knowing this had left her no wiser. She turned the radio volume back up. It was a discussion on the rise in chlamydia infections among schoolchildren. She wondered how many farmers listened to *Woman's Hour* as they worked, and whether it made them better husbands.

'How about you?' he asked.

She shrugged, ashamed at appearing like a bored child. 'Nothing really. I ought to go and check on Dido. Fetch her from Molly's.'

'I can run you up in half an hour.'

'No, honestly. I feel like a walk. This place must be getting to me. I *never* feel like a walk!'

So he gave her a lift in the tractor to the nearest point where she could scrabble over a hedge and onto the coast path. The route to St Just was quite simple, he said. 'Just keep the sea on your left and turn inland when you reach some cottages on the path above Cape Cornwall.'

She was prepared for the drama of waves on rocks but had forgotten the exuberance of Cornish coastal flowers. To either side and all over the steeply banking ground to her right were plush cushions of kidney vetch, thrift, policeman's buttons, even mats of naturalised exotica like hottentot fig with its flowers like stiff pink and yellow paper. More plant names came back to her as she walked, unused since biology fieldtrips out of school.

Not having glanced at a map first, she was unprepared for either the distance or the steep climb from cove to village and had a raging thirst by the time she arrived at Molly's terrace. But there was no reply and the door was locked. She walked on up the lane to the library but was told Molly was still on leave.

She had probably driven the girls down to the farm while Eliza was trailing along the coast path. Overcome with weariness, Eliza decided to be lazy and wait in the square for a bus that would carry her up Carn Bosavern to the caravan.

There was a bus in ten minutes so she slipped into the baker's shop, bought two saffron buns and a beaker of coffee and took herself to the churchyard wall to enjoy them. The coffee was filthy but the buns were fresh and good, authentically chewy, and restored her strength. She always found a cheap, rebellious pleasure in eating in the street because it was so strictly vetoed when she was growing up. When pressed, the only reason her mother gave her and Hannah against the practice was that people would think one was hungry.

'But I *am* hungry,' she would insist.

It was left to Hannah to explain, 'She means *poor*,' and earn herself a smacked hand.

'Well I *am* poor,' Eliza thought now as she licked the sugar off her lips and used a thumbnail to pick at a currant lodged in her teeth. Unbidden, the possibility occurred to her that Pearce was rich but she dismissed it. He was proud, perhaps, aware that inherited acres and a house with family connections was a burden of trust and duty but he was too careful even to be one of those comfortably off men who cultivated shabbiness as a kind of good manners towards the less fortunate.

Like the old houses around it with their swirl-carved kneelers, the church, she realised, was a small jewel. Lured inside by the ancient sundial above its porch, she was disappointed to find it had been zealously scraped of much of the character its exterior still possessed. Despite two drywork paintings on the plasterwork of Christ and St George, sure indications of the plaster's authenticity, some fool had not only removed most of it but had repointed the exposed granite with brown mortar, making a dark interior darker still.

Back outside she browsed through the small graveyard, reading the tombs. The range of names was as limited and local as those in the Polglaze family Bible. *By Tre Pol and Pen shall ye know Cornishmen* the rhyme had it but here it was all Eddys, Thomases and Clemenses. Heading back towards the gate, keeping an eye out for the bus, her attention was hooked by a familiar surname.

It was a Victorian stone, a tidy granite slab. *Near this spot lies Roger Trevescan of Vingoe Farm in this parish, courtier, composer, devoted son, loyal brother, who died in 1595 defending the honour of his kinswoman from Spanish raiders. This stone paid for by the Pentreath Society.* A few words followed in Cornish.

'The original's over there against the wall, Eliza.'

Eliza turned and saw that Molly had pulled up outside the bakers in her car. Eliza smiled sheepishly. 'I was just waiting for the bus,' she explained herself. 'Where d'you mean?'

'Behind that gorse bush there.'

Eliza walked a few paces to one side and found a sad line of broken or illegible stones tidied away against the yard's low wall so presumably separated from their graves.

Trevescan's was little more than a stump. . . . *evescan*, it read, in plainer lettering than the Victorian one. *Devoted son, loyal brother. Murdered in ye Spanish raide. Jan 5 1595. Requiescat.* A winged skull was now half-sunk in turf.

'Hop in,' Molly called. 'I'll run you up.'

'Where are the girls?' she asked. 'I called round.'

'They wanted a bigger bike ride than normal so I dropped them off on the edge of St Ives. They're coming back around the coastal route, through Zennor and Morvah. With the way my one dawdles and your one talks, it should take them most of the day. Was that okay? You didn't have plans?'

'No. I was just feeling a bit ashamed. All I was going to do was take advantage of the peace to flop.'

'So come to Truro. Keep me company.'

'I'm a hopeless shopper, I warn you.'

'I'm not shopping. Not really. I'm going to the Museum to look some things up for Lucy's holiday project. It's sort of a tradition with us. I do most of the work for her holiday projects in return for her doing all the washing up until term starts again.'

'Isn't that cheating?'

'Yes. But I make sure she understands it all and writes it up herself. I'd rather this way than spend the next eight weeks nagging her.'

'I thought she was bright.'

'She is for some things. Science things mainly. Anything involving the past is a kind of nightmare for her. She just glazes over.'

'What's the project?'

'Great-grandparents. They have to write a paragraph about each one and if possible find a photograph. Then they'll put them all together next term and see what patterns emerge. Who was local. Who fought in the Great War. Which families intermarried. How many died in childbirth or the great flu epidemic. I'm going to look up and copy the births, marriages and deaths for her and squirrel out the photos. She's got to do some work, though. Sorry. I'm kidnapping you. Are you sure you don't want to change?'

'Are these clothes very odd?'

'No!'

They laughed and Eliza asked at least to change into something a little more suitable for town.

'I drove round to Pearce's earlier, actually,' Molly admitted as they set off again. 'To pick you up. But you'd set off already.'

'Ah. Sorry.'

'That's okay.'

Eliza thought a moment. 'So you knew I'd spend the night there.'

'I knew what Pearce wanted. I hoped . . . I'm not going to pry, Eliza.'

'Okay.'

'But . . . Well —'

'— I spent the night,' Eliza said as simply as she could. 'It was very nice. He's a lovely man.'

'Yeah.' They began the steady descent from Newbridge towards Mount Misery and the main road. Eliza could tell Molly was searching for suitable words.

'And he's very . . .' Molly went on. 'He hasn't much *experience*.'

'You're not making out he's a virgin?'

'No, no. Not that. Not quite. God, I hope not! But . . .'

'Nearly.'

'Yeah. He's quite shy and the farm takes up so much time and the work's so isolating. And when we were growing up he was never much one for Young Farmers discos and stuff. He was never one of the lads in that way. Thank Christ. And then after Mum died he sort of got drawn into helping Dad out with things and . . . well . . . I suppose what I'm trying to say as his older sister I feel very protective towards him.'

'And you want to know if my intentions are honourable.'

'Oh dear. Well yes. I suppose I do.'

'Molly, I hardly know him. We've only just met.'

'That didn't stop you!' Molly said sharply then sighed and pulled herself back. 'Sorry,' she said. 'That came out all wrong. I just don't want him getting hurt,' she added more gently.

'And I don't intend to hurt him,' Eliza said. 'But we haven't . . . you know . . . *discussed* anything.'

'And he won't. Pearce can't bear talking about things. Not if they're personal.'

'Thanks for the warning.'

They laughed and the air cleared a little. Molly accelerated onto the dual carriageway with palpable relief.

'It's funny,' Eliza said. 'I'd never thought of myself in that light before.'

'I didn't mean —'

'I know, I know. But. Well. I suppose I *am* a single mother with an estranged husband and no job. And I've blown in from the big bad city with a dangerous lack of plans in mind. There's no one else at the moment.'

'Oh. Well that's good.'

'No. I mean is there anyone else? Is he *keen* on anyone right now?'

'Apart from you, you mean?'

'Don't be silly.'

'He's keen, you know. He'd never have moved so fast.'

'Well he was quite prompt,' Eliza admitted, thinking of a starry night sky.

'He's *really* keen.'

'Stop it!' Eliza laughed. 'So am I, all right? He's wonderful.

He's the loveliest man I've met in years. Now shut up and stop it!'

'Okay okay.' Molly smiled to herself as she concentrated on overtaking a lorry. She added, almost as an afterthought. 'No. So far as I know there's been no one since he had a hopeless crush on Maddie Nicholas.'

'What happened to her?'

'Got tired of waiting for him to say something, I think, and married someone else.'

'Ah. Did they . . . er?'

'I don't think so. No.'

Glancing across as they skirted a roundabout, Eliza noticed now the similarity between brother and sister. The features that looked simply blunt on him, their sculpture unfinished, looked too large and plain on her.

'That's his trouble,' Molly was saying. 'Most men – men like Morris – need a snog at the very least even to get them interested. But with Pearce the effect of just smiling at him and saying hello in a particular way could last for weeks with no further encouragement. I dunno. Women are meant to be the fantasists – they're always saying that's why men need dirty mags – but Pearce could dream me under the table.'

'All that being by himself and driving up and down alone with his thoughts,' Eliza said.

'Yeah.'

'And *Woman's Hour*.'

'Hmm.'

And for a few minutes they drove on in silence, contemplating the mystery of men. They passed the Camborne turn-off. Eliza sighed.

'What?' asked Molly.

'Oh. Nothing. Camborne, that's all. Reminded me of Kitty and how she'll want her place back and all the things we need to sort out.'

'Like what?'

'Like the house. My dead mum's house.'

'She was from Camborne?'

'No!' Eliza snorted, imagining her mother's genteel dismay at such an accusation. 'She was from Barnstaple. He was from Camborne and so was I.'

'You're kidding! You don't sound Cornish.'

'I do when I've drunk too much. Well he was the one with the accent and he left and she shouted at us if we so much as burbled our Rs so I never really picked it up properly. But yes, my sister and I were born in Camborne and went to school in Redruth.'

'Have you still got family down here?'

'Probably.' Eliza shrugged. 'I never thought about it. I never met any.'

'I bet you've got cousins at least.'

Molly's manner towards her now changed unmistakably. She had been friendly before but now was friendly and relaxed, as though the previous feeling had been not entirely trusting. It was touching, Eliza thought, that the mere accident of a place of birth could count for so much, this assumption that being Cornish would make her less likely to run away.

She never thought of herself as Cornish and researched Trevescan purely because his music spoke to her and no one else was studying him. Perhaps she would have had a stronger sense of roots had she been raised in an area more readily mythologised, like Mousehole or Lamorna.

Consulting the official records office required an appointment but, with a librarian's resourcefulness, Molly had tracked down an archive at the County Museum that was less formal. Up a flight of stairs off the museum's gift shop, the Courtney Library announced itself as *the oldest established Cornish history research centre in the county*, one of those proud claims which shrank in significance as one pondered them. It was a scrum of filing cabinets, bookcases, dusty albums and huge microfiche readers. After the sleek computer consoles and laptops in the British Library, these last seemed as cumbersome and quaintly antique as valve radios or early vacuum cleaners. The room's fittings did not appear to have been updated since the Seventies but it was a pleasant space. High windows gave out onto the bustle of River Street and between them hung a full length portrait of Arthur Quiller-Couch complete with tweed cap and pipe.

'Was that the one that believed in fairies?' Eliza asked.

'You're thinking of Conan-Doyle,' Molly told her. 'But Q-C wrote some good ghost stories.'

The few reading desks were deserted and the archivist seemed startled by their approach. As he found Molly the Newlyn microfiche 1890–1920 and fussily showed her how to use it, Eliza wondered what kind of person drifted into such a dry, remote sinecure. An historian, she supposed. Someone needing time for their own research into something so removed from daily concerns that they lost all ability to cope with the ordinary; the Development of Wood Joints in West Country Jacobean Joinery, North Devonian Chasuble Embroidery 1626 to 1702 or the Lost Madrigals of a Disgraced Elizabethan Courtier.

'And how can I help you?' He had turned to Eliza.

'She's with me,' Molly murmured, concentrating on finding Morris' grandmother in a raft of fishwives.

But Eliza asked, 'How far back do your records go?'

'It depends on the parish,' he said and she caught a faint whiff of some sad, dead smell; ear wax or a neglected tooth. 'Where a church survived untroubled they go back a long way. Paul was torched by the Spanish so the early records went with it.'

'St Just,' she said. 'Parish of St Just 1590 to about 1610.'

'Roseland or Penwith?'

'Penwith.'

'Nothing before 1595,' he told her without even needing to look. 'And it's very poor quality. Births, marriages or deaths?'

'Everything you've got.'

'Take a seat at the other reader please and I'll fetch it for you.'

She sat across from Molly at the second cumbersome microfiche reader. She clicked on the light and a fan whirred into motion inside. The screen seemed thick with dust but she knew better than to antagonise an archivist.

'What are you up to over there?' Molly asked, intrigued.

'Holiday project,' Eliza told her. 'Ssh.'

'Have you used one of these before?' the archivist asked, bringing over a roll of film tied with string and a brown cardboard label.

'All too often,' she sighed.

'Right.' He threaded the microfiche for her nonetheless and began to wind it. 'You'll have to go on a long way,' he said. 'The files you want are at the other end. And if you've used one before presumably you'll remember to hold this metal flap out of the way while you're winding or the film gets scratched.'

Left alone she held the flap obediently and wound. Thousands of records whirled by across the screen. Hundreds of hours of tedious, unvarying photography. Evidently others had repeatedly ignored his plea about the metal flap because the film was scored all over with scratches. They danced as she wound, like telegraph wires viewed from a train. Every now and then the screen went blank for a few turns before a fresh title page appeared.

'Bull's eye,' said Molly, finding the record she needed and making notes. 'One down, seven to go.'

Eliza reached the far end of the reel. *Cornwall Parish of*

St Just Vol 1 1595–1680 she read. The title page, like a blackmailer's demand or something waveringly held up at the start of an old cine film, was constructed from letters cut from a sheet then painstakingly lined up and glued to a backing card. The joins were clearly visible. *Filmed at the Penzance Library, Morrab Gardens, Penzance* it went on, in even tinier letters. *By permission of the Vicar of St Just. Filmed by the Genealogical Society, Salt Lake City, Utah, USA, January 1960.*

God bless the Mormons, she thought and wound on.

The word *BEGIN* squeaked across the scratchy screen followed by a photograph of the precious, leather-bound register, cruelly flattened out with its spine bunched up, the same register which could be viewed, and even handled, at the Records Office if one made an appointment. An elegant page of handwriting came next, describing how the original register had been rebound and restored in 1907, the then considerable cost of £4.10s and 8p being *defrayed by the Congregation*. And then the register began.

Poor condition was putting it mildly. The ancient pages, blackened by years of greasy finger marks, wood smoke, damp and, quite possibly, incense had been carefully patched and remounted only to be blackened further. Some pages were so dark they might have spent a year being kippered in a smokery. Beneath the surface stains, handwriting crept and spattered. Centuries of education and standardisation away from even the 1907 copperplate, much of it looked like the work of writers who were barely lettered. She squinted. She tried wiggling the focus knob.

'And another,' said Molly, taking triumphant notes. 'And a third. This is a doddle. Last year was wild flowers, which took for bloody ever.'

It was bitterly frustrating. If Trevescan's niece Rose married Michael Polglaze in 1615, and could be assumed not to have been around during the Spanish raid, when her parents were merely *betrothed*, it was a fair bet that her birth was recorded here. 1599. 1600. 1601. She could make out enough dates here and there to know she was in the right area of the register but the names eluded her.

'Something wrong?' Molly asked seeing her frown.

'No,' Eliza muttered. 'It doesn't matter really. Only idle curiosity.' Molly continued winding and making speedy notes then changed to the St Just records for the same period.

Someone cleared their throat. Eliza turned to find the archivist shyly offering her a small maroon volume.

'I know it feels a bit like cheating,' he sighed, 'But this is a transcript of the original. There are gaps but most of it's trustworthy, I gather.'

'Oh,' said Eliza, ridiculously pleased. 'Bless you!'

The pages were white, modern, barely read, the typeface a charmless sans serif. The printed text took up far less space than the scrawled original and in no time she found the pages corresponding to the murk she had failed to decipher. The layout presumably duplicated, more tidily, that in the original. Reading across the page there was the year, month, date, a surname, s or d depending on sex then the baby's name. She smiled to see so many familiar names, Penberthie, Tregerthen, yet more Roddas, and Cornish exotica like Jucca and Spargo.

The name should have jumped out at her but the quiet presentation fooled her and her eye swung past it before being drawn back. *1596. Trevescan* she read. *D. Rose Mary*. She made a note of the date, in case the family Bible should need correcting, then flicked idly forward through the burials to the marriages. She forgot the date she had read in the Bible but assumed Rose might have been an old woman of twenty at the time, so started at 1616 then worked backwards. She found her in 1612. A slip of a thing given away by her father at sixteen. She wondered if Michael Polglaze was a young swain or a ruddy-faced, advantageous older man, some friend of the family with conveniently placed fields adjoining theirs.

Once again, the surname was so familiar that she scanned it without registering it. Then, startled, she read the entry again to be sure. It was hard to believe that something so important, so important to a handful of historians and musicologists at least, should have sat so long unnoticed.

Rose was not given away by her father but by Roger Trevescan, Old Trevescan, Eliza's Trevescan.

Maybe the transcriber had made a mistake. A singer of madrigals himself, perhaps he automatically wrote the more familiar name without thinking? Eliza whirled through the microfiche, only remembering not to scrape the film when the archivist pointedly coughed into his *TLS*.

The marriage register was not much cleaner than the baptism one but she found the entry and, knowing where to look by referring across to the transcript, found the signature of the man who gave Rose away. It was a dark squiggle but there was an unmistakable loop midway, a 'g' not a 'b', Roger not Robert.

Feverish, not caring whether Molly was watching, Eliza flicked back through the register to the burials to find any male Trevescans who died in or after the year of Rose's marriage. Her heart was beating so hard she felt it like hiccups, in her neck and shoulders. There was the same roster of surnames. Jago. Penberthie. Thomas. A regular sad smattering of unattributed, genderless entries of *stillborn child*. She felt slightly faint and in need of fresh air. Perhaps he had lived into great old age? Perhaps there was somewhere a great cache of unpublished music, pasted into a wall or tucked beneath a floorboard or merely lost in an archive like this one?

But no. 1616. He lived to see Rose four years into her

marriage so he was, what? Forty? Forty-five? Well past an Elizabethan middle age, at least.

Sadly the microfiche readers were not the kind that could produce photocopies so she would have to lodge a request to copy the originals at the County Records Office. In the meanwhile, she copied the relevant pages from the manuscript then waited, like a hissing kettle, for Molly to find the eighth great-grandparent.

Molly looked up, saw her face and grinned.

'Do you need the loo, or what?' she asked and the archivist hushed her.

'Tell you in a sec,' Eliza whispered. Molly soon finished and, as they walked down the stairs, Eliza came out with it all in a rush. 'Which means he's your however many times great-grandfather.'

'Unless Rose was already due. I'm sure things haven't changed that much. I bet half the betrothals were shotgun.'

'So? He'd still be your step-ancestor and it means the madrigal is definitely his and has a flawless provenance. The dates were all wrong before but now they fit and, oh Molly!' She kissed her, unable to contain herself.

'I don't want to pour cold water or anything,' Molly began gravely.

'What?' Eliza felt her face fall.

'Well. That Roger who died might have been a son of Rose's named after her uncle.'

'But . . . Oh. God. Well yes, he could have been. But there's no record of a son's birth in the parish before that, and taken with Roger's presence at her wedding as well it would seem to be more likely that –'

Molly cut her short, flapping her in the chest with the back of her hand. 'I'm pulling your leg, girl. Of *course* it was him! Here. You'd better ring Pearce. He'll probably want to sell the manuscript now to build a new barn.'

She reached for her mobile and turned it on. It beeped. 'Hang on,' she said, holding it to her ear. 'Message.' She expertly pressed buttons without looking, straining to hear over the traffic and chatter about them. She hung up and instead of passing the mobile over, slipped it back in her bag.

'Well thank God we're over here, already,' she said, colour draining from her plump cheeks. 'We can drive up there in ten minutes. Oh Eliza. I'm sorry. It's all my fault.'

'What?'

'It's okay. She's fine.'

'Dido?' Eliza felt a spasm run through her. She felt sick with fear. Molly was already walking briskly towards the car park.

'She's fine,' Molly repeated. She's been in an accident and broken her leg but she's fine. The man took her to the hospital.'

'What man?'

40

Giles rose to a world transformed by the knowledge that he was about to become a father. It helped that there had been rain overnight so that the lush little garden outside the breakfast room windows and the boats moored in the dock had acquired an extra polish in the morning sun. His worries did not vanish with the good news. He still worried about how Eliza would react to her mother's death, still wanted to make his peace with Dido, and had not fallen suddenly in love with Julia.

She was not the same Julia, however. How could she be? She was now the mother of his child and by that simple formula of words his fate had been ordered for him. Where he had been at the mercy of impulse, shame and lust, now he found himself with simple obligations whose unambiguous clarity came as a relief.

He would make his peace with Dido and love her, always love her in a fatherly way, and he would set Eliza free while supporting her as he should but the bulk of his love would quite naturally flow to his own child, and his truest support to its mother.

Although marrying Julia before the baby was born would probably give legal protection to his rights as its father, he was at least sensitive enough to recoil from letting her believe that was his sole reason for proposing. So he had not raised the matter at all. She might not want to marry him. She was under no obligation to and she had certainly never dropped any dark hints before now. Not that he had noticed. He would let it rest and trust time to show him a way. Plenty of cohabiting couples had children without marrying. Why should they be any different?

The crab had given Julia a night fraught with bad dreams. Now that she was free to admit she had been plagued by morning sickness (and mid-morning nausea and afternoon pukes) he felt quite justified in ordering her up a paper and a leisurely breakfast in her room.

She laughed at his abruptly solicitous behaviour. 'I'm not going to fade away,' she said. 'I'm not the type. Sorry. Give Dido my love, if you catch them. We could always take her back with us for the first week of the holidays if Eliza could do with peace and quiet for a bit.

'Don't,' she warned as he stooped to kiss her. 'Sick.'

He had risen late and dawdled over breakfast downstairs – home-made bread, farm eggs – and the sun was already high overhead when he drove out of the hotel's tiny car park. His nerve failed him at the prospect of taking the steep road – little more than an unfenced slipway – which plunged down the side of the harbour. Turning right instead, he found himself heading out below the church and out of town along the promenade where there were already people strolling, sunning themselves, shading their babies.

Babies. Overnight he had become attuned to the idea of fatherhood and his whole world appeared to realign itself. He found himself noticing small children and their bulky paraphernalia: prams, pushchairs, carrycots, slings.

Missing his turning, he was forced to follow the seafront around to Newlyn where he picked up signs to St Just. A lane took him up through a thickly wooded valley to the road he must have taken last time only he had been in such a daze from his conversation with Mrs Barnicoat that nothing now seemed familiar.

There was no one at the caravan. Peering boldly in at the windows when it was plain nobody was going to answer the door, he found it hard to tell if anyone were still in residence. For all he knew the mess he saw, of rumpled bedding and muddled clothes, was Mrs Barnicoat's and Eliza had already headed back to London. The one garment on a hanger, a dark blue skirt with little glittery bits decorating the hem, was certainly not a thing he could imagine Eliza wearing.

Or perhaps they had simply gone into St Just for supplies? Perhaps they were off on a day-long excursion to the Eden Project or the Seal Sanctuary?

This was so ill-planned. The perky plaque of St Francis beside the door mocked his good intentions. He could not spend all day waiting here for Eliza to come home but neither could he bear Dido not to know he had tried to see her.

For want of any other paper he wrote a note on the back of one of the car hire documents. Dear Both. So very sorry to hear about your Mum/Granny. Since you don't seem to be in –

He stopped, realising how bizarre it would seem that he was there, with no warning or explanation, as though he were hunting them down. Which in a sense he was. Much easier to explain himself face to face. He would kill time then come back later.

Realising that the normal, loving thing to do in the circumstances was to buy a present for the mother-to-be, he drove down the hill into St Just. Flowers were out of the question here. Julia could buy more exciting bunches at their nearest roadside stall at home. There were a few little art galleries but they filled him with doubt and he suddenly realised he had no idea if Julia would prefer a tiny Cornish landscape or a bold, rough framed abstract. Earrings, perhaps, or a silk scarf? He guessed such things could be found in wealthier, more touristy St Ives so decided to drive on.

He had underestimated, from his glance at the atlas, how long the coastal route would take. The road not only followed the meandering, rocky coastline but often seemed to have been dictated by the arbitrary boundaries of ancient fields and farms. Wide enough through the former mining communities of Pendeen and Morvah, it became crazily narrow and twisty as it entered the wilder land above Zennor. Whenever he met an oncoming car or coach there was a wincing manoeuvre as one or both of them reversed into a point wide enough to let the other pass. A sign claimed St Ives was only a few miles ahead but it was hard to believe as there were little signs of civilisation beyond the occasional windswept farmstead. High moorland climbed to one side, tiny, stone-hedged fields sloped down to the sea on the other. It was pretty enough now but in midwinter, in the wind and rain, it would be desperately forbidding. Even now there were no boats in sight but distant trawlers and a fishing vessel so small it kept vanishing inside the swell.

Coming down the hill towards Zennor he swung out to make room for a small, red-faced boy having trouble with his cycle chain and remembered the importance of a bicycle for long summer holidays. He recalled the hours he would spend on his, idling, going nowhere in particular because the district was hemmed in by major trunk roads which were forbidden to him, but preferring to stay on his bike, bored and saddle-sore, ankles chafed, fingers oily, than to face the threatening, gin-scented longueurs at home.

As he climbed the hill on the other side, another child came flying down towards him, a girl in a baseball cap and spotty pink dress. She was going faster than she should, using one hand to smack her dress down as the wind lifted it over her knees, and was swaying wildly out into the road's middle.

He kept well to one side to make room and so as not to frighten her. It was only as she whizzed up to his open window that she glanced up at the boy in trouble ahead and he recognised her.

All he said was a fairly quiet, 'Dido?' but it was enough to make her glance sharply round at him then lose control of the bike. She let out a yelp and there was a clatter as the bike crashed into something.

Giles stopped the car where it was and ran back down the hill. The bike was half in a ditch, upended against the low stone hedge. Dido was sprawled in the road. He swore under his breath as he ran up to her. She had no helmet on, no visibility strap and the bike's brakes were probably as old and worn as the bike itself.

'Dido?'

She was crying.

'Dido, it's Giles.'

'I know!' she said furiously. She tried to move and cried out.

'Stay put,' he said, crouching beside her. 'What happened?'

'What do you – Ow!'

She was trying to lift herself onto all fours. Her hands were fine; grazed from hitting the road but fine. She had a nasty little cut on her chin. Blood dripped crimson on the hot tarmac and down her front. She tried again and again cried out, keening from the pain. Then he saw how one of her ankles was at a sickeningly wrong angle.

'Don't!' he shouted. 'It's your foot. I'll have to lift you.' He crouched down beside her. 'Put your arm over my shoulder.'

'No. Ow!'

'Dido, do it. I've got to lift you. There's no other way.'

Whimpering, she locked an arm around his neck.

'This is going to hurt,' he said, 'But we've got to get you off the road and onto the car seat. Hold tight. Both arms. That's it.'

Slowly he stood, half-suffocated by her furious grasp, and as soon as he could he scooped his arms underneath her to prevent any pressure on the fracture.

It must have been agony because she fainted. He hurried back to the car with her and had to lie her briefly on the verge while he opened the back door. Then he lifted her inside and arranged her across the rear seat. He held her in place as best he could with a seat belt so that she was sitting upright, her back against the farther door. Gingerly, holding it by the shoe, he straightened the broken leg before her. There was nothing he could use as a splint. He might have crippled her already. She moaned softly, coming round. He drew out the other seat belt and secured it around her thighs so she wouldn't slide off the seat if he had to brake suddenly. Then he leapt back into the driver's seat, swung the car around and headed back the way he had come, remembering seeing a turning for Penzance and praying it was a more direct route than the coastal one.

The red-faced boy was staring and Giles saw it was a girl. 'Where's the hospital?' he shouted to her.

'Penzance,' she stammered gruffly. 'The West Cornwall. But for emergency you'd better go to Treliske. That's Truro. Is she okay?'

'She'll be fine.'

He drove like a maniac at first then got a grip on himself, remembering she was not about to die unless he tried to kill them both. He glanced regularly over his shoulder at her. She was still propped up in the opposite corner to him and, soon after they hit the Penzance by-pass, he saw she had opened her eyes. The blood was drying on her chin and chest. She was not looking anywhere in particular, just whimpering softly and occasionally crossly scrubbing the tears from her eyes with the back of one grubby fist.

'Dido?'

She looked at him.

'Soon be there,' he told her, although the last signpost gave the distance to Truro as twenty miles.

'Good,' she managed.

'How's the chin?'

'Sore,' she said. 'I . . . I lost a couple of teeth.'

'Jesus! Where? At the front?'

'Back,' she mumbled and he realised she was turning the bloodied molars over in her hand.

'Where's Eliza?' he asked.

'Pearce's.'

'Who?!'

'Just for the night. I was staying with friends. Ow!'

'Sorry. Roundabout. Can't be helped. There. Sorry. Dido?'

'What?'

'Look I really know this isn't the right time but I wanted to see you, to talk to you. That's why I'm down here. Well. Partly. I'm on a sort of holiday with Julia. We're in Penzance for the weekend. But I heard about your Gran from Mrs Barnicoat.'

'Who?'

'The lady next door. The big lady in Camborne.'

'Kitty.'

'Yes? And . . . sorry. This is all coming out wrong.'

'Ow!'

'Sorry.'

'It *really* hurts.'

'We're nearly there, Dido. I promise. Soon be there and the doctors and nurses will make it all okay again. I just . . . I really wanted to say, to explain really, about that photo you saw in my office. I didn't want you to take it the wrong way or think I'm some kind of creepy perv.'

Briefly cleared of all whimpering and pain, Dido's voice was bright steel. 'Why didn't you tell me?'

'Well . . . I thought you'd be upset. Which, naturally, you were.'

'I had a right to know.'

'It was just a picture. Yes, though. Yes. You're right. You had a perfect right. I'm sorry.'

'I took it,' she said. 'If you were wondering.'

How many were there? He thought it was just the two. 'I got rid of the others,' he said.

'Bit late for that, isn't it? Now that I've seen.'

'Yes but I . . .'

'Just hurry. Please?'

'Yes, of course. Sorry.'

He put his foot down and shut up. What right had he to ask her forgiveness? He had no rights in the matter at all.

'Look,' he said a few minutes later. 'Truro. We're there. Hospital. See?'

'Great.' Her bravery astonished him. At her age he'd have been wetting himself with the pain. But then at her age . . . He tried to distract her. 'Guess what? Julia's going to have a baby. She's just heard. So early next year you'll have a little brother or sister. Stepbrother. Dido?'

'I won't. I won't have anything. Look. Hospital. Next left.'

Leaving her in the car, he ran after signs for A & E and at last found some paramedics who could fetch her on a trolley. They gave her a shot for the pain then manoeuvred her onto the stretcher as though she were made of glass.

'Don't worry,' one of them told her as they started to wheel her away towards the casualty department's entrance. 'Your dad's still here.'

'He's not my dad,' she said, fighting the sedative. 'He's just a family friend.'

Giles followed them inside. While she was borne away for X-rays and to have the leg set and plastered, he gave her details for registration and also filled out the necessary forms for any further procedures to be seen to on his private health insurance. Unbeknownst to Eliza, he had been paying premiums to keep Dido covered ever since Eliza left him. When the nurse passed him the consent forms for the X-rays he explained that no, he wasn't Dido's father but only her mother's husband. He did not go into detail; her aunt's estranged husband with occasional, unratified visiting rights sounded too suspicious for words, private health policy or no.

'So,' the nurse said, pen hovering, 'stepfather.'

'Yes,' he said then settled down to wait.

He was startled when Eliza appeared with a girlfriend in tow. He had not seen her for months. He realised the second she walked up to him how he had fantasised her into something she wasn't. In his head she had become either the mad destroyer or a helpless, depressive scatterbrain, the sort of woman who forgot to buy food for her own child. The Eliza before him was focused, trim, suntanned and really rather formidable. He saw at once how she, too, had developed a distorted view of him as the enemy.

He thought she would berate him, shout, ask him what the fuck he was doing in Cornwall but all she did was put her arms about him, kiss his cheek. He began to explain, very clumsily, that Dido had broken her leg falling off her bike, that he was on a short break with Julia, that it was probably his fault for startling her, when Eliza stopped him to say simply, 'Thank God you were there,' before hurrying off in search of her daughter.

The friend introduced herself as Molly and said how her daughter had rung her brother from a callbox in Zennor, who had then left a message on her mobile which was how they had got there so quickly.

By the time he had driven back to Penzance he was working himself into a state about not having told Julia what was going on but he need not have worried. Julia's slumber deficit had caught up with her and she had spent half the afternoon asleep.

'Don't worry,' she murmured sleepily to his hasty apology. 'I went out too for a bit. So sleepy though.'

He half-stripped and got into bed and snuggled into her back. But she was soon asleep again while he was left alert to his desolation. Nuzzling her hair, failing even to distract himself with its scented warmth, he wept in silence.

Waking, appalled because she had never seen him cry, she asked him what was wrong. He told a version of the facts, that Dido had broken her leg, that by some amazing chance he had been there to drive her to hospital and that she had seemed so brave and independent.

Hushing him, growing tearful herself, she assured him that just because they were having a baby of their own, he wasn't to worry that Dido would be any less welcome.

He thanked her, mastered himself, kissed her, braced by the sense that this was the moment where he ought to say he loved her but he couldn't lie to her. How could he tell her it was not a question of their excluding Dido but of Dido's excluding them?

41

Yes, Julia had been sick again but it was quite different now the reason was no secret. Giles might not have said he loved her but he was solicitude itself, almost oppressively so and she was happy to show apparent generosity in letting him off for a few hours in the hire car.

She enjoyed her breakfast in bed, and was sunning herself on the pretty daybed in the window, half listening to Alexy being interviewed on the radio, half reading a review of a client's recent recital when her mobile rang. She turned down the radio, picked up the phone and glanced at the display to see who was calling her. *Villiers* it said. She was tempted to press ignore and fob him off with her voicemail but she knew he was likely to punish her by calling the agency instead to leave a suggestively compromising message with Shawna. She had once told him, in a weak moment, she suspected Shawna of being jealous and of doing anything she could to undermine her. Resolving to have fewer weak moments now she was to become a mother, she answered.

'Villiers. How lovely.'

'Can you talk?'

'Yes.'

'Where are you? I hear seagulls.'

'A ravishingly pretty hotel in Penzance.'

'So you told him.'

'I did. I chanced my arm and told him and he's thrilled so we're keeping it.'

'We?'

'Yes, darling. We're going to be a family.'

'Oh. I'm so glad. I really am. Is it for public consumption yet?' He sounded uncannily sincere.

'No. It's far too early. I might lose it or something,' she said, stretching out her toes against a silky cushion. 'What can I do for you?'

'Why does everyone always assume I want something when I ring?'

Because they're too scared of the alternatives?

'Because we know what you're like. But you've caught me in a good mood so take advantage.'

'It's nothing, really.'

'Oh well, in that case . . .' she teased.

'Have you got a spare morning?'

'Funnily enough.'

'It's just that when Selina told me where you were, I thought it was too good an opportunity to miss. I want you to go and look at a house for me. And if possible get a peek at the owner. There'd be a lunch in it for you. It's perfectly legit but they've got something Mr Mister wants to buy and I need to know how badly they need to sell. Do they need a new roof? Are they loaded or *nouveau-pauvre*? What do they drive and how many? I'd feel I was imposing only I know how you love a good snoop.'

'What makes you think that?'

'I know you, Girl, like you know me.'

She checked out the distance on the framed map on the bathroom wall. She could be there and back within the hour. And Villiers was right. It was the sort of mission that piqued her interest. She called a taxi, stubbed the driver's curiosity with a flat, 'I'm here on business,' and had him drive her out beyond the Land's End airfield then down a pretty lane. 'Wait here,' she told him 'I won't be long,' and got him to park in a shady passing place while she walked on down the lane, over a little bridge and up to the house.

The air was loud with rooks, not the gulls that haunted Penzance, and swallows kept up their manic twittering on the wires overhead. It was a farmhouse, on a working farm judging from all the cattle shit. Not the wealthy manor she had expected, but old. One could guess that from the thick granite walls. Like a lot of women she had devoured *Rebecca* and *I Capture the Castle* in her early, dreamy teens but she had never fantasized about being mistress of a grand house. Dinner parties for six were frightening enough. The thought of having to cope with house parties and intimidating old retainers was horrific. From her time as a nanny she knew that such households still existed all over the country, less poetic than Manderley and whatever the Dodie Smith house had been called, but equally daunting to manage. She knew that their owners occasionally married wrong girls, girls like Julia, girls not raised to cope.

This house, however, had all the charm of a Manderley — surrounded by empty land, the sea nearby, a powerful sense of family history — without the unfeasible size. She walked closer. There was a footpath across the farmyard towards the sea, she had noticed, so she had a perfect excuse to be there. The paintwork was flaking here and there, she saw, and some guttering drooped. A rusted drainpipe had been replaced with a cheap plastic one. One of the chimney stacks leaned alarmingly inwards. A household, she gauged, that was patching and making do rather than thriving. The little garden seemed neglected, but then most farm gardens would be. She saw no car at first — and there was no garage — then she spotted a filthy and very basic green Land Rover, parked in one of the barns.

She walked on along the footpath to the back of the house where some horned cattle eyed her suspiciously from behind a barbed wire fence. The paintwork was worse here, where the weather hit it from off the sea. She knew she should be looking for signs of dereliction but found herself charmed. The floral curtains were old and not to her taste but she could see at once the place's potential and how simply someone like her could realise it.

There was a churning of gears and diesel engine. She turned to see a yellow tractor approaching from one of the seaward fields, every bit as old as the Land Rover. She began to walk on then realised how odd that would look when she stopped and came back the same way. So she turned at once and started back towards the taxi, needlessly nervous as the tractor approached her. The driver pulled past her and swung into the barn beside the Land Rover. She walked on but then the driver jumped down and called out to her, 'Lost your way? The path goes straight on the way you were headed. It's not very clear at the moment since it all got churned up down there.'

'No,' she said. 'It's fine. I was . . . I was looking for a friend, in fact. A friend of the family. She's staying in a caravan near here I thought. Eliza Hosken and her daughter.'

As he emerged from the shadows he smiled broadly, his teeth white in his filthy face. 'They're up on the hill.'

'You know them?' she asked, startled at being caught out.

'Getting to,' he said. 'Eliza's been around here a few times. You've just missed her, in fact. She should be back up at Kitty's caravan by now. I'll run you up if you like.'

'No thanks. I've . . . I've got a taxi waiting in the lane. It's up the hill a bit, then?'

Why did she ask? Because he had such a glorious voice, like the rich, brown voices of her childhood. And his eyes were a brown to match. And he made her feel at once delicately feminine and entirely safe. Fool that she was. He would be bound to remember her and mention her visit to Eliza now.

'That's right. Up Bosavern to the T-junction, left towards St Just then immediately right down a – oh. Sorry. Hang on.'

His mobile was ringing. She thought to slip away while he answered it but found herself rooted to the spot.

'Luce? Where are you?' There was a lengthy explanation. He frowned. 'Bloody hell. Where's your mum? Oh. Well don't worry. Stay put and I'll be right up there. Stay put.' He hung up then 'Sorry,' he said. 'Bit of a crisis. Sorry. Got to go.'

He ran over to a tap where he quickly washed his face and hands then ran on to the Land Rover and drove out up the lane as fast as its labouring engine would carry him.

'Not rich, I'd say,' she told Villiers when she called him from back at the hotel. 'But not hungry either. And not an idiot. And he knows Eliza.'

'I know,' Villiers said, enjoying capping her surprise with a bigger one. 'Didn't I tell you? I suspect he's her new squeeze. Thanks, darling. I knew I could count on you. Hang on to the cab receipt and I'll claim it off my expenses from Mr Mister. And we'll do lunch once you're back. Gotta run. Byee.'

42

Lucy was in a terrible state, having convinced herself it was her fault somehow. She was already fiercely protective of Dido. Pearce soothed her as best he could as he drove her home, but when Molly rang him from the casualty department, Pearce agreed that she should come back to take Lucy off his hands. He could then drive up with the Land Rover, better equipped than her little car to deal with a passenger who could not bend her leg.

His first reaction when he realised Dido would be fine but temporarily lame was guilty pleasure; he had been dreading them leaving Cornwall and it was now out of the question for them to travel. Dido was woozy with painkillers, all cheek and bravado gone. Eliza was worn and worried. The sight of them lent him the strength of mind to take control.

He drove them back to Kitty's caravan but only so that Eliza could help him pack their things to bring back to the farm. She made a token show of resistance but he could tell there was no fight in her. Besides, she knew a cramped caravan with no television was no place to be confined with a reluctantly grounded nine-year-old.

He carried Dido in and enthroned her on a sofa with extra cushions, a rug, a jug of juice and the TV's remote control. Dido was waking up and beginning to enjoy the drama. He was about to start fixing them supper when Eliza surprised him by saying she wanted to cook, that she had not cooked anything proper for ages.

'Because you can't,' Dido shouted from next door.

'I'll make us all a pizza,' she told him. 'It'll be fun.'

He was actually relieved because the next two stills of broccoli plants had been dropped off in the yard that afternoon while he was off at the hospital and needed attending to. He spread them out, tray by tray in long lines across the yard and mixed up some rabbit repellent in the knapsack sprayer. By the time he had sprayed all two hundred trays then stacked them back in the stills, the sun was sinking and smells of garlic, tomato and roasting cheese were coming out of the kitchen windows.

He came back inside to find Eliza playing a prom concert loudly on the kitchen radio in competition with Dido watching a game show on the television and a crackly atmosphere as though angry words had been exchanged while he was out. Or perhaps the anger had boiled up at the hospital and his absence had seen them spending time in adjoining rooms, not talking.

Eliza was hot and bothered. Now that he was inside, he could smell burning beneath the Italian richness but he did not feel he should comment on it.

'Smells good,' he said. 'I was longer than I thought. Sorry.'

'That's okay. Where do you eat when you're not entertaining?'

'Standing up, quite often. No. In here, anyway. But we can eat next door. Keep the young one company.'

He washed the repellent off his hands, scrubbing at his nails with a brush.

'What's in that stuff?' she asked.

'Dunno. Chilli, maybe. But it smells better than what Dad liked.'

'What was that?'

'Renardine.'

'Fox juice?'

'Something like. Made your clothes reek for days if you splashed it.' He came near where she was slicing the pizza on a bread board. 'Did I do the right thing, bringing you both back here?' he asked quietly.

'Yes.' Her tone was brisk. 'Of course. Why?'

'Nothing. It's just that I thought . . . nothing. I'm glad you're here. Are you hungry in there?'

'No,' Dido shouted back.

'Of course she is,' Eliza said. 'She loves pizza.'

He opened them a bottle of wine and they sat down to a rather spread-out meal, with he and Eliza at table and Dido several feet away on her sofa.

The pizza was not a success. Lacking yeast, Eliza had fallen back on something she dimly remembered reading in a newspaper recipe and made a base using a floury scone mixture which managed to be burnt around the edges and gassily undercooked in the middle.

Pearce was hungry and would have eaten anything, so polished off his helping with ease but when he answered Eliza's apologies with, 'No. It's good,' Dido said,

'It's disgusting.'

'At least eat the topping,' Eliza suggested but Dido slid her plate to the floor with a clatter.

'Giles' pizzas are much better,' she said rebelliously.

'If you can't be polite,' Pearce said, 'you'd better go to bed.'

'Can't make me.'

'Dido . . .' Eliza began.

'Oh I think I can,' Pearce said and, advancing on the sofa, slid his arms underneath Dido and picked her up.

She protested and swore shockingly, angry because she was

half-amused. All the way up the stairs she smacked at his face and pulled his hair but he was relentless and deposited her on the bathroom stool to brush her teeth while he fetched her crutches from beside the sofa.

He turned down the bed in her little room, switched on the bedside light and drew the curtains. Soon she was banging along the corridor to join him. 'Careful,' he told her, 'or you'll break the other one.'

She had changed into her nightdress, a long tee shirt with breakfast stains on the front. The fresh plaster cast looked doubly incongruous beside her other skinny leg. 'I feel like an elephant,' she said as she swung it onto the bed and pulled the duvet over herself. 'Or a hippo.'

'You'll soon get used to it.'

'Have you ever broken anything?'

'No. But you'll soon get used to it.'

'It *was* disgusting, wasn't it?'

'Yes. But when people apologize for bad food they don't really want you to agree with them. Your mum tried.'

'Huh. Suppose. I couldn't eat it, anyway. I was too sore.'

'In your leg?'

'In my mouth.'

'Where you cut yourself?'

'Inside.'

'How come?'

'Can you keep a secret?' she asked him solemnly.

'Depends who from.'

'If you tell her, she'll be really upset and we'll have to go back to London right away.'

'Okay,' he said dubiously. 'I can keep a secret.'

'Hold out your hand.'

When he did so, she reached out a hot little fist and slipped something into his palm. It was two teeth. Two large ones. Molars. Nothing apparently wrong with them.

He was shocked. 'Did these come out today?' he asked. 'When you fell?'

'If she notices, then they did. They got knocked out on the ground when I fell, okay? But she won't notice. She never notices stuff like that.'

'But I don't understand. Why don't you want her to see? These are big teeth, not baby ones. We should get you to a dentist. You could have them put back in somehow.'

She shook her head. 'No,' she said. 'But we've got to go back to see the specialist after the weekend because he wasn't there today. I'll need you to drive me. We can say it's just X-rays and stuff. She won't care.'

'She cares very much.'

'Yeah yeah but . . . you're not to tell her. Not yet. It's really important.'

'Okay. I won't. D'you want them back?'

She held out her hand for the teeth then pocketed them. 'I'll need to show the orthodontist,' she said and her quiet self-importance charmed him so much he had to make an effort not to enrage her by smiling. 'Can you tell her I'm sorry I was rude,' she said. 'It's just she really pisses me off sometimes.'

'You can tell her yourself. I'm sure she'll look in on you before you go to sleep.'

She opened her book. She had started *Finn Family Midwinter*. 'You do promise, don't you?' she said as he stood to leave her in peace.

'I promise,' he said.

'It's really important.'

'Okay.'

He joined Eliza on the sofa. He passed on Dido's apology but kept her secret, for now, not seeing what harm it could do.

'You were very strong-minded,' she told him. 'I just give in most of the time. She's so like Hannah in that way.' She slid her feet into his lap. 'I'd make a lousy farmer's wife, wouldn't I? Can't even make a pizza.'

'Most of the farmer's wives round here buy their pizzas in multipacks at Iceland. I think I love you.'

'I know,' she said.

'You don't have to say anything back,' he said, anticipating her silence. 'Just thought you should know.'

'Why?' she asked after a moment of absentmindedly rubbing her feet against his belt buckle.'

'Well . . . I . . . it seemed the sort of thing one should –'

'No, I mean why me?' she laughed. 'Why us? We are an us, you know. We're a package deal.'

'I know that.'

'So it would have to be all right by her as well as by me.'

'Sure.'

'Just so long as you know.'

43

Working in Pearce's small office would have been impossible. Eliza liked the idea of sitting at his desk, deep in his father's blue leather chair, but a rising tide of farm paperwork spilled over from the filing cabinets on one side of the small room to the computer and desk on the other. Eliza sensed he was one of those people who chose to work in a chaos only they understood but she needed room to spread out her notes and feared that by making space amidst the cattle passports, subsidy forms and muddy receipts for fertiliser and cattle, she would throw a delicate system into disarray. So she had colonised the dining room table instead. Her Trevescan thesis was spread out around her, removed from its files the better to rearrange it. While Dido watched videos, she was forcing herself to reread both the chapters drafted in prose and the pages and pages of notes, and as she read each sheet she sorted it according to whether or not it could still form part of the thesis realigning itself around what she now knew.

'Here on Magellan 16 our ways are different,' a woman said suddenly. 'We have only one child to every three of your generations. We live longer, see further.'

'Could you turn it down a bit?' Eliza asked.

Dido scowled to herself, rapt in the cultural exchange

between a woman with three eyes and another with a trunk like an elephant's.

'Dido!'

Dido fired the remote control and killed the television's sound altogether.

'I only meant turn it down.'

'It's okay. I can still follow the story.' Dido watched the alien women talk on. Her plaster cast was thrust out on a footstool before her, five filthy little toes peeking out at the end of it. The cat lay on her belly, one paw stretched up towards Dido's bandaged chin. Dido wore shorts and a baggy Eat British Beef tee shirt Pearce had given her. Since the accident, she had been in a stormy mood, casting baleful glances at anyone who tried to lift it by bringing peace offerings. The nurses had sent her home with a little compressed air canister connected to a thin pipe. If she used this to fire down the side of the plaster cast, it lessened the intolerable itching. Dido hotly denied the itching was bothering her at all but could be heard firing off the canister when she thought herself unobserved.

She had been so happy before her accident, blossoming into a new friendship, spending hours at a time out of doors, it was small wonder she felt a need to punish them for her confinement. Her pleasure when Lucy turned up with several taped episodes of her favourite sci-fi series was undercut when she realised Lucy would be spending the day outside, working for Pearce again.

Eliza found herself drawn in. There was an attack of some kind. Crushed by a fallen girder, the elephant woman entrusted a sort of pod, the slow-gestating future of her race evidently, to the three-eyed one, who wept in triplicate before fleeing to her space shuttle. Eliza was reaching the point of asking Dido to turn the volume back up when the telephone called her away.

She let the answering machine screen the call in case it was for Pearce. A couple of times she had answered without thinking and found herself faced with some agricultural query in impenetrable Penwith Cornish from a caller who plainly thought her simple-minded.

Pearce had given Dido her choice of bedrooms. She had chosen to stay in the little yellow one with a view into the branches of a battered pine tree. Eliza slept with Pearce at the other end of the long landing. He had put drawers and wardrobes at their disposal but was touchingly anxious lest she feel trapped.

'I can drive you to the bus station whenever you like,' he assured her. 'But until she's allowed to put any weight on her foot, Doe's better off here than high up in some tower block.'

That was her name now, apparently. Doe. The girls had cemented their friendship with a faintly defeminising name change. Lucy was Cee, which she elected to write as merely C. Eliza remembered the years at school when, seeking only anonymity, she was actually content to have people call her Leeza.

Pearce's gruff voice came from the machine. He gave his mobile number then said, 'Or you can leave a message for Eliza, Pearce or Doe after the tone.'

'Erm. This is a message for Eliza. From Anne Perry.'

Eliza grabbed the phone. 'Anne, hi. It's me.'

Anne was an eminently sensible university contemporary who had stayed put and carved a niche for herself in the English faculty. In an inspired moment, Eliza had remembered that Anne was partly involved in the setting up of a vast online poetry and song database which would eventually be accessible and searchable online. A mammoth work, it would contain every line of every English poem, prayer, hymn, song, folksong even pop lyric ever in the public domain. Heavily reliant on volunteer data entry, it currently stretched from *The Wanderer* to Dryden and from Hardy to the Lost Preachers, with substantial gaps. Eliza's hope was that, if the words of the mystery madrigal had been used elsewhere, even in a slightly altered version, Anne could tell her.

Anne gave her an address to e-mail the words to and asked the inevitable questions about whether she was *working* again and who was Pearce and so on. When she asked if she should update her address book, Eliza said, 'No, no. It's just a . . . well, a prolonged holiday, really. Just until Dido's leg's stronger,' and felt treacherous and confused.

She hurried upstairs, turned on Pearce's computer and opened the word processing program in which she had already made an initial stab at summarising her findings. The words to *Country Goodness* were already typed out. She copied them into an e-mail. The layout went wrong as she pasted it, however, running on lines which should be separate. Cursing softly, she ran through the text inserting line breaks. Thinking to make it prettier, she selected the text then centred it. Then she thought that looked precious so she selected the text again. By a slip of the mouse however she realigned it to the right margin instead of the left. She was about to correct this when she saw a new pattern.

By aligning the lines to the right, she found the last letters of each line in the second verse spelled out Rosy. She laughed. It was a happy accident, of course. The kind of coincidence that drove over-researched academics insane – the donnish equivalent of searching for hidden messages in the rustling of leaves or the arrangement of paving stones.

Elizabethan versifiers, like those in other ages, would occasionally play such games, of course, building a sonnet from the letters of a beloved's name or some coded refer-ence. There. The first verse line-endings spelled out nothing. YBOT.

She corrected the alignment to the left again and, out of idle curiosity, read off the first letters of each line. AMOE in the first verse and OEGE in the second. *Amo*, I love, but *Amoe*? An alternative spelling of *amow* perhaps, as in *amow amass I love a lass*? As for OEGE, it meant nothing that she knew of.

To waste no more time, she e-mailed off the text to Anne, who had promised that the department computer would take only seconds to search the database, then, ashamed of her rusty Latin, went on a browse through Pearce's bookshelves. He had thrown out nothing he had ever owned, from Caesar's *Gallic Wars Book II* to *The Five Children and It* and a Blue Peter album so it was a fair bet that he still had a schoolboy dictionary or two somewhere. He did not believe in alphabetic or thematic order so it took her a while to find an English dictionary, which offered nothing between *amniotic* and *amoeba* or *Oedipus* and *oeil de boeuf*. After another search, trying not to be distracted by other books along the way, she tracked down an ink-spotted Latin dictionary. This offered her *amo*, to love and *amoene*, meaning pleasantly.

It could not be Italian or Spanish because they tended to turn Oe words, imported from Greek, into E words. Old Norse? Anglo-Saxon?

This was ridiculous. She turned off the computer and was about to return downstairs to her notes and/or the further adventures of Elephant Woman's slow-gestating baby when she saw the doodles on one of the endless free pads Pearce seemed to be given by agrichemical sales reps. The girls must have been up here surfing the Net and Dido had covered the top sheet with Moomin figures. (She had discovered the books in Pearce's bookshelves and been copying the pictures from them ever since.) Eliza had always found the hippo-faced creatures sinister rather than lovable and hoped this was a phase that would soon pass. There were things in the books which had given her nightmares as a girl; the unfamiliar tall, thin Nordic stoves, the evocations of endless wintry darkness and the Hattifatteners, a band of malevolent little creatures like wandering condoms which were conjured up by electrical storms. She feared they might be making Dido dream too. But perhaps children saw so many strange things on television now that it took more than a whimsical novel to disturb their sleep.

Nonetheless she tore the page off, meaning to throw it away. On the next sheet down the girls had been having fun with their names. Entwining them as Didolucy, hybridising them into Dicy, Dolu, Ludi and so on. Eliza remembered their shouts of laughter when they found an online anagram engine which turned Dido Hosken into Die, Honk-Sod and Lucy Martin into Amy Run-Clit.

In one corner of the page Dido had drawn another Moomin, a kind of Moomin-girl with a gingham dress, a personal stereo, a handbag and a lipstick. She was peering at a mirror, refreshing the make-up on her hippo face and saying *I Dido* in a speech bubble. Her reflection, cleverly drawn, had a speech bubble to match and was saying *O did I?* Eliza smiled at Dido's ingeniousness. Then the girlish wordplay suggested something to her.

Too impatient to wait for the computer to warm up afresh, she ran downstairs and riffled through her piles of notes to uncover the original bass part, still tucked in its plastic Ziploc bag. Was it really possible? She stared at it hard, willing it to give up its secret, heedless of the fact that Dido had turned the sound on the television back up so that an intergalactic battle was raging about them.

The first verse was written under the music, the second, below the score, had been artfully centred so as to throw one off the scent with the misaligning of the crucial letters. *Ybot* was Toby backwards. Stupid of her not to see that earlier.

And *Oege*? She grabbed the Latin dictionary and almost tore its cheap little pages in her hurry. *Oege* was *Egeo* backwards which meant . . . Which meant *I am destitute* or, with the genitive, *I auctoritate*, whatever that meant. She was sure there were more meanings. Latin words, like Greek or English ones, acquired other meanings with time and usage.

Toby. My Lord Beaufort's godlike brother? Or a lover's pet name for him? It would not take a detective to check that one. She frowned in her effort to drag some significance into shape. Rosy. Rose Mary. The niece. The niece he passed off as, and loved as, his own. Amo Rosy. Amo-r osam would have been more convincing grammatically. And hidden in the other verse, his not so hidden adored downfall? The beauty of it was that the reference to loving the daughter-cum-niece was tucked away in the verse that spoke of the wrench of leaving his heart behind him in town, while the reference to Toby was hidden in the verse that spoke of *softer pleasures and a sweet obscurity*. The compensatory pleasures not of a new erotic love but of unexpected fatherhood. Pain and pleasure, remembered and present love simultaneously registered.

But why *egeo*? *I am destitute*? Destitute without Toby? Or impoverished because of what involvement with Toby brought upon him? Life at court was undoubtedly expensive but it offered unique chances of preferment and patronage which could never be his on a remote Cornish estate.

The noise from the programme was silenced so suddenly that Eliza looked up. Dido had switched the television off and was sitting up, listening as keenly as a hunting dog.

'What?' Eliza asked her.

'Julia,' Dido said.

'It can't be. They don't have the address here.'

'I know her laugh.' Dido lurched to her feet and began swinging out.

'You shouldn't go outside.'

'I'm not. I'm going upstairs. If she asks, I'm asleep or something.'

'But —'

'I don't want to see her. Okay?'

As Dido dragged her plaster cast and filthy mood upstairs, Eliza slipped into the hall and peered through the grimy window across the yard.

It was indeed Julia, looking at once countrified and elegant, and she was chatting to Pearce and, evidently taken with him, was backing him up against one of his tractor wheels with her charms. Pearce made best-be-getting-on noises and climbed up in his cab to drive back to the cauliflower field with another still of plants. Julia stood watching him go then gave the house an appraising stare. When she came no closer but started back towards her hire car, Eliza hurried out after her.

'What a surprise!' she called.

'Eliza!' Julia seemed so happy she began to bend forward to kiss then remembered who she was talking to and made do with a sisterly pat on the shoulder. 'I know you're hard at work so I didn't like to butt in on you but I thought, since you and Piers —'

'Pearce.'

'Pearce,' she sighed. 'How lovely. He's gorgeous! I thought, since Giles and I are so nearby, we should have the two of you over for dinner tomorrow. At the hotel. Nothing too smart but the food's great. Pearce seemed to think it would be fine.'

'Er. Yes. Sure. Look, Julia, I wonder if you could ask Giles —'

'How's the poor invalid?'

'What? Oh, Dido. She's fine. Cross but fine. You can imagine. Look, I need to know some Latin and I wondered if you could ask Giles.'

'Giles? Latin?'

'He's good at it. Didn't you know?'

'Another hidden depth.'

'Ask him if there are any meanings of *egeo* besides *I am destitute.*'

Julia frowned fleetingly, testing the message for barbs.

'I'd ask him myself,' Eliza explained, 'but, well, you're here and I don't have the hotel number and—' she broke off, watching Julia's automatic examination of her and realised she probably hadn't touched her hair since getting up. She was also in bare feet and Pearce's manky dressing gown. She guessed this was gratifying to Julia's self-love because Julia smiled almost warmly and said, 'You're looking so *well*!'

'But you'll ask him?'

'Yes, of course I will. And we'll see you tomorrow evening. Eight, say? Can someone babysit Dido? I thought just grown-ups for a change.'

'No. Of course. That's fine. Er. I'd offer you coffee but . . .'

'Scholar at work. I'll get out of your hair. See you.'

She shut part of her skirt in the car door. It flapped as she drove off. That and the invitation to dinner and Julia's general demeanour were so entirely out of character, weird even, that Eliza wondered briefly if Julia might be pregnant. But she was too keyed up to hold such a depressing thought for long.

'Wicked witch has gone,' she called up the stairs. 'Coast's clear.' And thinking two could play at that game, she set about washing up breakfast and last night's supper. Then she loaded the washing machine since they had no clean underwear left, no clean anything in fact.

When Giles rang back, while she and Pearce were eating bread and cheese for lunch (Dido was still upstairs in a strop), she had already talked Pearce excitedly through her discovery, showing him the hidden words on the manuscript and expounding her theory. The act of framing her ideas out loud had lent her conviction and for a moment, when Pearce held out the phone saying, 'It's him,' she had quite forgotten asking Giles anything.

'Hello, Giles.'

'How is she?'

'Fine. Bolshie but perfectly all right. Any joy?'

'What? Oh yes. I feel the lack of,' he said.

'I'm sorry?'

'That's what it means. Can mean.'

He was flattered by her remembering his well-drilled schoolboy Latin, as she knew he would be.

'I wasn't sure at first,' he said. 'But I slipped over to the reference library in Morrab Road to check for you. *Egeo* from *Egere*. *I lack* or *feel the lack of*. But in some contexts, with the ablative or something, I've no Kennedy here, it can also mean *I desire*. That help you any?'

'Yes,' she said. 'Thanks. That's brilliant. Thanks,' and she hung up before remembering to thank him for inviting them over for dinner the next night.

'I feel the lack of Toby, even as I desire him,' she said, returning to her place at the table where Pearce was peeling her an orange. 'I love Rosy but I feel the lack of Toby, whom I desire.'

'Do you?' he asked. 'Well that's all right, then.'

44

The news that Eliza had a new man in her life was only startling for a moment. As soon as Giles recalled how different she had looked at the hospital and the equanimity with which she had faced him, it made perfect sense.

Julia could not disguise the pleasure and relief the news had given her.

Giles had assumed people exaggerated when they spoke of unsisterly closing of ranks that occurred among women who were hitched towards those who became suddenly single. Seeing the process in reverse, he revised his opinion.

Having seen inside Eliza's flat at last, he knew he should be happy for her to be starting afresh, returning to her Cornish roots, but could not help being anxious that her moving down here meant losing Dido.

'Dido can still visit us,' Julia said, reading his mind. 'She can come for proper holidays. But I'm sure the schools here are much better than that place she's stuck at in London. The classes are bound to be smaller.'

That night at dinner, Eliza looked still better than she had at the hospital. She was not in a state, after all, and she'd had time to prepare.

The boyfriend was reassuringly not a beauty. He was, however, dauntingly male and by his mere handshake and lack of cologne made Giles feel effete and lightweight. Giles made the mistake of beginning their conversation with, 'So, Julia says you're a farmer,' to which, with a hint of mockery, Pearce said, 'Eliza says you sing higher than the average Cornishwoman,' and the gulf between them was marked out with smoking beacons.

Defensively Giles felt he must indulge in a little sabre rattling, with aggressive questions about foot and mouth, BSE and subsidies. Pearce proved disarmingly unaggressive in response, retaliating with quiet humour and an admission that British farming could not continue as it was and that most subsidies were probably unjustifiable.

For all his rumbling voice and big frame, he had the gentleness of a man who knew his strength and Giles found himself imagining what it would be like to be a child on such a lap, held by strong arms and read stories in such a voice. And he felt jealousy, not that this man was sleeping with Eliza but that he would undoubtedly prove a more effective father to Dido than he had.

The two other couples staying had both gone out to an afternoon wedding. This created the illusion – since the hotel was designed to feel like a private house – that Giles and Julia were entertaining in their own home and had mysteriously acquired a handful of servants and a cook. It was still light and the windows open on to the garden filled the sitting room with some rich scent. Lily, perhaps, or lilac. The sofas were old, deep and comfortable, one wall was lined with books one might actually want to read and the lamps shed a flattering light. A waitress brought them champagne and dishes of huge green olives. Glancing up at the tableau they made in the speckled looking glass, Giles saw this was the perfect place for them to meet; a civilised space where none of them belonged.

There was an initial flurry about Dido. Where was she?

With Pearce's sister. How was she? Cross. Then a brief embarrassment followed when the woman who brought in their menus was recognised as an old schoolfriend of Pearce's. Actually it was no embarrassment at all. Pearce greeted her, introduced her, asked after her children. To be embarrassed one had to be self-conscious and he seemed entirely lacking in that, merely calm, self-contained, faintly amused. Retreating, sabre lowered, Giles tried to despise him for wearing brushed denim jeans and great clomping, slightly orange boots which had probably come from the same farmer's supply depot as the jeans, but found he could not because it was so obvious that a man who wore such things did not care and would be impervious to fashion criticism.

When they were called down to the dining room, Pearce was drawn into conversation by Julia so, having handed round walnut bread, Giles turned to Eliza.

'I'm so sorry about your Mum,' he said. 'I know you didn't get on much but, well . . . she'll leave a mum-shaped space, won't she?'

'Yes,' she said. 'Thanks. She always liked you.'

'Did she?'

'You know she did. She thought I was insane to leave you.'

This silenced him. What could he say. *You were?*

'How's yours?' she asked.

'Sober. Scary,' he said. 'You look well. Despite broken legs, dead mothers and no visible means of support.'

'I feel well,' she said and grinned.

'So life is good,' he said.

'Yes,' she said without even needing to look at Pearce. She smiled almost wildly and, fluent in the signs, he wondered if she'd had some Dutch courage before she set out. 'In the most amazing and unexpected way, it does seem to be. I've almost finished the doctorate,' she added.

'Trevescan?'

She nodded, giggled at the unlikelihood of this and began to tell him a long, involved story about a family Bible and an unpublished manuscript she was convinced she could prove to be in Trevescan's own hand. While she talked, he found himself admiring her. He had not forgotten how pretty she was, but it had been so long since she was last deeply involved in her work that he had forgotten how enthusiasm lit her rather old-fashioned looks up from within so that she became almost beautiful. Her cleverness had always unsettled him – her conversation assumed a wealth of academic reference he lacked so that three-quarters of his responses were bluffs. At the same time it had always given him vicarious pride. He had loved it when she locked horns with some friend or colleague over dinner and became so involved she would forget to eat the food on her plate.

'So what happens when you finish?' he asked. 'Will you go back to Oxford?'

'I don't know,' she said and now she glanced over at Pearce, who had just topped up Julia's glass too fast so that it slopped over. 'Maybe just finishing it could be an end in itself. Maybe I'm too old for all that. I dunno.'

He saw that perhaps the thing with Pearce was not so far advanced as Julia supposed.

In his hours of wounded pride he had often entertained the fantasy that Eliza suffered terrible regrets, that when she left him for Paul Lessing and it had all gone wrong, she had been desperate to apologise and come back to him only to find the way barred by Julia. Looking at her now, he knew he could never believe that again. Whatever her fond delusions at the time, she had not left him *for* Paul. Paul had merely proved a means to an end. She knew that male vanity required the satisfaction of a rival, that he would never have accepted that she might simply have outgrown him. He could chat and smile at this new man in her life quite easily because she would be bound to outgrow him too. Seeing the grim little flat she had been content to call home, seeing her childhood house, he had wondered if marrying her had been a crazy error of judgement. Watching her now he saw that, on the contrary, he should be flattered she had ever been interested in him.

He knew Julia had brought them all together because she imagined he pined after Eliza and thought if he could see her with another man he would be spited out of love with her. They should have met up like this years ago, if only so that he could see that, on the contrary, he was cured and could view Eliza and their past together without passion.

Who was he trying to fool? Of course he wanted her. Seeing her curled up in a corner of the sofa, shoes kicked off, feet drawn under her in the gesture he remembered, hair golden in the lamplight, hearing her softly insistent voice again, only reminded him how painful her sudden betrayal had been. He remembered sharply how physically acute had been the ache left by a relationship he had tried to dismiss as largely a thing of the mind.

'I'm going to see Dr Goldhammer again tomorrow,' she said. 'Can you believe it? After all this time? I never thought she'd agree to it.'

And all his carefully erected defensive fictions came tumbling down in the warmth of her smile. His obsession with helping and protecting Dido was symbolic, nothing more, a gesture towards the daughter now that the mother was beyond his reach.

Over coffee Julia was grilling Pearce about how he *survived* out here without theatre and opera and concerts. Giles turned to Eliza and was startled to find her looking at him with equal interrogative directness.

'What?' she asked.

'Sod all this. Julia. Pearce. The house. Everything. I love

you. I've never stopped wanting you back. Just say the word and I'll do anything, get rid of Julia, move back to Oxford, even move down here if that's what you want. Anything!'

But of course he said nothing of the sort. Because he was too cowardly. Because the big man in the orange boots was so obviously, incontestably, a Good Thing. Because Julia took that moment to look across at him with his mother's hot, beseeching eyes.

So no. He leant forward, as did Eliza, and said, with all the cautious warmth of a second proposal of marriage, 'We've never discussed this, which is daft, but you know you can have a straightforward divorce whenever you like. I won't put up a fight. You can split me down the middle.'

'Thanks,' she said and actually grinned. 'That's so sweet. But I couldn't afford a solicitor. Why? Do you and Julia want to . . . ?'

'Oh. No,' he said a little vehemently. 'I mean, probably not. I dunno. It's all a bit meaningless really, when you already live together but, well . . . And there's always Legal Aid. You know I wouldn't want you to feel I was holding you back.'

'I don't, Giles.'

'Good. Eliza?'

'What?'

'I . . . I saw your flat. I had to check on you when the school asked about where Dido was and . . . Christ! I'm sorry. I had no idea. Look, if you divorced me and it was all sorted out properly and you'd have a settlement and . . .' Where was this coming from? 'even if we had to sell up or whatever. I worry about you. And Dido. And —'

'Because I'm so poor?'

'Partly. Think about it.'

'I will. Okay?'

45

Julia's idea in inviting Eliza and her new boyfriend to dinner at the hotel was ostensibly to clear the air of any awkwardness caused by Giles' involvement in Dido's accident. She justified it to herself by saying it marked the start of a new era in the life of the extended family in which, as part of a new, independent couple, Eliza could progress from the problematic role of errant and/or abandoned wife. Only now that the evening was not going according to plan could Julia admit to herself what her actual purpose had been. She was overjoyed that Eliza had found someone else, not for Eliza's sake but for hers and Giles'. At last Eliza could be established as something other than a hapless victim and by seeing her happily involved elsewhere, Giles could at last be brought to let go of past mistakes and move on.

Eliza had begun the evening appropriately enough, sitting by her former rival and drawing out Pearce to show him off when he was too modest to take his best advantage. But when they went down to dinner she neglected Pearce more and more to talk to Giles. Far from being embarrassed by this, Giles seemed not to notice and even encouraged her, asking her quiet, exclusive questions about music, murmuring things too low for Julia to hear or, when he did steer the conversation into more general territory, soon making it exclusive again by playing do-you-remember, indulging in reminiscences that meant little to her and even less to Pearce.

At first she thought Pearce was painfully shy. Having seen him filthily relaxed in his work things, she was startled to see him clean and assumed he felt restrained by smarter clothes. She was used to Giles and men like him, who always spoke first and were never short of something to say. Finding herself thrown together with this big, tongue-tied stranger made her shy too, and not herself at all. Not what she had come to think of as herself, anyway. Then she realised he was not shy at all, but attentive and uncompetitive. Before long he was drawing her out, topping up her wine, passing her vegetables, asking gentle questions.

'It can't have been easy for you,' he said abruptly.

'What can't?'

'All the . . . the mess. You must have been very young when you two met.'

'Quite young,' she said, flattered.

'Didn't you hope for something straightforward? Just a bloke and no baggage?'

'Oh I don't think there's any such thing. I bet you come with baggage.'

His eyes glittered with something. 'I've never been married.'

'No? But you'll still have baggage. Parents. Family. Even no emotional history – no relationships – is baggage of a kind after a while.' She summoned up a laugh she intended to sound carefree but it came out as a kind of bitter croak, so much so that Giles looked across at her and she had to reassure him with a quick, private smile.

'Shall we have coffee upstairs?' she suggested. She hoped that a move back to the sofas would shake up their configuration as two reunited exes and two spare wheels.

Eliza slipped away to ring the babysitter to check Dido

had gone to bed. Pearce shambled off in search of the gents. Briefly alone in the sitting room, therefore, Julia drew Giles down on the sofa beside her.

'He's lovely,' she said. 'Gentle giant. She's very happy.'

'Yes.'

'What about the baby? Have you told her?'

'Course not.' He seemed almost shocked. 'Did you tell him?'

'No. But why should it —?'

'It . . . it just seems an odd way of going about it. And . . . it wouldn't be very fair. She can't have them, remember.'

'You never said.'

'I must have done.'

'You never told me.'

'She might not have told him yet.'

'Oh God,' she said. 'Of course. I won't say a word. Our happy secret.' She smiled and touched his arm, hoping to draw him into a warm moment in which they might be discovered. But the coffee came in, borne by Pearce, who had relieved his schoolfriend of the tray. And Giles jumped up to take it off him and pour and Pearce plonked himself down where Giles had been sitting.

When Eliza came back in she had done something to her hair. Julia suspected she had washed it just before leaving and come out with it wet. It had spent most of the evening hanging rather limp, looking clean but gratifyingly lifeless. Evidently she had brushed it and now it stood out around her face and glittered. *Spun gold* Julia thought, picturing fairytale heroines. *Hair as yellow as corn.* She had also been playing with the bottles of scent in the ladies. As she kicked off her shoes and settled herself into a corner of the opposite sofa, Julia caught a little erotic message of stephanotis.

Naturally when Giles took her a cup of coffee and a little

saucer of chocolates, he settled down beside her and the tête-à-tête resumed.

'Lovely room,' Pearce said. 'My mum used to come here for toasted cheese sandwiches in the Fifties. It wasn't so posh then, I expect. Is this your first time in Penzance, Julia?'

'We're all snowballs,' she told him, unable to match his small talk.

'Sorry?'

'It's all a con, isn't it? This business of starting afresh. Start a new life somewhere else. Start a new relationship with a clean slate. We're snowballs. We don't start afresh, we just pick up more stuff as we go along. I was so nervous about tonight but the moment you two walked in I thought, "Marvellous! Look at them! Crisp and clean and in love. A new start. So we'll all get a new start now." But it's not true.'

'Isn't it?'

'Well look.' She waved her coffee cup towards the other sofa, not caring that coffee slopped into the saucer. 'He still loves her. He probably always will. If I'm to make it work with him, I have to accept that as part of his baggage. You too.'

'You . . . you think she . . . ?'

Something in his manner made her need to hurt him, just for a moment. Perhaps because she could see so completely the nice, steady appeal he had for Eliza and was envious that she should be in a position of such manly plenty. 'Oh just look at the body language,' she told him impatiently.

At that moment Eliza smiled at something Giles told her and, twining some golden hair in her fingers, wriggled herself deeper into the sofa cushions in a way that seemed to lay herself wide open to him.

'Of course she's still in love with him. You may be her new Good Thing but he'll always be her old favourite, always at the back of her head when she's with you, and there's no competing with that.'

Villiers could not have done it better. Her observation killed their conversation, left him looking so miserable she wanted to take his big hands in hers and kiss their scarred knuckles.

'Don't listen to me, Pearce. I'm just twitter and bisted.'

'No you're not,' he said kindly.

Damn it! She had kicked him when he was down and yet he could find it in himself to be kind to her.

He was still watching the others and when Eliza suddenly said, 'Is that the time? I've got an early train tomorrow. Take me home at once, Pearce,' his grateful smile was heart-breaking.

46

Pearce had approached the evening in such high spirits. In the light of their conversation the previous night, Eliza taking him to meet Giles and his girlfriend felt like a public declaration of which he could be justifiably proud. He knew that he should not overinterpret her actions and that there was probably an element of aggression, of getting back at her ex involved.

Only he wasn't her ex, of course, but still her husband and Pearce, in his cautious optimism, was quite unprepared for the shock of seeing how physically suited they were. With the same hair and eye colour and the physical ease between them, they might have been brother and sister.

He had thought he would at least have some advantage by being on home ground but the hotel was far smarter than he remembered it being and Giles somehow contrived to make it feel like his private house. Giles gave him the conversational upper hand by opening with some ignorant, third-hand assumptions about farming but, to his irritation, Pearce found himself cowed into politeness and came across as the quiet, dim country boy for which they took him. But it was the physical contrast between them he found most demoralising. Giles was film-star handsome, the sort of man who would welcome a camera from any angle. Pearce felt himself a great, hulking blob beside him.

He tried in vain to coax Julia into talking about herself, her house, her work but found to his dismay that everything led back to Giles; Giles' work was her work, Giles' house, her house. He was trying to ignore the way Eliza and Gile were getting on but Julia could talk about nothing else. She was frightening company. She might lose control at any moment and start shouting.

Then there was the horrible surprise when a voice behind him said, 'Can I take your orders for drinks?' and he realised that Janet worked there. He could not keep his back turned indefinitely so made a big show of asking her how she was, how Lance and the girls were and so on. But he saw how she read the situation and despised him even as he clumsily introduced her, because in his nervousness he said she had been to school with him and she did not bother to correct him. Luckily someone else served them during dinner. Coming upstairs again afterwards, he managed to catch Janet on her own as she brought coffee up. He took the tray off her, which made matters worse because it seemed like the equivalent of telling a servant they could take the rest of the night off.

'Old friends,' he told her. 'Haven't seen them in ages.'

'Better get back to them quick, then,' she said. 'If they want liqueurs, they're inside the desk with the honesty book.'

Worst of all, however, was the way Eliza talked to Giles about *Country Goodness*. She talked about music more generally too but in specialised language that excluded Pearce as completely as if they had been speaking a foreign tongue. She talked about recognising its style and handwriting, about her trip to the British Library and her breakthrough in the Truro archive as though all that mattered was Giles' approval. To Pearce's ears – straining to pick up sentences even as he pretended to listen to Julia – she made her trip to Cornwall sound like no more than a research visit, a brief, lucky diversion from her career elsewhere. She touched Giles on the elbow, the hand, even the knee. She did not touch Pearce once all evening. When he turned back to Julia, hoping for relief, she merely held up a mirror to his jealousy, being similarly tormented, so that they ended up less as fellow performers than as spectators to the main event.

'What an ordeal,' Eliza said as soon as they were alone in the Land Rover again. 'Sorry to put you through that. They're desperately unhappy, of course. It comes off them in little waves.'

'Do you think?' he gently encouraged her and she spent the drive home pinpointing the ways in which Giles had been rude or Julia catty, analysing how badly they were suited.

'He's scarred emotionally,' she said. 'I never really noticed before, as if he had one skin too few.' As they stopped for the traffic lights at some roadworks she said, 'I ought to divorce him properly. Cut loose from the whole tangle. Would you mind very much if we never saw them again?'

'Of course not,' he said. 'Whatever makes you happy.' He glanced across and saw her abandon herself to a great, hands-free yawn. She had never looked so lovely to him.

47

It was the first time Eliza had been back to Oxford since she and Giles moved to London. Her initial impression was that nothing had changed. The old buildings were as arrogantly lovely, the lawns as immaculate. There were the same impossible tangles of locked or dismembered bicycles at college entrances, the same sense of lofty removal from the encroaching commercial world, the same sensation that, even in summer, the air was several degrees colder.

Most of the buildings had been cleaned, however, Italian-American coffee bars had proliferated and the shops along the High Street were far smarter than she remembered them being. Most startling was how very young the students seemed. It being the long vacation, undergraduates had vanished but the summer influx of overseas language and culture students milled about lodges and sprawled, Mediterranean fashion, on lawns and steps where the locals never sat.

Entering her old college and telling the porters who she was there to see, Eliza felt more like a parent on Open Day than a returning scholar. One of them remembered her. Half-remembered her. He called her Lisa.

As College Organist, Dr Goldhammer occupied a set of rooms at right angles to the chapel, enjoying views of the stained glass on one side and a secret, ferny garden on the other. She shook Eliza's hand and ushered her in, typically behaving as though this were just another weekly tutorial, not a reunion after an eight-year absence. She pointed Eliza to an armchair, poured her strong tea from a pot she had already started then sat behind her desk. Eliza noticed at once a print-out of the fistful of pages she had sent ahead of her by e-mail.

Dr Goldhammer picked the first page up, glanced at it then set it back on the pile.

'This is all rather extraordinary,' she said coolly. 'You're an extremely lucky woman.'

'I know.'

'Nine-tenths of doctoral research in this period is merely rearranging known material. The challenge is usually to make the old seem fresh. By presenting us with entirely fresh material you steal a considerable march. But then you know that. Is it any good?'

'The madrigal? I only heard it sung very badly, but yes.'

'Better than just interesting.'

'Yes. Publishable. Good enough for me to feel sure it was by him the moment I heard it. And then of course there's the personal significance.'

The glasses went back on. More pages were turned back and forth.

'Well . . . your evidence for *that* is pretty scanty still. I mean, you *make* it fit but I can unmake just as easily. A literate man, an adept amateur poet of the period would hardly have left half his hidden rhyme in English, half in Latin, surely? Amo Rosam et Tobiam egeo would have convinced me more than your, what was it, *Amo Rosy e(t) egeo Toby.*'

'Yes, but that would have given him two verses of five lines instead of two of four,' Eliza began warily.

'Or two of four followed by a couplet. A sonnet, in other words. A versifier of any skill, as we know Trevescan was, if only on the basis of his words to *Go Dissembler*, would surely have taken the letters of his hidden message as his starting point then built the verse from them. An extra line per verse would have been neither here nor there. You need more examples to back up your case. Look at some Sydney. Read Shawcross on riddles and perhaps work up a reference or two to Mary Trelford's work on Elizabethan code systems . . .'

Eliza made notes in her pocket diary and wished she had thought to bring along something more convincing, like a file or a box of index cards.

'Your bibliography's a bit scant, too. I know I've always admired a lack of padding but it won't be me who does the assessing. Your examiner will almost certainly be Joe Rhodes or Anthony Trickett and they're both, well . . . Just pad out your secondary sources a bit. They'll appreciate that.' She pushed the pages aside. End of subject. Eliza sipped the tea although it was tongue-curlingly bitter.

'Tell me about the manuscript,' Dr Goldhammer went on. 'You say that it's glued in the back of a Family Bible?'

'Yes. Torn from four original copies of East.'

'The Fourth Set of Books?'

'Yes. 1618. Obviously a next step will be to put out a search for the set with end pages torn out then research its provenance . . .'

'Will your Cornish friend release his pages?'

'No. They're of family significance.'

'Pity. When you've published, he could sell them for a fair price, you know.'

'Would the college be interested?' Eliza had a bright image of Pearce with a shiny new tractor until Dr Goldhammer made a face.

'The old story,' she said. 'Rich on paper but not in practice. I had to go cap in hand even to persuade them to buy us the New Grove. They wanted us to make do with the online version. Villiers Yates, however, would almost certainly be prepared to spirit the manuscript off to that Texan collector he buys for. Byatt.'

'Has Villiers spoken to you?' Eliza asked defensively.

'He put out feelers. In the meantime I suggest you persuade your friend to let you have the four pages scanned onto disc. If you could then get someone in Computer Sciences to compare them with scans of the Dublin and Bodleian manuscripts you'd have expert verification for joint penmanship at least. Yale – was it? – came up with a program for sourcing typeface in the Gütenberg Bible years ago, we must have something similar by now.'

'Right,' said Eliza, thinking at once of Anne Perry, her friend in the English Department. 'I think I've got a good contact for that. So . . . you think it's worth pursuing.'

Dr Goldhammer cast another critical eye over Eliza's inexcusably scanty bibliography. 'If you don't, I can think of at least three keen young things I could put onto it.'

'Oh no. I mean I do want to follow it through it's just, well, I've been out of harness for so long I was worried I'd started to lose my sense of perspective. And I . . .'

'Can you imagine pursuing further research when this is done? Or lecturing and teaching?'

'Well . . .' Eliza tried hard.

'Not that we could make any promises of offering you a post. The competition is fiercer than ever but . . . If you were prepared to travel to wherever the offer came from, I've no doubt this could prove a useful calling card for you. A conference or two, always assuming you find a publisher for your research . . .'

'Yes. Perhaps. I think I should take it one stage at a time.'

'Very good. But I'm still nominally your supervisor and I think we should agree a provisional delivery date, don't you? Since it's been so very long in coming. How does

November strike you? November 1st. Then we can have another meeting to discuss any tidying up before you submit the thesis officially before, say, the end of January.'

'All right.'

'Good.'

Dr Goldhammer stood and saw her out. As dryly matter-of-fact as ever, she closed her outer door firmly before Eliza had even left the landing.

Uncertain whether her train from Penzance would be delayed or how long the meeting would last, she had kept her options open, vaguely thinking she might turn up on Anne Perry's doorstep to beg a sofa for the night. But the lanes seemed full of pretty things in summery dresses and, with only her battered shoulder bag and pocket diary as defence, she felt neither sufficiently lightweight nor scholastic enough to linger. Dismissed from Dr Goldhammer's presence when she had expected – what? Some kind of donnish celebration? A judiciously small glass of sherry? – she felt dismissed by the town, lacking in youth and application. She would return when she was better prepared and fully armed. For now, she returned to the station and began the long journey home.

Whereas the trip here had been swift and fairly direct, she was going to have to change repeatedly on the way back, which seemed to heighten her folly in coming all this way for half an hour with a dried-up, passed-over sourpuss.

What did she want out of this? Could she really see herself as a Dr Goldhammer? Dr Eliza Hosken, immured in a set of rooms with a clavichord, two hundred books and a regular misericord in the college chapel?

But of course she could never be like that, because she had Dido. Dido could go to a good school here and have suitable friends and they could live in careful, colourful economy in a cosy cottage on the cheaper side of the station and canal. She would ride a bike again to get fit, ride a bike on her way to give surprisingly popular lectures.

But something was missing from the fantasy and she suspected she knew what. Who, rather.

She bought herself a half-bottle of nasty, brackish wine from the buffet car and found a window seat where she was soon hemmed in by a large man with a suit carrier and a laptop. He had run for the train and sweated profusely as he made a series of extraordinarily tedious phone calls to colleagues and friends.

At the bookstall she had bought a bargain copy of *Jane Eyre* to help pass the journey but her eyes soon slid from the cramped text to staring out of the window at passing fields. She watched a Sunday farmer using his tractor to pull some device across the side of a grassy hill and felt hemmed in suddenly by daunting possibility.

48

Julia was left so restless and edgy by the little dinner party that Giles fully expected her to wake demanding they fly home a day early. She slept badly. He knew this because he had twice woken as she slipped out of bed and padded to the bathroom. A third time, towards dawn, he'd rolled over meaning to slide a leg between hers for comfort and found the mattress coldly empty beside him. He'd turned to see her huddled on the daybed, wrapped in a blanket, staring out at the boats and dangerously pensive.

Woken later when breakfast was brought to their room, he was ashamed that there was no sign of her, as though they had been caught rowing in public. She bustled in with a raft of Sunday papers half an hour later, however, and announced that she had reserved them two bicycles at a hire shop on the other side of the harbour.

'It's another lovely day,' she said. 'I thought we could ride along the cycle track around the bay to visit the Mount. They told me it's one of the days when Lady St Levan opens her gardens for charity.'

Giles, terrified of London traffic, had not ridden a bicycle since his student days, apart from when he played Apollo in a very childish production of *Death in Venice*. For much of its length the cycle path was far from the road and ran, carefully fenced, between railway lines and dog-haunted beach. The only danger was posed by other cyclists, many of them wobbly children, and the occasional bloody-minded cluster of pedestrians.

It was low tide so when they reached Marazion they were able to lock their bikes to some railings and walk out to St Michael's Mount on the rounded rocks of a still glistening causeway. Julia was in one of her brittle, glassy moods, furious about something it would be up to him to divine. She fell to sightseeing as though it were her last allotted earthly task. She marched up the vertiginous path that was dark with shrubbery, itchy with little flies, to the fort-turned-mansion.

Only those parts of the house that must have been most expensive to keep up – the rooftop apartments and fanciful battlements – had been handed over to the National Trust. The St Levans still lived there in some style presumably, in rooms tantalisingly out of view. After sweeping through the public areas, peering through every window and reading every little card with a kind of thin-lipped piety, Julia slowed down a little when they descended to the gardens but even there she acted as though someone were taking notes on her cultural seriousness.

Giles could not tell an asphodel from an allium but even he had to concede that the gardens were a triumph of ingenuity over nature. Where the house seemed to grow out of the rock, the gardens had been painstakingly carved out of shelves in the seaward cliffs below it. Steps in the rock and snaking paths led one through a sequence of rooms built of plants, many of them hot flowered exotics which drew precious comfort from the sun-warmed rock that they could not find in the sea winds and Cornish weather.

But it was only a garden, not the Piero *Flagellation*.

'It's so clever,' Julia said. 'Do you see how none of the

plants can grow very tall but you don't notice because of the angles and the way the borders climb up above head height? And that's pretty. Is it an abutilon or a . . . What is it, do you think?'

'No one's keeping score, Julia,' he told her. It just came out and far more bitterly than he had intended.

'What?' she asked, perplexed.

He thought it best not to repeat himself in case she really had not heard. 'Is all this racing around good for the baby?' he asked instead. 'You had a rough night. Shouldn't you be taking it easy?'

'There is no baby,' she told him.

They were standing at the foot of a little flight of steps by a bank of some succulent that was evidently a feature of the place because passers-by stopped to caress and admire it. There was a clutch of older women discussing the plant now.

'Is it a sedum?' one was asking.

'Or an echeveria?' a companion said.

'It's an aeonium,' said Giles, who had spotted the sign and hoped they would pass tactfully on their way. But they loitered, oblivious to the painful scene they had blundered into.

'Oh yes,' the first one said. 'There's a sign. Look. *Aeonium Schwarztopf.* I always thought it was *kopf.*'

'That's the soprano, dear.'

'Oh yes.'

And on and on, so Giles tried to move on instead but Julia was rooted.

'I lost it,' she said.

'When?' he asked, appalled.

'This morning. Last night.' She shrugged, sapped of all energy now she had spoken up and he saw her manic tourism for what it was, a wild attempt at diversion. She was beautiful to him now, so defenceless, all elbows and proudly jutting chin.

Heedless of their audience, who at last had sensed they were overhearing what they should not and begun a pantomimic retreat, their exaggerated discretion only drawing attention to their presence, he drew her to him and kissed her hair.

'You should have said,' he sighed. 'You should have woken me, Babe. I'm so sorry. Jesus. And we were so excited.'

'Were we?' she asked.

'Don't be silly. Of course we were. I've been walking on air since you told me. I mean I had been. Jesus.'

He noticed she was not holding him in return. He stood back a little, still holding her. She looked aside, avoiding his gaze as though ashamed.

'Maybe I didn't lose it. Maybe I was just late. It happens, especially if I've been skipping meals. Maybe my last one was early.'

'Have you?'

'Have I what?'

'Been skipping meals?'

She smiled at him now but in a way that chilled him. 'I eat about one to your every three,' she said.

He was going to ask her why or apologise or say something crass, which she anticipated and prevented with another shrug. She turned aside and continued through the gardens. He noticed she was looking at nothing now, merely walking. He caught her hand to slow then stop her.

'Listen,' he said.

Her expression was a silent, uninviting *what*?

'I was going to ask you to marry me,' he said. They had witnesses again, a young couple coming the other way, each with a baby in harness, a matching set. 'I mean I am asking. Will you? Please?'

49

'I was going to ask you to marry me,' Giles said.

He was holding her hand, admittedly only to stop her walking away and to grab her attention but in this setting it felt as public as a passionate kiss would have done. Julia found herself transfixed by the faces of two wet-lipped, passing babies. Strapped to their parents' backs they performed a simultaneous eyes right, as though sensing not an irrelevant argument but a great, milky pap.

Giles squeezed her hands. She looked at him instead.

'I mean I am asking,' he said. 'Will you? Please?'

She pulled her hands away as gently as she could and continued walking, drawing him with her. They attracted too much notice standing still against the flow of visitors. 'You don't have to do this,' she said.

'What do you mean? I know I don't have to. Will you?'

'You're a bit late,' she said as they stepped under the trees and began their descent down the rocky path to the harbour. 'If you'd asked me when I first said I was pregnant, at least that would have made sense. There are advantages to a baby having married parents. But now?'

'I thought you'd be angry if I'd asked you then, as if that was the only reason.'

'Wouldn't it have been? And a good practical reason. But

asking me now is . . .' She was so angry that her voice shook and for a few paces she had to avoid looking at him. People passing them in the other direction would be carrying away two hot, cross faces and enigmatic conversational morsels. *Asked her what? If she wanted the dining room painted blue? If she wanted friends to join them on holiday? If she wanted a threesome with him and a best mate?*

'Your trouble is you're too sentimental. You're a pathos-junkie,' she said. 'Eliza. What could be more pathetic? The unworldly, donnish Eliza with a baby in tow. And Dido. Christ, *she's* practically a foundling! That's pathetic. That really gets to you. And now me. Who'd have thought it? Now that I lose a baby I stop being just good old dependable Julia, always good for a shag or a flower arrangement and turn into poor Julia-who-lost-her-baby.'

'Is that really how you think I think of you?'

'But most of all it's you, isn't it? The pathos of you that really gets your juices flowing. Christ, your alky mother did a thorough job on you! You're probably creaming yourself already at the thought of jilted Giles.'

'Shall I take that as a no, then?'

'Giles please listen.' She stopped. Spoken, her anger had evaporated as swiftly as it had come to the boil. The tide was in now so there was a stream of people around the harbour wall to catch boats back to Marazion. She sat on an isolated bench rather than join the queue while it was so long. Giles sat beside her. Now she took his hand.

That distant wooden creaking you hear, she told herself, *is the turning of tables.*

'What is it?' he asked.

'Do you love me?' she asked quietly.

'What? Why are you –? Yes of course I do.'

He was not smiling, she noticed. There was no surprised

laughter, no honest relief that the question required only a simple answer.

'Say it then.'

'But . . .'

'Say *I love you, Julia.*'

'This is stupid. You know I do.' He sighed then said, 'I love you, Julia,' with as much sincerity as a small boy prompted to say thank you for a dull weekend.

Still holding his hand, she made sure she took a good look at him saying it. The hair was still blond but its curls would look less angelic as they turned grey. She suspected he had not yet noticed it was thinning at his crown. The worry lines in his face were winning out over the laughter ones – frowning was his habitual expression when singing florid passages – and would soon set the mood of his face at rest. After a succession of hairy lovers, she had been charmed at his smoothness, at the cradle-snatching comfort of kissing someone whose jaw was never significantly bristled. But as he aged was there not something of the old child about it? Something unpleasantly immature? She withdrew her hand.

'That took about twenty seconds too long,' she said. 'Or should that be four years and three months?'

'I'm so sorry, Babe.'

'Don't apologize. It was a kind lie. It's my fault for forcing it out of you. Shit.'

She wanted to stand and hurry to one of the little boats which was now awobble with boarding passengers but found herself sapped of strength and sat on, feeling her face grow stony as the full boat chugged away and another came to take its place.

'What do you want to do?' he asked at last.

'I don't know,' she said, feeling close to tears and driving her nails into her palms to save herself. 'We've lived together all this time without it being an issue but . . . I don't know.'

'No,' he checked her with a touch to her forearm before she should say too much. 'I mean, what do you want to do right now?'

'Oh,' she said and laughed. 'Sorry. Erm. God. Shall we go back to London?'

'Of course.'

'I'm sorry. I don't think I can stand another night here.'

'No. Of course you can't. You poor thing.'

'Don't, Giles.'

'Sorry.'

He touched her elbow as they rose and the small contact was trigger enough for them to fall into each other's arms for a brief, desperate hug then they went on their way to the boat.

The business of travel would absorb them as tourism could not. Packing, driving to the airport, waiting for a plane, flying home, catching a taxi, unpacking, opening mail, concocting some kind of Sunday supper.

Who was to say that these activities would not let them slip back into their quiet routines just as before? As they shuffled down the wet steps and were handed into a bobbing boat by its walnut-faced pilot they were just another pair of summer trippers and for all she knew Giles was now as placid as he seemed.

Her mind, however, was tangling itself in knotted possibilities. He had not repeated his proposal but she could still accept it. And perhaps she could not? Perhaps he had only asked her on a charitable impulse and now considered himself reprieved? Ridiculous! Of course they could not live on together as though nothing had happened; the assumption that he loved her or was on the point of discovering he did was quite different from the unadorned knowledge that he didn't. Being ruled by fear, her instinct had always been to cling to security rather than dare to entertain alternatives. For days she had been wavering between embracing motherhood and continuing childless and either option had seemed tumultuous at best. But that was nothing compared to suddenly imagining life without Giles. Unprotected by his money, house and status, obliged to rely on her own income, to find somewhere of her own to live, she would have to fall back on her own friends and she had few who predated Giles and thus were not shared territory.

Unable to imagine a future without him, she cast her mind back to her life before they met. She had shared a small flat in Hackney with a young man and woman who had advertised for a flatmate. They had little in common. They maintained closely guarded, separate shelves in fridge and larder. Quarterly bills had been a source of strife and acute anxiety. Not a happy time.

Repelled, she made a conscious effort to be calm. Hundreds of couples did not love each other yet stayed together. But presumably they had loved each other once and the feeling had decayed. Or did they merely stay together from fear of the alternative?

One day at a time, she told herself as they cycled glumly back around the bay. *We'll do nothing hasty and take this one day at a time*. There could be no thought of domestic upheaval with Giles' first night only days away or of her making decisions with her hormones still out of kilter.

The man at the cycle hire shop was greeting the returning couple in front of them with mockery at their failure to fulfil their plan of riding to Land's End and back. But turning to Giles and Julia he read the grimness in their faces and his banter dried up.

They climbed in silence the little hill from the harbour's edge and re-entered the hotel.

'If you can face dealing with the airline,' she told him as she picked up their key, 'I'll go upstairs and do the packing.'

'Okay, darling,' he said with a cautious little smile.

He never called her darling. It made her feel like his old boot of a wife, which was either sweet or cunning of him. It also made them sound like a couple that had just suffered a tragic loss, which in a sense they were. As she zipped up their wash things and gathered books and belongings onto the bed then folded away the few clothes she had unpacked, it was with a bereaved woman's sense of the cruel persistence of ordinary things in the face of savage change. Here was a bottle of eye drops bought before her first bout of morning sickness, which was still safe to use for another two weeks. Here was the silver bangle he had bought for her last birthday, before she had realised he did not love her, before she noticed that he had always signed his notes or cards to her Giles XXXX rather than love, Giles. She had always taken those Xs at face value, as a row of kisses, as a reticent mark of feelings he was simply too restrained to discuss. Now she saw they had always been merely the algebra of a misunderstanding. Maths had never been her strong point.

50

Molly and Pearce sat at the kitchen table outside the back door of the farmhouse, enjoying the afternoon sun and desultorily picking over the Sunday papers she had brought with her.

Instead of the usual Sunday lunch at her place, to which Morris was always invited too to coerce him into spending time with Lucy, the three of them had come to the farm. It was easier to accommodate Dido's broken leg that way. Besides, St Just was noisy with an open-air Cornish mystery play in the Plan an Gwarry and they wanted to escape the crowds.

It was the first meal Pearce had taken outside that year, not counting sandwich lunches in the tractor. They had eaten roast pork, through force of habit, but with salads and lemony roast vegetables instead of the usual Sunday roast padding.

As well as the sleepy cooing of the collar doves on the nearest barn, regular thunks and clatters reached them from the far end of the yard where Morris had been persuaded to teach Lucy how to shoot beer cans with Pearce's boyhood air gun. She had expressed a wish to shoot for a while and he had hopes she would take after Morris, proving a better shot than Pearce was, and so be able to do something about the farm's perennial rabbit plague. And the collar doves.

Molly had made Pearce put on sunglasses because he always suffered from headaches in the summer and she was sure they were light-related. She wore some too, big, tortoiseshell, Jackie O ones that made her look at once tough and intensely feminine. The impenetrable glasses made her face utterly relaxed and impassive and he felt them do the same to his. Thus masked, he might tell her any-thing.

Lucy at last succeeded in shooting a can off the hedge. As Morris ruffled her hair, she turned towards the house for approval so brother and sister clapped her.

'So what's Eliza hoping to do up there?' Molly asked, pouring them both more wine.

'See her old tutor,' he said. 'She reckons she's found enough material to finish her thesis. Become Dr Hosken.'

'He's not Cornish, is he? The husband?'

'No. Hosken's her maiden name. Don't think she ever really used his.'

'So what's he like?'

'He's okay. For a Londoner.' He grinned, as did she. He knew she was thinking of their father who always said of Londoners *they think they bin and they bain't*. 'He thought I'd like him more if he told me he listened to *The Archers*. He's a bit prissy, really.'

'Pretty?'

'Prissy. And pretty. Handsome. He's still mad about her.'

'So why'd his girlfriend ask you both?'

'You're the woman. You tell me.'

'Do you think Eliza'd ever —?'

'No.'

'All right. All right. You sound very sure.'

'She said. I believe her.'

'But if she's still wanting this doctorate —'

'— then she'll have to go away. Living out here's all very well if you're content to grow broccoli or write novels but academics need to be where the libraries are.'

'And the students. She'd be expected to teach. Would you mind her going away, Pearce?'

'Course I'd mind. I . . .' Even with the glasses on he felt inhibited. Her romantic life had proved so unromantic, so curtailed by necessity and disappointment that it felt insensitive to tell her of his happiness. Or risky, as though her unlucky glance could scorch it.

'Has she really got to you?' she asked tentatively.

'Yeah,' he said. 'Molly, I'm as crazy about her as Giles is.'

'But she's got so much baggage.'

'You're not the first to tell me that. And no, she hasn't.'

'She's got a kid.'

'So? So have you. I like kids.'

'But don't you want some of your own?'

'Yes, but . . . There's no point saying all this if they're going away. Why not just enjoy it while I've got it?'

'Because they might *not* go away. And then you'd have to deal with it. God!' She sloshed more wine into their glasses.

'What?'

'You're such a . . . such a bloke, sometimes. I forget, because I'm not married to you. You can't just bumble along without looking ahead, Pearce. That's why there are so many men with the wrong women. They bumble. Then they wake up and it's the woman who gets punished for it.'

'Yeah well she's *not* the wrong woman, okay?'

'She can't even cook, Lucy tells me.'

'So? You're not exactly Gordon Blue. And neither was Mum. I'm glad. I like that she can't cook and dresses funny. It's because she'd rather be thinking and frankly, around here, given the sort of women I meet, that makes a fucking change.'

'Well if you got out more, you'd meet more women.'

'What is this? I like the woman I've met. Very much. I'm mad about her and if she wants to go away I'll . . . Christ.

Listen to me. I've even been thinking about selling up and following her.'

Molly was stunned into a satisfactory silence.

'That's how serious I am,' he told her.

'Does she know?'

'Course not. It wouldn't be fair. If she stays it has to be because she wants to and because the kid wants to, not because they feel they should.'

'Oh don't worry. I'm sure Dr Hosken will do exactly as she pleases.'

'Why don't you like her?'

'I do. Oh, Pearce, I do. She's great! If she walked into the library after a job I'd give her one like a flash. It's just that she's got a track record. She's a liability as a . . . as relationship material.'

'And I'm not. Just because I'm your brother.'

Molly looked at him flatly for a moment or two while she worked out what he was hinting at. 'It's okay,' she said at last. 'I know. I know you're a grown-up with a love life and complications and . . . Sorry. I'm being a cow. I just wanted to be sure. I've wanted something for you for so long. You know that.'

'Oh. Well great.'

'And in case you were worrying about it, I wiped the address for that seedy chat room you've been visiting off my computer's history files. I'm assuming it was you going there and not Lucy. Or I've really got my hands full.'

'No. It was me,' he admitted. 'Thanks.'

'Now you're angry.'

He sighed. 'No. I just wish – Hey!' He clapped again. Lucy did a butch little victory wiggle like a goal scorer while Morris set up another can for her.

'Would you marry her, if she was free?' Molly asked.

Pearce looked away. 'In my dreams,' he said.

'Even if she didn't want any more kids?'

'Has she told you she doesn't?'

'No. But would you care?'

'I dunno. No. Probably not. Her decision. Anyway, Dido'd be more than enough. And it would be nice because, well . . . she's not really her kid either so it would make it easier.'

'Because Eliza didn't have her with another bloke, you mean?'

'Probably.'

There was a clatter from inside the kitchen as a crutch fell onto the slate floor. A muffled curse followed. Pearce winked at Molly over his sunglasses.

'She's such a *sweet* girl,' Molly enunciated loudly. 'But she's got *such* big ears.'

'I heard that,' Dido said, hobbling out to join them.

'You're meant to be lying down resting that bone of yours.'

'Simkin kept lying on me and I got hot. Anyway, I could hear you both even from in there. But I didn't listen.'

'Oh no?' Molly teased. She pulled out a chair so Dido could sit herself more easily.

'No. When you two talk on your own you get really Cornish.'

'How do we sound?'

'You sort of burble. She's going to have a baby, you know.'

'Who? Your Mum is?' Molly sounded as horrified as Pearce felt. Another woman's child was one thing, another man's . . .

'No,' Dido snorted. 'She's not that stupid. Julia is. Giles and Julia. He told me on the way to the hospital but I'd sort of forgotten.'

'Oh,' said Molly. 'Well that's nice for them.'

'Yeah,' Pearce agreed. 'They must be thrilled. I wonder why they didn't say last night.'

'Maybe it's a secret,' Dido said, scratching an itch inside her plaster with a fork left over from lunch. 'He often tells me things he isn't meant to.'

Morris was coming back with the air gun, in need of another beer, Dad-duty done for the week. Pearce showed Dido how she could scratch deeper if she held the fork the other way around. He had a picture of Giles and Julia side by side on one of the hotel sofas, because he could not picture their London home. Julia was immensely pregnant and Giles was beaming with paternal pride. Even as Pearce suspected the news would cause Eliza a certain covert pain, he felt an immoderate swell of content.

51

Pearce was driving over to Leedstown to buy spare parts for the tractor and had given in to Dido's plea to be taken along for the ride. Filthy weather had blown up overnight and Eliza was worried Dido would get rain on her plaster cast, had visions of the thing turning softly unsupportive, but Dido was adamant that her unstitched tracksuit bottom would be protection enough.

'I won't get out of the car,' she insisted. 'I just want the ride.'

'I'll bring her back the scenic route,' Pearce said with a wink. He helped her out and up onto the back seat of the Land Rover where she could sit sideways with her plastered leg stretched along the seat.

Eliza passed up her crutches then rode in the front. She had the family Bible on her lap, wrapped in a carrier bag from the Co-op. Pearce had agreed to let her scan the madrigal onto a disk at Molly's.

Dido was full of questions about the scans and how the university computer department could use them to find matches (or not) with the Trevescan manuscript in Dublin. 'Could they do the same with people,' she asked, 'to prove who belongs with who?'

'They already do,' Pearce told her. 'With fingerprints and

DNA and when the police are trying to find someone they use a computer to show him with and without a beard or how he might look with different coloured hair. When a kid's been missing for a while they can even show how they might look a year or two older.'

Dido turned back to Eliza, ignoring his contribution in the lofty way she had when she thought someone had strayed from the subject or wilfully misinterpreted a question.

'And if they can,' she asked, 'and you do prove the piece is by Roger, do you get paid?'

'No.' Eliza smiled.

'But do you have to become a teacher, though?'

'A lecturer. I could. Maybe. Dr Goldhammer said I might get offers from universities all over the place, depending on how the thesis goes down. I could lecture. I could get more funding for research. Maybe I could write a book.'

'But you'd have to go away? We'd have to go somewhere else?'

'It depends.' Eliza was acutely aware that Pearce was listening. 'Maybe.'

'I hate maybe.'

It was almost a relief for once to feel Dido slump back into her more usual sulk. She had spent most of the morning showing interest, humouring Eliza almost, in a way she only did when lying or breaking the rules in some way.

As they pulled down the hill into St Just, Pearce had to pull over to a verge to let a lorry past.

'Giles and Julia go back to London today,' Eliza said, amazed at how ordinary that sounded and how calmly she could say it.

'Good,' Dido said.

'That's not very nice,' Eliza told her.

'What did they do to *you*?' Pearce asked.

'Duh. Only broke my leg.'

'You did that yourself.'

'Yeah,' Dido sighed. 'But I wouldn't have fallen off if he hadn't been there. They're stupid. Piles and Poolia.'

Eliza caught Pearce's eye as they swung off the square towards Cape Cornwall. 'You're in for a cheery morning,' she said. 'Sure you can stick it?'

'I can always play the radio loud,' he said and flinched as Dido smacked him lightly on the back of his head.

'You don't have to go in the car, you know,' Eliza told her. 'You could always come to Molly's with me, hang out with Lucy for a bit.'

'No no!' Dido exclaimed in an *I'll be good* voice. 'I want to see more Cornwall.'

'Did you and Lucy have a row?'

'Nope.' Cornered, Dido had to confess. 'Not really . . .'

'What about?'

'It's nothing. Don't worry. Work hard. See you later.'

'You will, child. You will.' She leaned across to kiss Pearce quickly. 'Thanks,' she told him.

'Pleasure,' he said. 'Do you want to hang on so I can pick you up later? I don't know how long we'll be.'

'No, it's fine,' she told him. 'I can walk back or Molly can run me over. The rain can't last for ever.'

'It can,' he said. 'It does. Bye, then.'

Dido smiled at her sweetly as they drove off, happy, apparently, now that she had Pearce all to herself.

Eliza hurried up Molly's path, clutching the bag to her chest in an effort to keep the Bible dry.

Lucy opened the door. 'Oh, hi,' she said and walked back to the television. 'She's upstairs.'

Molly emerged from her bedroom, dressed a bit smarter for work.

'God, I forgot!' Eliza said. 'Have I made you late?'

'It's fine. We don't open until ten. The computer's in here.'

Her manner was strangely terse and she seemed to be avoiding Eliza's eye.

'Is something wrong?' Eliza asked her.

'No.' Molly met her eye and shrugged, confirming that there was. 'Luce?' she called down the stairs.

'She's watching television,' Eliza told her.

'I know. I just wanted to be sure she had it on loud enough. Come on in.' She led the way into Lucy's bedroom.

The top half of a bunk was made up as a bed. The lower half was a sort of nest, draped with camouflage netting. A St Piran's flag was pinned across the ceiling along with pin-ups of the Cornish rugby team and Gary Cooper in various Westerns. Elsewhere the room was extraordinary in its neatness. Clothes were put away, the few books stacked tidily at one end of a small shelf, an Action Man in cowboy gear sat incongruously in the lap of a brown monkey at the other. Apart from the computer and a pot of pens, the desktop was virtually empty.

Molly saw Eliza taking this in. 'I know,' she said. 'Control freak. It's one of the ways they've bonded.' She sighed, turned on the scanner and clicked the mouse to open an image-handling program. 'Give us the book, then.'

Eliza sat beside her and drew out the Bible. Practised, Molly turned directly to the back pages and flattened the soprano part out against the scanner bed. Eliza winced at the violence this did to the book's overburdened spine but watched the screen hungrily as the scanner hummed into motion and a dialogue box announced that a scan was in progress. At last a detailed image of the page appeared.

'Right,' Molly said. 'There you go. Page one of four. You can adjust brightness and definition like so, crop it if you need to like so then save it to your floppy. You can do the rest yourself, can't you?' She stood.

'Molly, what's wrong?'

'Nothing. I've got to go to work.'

'It's not quarter to yet. What is it? I feel as if I'm in trouble and I'm not sure why.'

'It's not you.' Molly sat down again. 'It's . . . it's just everything.'

'Morris?'

'Yeah.' But she was lying. 'No. It's Lucy. She had me up half the night having nightmares. I know she comes across as tough but it's all a front really. But she hasn't had bad dreams for months. Not since Morris lost the farm and we moved out.' She started to stand.

'Sit, Molly. What about?'

Molly sat again, reluctantly.

'What about?' Eliza repeated.

'It was daft really. I mean dreams always are in the morning, aren't they? She thought her face was changing shape. Melting. Like wax. I had to have her in my bed in the end and she was still tossing and turning. At one point I even woke to find her staring at herself in the bathroom mirror. Checking. She wouldn't talk about it at first. Clammed up. Pretended I was exaggerating. But I had a go at her over breakfast and she cracked and told me. Showed me, really.'

'What?'

Molly glanced at her watch then clicked with the mouse to bring up a series of saved images.

'I promised her I'd wipe them off. She's scared to death of them but she can't stop going back to look. I thought they were just playing up here downloading pictures, playing around with scans and games but, well . . . You look.'

The first image was familiar, the crumpled dressing room snap of Dido Eliza had been missing from her wallet for several days. Molly clicked impatiently to move on to the next. This too was familiar. Moominmama, not unlike the repeated sketch she had seen on the pad the other day, the hippo-faced creature with her signature black handbag. Molly clicked again.

Eliza felt slightly sick with anticipation. Dido had cunningly blended the elements of the two previous pictures so that her own smiling eyes and unruly hair sat behind Moominmama's face. Eliza forced herself to laugh. 'I didn't know she'd learnt how to do that. They're just messing about really. You're saying this gave Lucy nightmares?'

'No. I think this did.' Grimly, Molly clicked again. 'Look at that. I mean, I know I should feel sorry. I do feel sorry but . . . However you look at it, that's a monster.'

They both stared in silence at the image. For some reason, the mention of the Internet perhaps, Eliza had been bracing herself for pornography of some kind. This was so complete a shock she was frozen, unable to speak.

'I'll wipe it off now you've seen it.'

'No.' Eliza caught Molly's hand before it reached the mouse.

'It's horrible.'

'It's my sister.'

'What?'

Deep breath, Eliza.

'It's my sister,' she repeated. 'Dido's mother. It's Hannah. Cover the lower half of the face and you'll see the likeness to me and Dido. Here. Let me.'

She held a piece of paper over half the screen. Even allowing for their slight protuberance, Hannah's eyes were hers and Dido's, as were her forehead and ears.

Now Molly was reeling almost as much as Eliza. 'I don't understand,' she said. 'I thought she died in a climbing accident.'

'She did. She did. It was a trek for the charity she worked for. They look after people whose faces are damaged or . . . or like this.'

'Jesus.' Molly looked back at the page more closely. Eliza could tell she was looking for the humanity beneath the monster mask; it was a look she had seen so many times before, on startled Jehovah's Witnesses, on friends who came to play.

'It's a very rare bone disorder,' Eliza said, 'thank God. But it doesn't kill you. Cherubism. A *kind* of cherubism in her case because it didn't conform to the medical stereotype. I mean it's so rare that every case adds a bit to the slender sum total of their knowledge. Sorry. I'm rabbiting.' She took a deep breath, looking at the photograph for inspiration. Where to start? 'It didn't show up until she was about nine. Ten. By the time she'd stopped growing she could have had operations to correct it a bit.' She checked herself, hearing Hannah's indignant rebuttal of the word *correct*. 'Reduce the jawbone. Things like that. But she refused. She was amazing, really. She said, "This is who I am. I'm happy with it. I'm different. Get used to it."'

'What about Dido?'

'Like me she probably has the gene and could pass it on. But there's a chance she won't develop it and I . . . I wanted to protect her.'

'She didn't know any of this?'

Eliza realised she was weeping, the taste of her tears sharp on cracked lips. 'Where did she get this picture? Could she have downloaded it from the charity's website?'

'It's a scan. Not a download. You can tell from the heading.'

Eliza looked deep into her sister's face, reminding herself of every detail as she spoke 'I wanted Dido to have as normal a childhood as possible for as long as possible in case she did develop it. I didn't want her to feel shadowed by it the way I had, having Hannah for a sister. Giles always agreed with me.'

'Giles?'

'My husband. Giles Easton.'

Saying his name was like releasing the catch on a door deep within herself. Anger had been admitted. Eliza forgot all about the scanner, the Bible, Trevescan, and thought only of Dido discovering all this alone and unprotected and the swift, careless ruination of one of the few well-laid plans in a haphazard life. Giles had the only surviving pictures of Hannah as an adult. Early in their marriage they had agreed to hide them away in an envelope in a locked drawer in his desk. In the rushed drama of leaving him, she had not thought to retrieve them. It had occurred to her since to ask for them but she had decided, fool that she was, that Dido was far less likely to stumble on them in his more regimented household than in her own chaotic one.

'I need to use your phone, Molly.'

'Sure,' Molly said. 'Shall I, er . . . ?'

Wipe this off, she meant but could not say.

'Yes.' Eliza watched as Molly clicked *delete* repeatedly, removing Hannah, Moominmama, Dido and the picture hybrid labelled *Moomindido*. There was a fifth picture file. Molly highlighted it, prepared to delete. 'Wait,' Eliza said.

'You don't want to see that,' Molly said, 'Trust me,' and deleted it but not before Eliza read the title, *Handido Hobbyarrr*, and had started picturing its contents: Dido's laughing eyes and button nose above her mother's slightly spotty lantern jaw and carefully, vivaciously made-up lips.

She hurried downstairs to Molly's kitchen, riffled through the yellow pages to the hotel section, found the number, grabbed the phone. Molly came in after her and stopped in the doorway, held back by the force of unfamiliar anger which was causing Eliza's hand to shake as she gripped the receiver.

'Oh. Yes. Hello. I wonder if I'm still in time to catch Giles Easton?'

'Yes, you are. That's his friend, isn't it? You were in for dinner on Saturday.'

'That's right.'

'I'm Janet. I brought your drinks in. Their flight isn't until one. He's in the garden. Who shall I say is calling?'

'No. I don't want to speak to him. Just tell him his wife is on her way over.'

'His *wife*?'

'On second thoughts no. Don't tell him anything.'

52

At nine and three-quarters, the age when all her friends started to grow, Hannah grew too, but not just in the legs and spine. Her jawbone and chin also grew, did not stop growing. At first it made her look merely obstinate, then the area below her mouth grew to the point where people pointed her out to one another and women murmured sympathetically in bus queues. She was nicknamed Desperate Dan. Her friends began to shun her. To make matters worse, her warm brown eyes, which had been one of her best features, became enlarged and protuberant. By eleven, she had become a grotesque, an infamous local freak. But only when the family dentist, alarmed at the malformation of her teeth, insisted she was not simply ugly but suffering from a bone disorder, were specialists consulted.

No one in the family had looked like this and her mother assumed this was some correctable hormonal imbalance. The verdict was crueller: a disorder on a cellular level, genetic, inherited. The bony swelling grew progressively worse so long as the patient was growing then halted leaving them with benign bone tumours that displaced their teeth and gave them a look as inbred as any renaissance prince. Boys could at least mask the worst effects by growing a beard. In the past there had been little option left to girls beyond joining a circus.

Suddenly the childhood photographs of Hannah, pudgy cheeks puffed as if to blow out non-existent cake candles, gappy teeth bravely displayed, were revealed as sinister warnings her parents had ignored in ignorance.

Their father finally made a show of remembering that he had a great uncle who was similarly afflicted. He produced a photograph of a young man whose best tweed suit, snappy tie and slicked down hair only emphasized his inflated jaw and gobstopper eyes. Their mother was appalled then furious at what she saw as a deliberate deceit. There were no grand rows, because of the embarrassment both essentially kind-hearted parties felt at appearing in any way to devalue Hannah's looks – merely muttered, encoded skirmishes. The marriage never recovered and, when Eliza was just ten, her father went to a conference on mining technology and never returned. He vanished without trace and was not greatly missed. There was no divorce. No maintenance payments. No parental visits.

Hannah was prodigious. She shrugged off her old friendships as evidently valueless and made new ones through sport. Sport became her passion. She fenced, she swam, she ran, she cycled. It was as though she wanted to compensate for the dereliction of her face by pushing the rest of her body to the limits of endurance. She avoided team games, where her outlandish appearance could too easily give rise to humiliations, and concentrated on sports based on personal bests. She made new friends among her fellow athletes – less pretty, less clever, less cultured than her old cronies but more trustworthy in their clannish dullness. Many of them, she realised, were also proving themselves in the face of academic failure, criticism from teachers or simply chronic shyness. Compared to most of them, she was sharper, more resilient and certainly more courageous. By the time she was finishing her A-levels, Hannah had been adopted by the school as a kind of mascot, a demeaning process she merrily subverted by refusing to appear either grateful or meek.

She had difficulty finding a good university place. She was no academic, certainly, but she gained respectable grades. Confronted with her huge face in the interviews, however, numerous admissions staff assumed she was retarded. Then a cunning teacher put her forward for a sports scholarship in America, a land where physical perfection was God, certainly, but also a country where the empowerment of minorities was fast becoming a kind of religion.

And somewhere between the sunny campus that welcomed her and the Himalayan mountain that destroyed her, Hannah conceived a child.

53

When Giles rang he found the last remaining Sunday flight from Newquay was already fully booked. There was such demand at that time of year that he found he could not even move them to an earlier flight on Monday morning or squeeze them onto flights to Stansted instead of Gatwick. They could have damned the expense and driven the hire car all the way back to London but close confinement for six hours or more seemed worse than staying put. So they were faced with no option but to spend another night in Penzance.

Curiously they fought no further. The loss of the baby and Julia's refusal of his proposal were a shared burden. Like fellow flu sufferers, they were hopelessly, wretchedly solicitous of one another's comfort. *How can I make myself least repugnant to you?* was implicit in all their actions.

Another dinner in the hotel's small, pretty dining room was out of the question; their pained lack of conversation would have been too exposed there. So they went, impulsively, to the cinema, thinking that two hours not talking in a darkened room would at least eat away a good chunk of the evening.

There was a small cinema on Causewayhead, divided into three even smaller ones. One of the oldest cinemas in constant use in the country, apparently. The choice was a cartoon about beetles, a horror film called *Cleaver* and *In Health*, a romantic comedy. They opted for the comedy as the lesser of three evils. But far from clearing the air, the film weighed down on them both and they returned to the hotel in stony silence. There was a bar and honesty book hidden in a writing desk in one corner of the sitting room. Without needing to ask, Giles poured them both big slugs of brandy. Taken on an empty stomach it ensured that Julia, at least, was deep in corpse-like slumbers within minutes of lying down.

Giles lay beside her until the need to wrap her in his arms drove him to run a deep, hot bath and soak in that instead. He lay with foam tickling his chin, feeling a distinct draught on his toes through the overflow holes and trying not to think of their unborn child tumbling helplessly into the restored Victorian lavatory across the room from him.

They had not discussed the future at all. She had said she was no longer pregnant or never had been. He had asked her to marry him. She had said no. Or rather, she had pointed out some brutally good reasons not to say yes. And there the subject had closed. Was she leaving him? There was no reason why she should, necessarily. They had lived together for several years without marriage being an issue. But to do so after her rejection of him seemed forced.

She had hit home. He *did* ask her because he felt he should. In part. First he'd felt he should ask her because she was pregnant with his child, then because she no longer was and he did not want her despising him for only asking her out of duty. For a second, when it had become clear she was turning him down – it took a moment or two for his brain to catch up with her sharp speech – he felt something approaching euphoria, a mad, bad stab of born-again bachelor wey-hey.

But that response was no sooner registered than swept aside by regret that was more than wounded pride. He was desolate at the thought of being alone again, of rattling around in the house. He pictured a descent into squalor or taking in lodgers or a now inevitable divorce from Eliza and a move into somewhere small and cheap and unpleasant ungraced by either woman's influence.

Perhaps Julia was not leaving him though? Perhaps she merely needed time to adjust? Rebuked by her, he could see now that it would be only decent to put things in more honourable order, to divorce Eliza then propose to Julia again.

But now he lay in the cooling water feeling his fingertips turn pruny and remembering how transfigured the world had seemed to him when she said she was expecting. Now he knew it was fatherhood he most regretted. The prospect of a child had shed a new light on their relationship as much as on the world beyond, changing emphases and priorities, freeing them from the tyranny of choice by a removal of options. And the closing off of that prospect brought, oddly, less a return to former freedom than a dulling to dimness of what had formerly seemed bright. What had been just a relationship was now a *childless* relationship. They had gone overnight from being a couple who chose not to have children to one that failed to keep them.

He woke with a jolt at the gunning of a boat's outboard motor, jumped out of cold water, dried himself and hurried to bed. Perhaps sleep had made Julia forget their situation for she shuddered in her slumbers and, half waking to the coldness of his limbs, drew him against her so they fell asleep in tandem normality.

Normality still reigned when they woke, ravenous, break-fasted, packed, settled the bill and started to load the car to drive to the airport. But then one of the waitresses, Pearce's slightly flustered school chum, slipped out to warn them that Giles' wife had just telephoned and was coming over to speak to them before they left.

'She didn't want me to tell you,' she said, 'But Hell, you're the guests, not her . . . If you like I'll say you'd gone before I could stop you.'

Horrified at the thought of missing their precious flight, Julia was all for this but they still had plenty of time and Giles was worried it might be a message about Dido. So they waited, rather formally, on the sofas to either side of the sitting room fireplace while the waitress followed them back in and hurried apologetically through her dusting.

Giles began reading the morning's paper and was soon drawn into an article previewing *A Midsummer Night's Dream* which hinted darkly at the sensations promised by the director's past record and unconventional casting of Dewi Evans as Puck. There was also a rather good photograph of himself in rehearsal, dancing palm to palm with his luscious Titania, and he was about to show Julia this when Eliza burst in like the wrath of God, startling them both and sending Pearce's friend scurrying from the room.

'Who the fuck gave you permission to fuck up my daughter's life?' she shouted. Eliza never swore and never shouted. The effect of her doing both was electric. She ignored Julia entirely.

'Sorry?' he said, stalling.

'I've seen the photograph,' she told him witheringly. 'She's been copying it all over her friend's computer and scanning it and e-mailing it for all I know. It's probably posted on some website by now.'

'Jesus!' he said. Eliza seemed angry enough to call the police. He had woken daring to entertain a careful fantasy of a future in which Julia and he grew old together as a sophisticatedly childless, unmarried couple while Dido visited them for a week at each school holiday, giving Eliza time off for lecture tours or driving combine harvesters or what-have-you. In an instant his future shrank to a stark cell on a nonce wing. 'It's not what you think,' he began.

'Oh I think it is.'

Julia slipped out of the room. Giles could not tell if she went to fetch help or to stop them being interrupted. Or perhaps she was going to jump into the car and catch the plane without him?

'It was just a photo. She looked so sweet and I thought I'd just –'

Eliza cut him short with an acid laugh. 'Hannah was called a lot of things in her time but *sweet*?'

'Hannah?'

'Yes.'

'You're talking about Hannah?'

'Of course I am. Who the –?'

'I thought you . . . Sorry.' He sat and only just stopped himself from laughing with relief.

'No,' Eliza pursued him. 'What did you mean? You said it was a photo.'

Shit. Mentally he took a deep breath. He became aware that Julia had turned back in the doorway and was listening intently.

'I took a picture of Dido while she was asleep,' he said. 'It was silly of me really but she looked incredibly sweet and young and I thought you'd like a copy. But then I printed it out a few times and realised her shirt had ridden up and it looked like kiddie porn so I . . . Well I thought I'd destroyed it. I had. But. Oh shit.'

At last he realised what a fool he had been, and which photo Dido had been talking about in the car to the hospital. Slower to change gear once her speed was up, Eliza was still angry with him.

'I thought we'd agreed. I even remember you saying "We must give her as normal a childhood as possible for as long as possible." And now you go and screw it up just when she's the worst possible age to –' She broke off, aware now of Julia who had stepped back into the room and closed the door behind her.

'I showed her,' Julia said. 'He didn't know a thing about it. I knew where the picture was hidden and I told her where to look for it.'

A waiter appeared to take their orders for coffee but was warned off by a glare from Eliza.

54

Giles jumped up and they both looked at her so sharply that for a second Julia thought they might turn on her like dogs interrupted mid-fight.

'I told her,' she repeated. 'At the time I honestly thought I was doing it for her own good. I felt she had a right to know and was old enough to deal with it.'

'What the fuck made you think it was any of your business?' Eliza was incredulous.

'I'm very fond of Dido,' Julia told her. 'No. I love her. But . . . I wasn't supposed to tell you, Eliza, but it can't do any harm now. I was pregnant when I found out. And I think it was making me a bit mad. I think I was trying to protect the baby.'

'It's not *catching*,' Giles said.

'I know that. I'm not a fool,' she told him then turned back to Eliza. 'I think I was unconsciously clearing the nest a little,' she said. 'They were too close. He wasn't even her father. I . . . I'm sorry. It was a horrible thing to do.'

'But it worked.'

'Yes. I'm sorry, Giles.'

Giles said nothing to her. He had slumped into a chair by the desk.

'None of this would have happened,' Eliza told him, 'If you hadn't told *her*.'

'I didn't,' he began.

'I found the picture,' Julia confirmed. 'I recognised her. Hannah.'

'But how . . . ?'

'When I first met you I thought you seemed familiar but then I thought, 'No. It can't be.' I only knew you by your maiden name, of course. And when you were a kid you had short hair and everyone called you Leeza, didn't they? Leeza or Diz.'

'Yes,' Eliza said, frowning, no longer angry but wary now. 'Yes they did. I hated it. But —'

'But then I found the photo a couple of weeks ago. And I realised who you were.'

'But who are you?'

'Julie Dixon. You won't remember me. I wasn't very memorable. I was in the year below you, besides, so you'd have no reason to. We lived at Illogan, in one of the new houses above the sea. But you lived in Furnival Road, Camborne. I remember because I followed you both home from school once, all the way along Trelowarren Street. I used to watch out for Hannah. My dad was the groundsman at a campsite at Hayle Towans. My granddad had one of those beach cabins there. My mum ran a kennels from home. Dogs and cats. And she was a dinner lady at school. She always did the potato. Smiled a lot.'

'I remember her. Big hair.'

'Very big. Hannah was amazing, Eliza. We all looked up to her. She was a kind of hero, in spite of how she looked. You should have been proud of her not hidden her away like a dirty secret.'

'Yes, well, that was for me to decide, wasn't it?'

'Yes. I'm sorry. It was. I should have talked to you, not Dido. But we don't really talk, do we?'

'Shit,' Giles said softly. 'The time. I hate to do this but we've got that plane to catch. I've got a costume call this afternoon. We should go.'

'You go,' Julia said, still watching Eliza. 'I'll come on the train later.'

'But why? That's silly. The tickets are all booked and we've got the —'

'Leave my bag in the hall. I'll come on the train.'

'I don't understand.'

'I should go,' Eliza said, sensing trouble.

'No,' Julia told her. 'Sit. Stay. Giles, I'm leaving you. I'll drop by to pick up my stuff during the week.'

Eliza was frantic, 'I really should go.'

Julia held her arm this time. 'No,' she said. 'I want to talk to you. Go, Giles. Quick. You'll miss your plane. We can talk later.'

He went surprisingly quickly, defeated by timetable and career, not looking at either woman.

'Poor Giles,' Eliza said when the door had shut again. 'That was cruel.'

'At least I told him to his face,' Julia reminded her. 'Because he never heard it from your lips it took him weeks to accept that you'd gone. He won't have the same trouble with me. It's far crueller to be nice, sometimes, and let things drag on. He's been trying to leave me for years but he hates to be in the wrong. I just made it easier for him.'

'Why did you make me stay? That was awful.'

'What is it the self-help books call it? Closure. You needed closure.'

'But you seemed so happy together. A good fit, I mean.'

'Liar.'

'Weren't you?'

'He still loves you. I never stood a chance.'

'But . . .' Eliza glanced towards the door and Julia knew

she was wondering whether to run after him and flag down his car. 'I'm not available.'

Julia laughed. 'Since when did that make a difference?'

'Poor Giles.'

'Oh he'll be fine. He's beautiful.' She looked at Eliza's golden hair and shining blue eyes. She was wearing crazy clothes but she could wear a bin liner with holes cut in it and still look innocent and clean. 'Beautiful people aren't necessarily happier but they get more opportunities than the rest of us.'

'You're beautiful.'

'Gee. Really? No, I'm not, Leeza. I just dress with tremendous care.'

'You called me Leeza.'

'Sorry. Eliza.'

'I don't understand. You're so posh.'

'I'm not. I never lied. I never pretended to be what I wasn't. Except for, maybe, changing Dixon to Forbes Dixon, but Forbes was my mother's name so . . . I just left things unsaid, let people join the dots with their own conclusions. I can still talk Camborne.'

'Go on.'

'You made a proper job of that, me handsome.'

Eliza grinned. 'Julie Dixon.' She relaxed her own accent to match. 'As I live and breathe.'

55

'I hated doing that,' Pearce told Dido as they drove out of St Just. 'Do you lie to Eliza often?'

'No,' she said. 'Only sometimes. To save her feelings or stop her worrying.'

'Does she worry much?'

'She's seeming very selfish at the moment but that's just because of work. Trevescan. But sometimes she . . .' Dido dried up.

'Well?' Pearce asked.

'Sometimes she gets depressed.'

'We all have bad days.'

'No, I mean really depressed. She just goes to bed and stays there. She'll pretend to have got up and done things while I was in school but I can tell when she's lying and I know she hasn't moved because everything will look just the way it did when I left the house.'

'And that's when you might lie to her.'

'Yes. Or before. When she's okay, to stop her getting like that, you know, depressed.'

'But if she thinks we're buying tractor spares, shouldn't I at least stop by Leedstown on the way back to buy some in case she asks?'

'She won't ask. She won't be interested. She only notices

what interests her. You've seen the way she dresses.'

'Hmm.'

'I mean, you can if you like. But I wouldn't bother.'

'Okay. So how did you get to see the orthodontist so fast? Since it's not an emergency.'

'We're going private.'

'You're kidding.'

'Giles is paying,' she said airily. 'He felt guilty so he'd have said yes to anything. But I'm on his insurance plan in any case. Mum doesn't know.'

'You mean you lied to her.'

'No. She just doesn't know. She wouldn't approve. Politics.'

'And the fact that it's Giles.'

'Yeah. But it's okay. I mean, he made me fall off so he can pay. There's just one thing.'

'What? No more lies.'

'No but . . . well. They'll probably think you're him or my dad or, yes. They'll probably think you're my dad and it'd be easier if you let them think that.'

'I can't do that!'

'You've got to.'

'Dido, it'd be against the law. Look, this is ridiculous. I'm sorry. I should never have – I'm turning round at the next roundabout, okay? We've still got time. We can whizz back, pick up Eliza then come here again with her. We can ring the hospital and say we're running late.'

'No.'

'We'll have to. I can't lie.'

'No!'

'Dido, I know you're used to getting your own way but that's going to have to change if you want to live with me.'

'I don't want to live with you!' she shouted, on the edge of tearfulness.

'Fine,' he said, wounded and getting angry despite his better judgement. He had always despised parents who let their children manipulate them into spoiling them. 'Fine. No problem in us going home, then.'

Dido did not throw a tantrum or scream or lay it on thick to beat him into submission. If she had, resisting her would have been easy. Instead she cried in a terrible, quiet, dry way, more like a terrified child than a frustrated one. Rather than double back at the roundabout, he found himself driving on towards Truro. He stopped, however, in the first lay-by they came to, cut the engine and turned around on his seat to confront her.

She twisted her face away from him, trying to hide her tears. He saw how the hand nearest him was crushing the seat cushion, clawing into the harsh material in her effort to regain control.

'Look,' he said. 'It's okay. I haven't turned back, all right? Dido? Here. Stop. I haven't got a handkerchief. Have you? You should blow your nose. You don't want the doctor to see you like that or he'll think you're not brave, eh?'

She muttered something incomprehensible.

'What's that?' he asked.

'I'm not brave,' she said.

'Oh, I don't know about that.'

'I hate crying.'

'Another thing you've got in common with Luce. So stop. Breathe. Take deep breaths. You'll soon stop. That's it. So. What time's your appointment?'

'Ten thirty.'

'We better get going then. But let's strike a bargain before we do.'

'What?'

'I'll only pretend to be your dad if you treat me like one and tell me what's going on. I hate secrets. Always have. Can't be doing with them. My parents always hid things from us and I hated it.'

Dido blew her nose, tidied her handkerchief away again and took a few breaths. 'Teeth,' she said at last.

'Your teeth. The ones you knocked out?'

'Yes. I didn't knock them out. I told you. It's something else.'

'Are you sure?'

'Yes. No. Not really but I think so. That's why I lied. I knew if I said the teeth had been knocked out they'd be more likely to do X-rays of my jaw as well as my leg and let me see an orthodontist. Especially if Giles was paying.'

There was something so touching about the way she had mastered the word *orthodontist* but he suppressed the impulse to touch her, even to pat her arm, because a small part of him suspected he was still being manipulated.

'Tell you what,' he said. 'Speaking as your fake father. If it turns out there's nothing wrong and they *were* knocked out or fell out naturally, do you promise we can make a clean breast of this and tell your mum everything? Only I haven't known her long and me telling her lies isn't a very good footing to get off on.'

'No. I mean it isn't. So okay.'

'Good.'

He never had to lie. The nurse who dealt with the insurance details was confused at first because she had called Giles first thing for confirmation that his daughter was coming in and assumed this was Giles before her now.

'No,' Dido said. 'This is Mr Polglaze. He's with my foster mother. She and Giles are separated.'

'Ah. Fine. Sorry,' said the nurse.

'But I've got a parental consent letter,' she went on.

'No. That's fine,' the nurse said. 'You're not down for any treatment this morning and we already took the X-rays on

Friday, didn't we? Yes. With your father's consent. So that's fine. Wait here please.'

'What letter?' Pearce muttered as the nurse retreated and he helped Dido into a chair.

'I typed it up on the computer in case,' she said, patting her pocket. 'I've been doing her signature since I was eight.'

When the specialist came out and everyone introduced themselves, he was all set to take Dido in on her own but she turned and said, 'Could he come too, in case there's anything I don't understand?'

'Yes. Certainly,' the orthodontist said, so Pearce followed them in and sat to one side of the consulting room. It looked like any dentist's surgery, only larger and with more machinery.

'So,' the orthodontist began. 'We've got your X-rays up here on the screen, Dido. That was quite a bump you had.'

'I know.'

'No concussion, though.'

'No.'

'You told the radiology nurses you lost two teeth.'

'Yes. I've got them here,' she reached eagerly into her pocket and produced the same molars she had shown Pearce. If the orthodontist was taken aback, he was too professional to let it show.

'Ah. Excellent,' he said and made a show of examining them and their roots. 'Nice healthy teeth. Good girl. Now. If you'd lie back on the chair here while I tip you back and take a closer look. Open wide. That's it. Good. Goodness yes. Now the other side? Hmm. Yes. Thank you, Dido. Let's get you back up again. No drilling. Nothing nasty. Now. Those teeth of yours. They didn't fall out when you came off your bike, now did they?'

'No.'

'I thought not. When did they come out?'

'Two weeks ago now. About. In London. Just before we came away. It didn't really hurt or anything. They just sort of came loose.'

'And are any of the others loose?'

'A bit.'

'Front or back teeth?'

'Back. At the bottom. Next door to where the others were.'

'That must make it hard to chew.'

'It does a bit. Hard things are hard to chew, like pizza crust.' She glanced at Pearce.

'And you're Dido's stepfather?' the orthodontist asked him.

'Er, no.' Pearce said.

'He lives with my mother,' Dido chipped in. 'My foster mother. My real mother died when I was a baby so I live with my aunt. No one knows who my father was.'

'Ah. Well. Look over here at the X-rays. Now. This one's you. See? D Hosken.'

'Yes.'

'And this one,' he hooked up a second one, its name covered over with tape. 'This one is of another girl your age. And so is this.' He hooked up a third. 'Do you see any difference? Particularly in this area.' He pointed at the jaw bone.

'My one's thicker.'

'Yes. The thing is your teeth shouldn't have come out. Unless you were rotting them with sugar, which you plainly weren't, they should have stayed put for years, maybe all your life. What happened was that your jaw pushed them out by doing some extra growing here and here.'

Dido reached into her pocket where the teeth had been and produced a small, crumpled colour photograph. 'Am I going to look like this?' she asked, very calmly but with real curiosity and passed the picture over.

Pearce strained to see but caught no more than a flash of colour and skin tone before the orthodontist turned it over to look more closely. He was obviously unnerved. Pearce saw the colour actually drain from his face. This was, he realised, a terrible ordeal for the man, an interview he had been dreading, for all his smooth chairside manner.

Instead of answering her directly, he asked a quiet question of his own. 'Where did you get this?'

'From home. It's my mother. The dead one. She had cherubism.'

'Yes. Yes she did. She lived near here, didn't she?'

'When she was young.'

'I thought so. She was quite famous. I met her when I was training, met her as a doctor.'

'Did you really?' Dido had briefly forgotten her first question. 'What was she like?'

'Formidable. Very brave and rather frightening. You see, doctors are used to being able to hide things from young patients but there was no hiding anything from her because she'd done her homework. A bit like you.'

'So I do have it?'

The doctor handed her back the picture, took off his glasses and rubbed his hand across his eyes.

'Christ,' he whispered, quite audibly, a prayer as much as a curse. For a moment Pearce thought he might start crying. 'Yes,' he said. 'If she was your mother, and given these X-rays, and your age, then yes. It's very probable that you do.'

'What will happen to me?' For the first time since leaving the Land Rover her voice showed signs of strain and wavered slightly.

'Your lower jaw, your maxilla it's called, will continue growing to an abnormal size. Perhaps to double what it should be. You'll probably lose some more teeth in the process but it won't hurt. The rest of you will be growing

439

anyway as you reach your early teens, your legs, and arms, all of you. So you'll be a bit tired but no more than any other teenager. Your skull may grow a bit too. In a way it shouldn't, which might push your eyes outward slightly but mainly, as in your mother's case, it'll be the lower half of your face.'

'Is there nothing you can do?' Pearce asked, unable to keep quiet. The orthodontist seemed grateful to be reminded there was another adult present, not just this curious, severe little girl with the pocketful of horrors.

'Yes there is,' he said, addressing them both. 'And obviously this is something we'll need to discuss with you and your parents, all your parents, later on. Your mother refused all treatment,' he said. 'I remember. She was known for that. But things are far less crude than they were twenty years ago. Plastic surgery is a real art now. Thanks to the techniques we've developed for people hurt in car crashes or by bone cancer we can operate on the bone, on the jaw bone that is, and reduce its size and bring your face size more or less back to normal. I can show you some pictures if you like.'

'No thanks,' Dido said.

'Maybe later.'

'When would you do this?' Pearce asked, feeling as he spoke that his voice was choked up with swallowed tears.

'Not for a while,' the orthodontist sighed. 'It's a genetic disorder so we'd have to let it run its course at first, let the jaw grow and finish growing, before we could interfere surgically, otherwise more distortion could follow.'

They walked back to the Land Rover in silence, except for the rhythmic thud-thudding of the wooden block in the base of the plaster cast. Pearce opened the rear door and passed in the crutches first then lifted Dido up onto the back seat. 'Can I see?' he asked. 'The picture of your mum?'

'Sure.' Dido took it out and passed it to him. He climbed into the front seat then made himself look hard at the little picture.

It was bad but not as bad as he expected and he realised this was because he could see Eliza in the leonine hair and clever eyes and because he was able to read in elements of Dido and Eliza's characters, to humanise what he saw. He handed it back to her. 'Thanks,' he said. 'Thank you. Jesus, Dido. It's going to be so hard for you.'

'I know.' Her voice sounded tiny. She was looking at her mother again.

'I don't want you to leave. I think you should stay with me. I think you'll do better down here with —'

'Yes,' she interrupted him.

'But if your mum goes to be a lecturer or whatever —'

'She won't.'

'She might have to.'

'Can't you tell her you love her?'

He smiled, patted her plaster cast as that was all that lay to hand. 'I wish it was that simple.'

'I think I know a way.'

'No, Dido. No more scheming or lying.'

'I won't have to lie.'

'And when we get back we have to tell her. Tell her everything.'

'She never told me.'

'You got the photo, though.'

'Not from her. I nicked it from Giles' house. I think she's scared.'

'No. She can't be scared of her own flesh and blood. If she didn't tell you it was because she was hoping it wouldn't happen.'

'She was scared, then.'

'Oh all right. So she was scared. Do you blame her? She loves you. She doesn't want bad things to happen to you. She probably hopes they'll go away. We tell her when we get back.'

'Yes. I'll tell her, if you like.'

'We'll see. Come on. Belt up, now.'

But Eliza did not need telling. She ran out to meet them as they drove into the yard and she seized Dido in a passionate hug as soon as she could tear the door open and everything came spilling out on either side; a great store of fear and bitterness mixed with love and reproach.

'I want to see her grave again,' Dido said, after Pearce had made them eat some lunch.

'She's not there,' Eliza said. 'Not really. She was cremated in Nepal.'

'Yes but still . . . couldn't I see it again?'

'Of course,' Eliza said, wearily. 'I expect we can catch a train this afternoon, get a bus into town then catch a train to Camborne.'

'No you won't,' Pearce said. 'I'll drive you. I'd already given up doing the planting today. I've nothing on till tomorrow. I want to see too. I want to see Dido's house.'

So they had a strange excursion to grim old Camborne, their spirits faintly hilarious, giddy from news and a sense of tumultuous change. They saw the graves first, Eliza's mother's, which still had no stone, and beside it a small granite slab that read,

SACRED TO THE MEMORY OF

HANNAH HOSKEN

1967–1993

BELOVED SISTER, DAUGHTER **&** MOTHER

Fear no more the heat o' the sun

It transpired that Dido had looked up the quotation on her first visit and she persisted in reciting the Dirge from *Cymbeline* over the grave until Eliza told her to stop it or she'd make them all cry.

They left flowers for mother and daughter then went to admire Dido's still unsold house from the outside. They were excitedly invited for tea by an enormous woman in the bungalow next door so Pearce was at last able to put a face to Kitty Barnicoat. As she poured tea and buttered slabs of saffron cake and fired off salvos of questions, Pearce felt all sorts of gaps in his understanding of Eliza filling in, and began to see how she came to be who she was.

He woke in the night smelling burning and hurried to the window. He had a farmer's horror of fire, having seen first-hand the ease with which damp straw or oily rags could heat up and spontaneously combust. At this time of year, only weeks before the barley harvest, there was little straw left in storage but his first instinct was still to glance that way. Seeing no flames in the barn he pulled on a dressing gown and crossed the landing to look out at the tinder dry barley fields. No fires there. He headed downstairs. The oil-fired boiler was an ancient, untrustworthy one with a time clock made the more erratic by frequent power cuts. Possibly the smell which woke him had been the boiler firing up to heat the water hours too early. But the boiler was silent. Then he heard a ripping sound and turned back towards the sitting room.

Dido was sitting by the fireplace, lit in the sudden flare of burning paper. The family Bible lay on the rug between her stretched out legs. Pearce watched as she tore the last glued-on page of the madrigal from its binding and threw it into the flames.

She did not jump when he spoke. She must have heard him come downstairs.

'I'd been offered serious money for that,' he told her. 'A lot of money. It would have paid for your operations.'

'I don't want any operations,' she said as the last page

flared up and died down. 'I've decided that. I think Mum was right. Hannah-Mum. It'll still be my face. Why should I change it just to suit other people?'

'See how you feel about that when you're a boy-mad teenager,' he said, picking up her crutches in the moonlight and helping her to her feet.'

'I'm never going to be boy-mad. I'm going to work with animals.'

'Oh yes? It's very hard to be a vet, you know.'

'Then I'll be a farmer,' she said. 'Or a kennel-maid. And I'm staying here. We both are. I've fixed it. She'll have nothing to leave for now.'

'Will you promise me something, Dido Hosken?'

'What?'

'Never tell your Mum you did this.'

'Why not? She'll find out. She has to.'

'No she doesn't. Never tell her. Okay?'

56

Eliza had on their mother's old wedding dress, a close-cut oyster silk bodice, hard with stiffening panels and seed pearl embroidery, over a full, New Look skirt. They were of a size so it had needed no adjustment. Hannah was putting up Eliza's hair, which had grown magnificently, rolling it around little pads and pinning it up. She was dressed in Nepalese national dress.

'There!' Hannah said. 'Exquisite. Who'd have thought the old bird would ever have bought something so sexy for herself! And now . . . Oh this is such fun! I've always wanted to be a Matron of Honour. It sounds so butch.' Biting her lip with excitement, she turned aside to pick up a long length of antique lace, worn by three generations of Hosken brides before this. Spreading it out with her fingers, she prepared to lower it over Eliza's hair and face but smiled at her in the mirror before she did so, smiled a goodbye.

'Oh no. This is only a dream, isn't it?' Eliza said.

''Fraid so. But you still look lovely. *Fear no more*, darling.'

Eliza felt a tremendous wish to cry but woke instead.

There was a faint light coming in at the window and she had not yet adjusted sufficiently to country living to tell if it was moonlight or the first, colourless glimmer of dawn.

Pearce startled her. He was sitting up, in his father's silk dressing gown, leaning against the brass bedstead by her feet. She realised he must have woken her by touching her feet or murmuring her name.

'What is it?' she asked. 'Pearce? What's the matter?'

'Ssh. Nothing. Sorry I woke you. Go back to sleep. I shouldn't have woken you.'

'No. What?'

'I . . . You. You took the Bible to Molly's this morning, didn't you, to scan it?'

'Yes. Why?'

'And the scans came out okay?'

'Well I didn't see them, because I had to rush off. But Molly finished them for me later. She dropped the disk off with the Bible while we were in Camborne. Why?'

'Eliza do you love me back? Even a bit?'

'Yes. Yes I think I do. I realised it today. I started to suspect it in the hotel this morning when Julia said I could run after Giles and he'd take me back. And I knew it was so completely what I didn't want. The rest fell into place this afternoon when we were saying goodbye to Kitty. She sort of patted your arm and it made me think, *He's it. He's the one.*'

'Oh. Oh good.' He crawled up the bed to her end and kissed her. She ran a hand through his hair. He smelled of bonfires for some reason. And brandy.

'Have you been drinking?'

'Yes. A bit. I started then I couldn't stop. I . . . Eliza, I love you.'

'That's good.'

'I love you so much. And I did it because I don't want it to take you away. I burnt it. Not the whole book but I burnt the manuscript. It's gone. Completely gone. I'm sorry. I don't know what came over me. I thought it would stop you going but of course it won't because you've got the scans and you've got the transcript and . . .' He started to laugh nervously then stopped, unable to read her reaction.

Eliza felt as she had when told of Hannah's death, or her mother's; acutely aware suddenly that she was a person who had lost something of immense importance and that a strong reaction was expected of her but unable to register anything in the immediacy of shock. In all three cases she knew blankness was inappropriate. A reaction was called for. She ought to feel outrage at loss. But the blankness was a kind of safety curtain, dropped at the first guilty, flickering sense of a burden lifted.

57

Giles had already received his final call for his Act One entrance and was on his way to the stage when another bout seized him and he had to rush into the nearest gents to throw up, taking practised care to get nothing on his dressing gown. Inured to this grim routine he flushed to clear the smell as soon as possible but continued to crouch, still clutching the sides of the bowl, braced, gulping. The spasm had passed. He stood then, breathing deeply, walked to the sinks to rinse his mouth and gargle. He drank fresh water to kill the acrid taste then reached into his dressing gown pocket for a breath freshener.

Listening to the audience buzz over the monitors, he breathed deeply, drawing the chemical mint scent into his system. He had been suffering from stage fright for years and knew this brand would not affect his voice the way some could. A dancer came in to piss. Giles said a quick hello but slid out to avoid any camaraderie.

The costume calls had fallen a few days ago, on the afternoon he returned from Cornwall. Several times since then he had heartily wished Selina dead for the slyness with which she had trapped him into this but he was powerless. To drop out now, even with a genuine tragedy or illness as excuse, was to lose face and risk blackballing.

He was not the star, after all, but the star's last minute stand-in.

The poor wardrobe mistress had been through many awkwardnesses in her time from unexpected pregnancies to wigs and colostomy bags. She had dealt tactfully with hand-me-down *Salome* body stockings distended from use and a Swedish Octavian who had calmly removed every stitch for her fitting. But nothing had prepared her for this production.

'That's it, I'm afraid,' she said, handing Giles his costume, 'And then this for the second act.' She had tried to hang them on coat hangers to make them look more substantial and he felt deeply sorry for her. 'You'll be decent from the front, at least,' she said, looking at his face rather than the things on the hangers, 'Sort of. There was talk of a silver cape when it was for Mr Wilson but I'm afraid it was decided no in your case. You should be flattered, I suppose. It means you've got nothing to hide. Oh dear. Just call me when you're ready and I'll pop back in to check the fit.'

And now they were about to start the final dress rehearsal – hence the audience. Friends of the Opera House could buy tickets to dresses, and contacts and relatives of performers could usually be found seats too. His mother and Ron were out there in the middle of the dress circle. He wondered if they would walk out. It was more than likely. The removal of alcohol from their lives seemed to have created more energy for disapproval.

He slid up in the wings to join the others. The stage manager saw him and glared. He mouthed *sorry* at her. The French Titania took his hand.

'*Courage, mon beau*,' she whispered gutturally before remembering that she was on the wrong side of the stage. She giggled and slipped off in the semi-darkness, her silvery cape flickering green in the emergency exit lights.

The house lights dimmed. There was a wave of shushing from the auditorium, broken by a brief chorus of *We love you Dewi!* from some schoolgirls in the gods, then more, louder shushing. The stage manager began her quiet murmuring of technical cues into her headset, eyes glued to the computer screen and monitor before her. Then the applause came for the conductor. Then silence. Then the characteristic growlings of bass and cello glissandi which always seemed to Giles like emanations from the darkness itself, mysterious stirrings in Britten's fairy forest.

The curtain was up already. The set was an anti-set, cunningly designed to look like only darkness except for the floor which was a vast array of mirror, painstakingly polished for the last time only minutes ago.

'You are the scenery!' Grover had explained to his assembled cast at the first technical run-through.

The glittery fairy music began and on trooped the fairies. There were audible gasps from the audience. Not even the leaked news of Dewi playing Puck had prepared them for this.

Grover's production was all about sex. The *Dream*, as he saw it, was just that and thus all about the unleashing of our forbidden sexual urges. He had toyed, apparently, with the idea of naked boys, ones as near the illegal age as possible but abandoned that since none could be found who were both willing to strip and able to sing treble. Instead he had gone to the other extreme and hired an adult chorus of women and treble-pitched counter-tenors, padded out with several miming performers selected for their extra fatness, thinness or want of inhibition. They were all naked except for silver afro wigs and silver body paint. Instead of the boisterous gang of chirping schoolboys in gauze and chaplets envisaged by Britten and Pears, the first tableau was thus one of the more extreme illustrations by Beardsley.

A world famous Welsh voice murmured a sexy, 'How now, fairies?' through the sound system and Puck emerged through a trap door in the chorus' midst, scattering them. With no reluctance at all, it was said, Dewi Evans wore simply his own furry skin, discreetly bronzed, with his muscular legs tightly wrapped in something remarkably like the back half of a zebra. The wardrobe mistress had even conjured up footwear which looked and sounded like little clopping hooves, possibly recycled from the rear end of a pantomime horse.

Due to Grover and Dewi's recent absence, rehearsals had been frantic and virtually non-stop all week which had proved a mercy. Giles had been eating in the opera house canteen then going home like an automaton merely to shower, sleep and shave. He was ignoring mail, ignoring the answering machine, ignoring everything. Only last night, when he could not avoid ringing up his mother to tell her there were tickets for her and Ron if they wanted them, had his sense of crisis been allowed to well up and then it took the unexpected form of a sudden need to confront her and make her admit, as she had never done and he had never tried to make her, the damage she had done him as a child.

The dreams about Dido had redoubled in intensity, dreams in which he watched in mute horror as he did to her the things his mother used to do to him. And they leached out ever more into his waking moments, blurring with his memories so that he would become distracted during a rehearsal and miss an entry because he was picturing his nine-year-old self frantically scrubbing at his penis till it bled in an effort to remove the oily traces of his mother's slobbered lipstick.

He might be neglecting to eat properly or do his exercises or read mail but he had one thing all planned out and went over it repeatedly like a murderer rehearsing his moves. He did this even while Grover was rehearsing for the lighting technician's blocking of each scene. If they had taken up his offer of tickets and were there at the stage door afterwards, he would steer them out to a smart restaurant and do it there. If not, he would catch a train down to Winchelsea and do it to her in her lair. With Ron in attendance.

And here our mistress. Would that he were gone.

His cue. As a pair of hands twitched the dressing gown off his nakedness and he stepped out of the wings, there was a momentary chill of air hitting the patches where the gold body paint was not quite dry or where nervous sweat had pooled, then the great heat of lights and full auditorium swept over him. He felt more acutely than when in a less minimal costume, the presence of hundreds of people, their breath, their eyes, the glitter of countless pairs of opera glasses.

There was no comfortable recitative to warm one up. Britten gave Titania and Oberon some of their hardest, most florid music the second they first appeared. Elena was striding across the stage towards him to deliver the smart smack on the cheek off which Grover wanted their argument to launch. There were audible titters and even a distinct, disgusted *oh no!* as her cloak fluttered back to reveal her magnificent silvered breasts, bright blue, tassled nipples and outsize, strap-on scarlet phallus.

Giles would wear his own copy of the phallus later, once the gender balance between them had been symbolically restored. For now he wore engorged labia that would have raised a blush in Georgia O'Keefe. The thong which held them in place was intolerably itchy and he was acutely aware of the line it cut between his naked buttocks.

He hoped his mother was watching. He hoped she and Ron

were trapped in the middle of a long row, unable to escape without fighting.

He was feeling sick again. He wanted to scratch. He wanted to hide. Then Elena slapped him savagely and, like a newborn, he began to sing.

58

Now that she was gathering her things together, it surprised Julia to discover how little she possessed. Unlike Giles, she was not a great reader of novels, preferring newspapers and magazines that she could throw away. She had always been rigorous about giving to charity shops each Spring any clothes or shoes she had not worn within the last year, and maintaining a highly adaptable capsule wardrobe. She owned no art and no ornaments. She had always relied on whoever she lived with having a television and stereo system. Her only recordings featured clients, so she kept them at the office for ready reference. The clothes fitted into two suitcases (a present from Giles), her few bits of jewellery and the contents of her dressing table into a ludicrous matching vanity case (ditto). That left Jane Grigson's fruit and vegetable books, a wide blue glass ashtray Selina had given her when she first noticed neither of them smoked and a teak steamer chair she had bought for the garden and was damned if she would leave behind. She made one last, painstaking tour of the house, starting in Dido's funny little room in the attic and working her way down. She noted the contents of each room with a mournful attentiveness but found nothing else she wished to take.

It was a beautiful house and she had helped it become so

but she had done it with things paid for by Giles and, in any case, they were chosen for just this setting and might be less beautiful elsewhere.

She had bought a car, small, sweet and Italian, on an interest-free credit scheme. The trip to Cornwall had awakened a yen to leave town more often and she would be living now in a much cheaper district where one did not need an expensive permit to park. By the time she had heaved in the three cases, the teak chair and a bag of small miscellanea gathered on her rounds of the house, the front and back seats were crammed.

It was not that she had been a kept woman. She had always paid her way. But the things she paid for from her own purse tended to be expendable and practical, like food or housekeeping, or else for the garden. She had loved the garden and would miss it.

She let herself back in then walked out to the back to take one last look. The sun was low in the sky, slanting across the neighbours' walls and hedges. The Brandons at number six were throwing a barbecue. She caught the smell of singeing chicken fat and the murmur of polite, cultivated conversation. She knew these neighbours a little. Later wine would flow more freely, dance music would break the spell and food would burn, neglected. But for now the distant, burbling voices and clink of bottle on ice bucket stood for all she was about to renounce.

With the attentiveness to detail she had brought to her last walk around the house, she noted the pot of deep blue agapanthus in full flower, which would not see another summer because Giles would not know to bring it indoors before frosts turned the tender bulbs to pulp. She noted that the ring of box hedging around it needed trimming and tried to picture the clump of little trees it would become through lack of care. But she noted too that the sounds from the nearby party were churning up in her familiar social fears she need never feel again.

She and the baby would be all in all to each other for a while and then, as she re-entered the world, she would do it with more recklessness, she had decided. She would follow her heart, not her reason, befriend no one who frightened her into being someone she wasn't. She had not yet decided how far to take Selina into her confidence. Selina dearly loved a secret and could undoubtedly keep one, but the knowledge might prove too weighty a bond between them and would surely prove a source of anxiety.

Until Eliza burst into the hotel in her fury, Julia had been all set to return to Islington with Giles and secretly keep her appointment at the clinic, for the sake of saving a relationship it was clear could not survive parenthood or any enforced lurch towards marriage. She decided to leave him but keep the baby in the seconds after he stammered out to Eliza the unexpected story about taking nude pictures of Dido while she slept.

Of course he was not a paedophile; she would have sensed such a thing by now. But the idea of him creeping up on Dido in the vulnerability of sleep, admiring her nakedness and capturing it on film inevitably made her doubt him and imagine how she would feel if he did the same to a child of hers, if not this baby then the next. Men were often jealously possessive of a woman's past. Why should Giles' desire not also be transferable to her childhood self, as presented in her child?

She knew her revulsion was neither fair nor entirely sane. If his desire for Dido had been real, Giles would have had more sense than to blurt it out to the two women who had been mothering her. But she found reason not enough to dislodge it. Long before her train had brought her back to London and she was sat at her desk in the agency poring over lists of flats to let in the few, far distant boroughs she could afford, she had made up her mind that she wanted the baby, not the father.

She had found a tiny flat above a greengrocer's at the western extremity of Goldhawk Road. One room, a bathroom and a sunny, noisy terrace on the shop's flat roof. Anonymous, easy for work, not too far from a hospital, it was hers for six months while she found her feet. As when grieving for a loved one it was unwise to make any major commitments soon after the death of a relationship.

Weary, giving room to reluctance, she sat on the garden bench and was enjoying the scent from the bed of lilium longifolium she had planted where the unproductive apple tree had been torn out. It was time to go. She forced herself to stand and go back in, double locking the garden door behind her. Giles would be back before long and she had a horror of dealing with him face to face. She had always despised Eliza's cowardice in leaving him with no more than a written explanation but could see now that it was only Eliza's presence in the hotel that had lent her the courage to tell him to his face.

The heavy scent of lilies seemed to have come into the house with her. The lily bed was the spot where weeks ago Eliza had assumed they would not mind burying a dog. Which was why, halfway through setting the burglar alarm, she remembered that the bloody dog was still in the freezer.

She pressed *abort* and went down to the utility room to swing the freezer's lid up then slammed it down again in disgust. There had been no miracle. The full black bin liner was still there, huddled in the opposite corner from the frozen yoghurt, peas, apple pieces and bagged up beef.

She grabbed a pad and started to write him a note along the lines of I've called in to take my stuff and leave my key. Oh and your dead dog is wrapped up beside tonight's supper. She realised it was an impossible task to do so with decorous neutrality however, and besides, he was due back any moment and she ran the risk of the messy parting she had hoped to avoid.

She flung the lid up again, grabbed the bin liner and slammed the lid shut. This thing was best done without thinking too much. There would be a skip somewhere. There was always someone in this jumped-up neighbourhood restoring or rebuilding a house. She would find a skip, dump the bag and drive on. Eliza need never know that her wishes had not been carried out to the letter. Assuming Eliza ever told him, Giles could harmlessly believe his old pet was mouldering under his lily bed.

She set the burglar alarm again, appreciating the haste it imposed on this last departure, forbidding nostalgia or brooding, hurried out of the front door, locked it behind her and tossed the keys through the letter box. Assuming he noticed them, they would be Giles' first indication that she had visited in his absence.

She drove with the bin liner on her left, in the passenger foot well, and both windows open in case it began to thaw and smell.

The first skip was worryingly full and was just outside a supermarket. The second was in sniffing range of a nursery where local working mothers left their babies, so that did not seem right either. She drove on towards King's Cross. There was sure to be another before then. But there was nothing so, caught up in the flow of heavy traffic, she was forced to drive all the way to Shepherd's Bush. There the traffic did not permit her to stop, so she was forced on down Goldhawk Road, where there was a galling lack of skips. Could her new neighbourhood be so lacking in aspiration? She drove as slowly as she dared, scanning the passing turn-offs as she went and feeling seedy.

Frustrated, she parked in the shadiest space she could find and lugged her cases one by one along the pavement and through her skinny new front door, waving to the shopkeeper who was now her landlord.

It was smaller and noisier than she remembered. The air felt stale and somehow cooked and all the knobs and handles were greasy from decades of unfiltered cooking fumes from the cramped kitchen area. The dining table was a flap of Formica that swung back against the wall when not in use. Its ingenious use of a tiny space was even more depressing than the fact that it could never seat more than two.

She brought in the rest of her things. She left the bin liner in the car and decided that, once it was dark, she would venture out to sling it in one of the big dumpsters at the back of restaurants. Restaurant waste was taken away every day. No one would know.

Exhausted, she brewed herself a cup of tea in her new mug then, because there could only ever be a sofa or a bed here but never both at once, she made up the bed with the new sheets, bought like the mug during that day's lunch hour, and flopped onto it to drink her tea.

From bed the room looked slightly better. It had pretty plasterwork and a view across the so-called terrace into the leaves of two tall trees she did not recognise. Where their bus-battered branches did not quite meet yet she had a view of the shops and houses opposite.

During her first, disastrous visit to Giles' mother's house, Julia had been subjected to a great outpouring from Trudy Easton about how much she used to drink, what she drank, how much she would spend on it, how she would hide the bottles from herself, how she would pass out in shops. It was more information than Julia felt remotely comfortable knowing about this scary woman she had barely met but she felt she must enter into the spirit of the conversation.

'So why did you drink?' she asked her. 'If it was so awful and so bad for you. What were you trying to forget?'

And Mrs Easton grasped her hand, which was even more disturbing than all the details about her years of degradation. 'I didn't want to forget,' she explained. 'I was after courage. Dutch courage. It's true. It works. I was scared of everything and everyone. Scared all the time!'

At the time of their meeting Julia had thought that Trudy took against her because she recognised another woman who wasn't all she appeared to be and was worried of exposure by association. Now that it no longer mattered, she lay looking out of the windows and realised that it was not fakery but the symptoms of fear Trudy was recognising.

Julia lay, a comforting hand on her belly, staring out of the window and realised she need never be frightened again.

The houses were dingy but there were several restaurants, a launderette, a newsagent and her landlord's stores. Across the road she could make out a chemist with a green neon cross in the window and a place with a sign that was a Dalmatian whose black spots lit up every few seconds with lurid pink and a Lebanese café called The Golden Star. She had been staring at the flashing Dalmatian for a few minutes, sipping her tea, wondering whether the curtains were going to be thick enough to blank it out at night, before she realised the sign's significance and hurried over there.

She waited her turn until a child with a mewling cat in a blanket and an old black woman with something mysterious and fidgety in a cardboard box had both been seen. The vet was good-looking in a dependable doctors and nurses fashion, an effect heightened by his white tunic and the jeans he was wearing underneath.

'Well hi!' he said, smiling, for all the world as if he knew her.

'I've a dead animal to get rid of,' she snapped. 'A dog. Can you help me out?'

'Of course.' He looked suitably solemn and she regretted her abruptness. He was only being polite after all.

'It's in my car. Just round the corner. It's a dog.'

'Large?'

'Fairly.'

'Do you want a hand getting him in here?'

'That would be very kind.'

He slipped out ahead of her and let her lead the way.

'It's been frozen,' she explained, as he lifted the bin liner out of the car. 'He died a few days ago and I haven't had time to . . .'

'That's okay,' he said. 'Easier to carry like this.'

She followed him back through the waiting room, through the surgery and over to a little alcove where he laid the bag on a table. There was a garland of drying hops above a reproduction of an old painting of St Francis. It was, she realised, a kind of chapel of rest.

'I'll give you a minute or two to say your goodbyes,' he said quietly and began to back out.

'Oh, that's okay,' she said. 'It's not my dog. I mean . . . well. It was my boyfriend's. Sort of. It's . . .'

'Complicated?'

'It was. Yes. It isn't any more.'

Now that she was about to get shot of the dog Julia felt strange. Perhaps relief at the last practical task of a difficult day was letting in something more confusing than mere exhaustion. She felt giddy and slightly churned up.

'What do I owe you?' she asked.

'Normally quite a bit,' he said, 'for cremation. But you're in luck. I had to put down a cat and a guinea pig this afternoon.

The man I use does a job lot and their fees will more than cover the cost. Unless you or your –'

'He's not. Not anymore.'

'Oh. Right. Well unless you were wanting the ashes back.'

'No. Not at all. And neither will . . . No. No ashes.' She dithered. He made to leave her alone.

'Sure you've said goodbye?'

'Sorry. Yes. Absolutely.' She still did not move.

'You don't remember me, do you?' he asked, sounding amused and she caught just a trace of a familiar accent.

She looked at him again, tried to picture him without his veterinary tunic, which was easily done. He had just cut his hair; there was an untanned stripe where his nape had been clipped.

'Maybe if I fainted, you'd –'

'Colin,' she said, remembering now. 'Colin Thomas. You said you lived in Trelill.'

'I said my *mother* did,' he corrected her. 'I live upstairs.'

'Oh,' she said. 'I've just moved in across the road.' She was about to say *over the greengrocer's* then remembered she barely knew him.

'That's funny,' he said.

'Yes.'

He took a breath. 'I'm sorry about your –'

'That's okay. He was a good age, apparently. Standard poodle.'

'I meant your boyfriend.'

'Don't,' she said. 'Don't be nice.'

'All right then,' he said. 'You'd better go. So I can shut up shop.'

'Yes. I will. But thanks.'

'That's all right.'

She edged past him and opened the door to the street.

'I'll see you around, then,' she added.

'Yes,' he said. 'I expect you will.'

The giddiness increased as she found herself back on the pavement. She needed food, blood sugar. Bloody baby. It was Friday. She remembered too late she had not cancelled her appointment at the clinic.

'Julie,' he called after her.

She turned.

'Julie Dixon. From Illogan.' He was smiling.

59

They were planting the last variety of broccoli, the last of the last variety. Pearce's back was beginning to move beyond mere ache to hurt. He was too big to fit comfortably onto the broccoli planter seats without stooping painfully to reach the planting wheel with each seedling. This was one of the longest fields on the farm, Tippett's Gift, and would be every bit as punishing to harvest in midwinter as it was cruel to plant out in the glaring sun. The glimpse of the end of the long row coming up to meet them was a welcome sight. Beside him Lucy was about to run out of plants so he quickly grabbed a fistful of the ones from his tray and dumped them on hers. She was hoping to have earned enough from all the sessions she had put in on the planter to pay for some shooting lessons; once again, she had found Morris wanting.

The row they were working on did not finish neatly at right angles to the end of the field. It was shaved off in one corner by the headland, the area along the field's perimeter which they would use as a track during harvest. So they needed to stop planting one by one to leave room for it. Being used to this, Pearce kept one eye on the plants in his hand, one on the approaching headland.

'Okay, Eliza,' he called.

Eliza stopped planting. She slipped off her seat, scratching her scalp under her hat, then walked back with a handful of plants to fill in spaces where she had missed a few. It amused him that although she claimed that nine-tenths of the tasks around the farm were a mystery to her, she was already so conscientious. He had caught her reading *Farmer's Weekly* several times, or poring over ministry leaflets.

'Okay, Joe.' A friend of Morris' who was helping out that afternoon sighed with satisfaction and stopped his planting but stayed put on his seat, lighting a roll-up the moment his hands were free. 'And okay, Luce.' Lucy stopped. She played a favourite game which was to lean as far back in the seat as she could without falling off, watching the plants recede behind her upside down. Pearce carried on planting until the end of the row.

They banged the remaining plants out by tapping the trays against a hedge then slid the empty trays back inside a still. Morris drove the planter back. He would park it in a corner then speed on to another farm where he had agreed to help with a second silage harvest. Pearce drove his own tractor, towing the trailer with the emptied stills on it. Lucy and Joe hitched a ride on the back, swinging their legs. Eliza climbed up in the cab with him. Her bare arms and face were grimed up with earth and sweat like his. She was too tired to talk but sank onto a pile of old sacking and leant against him as he drove, pulling off her hat to indulge in another luxurious scratching session.

The radio was tuned to the five o'clock news. Suicide bombers in Israel. An assassination in Holland. Nervousness about the shift to the far right in European politics. Placid bulletins from a noisy world.

'Who's that?' Pearce asked. There was a man in the yard talking to Morris through the open tractor door. Morris gestured back at Pearce's tractor and the man looked their way and thanked him as Morris speeded away.

He was extremely tall and thin and had on a pale, grey-blue linen suit over a white tee shirt. The effect would have been that of a humanised heron only he was completely bald, shinily so, and had eyebrows of flaming ginger.

Eliza was struggling to peer through the muddy glass down at her level. 'Villiers!' she exclaimed. 'Villiers Yates.'

'Oh fuck,' Pearce said, remembering the phone number he had written down and since lost.

'You don't know him?' Her voice was alarmed.

'No. It's nothing. I was thinking of something else.' He was thinking of money, of the secret ransom payment which the madrigal would always represent for him.

Just how tall their visitor was only became apparent when Eliza jumped down to greet him and was immediately dwarfed. The poor man must have gone through life with permanent back ache from bending and a bruised forehead from when he forgot to, never fitting comfortably into cars or public seating, too long for any bed, unable ever to blend into a crowd. Closer to, Pearce saw he was younger than the baldness made him first appear, probably mid thirties like Eliza.

He was so very immaculate and Eliza so very dirty that theirs was a meeting of aliens, a comical effect heightened by his genuinely failing to recognise her when she first approached.

'Is that really you under there?'

'Yes,' she laughed. 'And this is Pearce.'

The heron turned to look at Pearce and did himself credit by holding out a hand to shake despite the state of Pearce's.

'Pearce Polglaze, isn't it?'

'And I owe you an apology. I should have rung you back weeks ago.' Pearce raised a hand to wave at Joe and Lucy who were just leaving together, then turned back to him.

'You haven't sold it to someone else?' Villiers asked.

'No, no. The thing is. It's . . . it's not really accessible at the moment.'

Eliza was aghast. 'Villiers, you haven't come all the way from London just on the off chance of seeing the rest of the manuscript?'

Villiers looked deeply embarrassed and blushed so hotly Pearce revised the opinion he had formed from the phone message and warmed to him instinctively. 'Mr Byatt got awfully keen,' Villiers explained. 'His wife has Cornish connections – she was a Rod? A Rudd?'

'A Rodda,' Pearce supplied.

'That's it. How clever of you. So the second she heard the name Trevescan she was on at him to buy.'

'It's not for sale, Villiers.' Eliza said. 'Not at all.'

'I was afraid you'd say that. Blast. Well at least I can tell him I tried. They'd have paid far more than the going market rate, you know. I even came with a blank cheque.' He patted his breast pocket causing Pearce a twinge.

New rotovator, Pearce told himself wistfully. *New diesel tank. New combine.*

'You must stay the night,' he said out loud. 'That's the least we can offer you.'

'I'm booked on the sleeper.'

'Ten o'clock. So you can stay for supper, then,' Pearce said. 'We'll drive you back in.'

'Would you really?'

'Of course,' Eliza agreed. 'Come in and have a glass of something while we get cleaned up.'

As Pearce climbed back into the tractor to drive it into the barn for the night, he heard Villiers say, 'Wonderful. In *every* way. I understand completely,' and heard Eliza giggle in response.

When he came in he found Villiers already settled in the garden with a glass of wine chatting with Dido and obliging

467

her by putting much thought into composing a limerick to write on her plaster cast. Through an open window he could hear Eliza singing upstairs as she took a shower.

'I feel bad you came all this way,' he told him. 'If I'd rung, you wouldn't have come. At least let me give you something towards your train fare.'

But Villiers waved the offer away saying it was good to get out of London and that everything could be claimed back off his American's expense account.

'You'll stay to supper, though. I'm afraid it's only cold meat and salad. But there are raspberries too.'

'That sounds lovely.'

'Do you think it's warm enough to eat outside?'

'What do you think, Dido?' Villiers asked.

'Outside,' Dido said. 'No question. Do you have to go back tonight? You've only just got here.'

'Work,' Villiers told her. 'London. Bills to pay.' And, for a bald heron, he looked crestfallen.

'How do you make your head so shiny?'

'I polish it,' Villiers told her gravely, concentrating on a penultimate line for his limerick. 'Every morning. With a square of antique silk.'

Pearce fetched potatoes, herbs and salad from the vegetable patch, set the potatoes to boil then went to shower. As he came back down he heard someone playing *Country Goodness* on the harmonium. It was Villiers. Eliza was busy in the kitchen and talking to Dido though the open door. Pearce went to stand at Villiers' elbow. Nobody had played it this well in years.

'Extraordinary,' Villiers said when he had finished. 'I can see why she's so sure. That last cadence especially. And you copied this out?'

'After a fashion, yes.'

'So you're a musician as well as everything else?'

Pearce shuffled his feet. 'Not remotely.'

Villiers had swung his stool round and was looking at him, fascinated. 'Eliza told me,' he whispered. 'How she tore it up and burnt it so it wouldn't come between you.'

'She said that?' Pearce asked, glancing up to see Eliza carrying a platter of ham and chicken out to the table.

'It's funny. I'd never realised she was so passionate. Of course there are still the scans she took. And your sister's madrigal group. If they've really got it memorised Eliza could sit there like Mozart hearing the Allegri *Miserere* and write it down note for note. She must be crazy about you, though. She's happier than I've seen her in years.'

'Have you known her a long time?'

'Oh, I've known her so long I'm to blame for everything. I introduced her to Giles.'

'So he's *your* fault . . .'

'He is rather. I was very, very in love with him when we were students and since I couldn't have him I decided the least I could do was to throw him together with the sweetest girl I knew. A bit like flower arranging, really.'

Eliza called them out to eat.

Over supper Villiers asked all the questions Pearce had not yet mustered the courage to pose. So by the time they were racing their guest into Penzance to catch the sleeper, Pearce was a happy man. Eliza had thought long and hard about completing her thesis, apparently, and had decided she would, if not for the sake of a further degree, then simply to prove to herself, and to Dido, that she was capable of it. But she was adamant that this was where she wanted to remain. This valley, above this rocky cove with this farmer.

'*Country goodness and a sweet obscurity,*' Villiers quoted at her, singing the line in a scholastic tenor that went perfectly with his heronish thinness.

'Yes,' she said. 'Exactly.' She explained that she had come back from talking to the school about enrolling Dido for the autumn (which Pearce knew about), full of the possibility of becoming the new music teacher there (which was news to him). He knew she had explained Dido's condition to the head teacher and been heartened by his attitude.

As Villiers gave his name to the night guard and climbed into the sleeper carriage, Pearce pressed an opened bottle of wine onto him along with some cheese, two peaches and a photocopy of *Country Goodness*. Villiers startled him by kissing him warmly on the lips then hung out the carriage's window and waved to them as the train pulled out around the bay, much as if they had been old and cherished friends. Which left Pearce feeling oddly as though they were.

'What a nice bloke,' he said, as they walked back to the Land Rover.

'Villiers? *Nice*?'

'Yes. Strange but nice. You can ask him to stay anytime.'

She was quiet on the drive home, exhausted from planting broccoli probably. In any case the Land Rover was so noisy when in motion that it did not lend itself to the sort of sentimental murmurings Pearce felt welling up inside him. He contented himself with holding her hand in between gear changes.

Describing why she and Dido were staying put she had twice used the word *safe*. 'It's so safe here,' she had said.

Pearce let go of her hand suddenly, needing both hands on the wheel to swing around a badly parked lorry.

Fear had never been a common emotion of his; boredom had, often, and irritation. Very occasionally a mild anxiety had penetrated the continuum of his quiet resignation, his sort of contentment. But now that he had a chance to be truly happy he found he was frightened every day. It was as though by giving shelter to Dido and her mother he had taken on their fears as one might take wet coats from visitors, without much thought about where to hang them. He lay awake and worried on their behalf. When Eliza made a first attempt at learning to drive he felt a stab of fear, as he did when Dido announced that she wanted to take rock-climbing classes once her plaster cast was off. But it was a good fear, he realised, a proof that his life had acquired ramifications and significance. These were coats he would gladly hold all evening.

Author's Note

Apologetic thanks to Ken Northey and Sue Visick whose lovely madrigal evenings in Goldsithney gave rise to the dream that gave rise to this novel. The conservatory and repertoire are similar but there the similarities end.

Heartfelt thanks, too, to Sally Donegani, for letting me steal her job, to Fanny Cooke, for letting me crib her A-level Music notes, to Doctors Celia Hicks, Catharine Gale and Jonathan Gale for their medical input, to Nicola Barr and Rupert Adley for their sharp eyes and wits and to Caradoc King for his powers of persuasion.

My deepest debt, however, is to my editor Patricia Parkin who deserves a medal for inimitable grace under extraordinary pressure.

Lastly I must acknowledge the profound, all unwitting contribution of Vicky Lucas, a young woman with cherubism to whose wit and defiant courage this novel remains an inadequate tribute.